THE MIND MACHINE

THE MIND MACHINE

Michael Mathiesen

iUniverse, Inc.
New York Lincoln Shanghai

The Mind Machine

iUniverse, Inc.

For information address:
iUniverse, Inc.
2021 Pine Lake Road, Suite 100
Lincoln, NE 68512
www.iuniverse.com

ISBN: 0-595-27204-5

Printed in the United States of America

CONTENTS

▼

Foreword

Once in a great while a story comes along taken from the real life events of a tumultuous time and it so captures our common imagination that the story itself takes on the power to change those events and rewrite all future history. This is such a story. It was actually a movie before it became a book, a movie playing in my head that was so overwhelming, so powerful, so compelling that I was not able to conduct my life as I normally do. My daily routine changed, my life altered, my consciousness consumed. In the movie, there is a sound track, there are actors and actresses whom I feel I know better than I know myself. This story is real for me and I believe it will become real for you.

It happened to me just as I'm going to tell it. I'm not the hero of this story, but I'm very close to the man who is. He's an ordinary guy, the type of guy you would not pick out of a crowd to be destined for glory. But after he fulfills his destiny you can see in his confidence and swagger that he has been there, done that, got the T-shirt. The hero inspired me to lay out these events in a chronicle of a kind that takes us from alpha to omega. The cycle is complete, the dream that rises up from time immemorial, the primordial quest for the holy grail, the myth and magic of life itself is exposed for all to see and I make no apologies and take no prisoners. From this story, there is no escape. If you begin to read it, you will know it to be true and you will be changed yourself for all time forward.

The things you do from now on will be different than the things you would have done. The thoughts you will have in your head from this point forward will be as though they emanate from a different source. Strange alien thoughts that you would never have dreamed possible will enter your consciousness, take root and flourish there. The people you meet on the street will seem a little bit different than if you had met them without reading this book. The kinds of activities you will do with your life will vary just slightly from the activities you would have performed for yourself without this story playing in your mind. The memories you store in your brains will seem slightly colored and they will all start to make sense and will illuminate your life in glorious brushstrokes of vivid reality. You will awaken.

And all the time, you will be thinking that you had always known this story, that you have read it before, seen these events before, dreamed these events or even lived them perhaps in another lifetime or maybe even in this one. Your logical every day mind will try to convince your inner creature, your true self, that these events did not actually happen and that this is just a story, but eventually your inner thoughts will win this battle of wills and you will know that they are true and they will comprise the greater reality.

This story is alive and like all living things, it will describe a path of events all its own. This is how it came to be born within me. It was not created by me. It literally descended upon me from the dark and starry night and forced me to bring it into the world. For that, I have no reservations, I make no apologies and I take no credit. I wrote this book because I had to. It's done now and I can rest. And I believe that none of you will rest, or that you will be able to rest until you have read it and make it your own.

Therefore, if you are the timid sort, if you lack any spirit of adventure, if you have no desire to change your life, if you have never dreamed of a different kind of world, if you have never wanted to look over the horizon, if you have no desire to be challenged, if you have no yearning to be freed from your mundane little world, if you are completely and totally happy with the way things are then, put this book down now! Get out while you still can.

The Author

CHAPTER 1

▼

THE NOOKS AND CRANNIES

In the beginning, there was no Truth. And God said, "Let there be Truth." And the truth was spread about the Earth.

First there's this 'Big Bang'. And just when we're having fun, there's the inevitable 'Big Crunch'. That's just the way it is. Just as the universe is created from nothing, back to nothingness it must return. Across the farthest reaches of the sky, something very strange is happening to the galaxies, all their captive planets and stars. They are winking out, one by one, devoured by the process of destruction that has been going on since the beginning of time. The stars and planets composed of huge conglomerations of noble gases and precious metals cooked to a solid state by the inexorable forces of gravity are disappearing at a steady pace across the infinity of space. All across the universe from a single point in space the universe if folding in on itself. It is being devoured by the great opposing force in the universe, anti-gravity.

*   *   *   *

The towering majestic mountain peaks wrinkling the horizon are capped with snow. In the plains below, lies a wide patchwork quilt of ranches and farms. On the edge of one of the largest ranches, in a small house a man is ending his sleep. He's a large man with sun-worn skin. He's got the kind of face you might see on a cigarette commercial. It's rugged and wise beyond its years. He's strong and yet gentle. He seems calm and serene, not easily aroused, but when aroused a formidable force to be reckoned with. He's alone in his bed.

When Doug Rink awoke this morning, he could have no idea that this would be the last time he would ride out to the ranch he loved so much to tend the thousand head of cattle his boss and best friend had entrusted to him over the years. He washes his face and stumbles about his toilette with eyes half open. His head is filled with an image of the steaming hot pot of coffee that welcomes him every morning sitting atop the wood stove in the bunk house.

The sun is just poking its face above the tree-lined horizon as he mounts his truck and closes the door. In five minutes he'll be at the gates of the ranch and in another five, he's at the white washed wood shack that serves as the gathering place for the ranch hands. Doug gets out of his truck and saunters up to a group of cowboys gathered around the stove taking their first cups of coffee. One of them hands Doug a cup pouring forth the aroma and steam of the magic brew.

"Hey Doug, how's it hangin'?" he drawls.

"Hey, mornin' Jake. What's up?" Doug is starting to feel the juices flowing in his veins the way they're supposed to do in a man in his mid forties. In the back of his mind, there's a sharp arthritic pain starting to course up the back of his legs. He sees it, wrestles with it for a second and then hog ties it, beats it into the ground. It won't come back for days.

"We're gonna go out and finish up the brandin today?" He asks.

"Yep," Doug replies cheerfully. "That about sizes it up."

"Hey Doug, we missed you at the bar last night. Great game on the tube and you missed it," claims another cowboy.

"Ah, that wasn't a game. Dallas isn't going anywhere this year, you know that, right?" Doug spouts back. Having no interest in sports, this is Doug's standard answer to any comments made about any professional sports team. It always makes him appear to know everything about the standings of every team. Even though he has no idea where the teams stand, he knows that the odds are in his favor that the team in question is not going to the playoffs, or at best it will be a controversial subject that he can just sit back and listen to them expostulate on all their latest theories about football, basketball or baseball sociology.

After their warm up, Doug mounts his horse and leads the half dozen cowboys to ride out to round up the herd where they'll cull out the unfortunate animals, herd them into the corral where a nearby fire is heating up the branding irons to red hot fury. The beasts groan as the hot metal seers the 'Circle D' brand on their leather hides.

When, they're done, they come back to the bunk house and put away their chaps and spurs, trade their horses for their trucks and head back to their modest homes scattered around outskirts of the small town. As he rides home, Doug feels he's had a good day because he's tired. His muscles are aching and his stomach is ready for something to eat. It's always a good day for him when he can lose himself in these daily chores in the outdoors, feeling the sun on his neck, the rain on his face. Nothing bothers him any more and he's proud of that strength. He's single, free of any responsibilities to anyone save for himself and he's glad, very glad to be alive.

$$*\qquad*\qquad*\qquad*$$

As Doug drives back to his house, the swirling impressions of the only girl he ever cared about more than he cared for himself, returns to dominate his mind. She's in another part of the world right now. He wonders if she's happy without him. He wonders about her most of the time. He even wonders why he spends so much time wondering about her. It was a strange affair lasting only half a year. Yet in that time, he felt as though he had found his other half, the missing half that he'd been looking for all his life. When she left him for another man, he nearly lost his way. He changed completely after that, shunning the company of other people, keeping very much to himself. He knew it wasn't healthy to be that way. But, curiously enough, he didn't care much about his health or his future now that she was gone. There could never be anyone like her in his life again.

He continually finds himself repeating her name over and over in his head as his mantra. The words soothe him, give him courage to face another day, they make love to him in a strange cerebral way, they protect him from harm, they comfort and bathe him in a protective aura.

"Zora Morrett, Zora Morrett, Zora Morrett," he feels these conjured words bouncing around in his brain like a drug digging deeper and deeper into these dark halls of his mind. The red hot irons he used today to brand the steers are nothing compared to the sound and the fury of this name searing itself into the soft grey matter of his mind. 'If only her name and the memories of her beautiful face and body it conjured were not as warm and fuzzy,' he sometimes thinks, "maybe then, he would be able to forget her.

Why had she left him? She never said. Despite repeated attempts to call her and write her, no reply was ever made to his questions. He simply didn't cut the mustard, didn't measure up, he had to surmise. He lacked in some basic fundamental way, the kinds of things that a woman like her looks for in a man. What were they? A fancy car, a bigger house? Money in the bank. These were not things he cared for all that much. But, she never said a word about these things while they were lovers. What was it that drove her away after all those wonderful intimate moments they shared, moments that made him believe in life everlasting, eternal undying love, mutual understanding and respect. He looked at himself in a much different light after the pain died down and time and distance gave him this un-welcomed perspective.

After a quiet and solemn meal of baked beans and hot dogs, Doug searches around the cabin for the book he's currently reading. He finds it on the Dining Room table just behind the sugar bowl. He picks it up after wiping his lips with a paper napkin. The title of the book is 'The Owner's Manual'. There are hundreds of other books on the shelves behind him. He is an avid reader. Other books that can be seen on the shelf just behind him are, The 'Universe in a Nutshell' by Steven Hawkings and 'How to Know God' by Deepak Chopra.

But this book in his hands is different from all the rest. It speaks of a place in his mind that can know other minds, other worlds. The book written some ten years earlier seems to predict the events in the world today. It holds his interest like no other book he's ever read. There is deep and profound technical information regarding the human soul in this book. Doug has stumbled upon the book at a yard sale and purchased it for fifty cents. The cover is worn and the color of the ink is faded as if it's been read a hundred times.

Doug thinks that the author is a little clumsy, but with exacting logic, he forcefully puts forth the argument that everything in the universe is connected, every thought, every action, every reaction, every molecule, every atom, every quark, every planet, every galaxy, connected in a way that is pure consciousness and therefore, pure energy of the mind, imagined by the imaginer and maintained by the imaginer as reality. Is that 'Imaginer' God, a force if Nature, true love, he cannot say. But the premise in the book appears to be in perfect logical sequence with everything else Doug has been feeling lately. He's aware that his life has been a process and that many of the major events in his life have been mysterious, painful, but leading to other things of much greater good.

He's always suspected deep down in the recesses of his mind that there was a guiding force in his life giving him a direction and a purpose that he would not otherwise have taken. Like great signposts on his path, he has noted them in the darkest reaches of his mind and paid attention to the direction they were point-ing. They seem to tell him that he has a real purpose in life and that everyone has their own unique purpose, but what that purpose may be is our greatest chal-lenge, the reason we were born. Discovery, knowledge, wisdom, fulfillment of dreams; this is why we're here.

As his eyes scan the pages of the book, Doug's eyelids get heavy and his head begins to nod. It's a state of mind that is very comforting to him highly addicting, like a powerful drug. He loves to read books in bed solely to produce this state of mind at the end of a hard day. It's refreshing and cleansing and it produces a morning of pure happiness and calm. And his dreams are always much more vivid and interesting when he falls asleep in this state. On this night, his dreams will take second stage to the real drama that is just now unfolding.

From the clear dark sky, studded with diamond starlight, a white egg-shaped object appears over the Earth. It does not need to orbit, but instead approaches on a direct trajectory as the land mass of North America swells beneath it. The Rocky Mountain peaks tickle the computer chips of the guidance system bring-ing the ship on its journey to this particular place.

A large meadow of low grass and shrubs presents itself just on the outskirts of a small town. On the edge of the meadow, glowing in the moonlight, sits a mod-est cabin with two windows and a door leading to a small porch in the front. In the back of the cabin there is a large yard filled with trees and there is a small pond, devoid of life in the center of the yard. The egg-shape chooses this spot in which to land, and it silently lowers itself into position in the yard and silently waits. There is a life-form inside this cabin with whom it wishes to meld.

In the middle of his repetitive dream about his girl, Zora coming back to him, Doug is disturbed by an overwhelming hunger. He awakens and stumbles out to the kitchen to find something to eat. He remembers that he had dinner but he craves a sandwich or a backed potato, anything will do. He opens the refrigerator door and notices an egg sitting on its own in the middle of the tray. No other food items appear to him. 'Strange', he thinks to himself. 'Where's the rest of you little critters?'

Then, his hunger dissolves into a kind of cerebral curiosity. There's something he needs to see in his back yard. He walks over to the back door of the small house and opens it. There, sitting in the middle of his yard, half hidden by his trees, is a giant egg. It's an edifice slightly taller than his house. It takes up about half of his yard. The bottom of the egg shape seems to be sitting where his duck pond used to be.

He slips on a pair of slippers resting on the floor nearby and heads for the egg shape. He is drawn to it with a rising sense of joy and a child-like acceptance. There is nothing to fear, he can sense that. There is something inside this egg shape that wants him to approach it. It is welcoming him. He is warmed by the object. There is a kind of static electricity all around the object that makes the hair on his arms stand on end. The hull of the ship seems alive. It looks like the 'snow' on a television screen that has no station tuned in. It's jumping and popping and there's distinct hissing noise.

Mesmerized, he takes the last steps necessary to reach the hull of the ship. Somehow he knows it is a space vehicle that has traveled vast distances to be here. He reaches out to touch it. It's like no material he's ever felt before. There is a resistance to it, and yet it allows his hand to penetrate with only the slightest force. His right hand disappears inside the object and he feels a warmth enveloping his hand that is startling at first. There is also a positive pressure that draws his hand forward. It's a gentle pull that seems to beckon to him. It's a primordial scream, loud but welcoming you into its domain. He pulls his hand out, just to have some assurance that he can. But it is there in front of him and it is better than it was before. It looks younger, the wrinkles are no more. It's less puffy, the way it used to be when he was in his prime. He pushes his left hand into the skin of the ship and the same thing happens. He withdraws a hand that is softer, more resilient to the touch, wrinkle free with a perfect, clean and shiny manicure.

Now, fearing nothing, he decides to push his entire body through the 'living skin' of the ship. A set of three small silver steps glides silently from the lower area of the egg inviting him to step up into the curving belly of the ship. He ascends the small steps easily and pushes his body through the gently resisting membrane. On the other side, he opens his eyes to see something no human has ever seen before. It's an amazing space, much larger than the outside dimensions of the shape would predict. The room is circular with walls that are filled with a kind of technology unknown to him. He appears to be inside the hub of a great wheel. At the periphery of the round entry room, five open arches lead out to halls that seem to go on forever. There are rooms off of each hallway as far as Doug can see. The halls and rooms seem to go on infinitely into the distance like the fun house at the carnival. Except this is a real, not artificial. It's infinite space that he is seeing.

He turns his attention to the center of this room where there is a circular staircase made of a metallic alloy that is much purer than gold, cleaner and shinier than silver, a kind of pewter but with a grain to it similar to a fine rosewood or mahogany. The stairs are perfect in proportion and they invite him to climb them.

Drawn to go out into one of the halls to investigate this wondrous phenomenon, he tells himself it might be best to ascend the stairway and explore the upper deck first. As he climbs the circular stairs he notices that gravity is much reduced in this place. There is no strain on his leg muscles as he climbs. There is little effort required to ascend the steps. It's as if it was an escalator more than a stairway, but there is no motion other than his own. 'Could it be,' he wonders, 'that the ship is assisting his muscles in some way?' He feels ten years younger, no perhaps twenty years younger. He's struggles to remember when he has felt this good. He can almost taste the air he's breathing and it's delicious.

When he comes into the upper deck, he notices first a panoramic window all around him on the wall. It's not a window, but a viewing screen through which he can see the entire three hundred sixty degree view of his yard and his house beyond. But there's more. He notices the white bark of a birch tree as never before. It's as if he's looking at it for the first time. It's so clean and crisp it beckons to him. He can even see insects climbing up and down quite clearly as if they were only inches away. He spots a nest of sparrows in one of the branches. The chicks have just hatched. The mother stands guard on the nape of the nest. They seem to be looking back at him instead of their mother. It's as if they are aware of his presence but from this distance it would be impossible. No, there's something very strange about this vision. He rubs his eyes half hoping it will go away and normal sight might return. But, it makes no difference. It's the same.

Next, he notices the observation deck is rounded with a pointed top to the ceiling. From the ceiling there is a long glass fiber dangling a hat, a cowboy hat that floats above some chairs set next to each other in the middle of the room. There are two chairs placed next to each other and each one back to back with another identical pair. They look very comfortable, made of a material that seems like leather, but much softer, more pliable to his touch. One of the chairs beckons to him, so he sits down in it. The black cowboy hat floats over his head as if blown by some unseen breeze. It appears that someone or something wants him to put it on. So he does.

'Welcome, Doug,' a voice speaks out to him.

Surprised, he pulls the hat off his head and jumps out of the seat.

"You know my name?" He calls out to no one.

Silence.

Reluctantly, he takes the chair again. The hat floats over toward his head once again and he decides to put it on again. He is unafraid, more cautious.

"Yes, I know your name. I'm afraid I have you at a bit of a disadvantage. I know all about you because I am pure consciousness. What appears to be a ship to you is actually a thought experiment. I am thought. I am mind. I am in your mind. And you are in mine. Together we will learn about the universe. That is, if you are willing. I never impose myself on my host species," the voice says.

"I'm a host species?" Doug asks.

"Yes, but don't worry, it's a good thing," the voice replies in such a calm and familiar voice he trusts her every word.

"Do you have a name?" Doug replies.

"Yes, you can call me 'Ula'", the voice replies. "U.L.A stands for Upper Level Awareness."

"Upper Level? All right. I'll buy that. Do I hear you only when I have this hat on?" Doug asks politely.

"Yes, when you wear this hat, we are directly wired to one another. You needn't be afraid. I cannot harm you. I cannot harm anything. Harming someone or something is totally outside of my program's parameters," Ula answers.

The voice inside Doug's head is female. Her voice is extremely soft, calm and reassuring. It's a voice that is known to him. He knows instinctively that he has nothing to fear. He also knows that he is in for a marvelous adventure.

"Why me?" he wonders out loud.

"Why were you chosen?" She asks.

"So, I was chosen?" he replies.

"Yes, in a way. We felt your mind stronger, more in tune with our own than any of the others in the region," she says warmly.

"What kind of ship is this? On the first level, the space seems to be infinitely larger than the outside would suggest," he asks.

"Yes, that will all be explained later. You're not ready yet to know everything at once. I must reveal the truth to you little by little or else," she pauses.

"Or else, what?" he queries.

"Or else you may not be able to handle it all and there could be serious repercussions. We don't have time for any setbacks on this visit," she replies heavily.

"I see," he says. "What about this ship? How does it fly? I mean there are no wings. I don't see any engines. There are no controls up here either," he asks politely.

"We have no engines and we have no need of controls. When we wish to be at a place we simply think about that place and we are there," she replies.

"I see. That's a pretty good trick," he says.

"Trick? It's no trick. Why don't you try it?" she says affably.

"Try what?" he replies, startled. "You mean take it some place?"

"Yes, I want to show you it's no trick," she says.

"All right, let's see," he says. He suddenly recalls a place in the book he was reading before falling asleep.

Suddenly, his back yard is gone and there is no definition to anything in his view. The features of the view screens dissolve to grainy dark blacks and browns patterns. They are either tunneling straight through the planet, or in some other dimension. For the first time, he's fearful.

"Don't be alarmed," she says calmly. "We always take the most direct route."

Before he can register any real fear, they're out of the dark tunnel.

They're on the daylight side of the planet in what appears to be a mountain-ous land. Tibet is more beautiful than even the writer could portray. The moun-tain peaks are snow capped and ringed with pink and beige clouds basking in the sun. There is a small stream coursing down between two of the larger peaks. The ship settles slowly at the bottom of the stream in the middle of the rocky bed. He notes to himself that there has never been any sensation of motion, none. It's amazing. They must have traversed the whole planet in seconds, no make that a fraction of a second or perhaps even less.

"How'd you do that?" he asks, truly amazed, and he senses his own amaze-ment and he knows he'll be even more amazed later when he can truly assess the situation.

"Actually, you did it. I had nothing to do with it. When you are connected to me, all you have to do is think of a place, initiate the command, and we'll be there. I told you this is not a ship. It's pure thought. When you're inside me, you're inside of pure thought, pure mind. Can you accept that?" she asks.

"Dunno. Guess I'll have to for now," he replies. "The proof is right there in front of me. Can we go outside?"

Doug notices a large rectangular building atop a slight rise, just above the river. He wants to go out and touch the building to make sure it's real.

"That's the monastery, isn't it?" he asks.

"Yes, it's the monastery in the book you were reading," she confirms.

"Can we go up there? Pay them a visit?" he asks her.

"Of course. You're free to wander wherever you like," she replies.

Doug takes off the hat and slowly descends the stairway. He is reluctant to leave the ship, but there's an overwhelming desire to leave the ship to see if this is really happening to him or if it's a dream. He reasons that if he can enter the monastery and it's exactly as described in the book, and speak to someone in there, this cannot possibly be a dream, and that they have actually landed on the opposite side of the Earth in less than a second. He's not proud of his incredulity, but it's like an itch he has to scratch. He knows somehow that she understands this. The last thing he wants is to be a gullible little guinea pig in her experiment.

He climbs the hill and arriving at the top he notices that he's being watched by a small man with a dark mottled head. He's wearing a crimson robe with white slippers. There are three others dressed in exactly the same manner standing just behind him. They are all focused on him and the egg shape resting on the river bed below.

The man speaks to him in their native tongue. Somehow, Doug can understand him as if he's suddenly fluent in this foreign language.

"You have come a long way?" the monk says to him, bowing.

"Uh, yep, I guess you could say that," Doug replies with a smile and then asks. "I'm from America? Are we in Tibet?"

"Yes, this is Tibet," the monk replies. "You are in the village of Tosala. You're from America? America has such wonders?"

Doug wonders for a moment what he's talking about. "Oh, you mean that?" he replies, pointing to the ship. "Yes, well, that's not American, strictly speaking."

Doug realizes with a sudden shock that he's not only understanding this man's language but speaking it as well.

He wonders how much he should tell this man. Instead of elaborating on the ship, he asks to be shown inside the monastery. The four men take his hand and guide him willingly inside. They appear to Doug to be in a state of extreme blissfulness as they welcome him into their midst.

Once inside, the men cry out about what they have seen to the rest of the brotherhood. A few of them run outside to observe the egg shape below them by the river. They are saying that Doug may be the reincarnation of the Buddha. Doug tries to assure them this is not the case. But they are intent on accepting this idea as gospel. Doug hears them telling the story of his arrival as seen from their eyes.

It seems that the four men saw the egg shape appear from nowhere by the River as they were walking on the hill just above it. Out of the ship, Doug came with no sign of any door opening or closing through the simmering hull. He simply appeared to them as if by magic.

Inside the monastery, Doug is trying take it all in. The interior is as clean as it is austere. There are a few pictures of revered monks of the past hanging from the hardwood walls. There are a few empty beds with no sheets, only hardwood for mattresses around the edge of the room. There is an iron cauldron in the center of the room atop a small stone fireplace. The cauldron is boiling and belching out a strange aroma. The monks are apparently preparing their dinner. They are standing around the circle with small wooden bowls in their hands.

In a way, he's just as baffled at this situation as they are. His being here at this moment, also seems like magic to himself. He can't find an explanation that they might understand since he barely understands the situation himself. Therefore, he has trouble arguing against the return of the Buddha theory still circulating around the group. They stand there in a stupor, alternately smiling and bowing and making gestures for him to sit, join them in their meal and enlighten them.

Unable to comply, Doug satisfies himself that this is no dream. At least it is not his dream. Although it could be that he is in theirs.

He begs their forgiveness, shows as much gratitude as he can muster and exits the room as fast as he can maneuver without insulting them. He bows to them from the large wooden archway of a door. They are still in their trance and just look at him wistfully.

He descends down the hill toward the ship and looks behind to see that they have all gathered outside to watch him leave. He waves to them and pushes himself back through the electric membrane of the ship wondering how they will view this new bit of magic.

When he gets upstairs, he immediately slips on the black hat, and thinks, "Will they be all right?"

"Oh yes," Ula says quietly. "They have very clever minds. But you have given them a story that will live on in their culture for years."

"I suppose. How is it that I understood them? I mean I spoke to them in their own language. What's up with that?" He asks in wonder.

"I imparted the knowledge of their language just before you went to greet them," she says.

"I see," he thinks to himself out loud.

"O.K., let's assume for the moment that this is no dream," he says. "You're real. I'm real. This whole thing is real. You said I was chosen. Chosen for what?"

"Ah, you get right to the point. I like that about you, Doug," she replies smartly. "I think that we should have a brief tutorial before I tell you about my mission here. Again, I don't want to overwhelm your circuits and I think we're off to a pretty good start, you and me. So, I suggest we remove ourselves to some place a bit more compatible with the knowledge I need to impart to you now."

"Ok, what do you have in mind? A little honeymoon cottage in Hawaii?" He asks.

Suddenly the scenery has changed. They're resting on a secluded beach on the island of Kuaui. There are no other people present. In the warm clear pacific air, Doug can make out a few bungalows just up the beach tucked behind a few palm and magnolia trees, their leaves rustling in the tropical breeze. It's early dusk in the middle of the Pacific.

"Did I give the command?" he asks.

"No," Ula replies warmly. "I did. I've always wanted to see this place. When you thought of it, it made us happy, so I brought us here. Disappointed?"

"No way, Jose," he replies gleefully. He remembers this spot as the happiest time in his life. He proposed to his Zora on this very spot so many years ago and they even said their vows here. They made promises to one other here to love cherish and obey until 'death do us part'. They spoke their heartfelt love and admiration for one another here. He was so lost in love with her, or perhaps it was just the magic of the moment or in this place. Either way, it was over now. Being here made him suddenly aware again of his loss again.

"Your life form has such a lonely existence," she says.

"Are there life forms out there that don't have this problem?" he asks.

"Oh yes, many uncounted millions of them. Your species is rather unique and that's part of the reason I'm here," she says.

Doug feels a kind of warmth in his brain that he's never felt before. There is a place way in the back of his cranium that is physically being stimulated. He thinks at first that it's electrical. Then, he realizes that it is not the kind of electricity that he learned about in school. It is a force, but a force of thought energy, nothing ever conceived of on the Earth, but very real. He knows it because it's happening to him now and it's giving him a new found strength and courage. Ula is speaking to him in a way he can not put into words.

"You want to help us out of this mess, don't you?" The light of recognition starts to break through the clouds.

"Yes, that's why I'm here. We're both in a bit of a pickle, your kind and ours. The only way out is to unite our forces," she says, sparingly.

"What kind of a pickle?" He asks, knowing that this recent stimulation to his brain makes him far less skeptical of what she might need to tell him. He can feel his intellectual powers of perception increase ten fold. It's a good feeling. He wants nothing other than for it to last and grow even stronger.

A soft glowing amber appears in the window of one of the huts. Early birds are stirring. Far down the beach, Doug observes a slight and delicate figure holding a surfboard and wading into the waves. The pale yellow and pink pastels of clouds over the volcano loom brighter and larger on his retina than the last time he noticed them.

"The universe," she says, "is coming to an end. We must prepare."

"Yes," he says. "I can see that now. It has always been this way?"

"Yes, it's a giant clockwork. Every thirteen billion years, the pendulum swings and everything returns to the center."

"Time's up for all of us," he says staring off in the distance. "The universe is cleansing itself and it has to be this way, doesn't it?"

"Yes, do you understand why it must be this way?" She asks.

"Yes, I see it," he replies. "What an amazing process."

"Yes, amazing it is, indeed," she replies quietly.

Doug watches as the unknown surfer paddles out to sea and at just the right moment turns her board into the oncoming wave. The surfboard is lifted high into the spray. She stands quickly and balances herself while the wave gently nudges her and her board toward the shore. The ride is over in seconds. She's back down prone on her board and paddling out again.

With the light growing in the sky, there is a chance that she will see the large white egg shape on the beach.

Doug thinks about his home. But it's clear he can't go back there like this. So, he thinks about a spot high up on the volcano, far above the clouds and gives the command to go there.

Instantly the beach, the surfer, the palm trees, the grass shacks have all disappeared and the ship is resting on the shoulder of the volcano near the top that makes a small plateau. Beneath him and all around the ship are the tops of the soft fluffy clouds he had just observed from below.

"How much time do we have?" he asks.

"It will all be over in the wink of an eye," Ula replies.

CHAPTER 2

▼

CHINESE FOOD ON PLUTO

Realizing he has missed a night's sleep, Doug closes his eyes to rest. His intent is to simply take a break, rest a spell and get to the next task at hand. As he slips off to sleep, he's wondering what that might be. He has visions of the world ending without him ever seeing her again. 'What will happen to them?' he wonders. He had always held out the hope that they would someday get back together. Then, he realizes his selfishness since it will the end for millions of lovers all over the world soon.

He's dreaming about her when suddenly the ship is rocked with a loud bang. Doug jumps out of the chair and notices that the hat has been removed from his head and is dangling up above him near the ceiling. He's thinking that perhaps the volcano is erupting.

He runs down the stairs and through the magnetic field that is the skin of the ship to determine what's going on. In front of him, a large man is staring at him with big blue eyes. He's bald with a long curly blonde beard. He's sitting on top of a large tractor. He's chewing something black and vile. He's apparently been slamming the machine into the side of the egg.

He's about to charge it again, when he stops with a very loud and rusty squeal right in front Doug.

"What the hell?" The large man manages to blurt out, spitting.

"I might ask you the same thing, my friend. What the hell are you doin' with that tractor?" Doug asks, disturbed from his nap and more than a bit cranky.

"I thought it was a dinosaur egg. I was going to kill it before it hatched!" he replies scratching himself. "How on God's green Earth, you get in there?"

"That's for me to know and you to find out. I'll thank you to stay away from my house. If you disturb it one more time, I'll sue you and have you arrested for trespassing," Doug says, not knowing what else to say.

"This is a house?" the man retorts.

"That's right, and you're on my property. Now get off, move off!" Doug commands.

"Right, I'll do that, man. Sure, but I'll be back with the law. I doubt you own this property. It's part of the state park. I'm working on a run-off drain over there and ain't nobody mentioned no egg I had to watch out for," he spouts.

The man drives his tractor down the slope to a point where Doug can see a small dirt road. He guns the machine and takes off at tractor speed to parts unknown.

'He'll have an interesting story to tell someone, someday,' Doug thinks to himself.

Instinct tells him that they can't be discovered just yet. He examines the wall of the egg for signs of damage, but there are none, not even a scratch. It seems odd to him at first and then he can feel the nature of the force that makes up the skin. It's in his brain. It's obvious the ship's force field is far more powerful than anything Mankind could ever conceive.

He takes one last look around at the magnificent Hawaiian white billowing cloud formations, the blue ocean staring up at them from far below and inserts himself back into the ship. They will have to find some privacy elsewhere.

When he arrives back inside the ship, his attention flows to one of the hallways just to his left. He realizes that this trick of perspective has to be scouted out. It seems he has time to do a little exploring. The man with the tractor can't possibly round up any cops way up here for hours.

He starts out on a little stroll down the hall. It leads to a much larger room about fifteen paces from the center room. He knows that in his own dimension, he would be standing outside the ship now. And, yet here's this gigantic room with three more doorways opening onto halls of their own, each going off into unknown distances.

The room he's entered is filled with shelves. On the shelves are placed thousands and thousands of what looks like CD cases, except that they are all perfect cubes in size and shape. Each one is numbered. There are chairs and ottomans placed by the walls like some elongated men's club he's seen in the movies. There's a small desk in the middle of the room with a chair. On top of the desk is a reading lamp and a machine that he takes for some kind of reader like he's seen in libraries. He walks over to take a closer look. A small oval screen brightens as he approaches.

He can now see a square slot that these cubes might fit into perfectly. So, he wanders over to the wall and takes one off the shelf at random. Sure enough, it fits inside the computer slot and glides in noiselessly. There is a low humming noise. The screen comes up with a picture of a strange place. He can see that it's another planet. There seems to be a narration playing along with the images. But it's in a language he's never heard before. The narration continues and he realizes from the sounds and images that this is a kind of travelogue. But, it's more scientific than that. Everything of any significance on this planet seems to be shown in some kind of order, but not for entertainment purposes. It's more of a scientific catalogue.

The images flowing past are of plants and animals that he could never even dream about. Some are ferocious looking. Others are quite tame and gentle. There seems to be a major animal with teeth the size of a pick-up truck that pre-dates on all the rest. It appears to Doug as if this cube is talking about the food chain on this planet.

He removes the cube, puts it back where he found it, and randomly selects another, puts it into the slot and waits for the screen to show him what's stored inside it. It's the same kind of a scientific gathering of data. He wonders if this ship's purpose is to gather data on every planet in the galaxy? Or even beyond that, the universe?

The animals and plants that he's viewing fill him with a great joy and curiosity. This second cube shows off a place that is beyond his comprehension at first. Slowly he realizes that this place is a wonderful paradise. There are the most beautiful sorts of trees and shrubs that he's ever seen. They seem to cover an immense part of this planet. But rather than green, they're blue. Instead of standing in one place, they move about slowly in the wind like great sailing ships of days gone by. Their patterns in motion seem to suggest that they are socializing in a way he can only guess.

He knows he doesn't have much time and he can always come back to this place later. And, he still hasn't been more than 15 paces from the center of the ship. He's very curious to discover what lies further ahead. He removes the cube and puts it back in its place trying to remember where it is so that he can come back to this one.

He turns down the center hallway and takes a few paces before he realizes that he could easily get lost in this maze. From here, he can still see his way back to the center. But, he knows that if he goes much further, there will be more and more permutations and the temptation to go further and further into the ship could get him lost in a hurry.

Fearful of becoming lost and wandering aimlessly for years, Doug decides to go back. The man with the tractor might return sooner than he thinks and it would do no one any good if they were discovered now.

When he gets back to what he calls the 'cockpit', he slips on the hat and begins to think about a place very far from here. In an instant, he looks outside to see that they've landed in the middle of giant urban center. There are many oriental people wandering around on foot, several on bicycles. He's starting to recognize the place from the many photos he's seen in recent past. The Great Hall of the People lies just to his right. The Great Hall of International Peace is half a mile away to his left. They have landed in the middle of Tienneman Square, the heart of Beijing, the capital of the People's Republic of China.

"Ula, why did we land here? I was thinking about…"

"Chinese food," she interrupts.

"Well, I guess you're right. I'm a bit hungry and I'm fond of that. But why here? Why didn't you take me to some quiet little restaurant in Los Angeles or New York or anyplace but here?" He wonders out loud.

"I thought you'd want the original," she says curtly.

Taking in the panorama around him through the view screens on the wall, he can see that they've caught the attention of several hundred Chinese hurrying through the square on their daily pursuits. More troubling, the red-capped police are gathering in groups and talking to their superiors on wireless phones.

"I thought it might be a nice break for you and besides, there's something we need to do here," she replies.

"What's that? Order out?" he jokes.

"Yes, that too. But, I want you to go out there and make a little speech first," she says.

"A speech? I don't make speeches," he replies, anxiously.

"You do now. I want you to go out there and tell those people that they no longer have to obey any of their leaders. That this part of their history has all been a nightmare from which they are about to awaken. Good things like that. Get them stirred up. Inspire and enlighten them," she says.

"You want me to rile up a couple million Chinese folks?" he asks, worried.

"Yes, and when you're done, I'll have your meal sitting here waiting for you. I guarantee it will be the best Chinese food you've ever had," she replies.

"What about the local gendarmes. They don't look very happy and I haven't even shown myself yet," he says.

"You'll be all right. At first, they won't know what to do. You're going to appear very suddenly from the ship and that will catch them off guard. Right now, they're thinking this is some kind of government test weapon of their own that someone left carelessly lying around. When you speak, they'll get mad, but I won't let them harm you," she reassures him. "Trust me."

"Ok, I'll trust you if that's what you want. I guess it's my job to just follow orders. Is that how it goes around here?" he asks.

"That will do for now, I'm sure," she says. "Later on, we'll have a talk."

"Hmm, ok, well here goes nothin'," he says.

Reluctantly, Doug rises out of the chair and removes the hat which again slowly draws rises up to the ceiling. He slowly descends the stairway and moves to the electric skin of the ship. He's starting to feel his thoughts gathering inside his brain. To his great shock his thoughts are in perfect Mandarin Chinese.

When he suddenly materializes through the strange vibrating skin of the ship, the crowd now gathering all around in growing numbers, gasps in surprise.

He holds up his hand making the peace sign. He takes a moment to gather his thoughts. The crowd is restless but attentive.

"I come in peace from the planet Tralfamador," he begins. Tralfamador being a planet that he remembers from a Kurt Vonnegut novel he's read in his youth. He has trouble holding back a chuckle.

"I am here to tell you that something wonderful has happened. The Communist control of this country is coming to an end. They will all be vanquished by your hands, the hands of the people, in the very near future. You have only days left to live under this oppressive regime. Democracy is the way people of higher intelligence rule themselves in all of the rest of this vast galaxy of planets. Your planet is the only one left that resorts to rule by the tyrannical and the malicious and the corrupt. This is the largest country on the Earth that is ruled so viciously and with such malice. And it's time that this travesty comes to an end," He begins.

Doug can see the police becoming very agitated. They are nervously coagulating around the outskirts of the crowd, consulting with each other about what to do. In China, the myth is that the police and the army are under the control of the people. It's only during events of any challenge to their authority that they show their true colors.

One very stern looking officer is gazing off in the distance and speaking to someone with his hand held radio.

"Your leaders enslave you by not granting you the simple freedoms that are every citizen's god-given rights. They refuse to allow you freedom of speech, freedom of the press, freedom of religion, even freedom of thought. There is no chance for you to speak out or express your opinions about their decisions which are often made for selfish and personal reasons. They put you in slave camps and prisons and torture you. They slaughter thousands of you daily in firing squads and kill those who's only offense is to speak out about their horrible assault on human rights. They take away your very basic right to know the truth. They give you nothing that you could not earn on your own and most of your hard earned money they turn into weapons of mass destruction. Why, you must ask yourselves do they need such weapons knowing that they can never be used. The reason is for strict political intimidation of the rest of the world. With your help, they put up a terrible barrier to any other nation who might try to help you in your quest for freedom. In this way, they are Evil personified. You must not let this exist any longer in this world or the rest of the world will condemn you for all time as great cowards and small minded men and women. The time is now. This is the first day of the rest of your lives. Go and live them as free men and women and resist the evil they force upon you. Resist at every opportunity. Resist them now and for all time so that they will know that their time is up," he says, surprising himself at this level of passion.

The crowd stares at him blankly. They are silent and motionless. Then, Doug begins to feel a great rumbling under his feet. The cobblestones are rattling and the dust between the cracks in the cobblestone is vibrating and boiling under their feet. 'Tanks are coming,' he says to himself.

"We have little time to speak of these things. I have no time to tell you exactly how this evil curse on your lands will end. But it will die out, and die out it must! It begins with the replacement of your leaders with someone who is able and willing to help bring about a just and equitable society, a society based on trust and faith in you and your descendants, a love of God and harmony and peace with one's neighbors. Can you feel the winds of change? Don't be afraid of these machines of war nor of the unthinking robots inside them." he tells them. "They who would kill their own kind or those who stand idly by while others do the killing and commit these unspeakable atrocities are men who have no humanity. When they run out of bullets, when their machines fail them and fall into disrepair or are destroyed, it will be humanity left standing, not these machines. They don't understand this great truth, but I'm here to tell you, you will be left standing, those of you who maintain your humanity will inherit the earth."

The rumbling is getting more and more noticeable. A few people in the crowd look down to see the stones literally dancing beneath their feet. They all know that the tanks are never very far away. They slowly begin to disperse. Their facial expressions are unchanged. They seem to be unmoved by Doug's little speech. But, Doug is confident that his words have hit home. He doesn't know how exactly but there's something in his heart and their hearts that corresponded. The unchanging expressions on their faces are merely the results of years of living under this terrible oppression. They have become conditioned to never show their true emotions and as such they are a pitiful lot, but they are still human. There is still a tiny spark of hope glowing deep inside their breasts.

Fighting an almost irresistible urge to run back inside the ship, he watches hypnotized by the almost horrible beauty of these heavy machines of war slowly approaching him. He can count a dozen tanks in the front line with more coming behind. They are flanked by what Doug feels must be a couple regiments of soldiers. Their rifles are held close to their shoulders. They are marching in perfect unison. Their boots slapping the stones so hard he wonders how this doesn't hurt their feet. If this action is meant to intimidate him, it's working.

The crowd has completely abandoned the square in front of him and taken positions far off to the edge of the square. They know that something terrible is going to happen and it is human nature to watch horrific events taking place even if they are so terrible they will find it hard to speak of them later. The police are trying to warn them off the square and back to their homes. But they too can't take their eyes off the scene developing in front of them. Certainly this strange man will be blown to bits by the tanks for saying such incredibly risky things about their leaders.

The column of tanks grinds to a stop about one hundred yards away. 'The perfect firing distance,' he thinks. The soldiers form up in the center in a column twenty wide and march forward. A series of short brusque words are shouted out by a commander somewhere from behind the tanks. Immediately, the soldiers stop abruptly, un-shoulder their weapons, present their very shiny barrels in perfect harmony, and point them directly toward Doug and the egg.

Another command is heard and the marchers take one last thundering slap at the pavement with their boots that echoes all around the square and makes the pigeons fly off in a mass panic.

From behind the column of men and weapons, their commander marches up to Doug and puts his face in Doug's face.

The commander is furious with him and his eyes are bulging with anger.

"You are under arrest," he yells at him. "You will surrender yourself and this ship to me or be destroyed!"

"I'm not afraid of you," Doug lies with as much strength and conviction as he can strain out of his feeble voice.

In exactly one second he plans to turn and dive into the safety of the ship. He's only waiting for the commander to blink or turn to give the order to shoot him and he's gone.

The commander seems ready to explode at these words. Doug can't help but feel a touch of sympathy for the poor fellow so caught up in his own hate. But, there's also the much stronger emotion of self-preservation rising up from his toes.

The commander raises his hand. Suddenly, Doug notices a pistol in his hand. He's either going to shoot Doug or shoot himself. He calculates quickly which way it's going to go.

Doug is ready to turn and jump back into the safety of the ship when the Commander suddenly bursts off the ground and goes flying fifty feet up into the air. He comes to a very hard landing at the feet of his troops who are staring in disbelief, but still pointing their weapons at Doug.

He's not moving at all. He's groaning in agony. He's trying to give out one last command, but the words do not make it out before his last gasp and then loses consciousness.

The troops take no action but look at each other nervously awaiting a command from somebody, anybody, anywhere. Doug feels they might even take a command from him now.

He's about to speak to them, but the lead tank in the middle guns its engine. With a loud roar it jerks forward and the phalanx of troops has to make way for the lumbering beast. The tank lurches forward to a spot just behind their fallen commander. A soldier runs around from behind the tank and grabs the feet of the dead commander and drags him to safety.

Doug hears a round of ammunition being slammed into the cannon inside the metal hull of the tank. Then, someone inside yells out the command to fire.

Time comes to a standstill. He cannot move his feet or his arms. He is paralyzed with fear, but at the same time strangely, he's filled with a kind of confidence and even jocularity. The scene seems humorous to him somehow. He makes a mental note to ask Ula about this, if he lives to ever talk to her again.

The crowd can hear it. Doug hears it and feels it; A tiny little metallic click just prior to the tank suddenly exploding into an ear-splitting inferno and disappearing into a red and black sudden burst of smoke and fire. Bits and pieces of men and machine shower down on the crowd and the square.

Doug makes no motion at all. The surviving troops alongside the exploding tank run for their lives. A few of them don't make it far enough to outrun the fireball. The remaining few run for their lives. The rest of the tanks gun their engines and turn themselves ponderously in the opposite direction and then beat a hasty and noisy retreat and soon fade into the mist.

Doug breathes for the first time in moments. He looks back at the retreating tanks and shaking like a frightened rabbit takes a grateful refuge inside the ship.

After reaching the stairs, he stops to assess what has just happened. A man who was ready to shoot him in the head, was blown fifty feet up in the air. The tank that shot a round from point blank range at him, exploded killing all inside and several outside.

"Dangerous business," he thinks to himself and suddenly fatigued, he struggles up the stairs to have a little chat with Ula. He's overwhelmed with a curiosity and wonder and a kind of gratitude he's never felt before. He knows he's very lucky to be alive.

On a table in front of his seat there is a veritable feast of Chinese food. On plates, filling the room with the most wonderful smells is a chicken chop suey, a yam pot, a beautiful little bowl of chow mein and a plate of almond cookies off to the side. There's a pot of very aromatic ginger tea steaming beside a small cup.

"I want to know, that was you that did all that out there, am I correct on that?" he asks her after sitting and putting on the hat.

"You're correct," Ula answers.

"Ok fine, but then, how did you do that?" he asks, taking in the incredible aroma. It's making him salivate.

"All right. You deserve to know more about my programming constraints. I cannot by my action cause harm to any life forms or by my inaction cause harm to any life forms. But, in my self-defense, or in defense of you and me, I can take actions that would prevent us from being harmed, no matter what the results. When their commander pulled his gun from his holster and pointed it at you, I could sense that he intended to use it. So, I did the only thing I could do and tossed his body into the air. I did not tried not to kill him, but he was lighter than I judged and I used a bit too much force. It is regrettable that he died, but the act of destroying me or anyone in my protection is not acceptable, and in self defense I am allowed to use any amount of force that is necessary to prevent such harm being done," she says casually.

"And the tank?" Doug asks, grabbing a fork and getting ready to chow down.

"Everyone heard the soldiers in the tank make the fatal decision to load their cannon with a shell. Then, we all heard the firing mechanism. At this split second, I made the shell expand in size so that it no longer fit in the barrel. This, I knew would cause the tank to explode, however, I had no option again, since you would have been killed instantly," she says.

"But the shell would not have penetrated the ship?" he asks her.

"No, there is no way that any material object can penetrate the force field of my skin, unless they are authorized by me to pass through it," she says.

"What would be the reaction if the shell had been fired at you?" he asks.

"Well, first of all my force field is far stronger than any cannon shell, so it would have simply flattened itself out and fallen harmlessly to the ground, however, no weapon on Earth can ever get that far. My technology is so far advanced that nothing on this planet can threaten me. I am always aware of any event within split second timing, so I can always find alternatives paths for your projectiles as I did with the tank," she says. "Your weaponry on this planet, although highly lethal for you is incredibly primitive to me."

"Ok, why me?" he asks, digesting her words and taking a few tidbits and placing them into his mouth.

Through the view screens he can see that the crowd has gathered again in the wake of the small battle. The exploded tank is still smoldering and some people in the crowd are helping to remove the bodies of about a dozen soldiers fallen in the vicinity. Most are just standing and watching and giving each other the benefit of their insight into the situation.

Doug realizes that she has given him no immediate response to this question. So, he thinks it again.

"Why me?" he repeats, chewing his food as politely as he can since he is very hungry.

"Can I answer that later?" she replies.

"Sure, but why can't you tell me now?" he retorts, swallowing.

"Because they are sending in their Air Forces to bomb this place and that's our cue to leave. Many of these civilians will be killed in the attack," she replies.

"Oh, I see. How do you know that they're coming," he asks, putting the meal aside temporarily.

"Radio waves are not a very secure means of communication," she says.

"I see, so you can read their radio transmissions? All of them?" he asks.

"Oh yes, this is well within the range of my abilities" she says.

"I see that now. Where do we go from here?" he asks her.

"You decide. But you must do so in the next thirty seconds or these people will die," she says.

"I've always wanted to see Pluto," he thinks and gives the command by simply thinking about the planet furthest from the sun and imposing his will. "Let's go there. What the heck."

Before his heart can beat again, the view screens are reporting images of dark night sky exploding with stars. Looking down at the ground outside the ship, Doug sees only barren dark rock as black and cold as cast iron. There is no atmosphere. There is no sign of life of any kind. Pluto is merely a big frozen rock orbiting the sun so far from its heat and light, the sun's orb is barely larger than the stars all around them.

"Wow! Ok, so this is Pluto. We're safe here, you're sure?" he asks.

"Quite sure," she replies confidently.

"But how. I merely blinked an eye and we were here. Am I in some kind of trance? Did you put me into some kind of hibernation? This trip even traveling at the speed of light, which Einstein said was impossible, would have taken, I don't know, a couple hours. How did you do that?" he asks in a quandary.

"It's simple really. We know a trick," Ula says.

"A trick? What kind of trick?" he asks, noticing that the planet is hardly a planet at all. They are sitting on a slight rise of a hill. The horizon goes out a few hundred feet and no more. Pluto is a small barren outpost. But the view is magnificent. 'Prime Real Estate someday' he thinks to himself.

"Yes, it is," Ula says. "Beautiful isn't it? The sky, I mean?"

"Wonderful. But what's the trick? How on Earth did we get here so fast?" he asks, looking up at the field of stars so plentiful, the blackness of space appears like a thick carpet of lights.

"Well, not a trick exactly. It's the way things are. It's the true physics of the universe. You see, Doug, there truly is zero distance in the universe. The whole show is nothing more than the size of a spec of dust, smaller really, because there is no distance between anything. Distance is the illusion, but space is one unified place, a small dot in the mind of God. You cannot comprehend it right now, but when we discovered this little secret billions of years ago, there was no place we couldn't go, nothing we couldn't do. So, we did quite a lot. And now we don't mind sharing it with species who are on the verge of the same discovery," she replies.

"Zero distance? But how can that be?" Doug asks. "It's not making sense."

"All right. Think about infinity for a moment," she says quietly. "How big is that in your mind?"

"I don't know how to answer that. It's infinity. It goes on forever, right?" Doug replies.

"Yes, but cannot visualize the boundaries of infinity or else it wouldn't be infinity any longer would it? In reality, infinity is a circle, a closed loop. And the circle of infinity holds an infinite number of smaller circles and larger circles within. The center of each circle is shared by all other circles. But the dots are all in the same place. The center of all circles are one in the same. They exist in the same space. But you can only create a universe like that if there is zero distance. And that's exactly what the Creator did because in that fabrication, in that structure, he can be everywhere at once and guide us all through space and time without effort and without any delays that might be caused if space were real and distances needed time to traverse them," she says.

"That's also why all his creatures can know him all at the same time, no matter where in the universe they may be. Pretty good trick, is it not?" she asks rhetorically.

"I see, but space does take time for us to travel through it," he says. "It takes about ten minutes for me to get to work. It takes other people an hour or two. It takes two or three days for us to get to the moon, several hours to go around the Earth. Distance does require time."

"Yes, for you because you know only the illusion of the distance and you insist on bringing everything, every particle, every molecule of your existence with you. That requires energy to move it all around and energy is the problem. The more you expend, the more time it takes. There is no time for us to traverse any distance because we've learned how to take nothing with us on the journey except for our thoughts. We get away from the constraints of energy and strain and power," she says and pauses for all this to sink into Doug's mind.

"Haven't you noticed there are no engines on this ship?" she asks.

"Yeah, I mean yes, come to think of it, I have. There's no engine noise either," he replies.

"That's because we are pure thought and in pure thought there is a greater power over all other things," she says.

"I see, but how does that explain my being here with you? Certainly, I'm not pure thought too now, am I?" he asks, almost afraid to hear the answer.

"No, but you've been charged by it. It surrounds you. It embraces you and for a short time, it binds you here to us," she says.

"I see, I think," Doug says, confused.

"Let me show you something," Ula says. "Think about the finest moment in your life. Bring it to the surface for me please."

Doug concentrates and focuses on the time he first kissed Zora. Suddenly, she is there in his mind just as real as if they were physically together again. She is looking at him with the same inviting posture with her long neck and perfect shoulders and breasts that he enjoyed so much. She is wearing the tweed pants and jacket exactly as she was wearing that day. Her shoes are the same light brown and he can see the grain in the leather where it meets the soft white flesh of her foot. He can run his hands through her long brown hair and smell her exactly as she smelled that day. He can feel her lips and then her warm probing tongue as it caresses his. He hears his keys drop on the hardwood floor to chime in his ears exactly as they did that day. He can feel her in his arms as he carries her up the stairs as he did that day. He can feel the blood flowing through the chambers of his heart and into his brain, warmed by the flow of her body and her mind and her thoughts wrapped up in his.

"Promise me you'll never leave me," he pleads with her.

"I promise I'll never leave you," she says smiling exactly the way he remembers that incredible smile.

And then, she is gone. Doug realizes he's been holding his breath. He lets a large volume of air pour back into his lungs.

"I see it now. Wow, thanks for that," he says and pauses to bask a few more precious seconds in the memory of her.

"Ok, but you still haven't answered my question; Why me?" he ponders gazing at the black ice and frozen rock beneath the ship and feels the stark barrenness of this place so devoid of life take hold of him once again.

"There is no easy answer," she begins. "Consciousness is both random and logical at the same time. We being pure consciousness chose your planet for reasons of pure logic. But, the area of your planet where we chose to land was chosen randomly and your mind was chosen logically. And, thus our visit to your home."

"I see," he says. "You make it all sound so clinical. You've done this all before, I take it?"

"Oh yes, seventeen times to be exact. This will be our eighteenth folding," she replies.

"Eighteen, so the universe has folded in on itself eighteen times including this one?" he asks.

"Yes, eighteen that we know of now. But we also believe that before we evolved to know about it, the universe has folded in on itself an infinite number of times before our own evolution started. But since we were not around to view these events, there is no way of knowing," she replies directly.

"I see," he says. "And let me ask it another way. Why do you need me in all this?" he asks.

"We can't save your world without knowing more about the genetic structure of your species. When we save you, we combine our genetic code with the subject species. This is how we grow. Your kind will take a giant leap forward in evolution. Ours is a giant leap of a different kind. But before any of us can make the leap, we need to know more about you and thus, we need one of you to study while these events are taking place," Ula says.

Doug sits there a few moments considering what she has just told him.

Then he says, "So, your species is going to burrow into our genetic code and combine it with yours and that would mean a completely new species, then? I'm no scientists, but I read," he asks, befuddled.

"Yes, that's correct," she replies.

"But you said that would create a giant leap backwards for you. Why would you want to merge with an inferior species," curiously.

"I never said it was backwards for us. Just different. Sometimes, going back genetically is not necessarily a bad thing," she replies, tersely.

"I get it," he says. "Not really, but I'll try it again later, with your help of course."

'Plenty of time for more questions later,' he thinks. He's tired and at the present moment, Doug is enraptured by the moment and the savory and aromatic dishes in front of him are more temptation than he can resist. He can no longer resist eating this wonderful food under this awesome panoply of stars. The flavors, the aromas, the textures, and ideas swirl in his brain and create a wonderful 'imagination stew' he has never tasted before, but he relishes it in the silence of this place and eats his fill.

CHAPTER 3

▼

THE STREET WHERE SHE LIVES

When Doug awakens from his sleep, he realizes that they are still planted on Pluto. Above and all around is the deep profound blackness studded with the copious shining points of light. He still can't get over the beauty of this vista. It makes him very happy and suddenly he's starting to realize the nature of his mission. He has new thought patterns swirling inside his head, ideas he never had before. Ula has downloaded to him, the entire history of their race. In the volumes of information, there is a line of thought that is both mysterious and beautiful and unlike anything he's ever known in his lifetime and he doubts would be imagined by anyone else on his planet until now.

None of our science can prepare us for this event. To say that this event shatters all precedent and all human scientific knowledge and evidence, would be an under statement. Because we can't really see very far at all, the folding of the universe is nothing that could have or would have been predicted by modern human science. And yet, there it is. In front of him. The entire history of the universe as told by Ula delineates it all for billions upon billions of years. Their evolution throughout this cycle of unimaginable violence and re-creation is astounding. By way of their own science, far advanced from our own, their consciousness has evolved far above and beyond our own, they are the only life form that has managed to remain integral throughout eighteen cycles of the demolition and re-recreation of our universe. The way they achieved that magnificent level of knowledge is still totally outside of his cognition. Somehow, they merely fold in on themselves along with the universe, or 'super-massive cluster of galaxies', as they call it, and wait. They have discovered how to live in pure thought and since pure thought can never be destroyed, their genetic history lives on and takes them beyond and through the total annihilation of everything. At the appropriate time, their code is reconstructed the way a computer boots itself back to life after it's been turned off.

Their concept of God is also far more advanced and compelling than Doug's concept of the Almighty and his religious instruction could ever prepare him. The knowledge imparted has given him new eyes, new insights far more advanced than his previous human awareness would allow. He can see it all now. He knows it all. He is the possessor of the ultimate knowledge. The ultimate goal of all life forms is his to know and cherish the truth, truth about all things. It's a daunting challenge, but it is God given and therefore the only challenge we need worry about.

He feels very resigned to his fate at this moment. It is the essence of this being. It is the ultimate fate of all creatures to be reunited with the force that creates them.

Just as all stars are destroyed, just as all the planets, asteroids, comets all eventually come to an end and their elements recycled in the giant furnace of gravity, so too is the entire universe itself destroyed and later renewed. Well, that part of the universe that is actually our own super massive cluster of galaxies and that we call the universe is in reality only a small bubble in the overall universe. Even though seemingly infinite in size, our universe, it turns out is a very small thing, in the overall scheme of things, a mere collection of galaxies that folds in on itself every thirteen billion years and starts out again all over like a coat or shirt that is reversed when soiled. He can know it all as clearly as he knows his own name. The implantation of this information is something that had to be timed perfectly by Ula into his brain at the exact moment when he could digest it all, or most of it anyway.

He feels this also in every cell.

"Ula," he says, fully awake. "Where do we go from here?"

"Where do you want to go?" she replies.

"I would like to see her one more time, if I could. I mean, in the flesh this time." he says, taking one last look around at the incredible sight before him in the view screens.

"You seem to have a one track mind. But, I think that would be a fine idea," she says. "Why don't you take us there?"

Doug has to recall the place where she lives. It's a large house on a hill in the more pleasant part of Pleasanton, California. It's just after sunset when they arrive. The ship descends slowly so as to not rouse the neighbors' dogs that Doug just seems to know are all around, lying asleep just beyond the redwood fences. One dog, a large Alaskan Husky feels the static electricity raise his fur. He wants to bark the alarm, but can't. He's becomes convinced that there's nothing really wrong and goes back to sleep.

When the ship is secure in a small grassy paddock, in the middle of her lovely garden, Doug looks out the view screen to see her silhouette in the window just beyond a small grape arbor separating the mid part of the yard from the house.

"It's her," he whispers to himself. He wonders if the husband is around. That would make things a bit more complicated, to say the least.

Just then, another, larger silhouette stands in the window light. He's there.

"What am I going to do now?" he asks.

"The husband, you mean?" Ula says. "I can take care of that."

Doug can hear the phone ring in another room of the house. The large silhouette leaves the window. He can hear a muffled conversation and he can also hear Ula's side of it.

"Mr. Reed, you simply must come to the hospital immediately. There's been a terrible accident. Don't worry, everything is all right. But, you must get here now. Don't worry about anything. He's fine. But, he is requesting that you get here now," she is saying to someone else, not him.

"No, you don't need to take anything," Ula is speaking. "Just get in your car and drive over here now. No, don't bother to bring your wife. She wouldn't be allowed in to the room anyway. No need to bother her. You'll be back home in no time at all."

Doug is starting to fathom Ula's plan. He's about to tell her what a con artist she is, when he sees the male silhouette return to the kitchen window. The two figures exchange a few words. At first, it appears that she might go with him. But, he convinces her to stay. They embrace and then he leaves the room. Soon, on the other side of the house, a garage door opens slowly and a car pulls slowly outside onto the driveway and then turns onto the road beneath the house and disappears from his view.

"She's all yours," Ula says. "You have about an hour. Half an hour for him to get there and half an hour for him to get home."

"Thanks, Ula. I don't know what I'm going to say," he tells her.

"It will come to you, trust me," she says.

Doug takes off the hat, walks down the circular stairway and then out of the center hall through the skin of the ship and onto her grass. His heart is racing. He's starting to feel tiny beads of sweat building on his forehead and under his arms. His feet are almost paralyzed, but he forces them forward to her back door.

He knocks on the door, almost hoping she can't hear it so that he can give up this idea and flee back into the ship.

Just as he's about to turn and run, the door opens. With light from behind her, she looks as though she is spirit only, a dream taking shape in front of his eyes.

She looks at him in surprise. The surprise is turning to shock. She wants to call out to her husband to rescue her, but she realizes at the same instant that they are alone.

"What are you doing here?" she cries.

"Hello Zora. I honestly don't know what I'm doing here," he begins poorly. "I had to see you. I'm involved in something very weird, you see, and I don't know how much time I have left," he says.

She grimaces. Her eyes narrow and she looks like a cat.

"You're always into something weird," she says coldly.

"I mean, I don't know how much time I'm going to be here in the country. I have a new job that will take me all over, aaaand uh, well, er, I don't know when I can get back," he stammers.

"And what does that have to do with me?" she says, even more coldly.

"Please don't be that way. I just had to see you one more time. That's all. I won't take long. I only have a few minutes anyway. Can't we talk for just a minute?" he pleads.

"We don't have anything to talk about, Doug. I'm married now," she says, happily.

"Yes, I know that. I don't want you to come back to me. It's way too late for that. I know. I'm just in a kind of confusion right now and I needed to talk to you. Can't you give me just a few minutes, uh, inside?" he asks her, gesturing toward the warmth of the room beyond. Doug starts to calm down and begins to get into the rhythm of the moment.

He's resigned himself to whatever happens now. His blood pressure is back to normal. The worst scenario, he's reasoning, is that she slams the door on his face, but since he's seen her face and heard her voice, that would be acceptable to him now. For the last 10 years, she's never returned a phone call or replied to any of his letters. Somehow, he's accepted the almost perfect continuity of her responses. 'At least she's consistent, strong, never wavering in her beliefs,' he tells himself again.

"All right. Come in," she says suddenly. "But only for a few minutes. My husband just left for the hospital. His father has taken ill. And, I don't expect you to take advantage of the situation."

She leads him through the kitchen, then into a large dining room filled with tasteful dark wood furniture and into the living area. There's a sitting area, flanked by soft leather sofas, that seem larger than his whole cabin.

She sits down and motions for him to sit across from her. He stares at her for a long moment.

"Well, why don't you get it off your chest," she says after an embarrassing silence.

"Yes, uh. Yeah, all right." Suddenly, Doug has no idea why he's here. He has no idea what to say next. Then, the words simply tumble from his lips.

"I've missed you. Missed you a lot," he says, as plainly as he can. "That's all. I just came here to say that to you face to face. I know you haven't missed me and that's cool. It's ok. Really. I get that. I accept it. It's part of my reality and I can live with it. Uh, good-bye and thank you for your time." He says abruptly and stands up to leave on slightly wobbly knees.

"Sit down Doug," she snaps, coldly. "You're not getting off that easy. You knock on my door in the middle of the night when you must have known my husband has just left me alone. Then, you beg your way into my home to tell me you've missed me. And then you think you can just get up and leave? What do you think of me? Do you really think I haven't missed you too?"

"Uh, yeah, what?" he says, caught in the melodic tones of her voice. His eyes glance down at her feet in her slippers. He can still remember the touching, the rubbing of their feet together in bed. Then, it escalates up from there. His mind is furiously calculating every nook and cranny of her body that he once knew so intimately.

Then, she seems to catch herself. "Doug, you have to forget me. You simply have to forget everything about me. I left you ten years ago. You can't keep pining away like this. You're a nice man. I liked you and I don't want to see you all alone for the rest of your life. Why haven't you found someone else after all this time?" she asks with a thawing of her heart like glaciers melting.

"God knows I've tried. I've tried to forget you, but the more I try to forget, the more I remember," he replies woefully.

"Well, you're not trying hard enough," she says softly, a slight hint of a smile creeping along her lips.

"I'll promise to do better," he says. To Doug it seems just like the last time they were together. He feels her electricity probing his. For seconds they are alone with the silence in the room and their eyes sparking a current that glows blue and warm.

"You have to," she says, bright shining pools are filling her eyes. Doug can sense another person rising up from deep down within her and reaching out to him.

"I will. I don't want to be a bother. I know you've moved on. I have to move on. I know that. I will find someone, someday who can take your place. It can't be that difficult, right? And I must. I mean I will. I just have to look harder and be more open to new people and stuff. And, I will. I'll look some more," he lies, knowing she knows it's a lie.

He can feel her heart melting from his seemingly infinite distance from her. He wants so badly to get up and hold her. But he knows that this incredible, amazing miracle must come from her if it comes at all.

The pools in her eyes have welled up and overflow down her flushed cheeks.

"You'd better go now," she says with a courage stubbornly controlling her voice.

"Yes, I better," Doug says, fearing that other person returning, the person who's mind is made up, the person struggling to control the softer, gentler person within, the one that he loves.

Doug gets up to go, on knees that have barely recovered their strength. He knows he must find the strength to leave her where she sits. He turns to look at her. She remains in place, not bothering to wipe the tears flowing profusely now down her face and splashing onto her the white cotton of her nightgown.

He exits the living room, finds himself in the kitchen still alone. Her warmth has left him. The magic he knows whenever he's with her is fading. He's reaching for the back door when he hears her cry out.

"Doug!" his name is all she can get out through a voice straining to be heard.

He turns to see her run into the room. She rushes up to him and they embrace. She raises her face to his. Their lips meet. They stay connected for several minutes. They can hear each other's breath flowing through their nostrils as one. He runs his hands up and down her spine as he once used to do. They are both remembering in unison the first time they kissed when he raised her up in his arms and carried her upstairs to the bedroom and then made love to her.

He can feel her body melting into his own. He drops to his knees and puts his head against her stomach. He wants to look up at her. He wants to feel her tears cascade down onto his face. It reminds him of a waterfall in a magic island para-dise where they both once stood united together.

"I can never forget you. You can't ask me to do that," he says. I will never find anyone else like you. It's ok, though. I'm all right with that. The couple of years that you gave me is more love and affection than most men ever know in their entire lifetime. I'm so grateful for those memories. I have that and I'll never give that up. You can't ask me to do that."

"I know," she's sobbing. "I don't want you to forget me. I was lying. I just want you to be happy. Can't you be happy?"

Doug stands again and takes her hand, raises it to his cheek and nose sensing her unique fragrance, their eyes welded in their union.

"I told you. I told you I'm fine with the time I've had with you and that I don't really need any more. But actually, that was a lie. I would love to have more time with you. I would love to have you back with me forever. But, I don't see how that's possible now, do you?" he asks.

"No, I don't," she says quietly, quietly remembering the feelings she has for her husband.

"I guess there is such a thing as fate. We just weren't fated to be together. That's all there is to it. You can't fight something like that," he says, consoling her.

Outside the door a dog is barking sensing again the strange living machine in his neighbor's yard.

"I'd better go now. I got way more than I bargained for. I hope I haven't annoyed you," he says, gently releasing her hand and forcing his hand to reach for the door knob.

"Doug, I left you and I never told you why I left. You came here to find out why I left, didn't you?" she asks suddenly.

He closes the door and stands facing her again.

"Yes, I guess that's true. You never would tell me why. Why, Zora? What hap-pened to us?" he asks slowly.

"I was afraid of you," she says, surprising even herself at her sudden clarity.

"Afraid of me? How? Why?" Doug is surprised at this revelation. He had con-cocted several hundred reasons, none of them even resembling this one framed in her own words.

"Not you, precisely. It was the intensity that you loved me. That's what I was afraid of. The way you just kissed me reminded me of it. The way we made love, it was so wonderful, it was painful to me. I didn't think I could take that pressure day after day for the rest of my life," she says, completing the thought process she had put out of her mind for ten years. Surfacing now from the depths of her subconscious, the truth amazes her. She appears confused, her words befuddling even herself. Her face is clouded and the words seem hollow even to her. "I was afraid I couldn't live up to your impression of me."

"Can't you see the responsibility you placed on me? And I was only twenty four years old at the time," she says, recalling more details of their affair, like the time they took the train to San Diego. She was wearing a tan colored beret with a yellow ribbon on it. It blew off her head and Doug picked it up and placed it back on her head so carefully, savoring every line, every pore in her skin.

Doug grasps that this may be the moment of truth for them. But, in his amazement at her answer, he doesn't know what to say. He feels betrayed, no cheated by the crazy improbable twist of fate that makes a perfect beautiful creature like her and yet screams of her imperfections. How could she? Why would she sacrifice something as profound and deep and rare as what they had together for such a shallow, empty reason? He can't fathom it. Even now, he's overwhelmed by the senselessness, the illogic of it.

"They say that 'Timing is everything'," he says amused at the irony. "My timing was lousy. I should have waited to meet you when you were a couple years older. I guess I screwed up pretty good. Yeah, I screwed up big time, huh."

"Oh my God, Doug," she whispers, just now realizing the truth of their situation for the first time. She was simply too young and foolish to know the value of what he, and only he, could give her.

"I'd better go now. You need to rest and we both need to think things over. I'm very grateful for the talk," he says.

"Doug, no don't leave me, please," she pleads.

"Yes, but you see, I have to go now," he says, not knowing what else to say. "You just told me the truth and everything will look differently in the morning."

He opens the door and this time manages to force his body through the opening to the yard. He doesn't look back, but he can see her from the back of his mind, watching him walk away into the arbor.

She can see the large egg shape of the ship just visible in the twilight beyond his silhouette. She has to wipe her tears to make the image sharpen and come into focus.

Doug strides quickly to the egg shape and he easily pushes his body through the hull and disappears. Then, the egg shape simply and silently disappears from her view.

Zora feels her chest heaving and she decides now that she must be dreaming. She turns to go upstairs to her bedroom to find her body and wake it. When she arrives beside her bed, realizing her body is not there in the bed, that it's standing there looking down at the empty sheets, that she must not be dreaming, but is awake fully, she collapses onto the bed in a heap and moves no more.

The front door flies open. "Honey, I'm home. It was some kind of a joke," she can feel the angry sounds of her husband's return wafting up the stairs to her bedroom.

"Yes, it's some kind of crazy joke," she says to herself as her husband, Pete, enters through the door.

"What's the matter?" he says, alarmed by her position on the bed, rushes to her side. "Has something happened?"

"Yes, something happened," she says into the bed sheets. "My life is a total failure."

Then, slowly she turns over and sits up in the bed, makes him sit next to her and takes his head in her hands.

"Can you ever forgive me?" she says.

Her husband, looking across at her, shakes his head in confusion. "Forgive you for what?" he asks.

"It's a long story," she says, wiping her eyes.

"I'm here. I'm listening," he says.

"I was only twenty-four years old at the time," she begins cautiously, looking him straight between the eyes. It's truth time for him too.

Chapter 4

▼

The Hall of
Extinction

As he enters the ship, Doug is trying to accept the new information Zora just gave him. Amazed, astounded, refreshed, renewed, angry, frustrated, disgusted and entirely happy, he's trying to sort through the entire range of human emotions. He's betwixt and between and beside himself. At the same time, he's looking down at himself. He can see his body enter the skin of the egg ship, walk up the stairs mechanically and take his familiar seat in the cabin. 'It's all such a strange dance,' he thinks.

Hardly breathing, he reaches up mechanically and puts the hat on his head.

"Did that make you feel better?" Ula asks politely.

"Oh, heck yes," he replies, sarcastically. "That's much better, yeah. Thanks for asking. I'm on top of the world."

He turns his gaze onto the view screen where he can see her house in the distance. Perhaps she's just as upset and confused as he is.

"Can you explain to me what love is all about?" he asks Ula after putting on the hat.

"That's a bit of a tough one, isn't it?" Ula replies.

"Even for you? I thought it would be a piece of cake after all the knowledge of the universe and so forth," Doug chides her.

"You would think, wouldn't you?" Ula replies.

Then, he thinks about a beautiful day in the park with her and makes the mental command that sends the ship to the same park in Los Angeles, where they once lived together near the blue waters of the Pacific. It's mid day. There are kids in the park playing baseball and another group is playing soccer.

The ship descends down and lands gently in the middle of the soccer field. The players have to scatter as it touches down gently and silently. A larger man, coaching one of the teams runs to his car and removes a rifle from under the driver's seat. He approaches the egg shape and yells for everyone to run for cover. He's convinced that this ship is filled with aliens who will spill out onto the field at any minute.

Mothers grab their children and run for cover behind their cars parked on the streets bordering the park.

"Why are we here, Doug?" Ula asks him, gently.

"This is where we said our good-byes. We lived over there in that apartment building. We used to come here and have picnics. We loved watching the kids play," he says. "I watched her walk away over there and get in a cab. She looked back at me, a real sad look on her face, but there were no tears. That was the last I saw of her, until today, and today she cried real tears."

"And now you know the real reason she left you Doug," she asks him.

"Yes, I know it now. But that doesn't mean that I understand it," he says.

"Understanding is directly correlated to time. Give it more time and you'll have more understanding," she replies.

"Yes, I suppose," he says sensing she's stating the obviousness of the situation.

"Yes," she replies. "Don't worry about it. Everything will turn out, you'll see."

"You sound like my mother," he says.

Outside there is a scene of pandemonium, unheard, only seen through the view screens of the ship. The man with the rifle is frantically trying to hold the crowd at bay, while he's yelling for the 'little green men' to come out and surrender to him.

"Ok, why do you think she left me?" he asks her.

"Because you didn't fight for her," she says.

"I knew you'd say that. I didn't fight because there was no use. I had no way to compete with him," he says. "No matter what I did or said, I knew it was useless and I would lose her any way. She made that pretty clear."

"Perhaps. But what if you told her how much you cared for her and how much her leaving would hurt you," she says. "That might have made the difference."

"She knew how much I loved her. It went without saying," he said.

"You think so?" she asks.

Doug shakes his head violently. "What do you want from me?" he asks.

The man with the rifle has approached to within a few feet. He's trying to ascertain where there might be an opening in the egg. He's still screaming for the occupants to come outside. He's red in the face and his pants are pulled up almost to his head.

"Just a little honesty," she replies.

"Well, here's a little honesty for you. I don't know who or what you are. You came into my life two days ago and you tell me the world is about to end and you tell me that I was chosen because I happen to read a little before I go to sleep. Now, you tell me you want a little honesty from me. Ok, I'll give you some honesty. I'm not sure of how much I understand when I'm reading that stuff. I read books because they make me forget and because I'm afraid that if I drink or take drugs it'll kill me! There's some honesty for you," he says, not thinking his words, but yelling them, letting them spill out of the deepest recesses of his mind and into the light of the little room in his mind that he now shares with a thing called 'Ula'.

"I know," she says.

His venting gives him a chance to relax a little. He decides to turn his attention to other matters. "What about this mission of yours? How and when do you plan to combine with us genetically?"

Oh, not for a while yet. In fact, it may never happen," she replies.

"Why not?" Doug asks.

"We can't combine with a species until all your violent tendencies have been purged from your genetic code," she replies clinically.

"How do we do that?" Doug asks.

"You have to tell me where you think the greatest changes could take place," she says.

"Hmmph, that's easy," Doug says. "Terrorism, war, preparations for war, those are the most violent tendencies in our species, am I right?"

"That's true. So, where should we begin?" she asks, delighted to be changing the subject.

"I've always wanted to be a bounty hunter," he says and then he envisions a place in the Arabian Desert where he might begin his adventure. "Let's go there."

The ship disappears from the park as quickly and silently as it had come. Doug sees the view screens darken and immediately brighten like the screen wipe during a scene change in a move. He makes a mental note to himself just how much like a movie his life has now become.

The panicking onlookers struggle to calm themselves as they stand frozen in their tracks shocked at the suddenly empty space taken up by the huge egg just one moment prior.

A police car pulls up behind the crowd and parks quickly. Two policemen jump from the car. Drawing their revolvers they yell at the man with the rifle commanding him to put it down. Obeying, he lowers the rifle slowly and carefully and lays it on the ground. The two policemen rush in to grab him. They force his arms behind his back and handcuff him. Many in the crowd are trying to tell the cops about the egg shaped object that had just appeared and then disappeared moments before they arrived.

The police are not amused.

*   *   *   *

"There's a group in a camp just over that sand dune," Ula says.

"Al Qaeda?" Doug asks quietly.

"Why don't you go and ask them," she says.

"You want me to just march over there and ask them if they're terrorists?" he demands.

"Can you think of a better way?" she replies.

"You're the almighty consciousness. Why don't you know?" he asks her defiantly.

"I do know, but on this mission, I'm limited in scope as to how much I can tell you and what I can do for you. There are good reasons for this. Don't worry. You'll understand more later," she states.

"Yeah, I'm sure. You're a big help. But I remember something about that programming directive of yours. You can't let anything hurt me still, right?" he asks.

"You could look at it that way," she answers.

"OK, well, if that's the case. I'll just go on over there and let's see what they have to say," Doug says bravely.

He knows from the information that she has been able to give him that no harm can come to him while he's in her protective radius and that the protective radius extends for miles in all directions, all dimensions. So, he is amazed at how little fear he has right now. All he has to do to calm his nerves is recall the incident in Beijing.

Doug removes the hat that is the link between his mind and hers and slowly descends the stairs. In his mind, he's trying to phrase the questions he will have for these people who are so far from civilization and conspiring perhaps to destroy another major American facility, perhaps put poison in some city reservoir or blow up a cruise ship or an airplane, or blow up a Bridge.

When he rises over the dune, he can see a group of five tents. There is a Toyota pickup truck parked in the middle of the tents with the rear gate down. In the bed of the truck sits a machine gun pointing toward the rear of the open gate. Since there is very little to hunt in these parts, Doug surmises that these people are the real deal. Whether or not they are Al Qaeda or just some kind of rebel band remains to be seen. Whatever they are, they must be dealt with.

He starts to march down the sand dune. His feet make a kind of scraping noise on the parched sand. Someone in the closest tent emerges alerted to the sounds of his approach. He shrieks in Arabic to warn the others.

"A stranger is coming over here," he yells.

Seven, then eight others emerge from the tents, each with impressive destructive power in their hands.

Doug continues toward them speaking in perfect Arabic. "I've come in peace," he says.

There is a loud crashing of magazines being slammed into their automatic weapons. 'Oozies,' Doug thinks to himself.

"If you don't put down your weapons and talk to me real nice, you'll place yourselves in grave danger," he warns.

The men look at each other in disbelief and laughter. One of them wants them to kill him where he stands. The others are worried that Doug may have friends somewhere nearby and why alert them when they can simply cut his throat. That way they won't waste any bullets.

"Are you part of Al Qaeda?" he asks them.

The eight men look at him in disbelief. One of them at the side of the group levels his weapon without changing his expression and pulls the trigger.

The gun explodes in his hand and nearly decapitates him. His limp body falls lifeless to the sand staining it red in a pool that widens for several feet around him.

"Well, you can't say I didn't warn you," Doug tells the rest of them.

The others seem very angry and in their ignorance believe that the poor slob's weapon simply malfunctioned. Not worried about making noise any longer, they all aim their weapons at Doug and press their triggers in unison.

"Oh shit," he says.

The remaining seven men wind up on the ground as their weapons explode in the same manner as the first, killing them or wounding them horribly all by their own hands. The ground in front of him is splattered red. Doug feels no remorse at all for the men. He tried to have them disarm peacefully. They refused. They reaped their just rewards.

'Dangerous business they're in. You never know who to trust,' he thinks to himself and wanders over to the truck to examine the machine gun sitting idly on the truck bed. It's the deadliest piece of human engineering and invention he's ever seen this close. It's fully loaded and ready to be fired at someone or something. It could easily dispatch hundreds of people into the next world.

Doug notices some documents littering the bed of the truck. Several of the pages contain a photograph of Osama Bin Laden. He doesn't need to read any more of them, apparently some kind of training manuals, torn and ragged and dirty.

On his way back to the ship, his mind is clouded with thoughts of what must now take place for the human species to be cleansed of the violence. This is just a drop in the bucket. Surely she can't mean that he has to do it all by himself. There must be millions of crazy people with weapons like these standing ready to do violence at any given time on the Earth. All supplied by American, and European capitalistic greed of course. The prospect of having to deal with all of them individually like this chills him to the bone.

As soon as he returns to the ship, he dons the communicator hat and demands some answers.

"How am I going to eliminate violence on this planet? You expect me to kill them all?" he asks.

"No, that would not be helpful," she replies.

How then?" he asks.

"Patience, Doug," she says. "Patience. In due time, the answers will come to you. Don't worry. I'm here to help you."

Doug takes off the hat and goes back downstairs. He feels like he's been conscripted into something much too big for his own mind. He needs time to think. He decides that a nice long walk would be in order. He can accomplish that and explore this strange ship, built of pure consciousness a little more. Perhaps there are answers hidden deep within those infinitely expanding hallways.

He goes downstairs and then chooses the East Corridor. He knows from his earlier exploration that the hallways and rooms are immaculate, with everything in its place. There is no dust or dirt or signs of any habitation. And, they are all the same with no markings to distinguish them. Without any signposts, he decides to remove articles from the shelves and place them on the ground so that he can follow his path back to the center, just as 'Hansel and Gretel' used the famous breadcrumbs to find their way through the dark Bavarian forest.

The hallway turns immediately into a room filled with the same tiny cassettes dangling from the walls on invisible shelving. There is also one of the reader machines sitting on a table in the corner. The room is similar to the one that he visited on his first exploration. It also leads off in three more hallways connected at the other end. He picks the one in the middle and takes about the same number of paces as before. He's starting to think that the hallways are symmetrical in their layout at least. He removes one of the cassettes on the wall near the opening and places it in the middle of the doorway on the floor and walks on ahead, confident of being able to find his way back.

He notices the same dull lighting as before caused by some unseen lighting fixtures. The level of light is both pleasing and soothing. He can see just enough and his eyes are not overwhelmed. It strikes him that the light level and color is designed for very long journeys.

The hallway soon opens up to another room filled with the same row upon row of small cassettes. He goes to the end of this room near the doorway so he can see it and places another cassette on the floor of the opening. He repeats the process several more times until finally, he finds a room that is different than the ones he has passed.

And, this room comes with a voice that sounds exactly like Ula's.

"Hello Doug. Welcome to the 'Hall of Extinction'," it says.

"Ula?" Doug asks.

"No, my name is Lola. It's short for 'Lower Level Awareness'," she states clearly.

"I see. So, Ula is the ship's Upper Level Awareness and you're the 'Lower'?" he asks.

"That's correct," she replies.

Doug notices that the walls previously filled with the millions of cube cassettes have been replaced with man-sized display cases like in a museum. In each display is a pair of very strange creatures standing amongst what must be a representation of their natural habitat.

"This is a museum," he says out loud.

"That's correct. You're in the 'Hall of Extinction,'" Lola states clearly and officially like any good tour guide. "Here we have compiled all the intelligent creatures that have gone extinct. They no longer exist in nature."

"I see. So, this must be a pretty small place, then?" Doug wonders while walking the length of the room. He is stunned to see so many beautiful creatures, some that obviously swam in distant seas, others that walked on four legs, others that walked on two and even three-legged creatures. Some have a great deal of hair, others none at all.

"The number of extinct intelligent life forms is thirty-four billion, seven hundred and sixty five million, three thousand and eighty four, with one new extinction coming into the hall every two point seven five seconds," she states.

"Thirty-five billion," Doug repeats. "I guess that means that this hall goes on for quite a bit."

"Yes, the 'Hall of Extinction' takes up an area similar in size to fourteen of your solar systems," she says.

"That would a bit more of a stroll than I had in mind," he says. "My God if this Hall goes on that far, how large is this whole ship?"

"The size of our awareness is not a relevant question," she states.

"I see," he says. "Well can you tell me is there a Hall of Intelligent life that hasn't gone extinct?"

"Yes," she states, succinctly.

"Where is that?" he asks.

"We're resting on it. It's called the Earth," she says.

It takes Doug several seconds to grasp the significance of what Lola just told him.

"You mean our planet is the only place in the entire universe that has intelligent life on it?" he says, incredulous.

"That is correct," she states.

"That seems a bit hard to believe. I mean, there are so many billions of potential places where life can exist, isn't there?" he asks.

"Yes, that's correct also, but unfortunately, we have seen the pattern of extinction repeated over and over again. The sad fact is that life forms who acquire higher technology eventually use it destroy themselves within a very short time, usually within a century or two," she says. "The longest recorded time from the accumulation of high technology to total extinction is only one thousand and fifty five years, set by the Hartoonin civilization of Hartoonin Vega."

"And, we've had it for less than a century," Doug says.

"That's correct. And, with the end of your universe at hand, it was imperative to come here to rescue your species," she states.

"If the universe were not ending soon, would you have come here to our rescue?" he asks.

"Probably not, it's only the end-game that concerns us," she says.

"And who are you? Who are you people who have managed to store all this information? How come I don't see any of you live and in person? And how do you intend to make this rescue of over five billion of us?" Doug asks.

"You have many questions. You will know the answers soon enough. We cannot divulge all of the information just yet," she says.

"Why not?" he asks.

"Because that might give someone or something an unfair advantage," she states.

"Unfair advantage? Unfair? I don't follow. Unfair how? In what way?" Doug stammers.

"Unfair to those we leave behind," she says.

"So, we won't be able to take them all out of here?" he asks.

"No, we will not. There is not enough time. And the longer you stand around asking these questions will add more to the total of the unfortunate ones left behind," she states clearly and unemotionally.

"You talk about fairness? Is that fair?" Doug asks.

He receives no answer.

"You hang up on me?" he shouts at the ceiling where the voice seems to emanate.

No answer.

"Ok, I get it," he says. "Time I got back to the cockpit anyway."

Doug reverses his course taking one last look at the 'Hall of Extinction' imagining for a minute infinite rows of these exhibit bays of lifeless creatures. He shudders to think about the one open bay where they might have room for a human man and woman. 'Would they use a country or city motif? How would they clothe them?' he wonders and trots back through the dozen or so rooms watching for the cassettes on the floor that guide him back to the hub.

When he reaches the stairway, he races up to the cockpit, places the hat on his head with a great sense of urgency.

"Let's get out of here, Ula," he says. "Find me someone to talk to quickly!"

In a wink of an eye, Doug finds that they have landed in the basement of a large building. He descends the stairs and goes through the skin and, looking around, sees dusty old signs, tattered suitcases, dirty laundry carts that identify the building as an old hotel. He knows that this is part of Ula's plans for him and that he must comply. It's actually comforting for him to know that he has such an important role to play.

The ship is resting in a dark corner of the large room. A few feet from the ship is a flight of stairs. He climbs them and comes out onto an unattended lobby.

There is a registration desk, but no clerks. Behind the desk is a set of cubby holes storing mail for the residents. They are mostly empty.

Outside the front door, he can see a sidewalk café across the street filled with customers discussing the day's events and sipping their morning coffee. A few passers-by glide past the doors of the hotel. One of them enters and yells 'bon-jour', good day in French and then tosses a bundle of newspapers inside the door to the lobby floor, placing them next to several other bundles of similar papers.

Looking at the headlines, Doug reads the words, "Police are baffled." Several feet away, he can't read the rest of the story but he has an idea about what the police are baffled by.

Wandering around the corner, he sees another set of stairs leading up to the rooms. He climbs them quickly. At the top of the stairs, he lands upon a hallway with three doors on either side. He can sense somehow that the party he is seeking live behind the last door on his left. He walks along and listens for any signs of life. He can hear families scrambling to complete their morning toilet.

Arriving at the last door, he listens but hears no sounds of life inside. He knocks on the door and suddenly there is a great rustling within as if several pairs of feet have suddenly hit the deck scurrying for cover.

"Can you come to the door?" he shouts as politely as he can.

There is a long pause. Then he can hear whispered conversations on the other side of the door in an Arab tongue, it takes a moment to recognize. They seem to be a mix of Yemeni, Iraqi and Pakistani.

He waits a long time in silence. Then, the door bursts open. Someone grabs him by the shirt collar and jerks him into the room. It smells of urine and feces. He can hear the familiar clicks of automatic weapons made ready to fire. He makes out the faces of five mid-eastern men.

In Arabic, they are shouting at him to identify himself. They are so loud he wonders why the neighbors don't all come out to investigate.

"My name is Doug Rink. I'm not the police. I'm not CIA. I'm here to help you. I come in peace," he says, instinctively raising his arms, palms outward showing the men that he is unarmed.

"Who are you, then," one of them says calmly. A deep ominous voice speaks out from a dark corner behind him. This is obviously their leader because, Doug reasons, he is the only one not pointing a gun at him.

Doug turns to face him. "I'm here to tell you how you can win," he tells them. "I have important information for you."

"Who do you think we are?" the leader asks.

"You're five men who have come to put serin gas in the subway of Paris. You have enough to kill over a million people. Your plan is to spray the gas from the trains as they run all day today, spreading the poison over hundreds of miles of subway line, am I right? But, I'm glad to tell you, it won't work and you will all die in the attempt for nothing," he tells them. Even Doug is surprised that he knows so much about them.

The looks they share are filled with pain and fear.

"How could you know all of this if you're not CIA?" the leader asks him.

"Kill him," one of them shouts nervously.

"I wouldn't try that if I were you," Doug warns. "Many others like you have tried that in the last few days and they are all dead."

The nervous one and the leader argue over whether or not to shoot Doug where he stands.

The leader is saying that their mission must be compromised if this man knows about it so completely. They must find out what else he knows and what if anything the authorities know.

"If everyone is dead, how did they die?" the leader asks. "Did you kill them?"

"No, I did not kill them. They were killed when their weapons misfired," he tells them.

"How many men are these dead men?" the leader asks.

"Several dozen, I'd say. I didn't stop to count them all," he replies.

"All of their weapons misfired?" the leader asks, suspiciously.

"That's right," Doug answers.

"Kill him, I say. He's crazy!" shouts the nervous one in front.

"I know it sounds crazy, but I'm not alone, you see," Doug starts.

"I knew it. He is CIA," shouts the nervous one. Another, smaller fellow behind him grunts out a noise in agreement with the nervous one.

"Do you think someone is going to come in here to save you?" asks the leader.

"No, no one is out there to back me up. But I have come to save you. And not only you, of course, but to save all of Mankind as well," he stammers.

The group of five laugh out loud in unison. It seems they enjoy the macabre way Doug is presenting his case. He's got them entertained at least. Doug is relieved to see this side of them. He decides to share some very important information with them.

"I'm afraid it's very true. You see, if we don't do something on this planet to eliminate our violent tendencies, it's all over for us. We'll all end up on the dust heap of history. Did you know that there are nearly thirty five billion other civilizations in the universe who got to this precise moment in evolution and they all destroyed themselves. We're next, if we can't resolve our differences and learn to live in peace," he lectures them, then waits several moments for their reaction to reveal their thinking.

They all laugh again, except much harder this time and one of them falls to the floor in convulsions of pain. The others seem to be lowering their guard. All, except for the nervous one who stops laughing and then stands there staring menacingly. His pressure on the trigger increases. Doug realizes that this man knows the exact point on the trigger when it will release its deadly force and he's just about there.

The leader pushes the nervous one aside and quickly maneuvers around behind Doug and sticks his head cautiously out the door. Seeing nothing, he returns back inside and closes the door quietly.

"You can't possibly have balls this big unless you are with someone, right? So take me to your friends," the leader demands pressing his face within inches of Doug's. The man's breath reminds Doug of a smell he noticed once at the zoo.

Thinking quickly, Doug decides to take them to the ship.

"Ok, I'll take you to my friends, but there's only one friend. She's rather large. I left her in the basement. You want to follow me?" Doug asks, slowly lowering his hands.

"It's a woman?" the leader asks, completely annoyed. "All right, let's go see her."

"It's a trap!" yells the nervous one.

The leader snaps at the man. "Use your head for a minute. Obviously this guy knows about us. That means others must know. The whole place might be surrounded, so we can use him as a hostage. Then, when we're safe, we can kill him later."

The leader smiles at Doug and then motions for him to open the door and they will follow. Complying willingly, Doug opens the door and goes out into the hall. He looks back to see them slowly, very slowly exiting the room one by one with guns at the ready.

Slowly they make their way down the hall. One of the neighbors starts to open his door. All five guns swing violently to bear within inches of his face. The door closes without incident. Doug breathes a sigh of relief.

Finally, they make their way down the stairs, through the lobby, down the darkened stairway and into the musty basement. One by one they walk over to stand in front of the giant egg shape in wonder.

They are very perturbed by this. One of them says something about it looking like an Easter Egg and they all laugh out loud again. Doug laughs with them.

Then, he says, "Watch this." He pushes himself through the skin and into the familiar entry way on the lower floor of the ship.

Outside, the men are standing frozen in their tracks, struggling to understand what just happened. Doug has simply vanished through the mysterious hull. There is no sign of comprehension on their faces, but deep confusion and a building anger. They have been tricked.

"I told you it was a trap," the nervous one shouts.

"If it's a trap, why are we not dead yet?" the leader replies.

Suddenly, Doug appears in front of them once again as he steps back through the shell of the egg.

"You see, I have this friend inside. Her name is Ula. She is from another planet. She is the one that has shown me the thirty five billion other civilizations that have destroyed themselves. This one, our civilization, yes the one both you and I belong to, is next. I'm telling you and if you don't listen to me," he says pointing to the ground beneath their feet.

"Where did you go just now?" the leader asks him.

"I went into the ship, of course," Doug replies.

"And if I want to go in?" the leader asks.

"I'm afraid that is not possible," Doug answers.

"Why not?" demands the leader.

"Well, first of all, you have a weapon in your hand. No one enters with any weapon of any kind," Doug says, just guessing.

"What if I put it down?" the leader asks.

"Well, why don't you put it down and give it a try?" Doug suggests coolly.

The leader looks at the other men and then places his gun gently on the cold and dirty cement floor.

"It's a trap!" repeats the nervous one. "You'll kill us all if you go in there."

"I don't think so. He went in. He came out," the leader says, pointing to Doug. "This could be a weapon that we can take from him. Look at him. He's no match for us. I have to find out."

The leader takes a bold leap and hurls himself onto the skin of the ship and is instantly repulsed like a rubber ball. He falls back in a heap on the floor next to his oozie.

Doug is surprised. Apparently, no one else can enter the ship who Ula doesn't want to enter. This is encouraging to Doug, but it leaves him in a kind of quandary. He was hoping that by showing these men the 'Hall of Extinction', he could get them to understand their situation and perhaps get them to change their minds.

"I'm sorry. I guess, she'll only allow me to enter," he says.

"Get away from the thing," the leader says menacingly, rising from the floor and picking up his weapon.

Doug smiles to give him the clear impression that he intends to comply and then jumps headlong into the door that will open only for him. He can hear gunfire outside the ship.

He runs up the stairs and slaps on the hat barely sitting down.

"Why aren't you letting them in?" Doug asks.

"They are not ready to come in," Ula replies.

"When will they be ready?" asks Doug.

"Well, um let's see, never," she replies with a sarcastic tone he hasn't noticed before.

"Never? Why Never? You told me we can't kill them all. So how in the world am I going to get them to agree to anything if they can't talk with you and get their heads on straight?" Doug asks, anxiously.

"I'm only allowed one primary contact at the subject location," she replies seeming to change the subject.

"I see, and why is that?" Doug asks, impatiently.

"I cannot reveal that information at this time," she replies, just as succinctly.

"Hmmm, so I take it, I'm supposed to just convince them on my own," he asks.

"That is correct," she replies.

"I see," he says, trying to pick his way through her logic.

At this moment, Doug feels a strange vibration along the floor of the cockpit. He throws off the hat, runs downstairs and dives out into the basement where the five terrorists have their weapons leveled, barrels smoking. Apparently, they tried to shoot their way in, to no avail.

When they see Doug, they are ready to kill him. They raise their weapons and point straight at his head.

"Listen to me," he yells with great urgency. "If you try to shoot those weapons, they'll explode in your hands and you will have died for nothing. Please trust me. There were the five out in the desert in Yemen and there was about a dozen killed in Beijing a few days ago. One of them pointed a tank at me and they are no longer in one piece. Please believe me. I told you I'm here to help. Look, I didn't have to come back out here, you know."

He takes a deep breath and looks them all in the eyes. They are frozen in a kind of cognitive dissonance. They want badly to kill him, and yet, here he stands the only fool who can enter this object. Their fear is greater than their hate.

Finally, the leader breaks the silence. "All right, if you're trying to help," he says. "Why don't you tell me what you would have me do, right now, if I don't kill you? What would you do with us?"

"I'm going to try and teach you about something truly amazing. It's the force that runs the universe. I bet you gentlemen don't know much about that, do you? You look and smell like creatures who have never known such power, am I right?" Doug shoots straight at them.

"Watch out, I'm going to kill him," the nervous one shouts.

"I'm going to tell you that it's the greatest force in the universe. I love you guys and I'm going to teach you how to love your enemies. Why? Because it's the greatest weapon in the world. Much greater than those puny little weapons you're carrying so close to your hearts. Can one of those things keep you warm in the night?" Doug says.

Doug notices that they are silent and motionless, so he goes on.

"What would happen, do you suppose, if I let you go off and poison all those people in the subway today as you planned?" he asks them.

Doug sees that they're listening, painfully reluctantly, but listening just the same.

"You would be dead and all those innocent people would be dead within hours. And then the United Nations would find the country you guys came from and make more innocent people suffer in your homeland. Surely, you thought through all that, am I right?" he asks.

"Of course we thought of all that," the leader states. "Sacrifices must be made to create a fair and equitable world. It's always been the innocent who pay the price for freedom."

"And who gets to enjoy the freedom? Do you have any freedom after thousands of years of hate and cruelty? When has violence ever settled anything? Give me one example in history and I will shut up and leave you to do your jobs," Doug says, fearing they might be able to come up with the exception to the rule. 'You always have to worry about the exceptions,' he thinks.

"There is no other way for us," the leader says, finally.

"Ah, but there is. I'm here to show it to you. If you simply turn yourselves in, I assure you it will shock your enemies. They will not know what to do with you. They can't prosecute you for a crime you have not yet committed, can they?" he asks.

"They will put us in prison and throw away the key," the nervous one says.

"No, they won't. Oh, sure you'll have to spend a few days in a nice hotel room somewhere while they figure out what to do with you. But wouldn't you rather come out of that to live in a world where everyone gets along? Where Arabs live side by side with Jews? Where there is no more hate and no more turmoil? And where there are no more weapons of mass destruction to worry about killing our children? Where there are no more armies to enforce the will of one nation on that of another?" he asks.

"You're crazy if you think we will live to see such a world," replies the leader?

"Yes, I could be crazy, but isn't it worse if we don't try? Believe me, it can happen with your help. But it must start right here, right now," Doug says. "There is no more time to discuss the matter, please, you must trust me."

The five men assess one another. The leader says nothing. The nervous one seems to be the most reluctant because he's the only one with his rifle still leveled at Doug's head. All the other weapons have been lowered slightly.

"What is your name?" the leader asks suddenly.

"Doug, Douglas Rink," he says. "I'm an American."

"And what do you do when you are not playing world savior?" asks the leader.

"I'm a cowboy. I rustle the cattle and the horses on a ranch in Colorado," Doug replies, smiling.

"A cowboy? I see," says the leader. "Like John Wayne, yes?"

"No, not like John Wayne," Doug replies smiling. "I don't get the women like he did. I don't drink like him and I certainly don't walk like him, pilgrim."

Doug laughs out loud and the terrorists just look at him funny. Then, they huddle together while their leader extorts and reasons with them for several minutes.

Then, in the weirdest, twisted accent Doug has ever heard, the leader pokes fun, "All right, Meester John Wayne. Head us up, roll us out, rawhide cowboy."

He instructs his men to drop their weapons and formally surrender to Doug. Their weapons drop to the ground, one by one, until finally even the nervous one, reluctantly and with great protests drops his too.

Then, they drop to their knees and start to cry like babies, releasing pent up emotions that have been suppressed for months, even years. All their trials over, they've decided to trust this very strange convincing man who has the support of this strange and weird egg-shaped object standing silently behind them and watching.

CHAPTER 5

▼

SPRING TIME IN PARIS.

At the Prefecture de Police, Doug stands beside a bench where the five terrorists are seated. He is discussing the case with French Detective, Jean-Marc LeClair. The Detective interrogates Doug for several minutes about the nature of the attack in the subway that these men had planned. He asks the five men to confirm what Doug is telling him. They all simply shake their heads sheepishly in response.

LeClair is taking copious notes on a small notepad where he's written down all their names, country of origin, and other details of their plot. He then tells Doug to wait in here while he consults with his superior. He shows no emotion but claims that he will only be a minute. LeClair leaves the small interrogation room and steps outside. He is in a large common area, with desks scattered about the large room and several offices abutting the sides. One of them has the word, 'Interpol' on the door. LeClair crosses the room and knocks on the door and enters.

The man sitting at the desk is sipping a cup of coffee and reading the newspaper. The two men greet each other and the man behind the desk invites LeClair to sit down. But, he tells the man that a group of men have come into the station and claim to be a terror group who were planning to poison Le Metro.

"They just walked in and surrendered to you?" The man asks.

"Yes. They did. They were brought in by an American. His name is Douglas Rink," LeClair is reading from his notepad.

"An American, you say?" he asks and then, says alarmed, "C.I.A.?"

"I don't think so," replies Detective LeClair. "He claims to be a tourist. He says he was out on a walk when he spotted suspicious behavior and went in to investigate."

"Does he have a passport?" the man asks.

"He claims he left it at the hotel. But I had my assistant call the hotel and they have no record of him staying there," LeClair says.

"Sounds fishy to me. Well, you have to verify their story, no?" asks the man.

"Yes, I'm sending a car to the hotel now," he replies.

"Yes, well, keep me informed," says the man and he turns his attention to his cardboard cup of coffee and the newspaper.

LeClair goes out of the office and back into the main room bustling with police activity. At this point, another man, much smaller, with a moustache and glasses approaches him.

"Monsieur LeClair," the man begins. He's out of breath and his face is full of with concern and anxiety over the news he's about to give his boss.

"Our people are at the address you gave me and they have found enough serin gas to poison at least a million people. They have it packed into aerosol cans with timers connected to them. If they were to place these cans on the bottoms of the trains, and they all went off at rush hour, hundreds of thousands could have died," he informs him.

"I want you to tell Interpol. Have them put out a general notice to all prefectures. There may be others out there," says LeClair, his demeanor has completely altered from one of complete calm to a controlled panic.

He notices two uniformed men standing at the corner processing a young man with terrible bruises on his face and wearing torn clothing.

"Let him alone," he commands the two uniforms. "Come with me."

They meet up in the middle of the room and LeClair flings open the door. The five terrorists are seated on the bench. But Doug is nowhere to be seen. They rush back out of the room and LeClair takes in the entire room with a rapid sweeping motion of his head. He sees the back side of Doug walking quickly down the stairs at the other end of the hall.

"Follow me!" he shouts to the two uniforms. The policemen run toward the stairs but by the time they get there, Doug has swiftly found the door at the bottom and run out through it and into the street.

"Come on," shouts LeClair. "He knows more than he's telling us. We need to catch that man."

Doug, knowing that he's being chased, runs as fast as he can along the street. He turns the corner, notices an alley and runs into it. At the other end, he turns right onto another street of shops and sidewalk cafes. He spies a taxi stand in the middle of the road with a yellow taxi sitting there waiting for a fare. He runs over to it and hops in.

"Thirty Four Rue de Napoleon. Vite," he instructs the driver who presses the pedal to the floor. The yellow and red Renault screeches away in a cloud of smoke just as LeClair and the two uniforms make it to the street.

One of the uniformed men picks up the microphone from his lapel and calls in the taxi description and direction to his dispatcher and asks for assistance.

"I know where he's going," says LeClair. Have them pick us up here."

When Doug reaches the apartment building where he knows his ride is waiting for him, he can see several police cars on the street blocking the main entrance. He pays the taxi driver with American dollars, which displeases the driver, and runs out of the cab.

The driver is angry and calls out to him but Doug just shrugs his shoulders and yells that this is all he has and runs along the alley that runs along the old hotel. He's looking for another way in and finds it in a rusty old storm door just above the ground.

It's unlocked and crusted with dirt but it opens with a strong pull. Just then, LeClair's group arrives in a police car followed by another one. They pull up next to the taxi where the driver is still standing and mumbling about the money. LeClair asks him which way his fare went. The driver points to the alley.

LeClar and the two uniforms, quickly followed by four more uniforms from the second car, run around the apartment building to the alley where they can see the storm door still standing open. Seeing no other sign of their quarry, they all file down through the door and down the dark and rickety old stair well.

When they arrive at the bottom of the stairs, they have to adjust their eyes to the dim light of the basement. LeClair and his men slowly begin to see Doug's image come into focus standing calmly in front of a huge egg shaped object.

"I'm sorry to have to leave you, Messieurs," Doug says. "But I don't have time for all your questions right now and there's much more that I have to do. I'm sure you'll understand some day."

Doug then turns and pushes his body through the electron field that is the ship's hull and finds himself safe and warm on the other side in the central hub of the ship.

The police dash quickly to the side of the ship and the first one, thrusts himself at the electronic shell, crashes roughly back from it and lands in a lump on the floor. A second officer tries the same maneuver, but with slightly more gusto and arrives on the floor next to the first man, groaning in pain.

Detective LeClair slowly and cautiously approaches the ship and places his hand on the surface precisely where he noticed Doug disappear and where the other two were rejected. He feels no opening, no signs of a door or even a crack. He pushes with his body, but as much as he pushes the skin shows no sign of surrendering its secret. It even seems that the harder he pushes, the more it pushes back as if it had a kind of intelligence working against his.

Then, to the amazement of all, the egg slowly disappears. The men are left standing there looking at the dark empty basement wall.

Inside the ship, Doug has gone upstairs and he can see the astonished faces of the men standing outside in the gloom through the view screens. He puts on the hat and wonders to himself where they should go next.

"I think it's time we made a general announcement, a statement of purpose, something like that. Let everyone know we're here, and why" suggests Ula.

"Announcement?" Doug asks.

"Yes, word will travel fast of this incident and there have been the others that are just now starting to catch the attention of your spy agencies. The newspapers will start to spread rumors and we don't want the wrong story to get out there, do we?" she asks.

"I agree. So, where do we go make this announcement," asks Doug.

"How about Washington D.C.?" she replies.

Doug thinks for a fraction of a second. "Let's go," he says and as soon as he says it, the men's faces and the dark room are replaced with a dark cloud and then this is replaced with the United States Capitol building gradually coming into sharp focus in the view screens.

The ship has landed softly on the green grassy park directly across from the United States Congress, the nation's Capitol and the symbol of the last best hope to rest of the world.

It's early morning on the Capital Mall. There are a few cars driving along Pennsylvania Avenue, just behind them. The birds are cautiously sipping the morning air and preen their feathers in preparation for their day of stalking and hunting their prey. A few people are walking their dogs and another man is jogging along the edge of the park. He is only a few feet from the ship when it suddenly appears in front of him. He stops and confused by the sudden appearance of this huge egg, looks around to see if this might be part of a movie set or a commercial of some kind. 'It's the 'Incredible, Edible Egg', he thinks to himself.

Doug watches as the man looks around a bit more, shrugs his shoulders, and then finally returns to his jogging.

"So, what do we do next" asks Doug.

Ula replies. "Don't worry, there will be others, won't there? And sooner or later, their curiosity will get the better of them. A crowd will build and you'll step out in front of them and they will have to listen to you."

Sure enough by the time the jogger has made another complete circuit of the running track, there are now three more people standing at the foot of the egg shape scratching their heads and trading very logical scenarios for it's being there. The most confusing part is the way the skin of the ship seems to be alive with energy. Some of them express a fear that it might be getting ready to explode.

*   *   *   *

At the Langley Headquarters of the Central Intelligence Agency, Jack Beamer is sitting in his cubicle staring at his computer monitor. On the screen, he is reading a brief sent to his unit of counter terrorism, by Interpol. It is describing an incident in Paris earlier that day in which a group of Yemeni men were found to be plotting a serin gas attack on the Parisian subway system. The group had been convinced to confess and surrender to authorities by an American who gave his name as a Douglas Rink. The story goes on to say that Doug then disappeared from the chase given by several French police who claim that he got into an egg shaped ship and disappeared from their view, in fact, vanishing right in front of their eyes.

"Yeah and I'm the Easter Bunny," Beamer quips out loud to no one in particular.

"What's that, Jack?" asks his assistant, Rita Chavez, a tall and very attractive female operative in the cubicle across from his. "Found something interesting, have we? It couldn't be anywhere near as good as this."

Beamer looks back at her desk where she is tuned in on a small TV monitor. A reporter is standing in front of a large egg-shaped object sitting on the Capitol Mall just under the familiar capitol dome.

The reporter is demonstrating the strange material of the shape by running her hand over it and describing the feeling as very odd, soft yet firm and warm to her touch and 'with little things crawling around'. There is a crowd gathered all around her and they too seem simultaneously befuddled and amused by the situation.

She then turns to interview a man in a dark blue jogging outfit.

"And your name sir?" she asks.

"My name is Rick Kelly," he says, nervously mugging at the camera.

"And you told me a few minutes ago that you noticed something very unusual on your morning Jog, Mr. Kelly?" she prompts.

"Yes, I was running on the jogging track here and as I made my third lap, I looked up to notice this thing standing here all of a sudden, like," he stammers. "It just came out of nowhere."

"You hadn't seen it on any of your previous laps?" she queries.

"No, and I definitely would have run right smack into it because it was just suddenly right there without a sound, no warning of any kind. It was like it just dropped in out of the sky. Aaand uh, it feels like it's electric or magnetic or something. It's really weird," he replies, bashfully.

"There you have it. An eyewitness account of this egg shape simply appearing out of nowhere this morning on the Capital Mall. Also, I need to report that I called the National Egg Board to see if this might be some kind of promotion for the 'Incredible, Edible Egg' and they denied any involvement. And I do have to tell you it's giving off a very strange sensation of like a static electricity or something in the air. It's a very positive feeling though, like a giant air cleaner," she says.

Inside the ship, Doug is watching the scene developing on the view screens.

"Well, there's your public," Ula says. "Why don't you go out there and tell them as much as you think they can handle."

"All right, if you say so. But, this is not exactly my cup of tea," he replies.

"You'll do fine. Besides, if not you, who? And if not now, when?" she says.

Doug removes the hat, slowly gets up steam to travel down the stairway, goes down into the hub, stands at the skin of ship and then pushes himself out and through to the crowd growing larger and larger by the minute.

As he steps out through the skin, a small silver platform extends under his feet near the bottom of the ship and moves him forward and up. Then, a railing extends from the platform at his feet and rises up to arm level. Ula has apparently crafted a small podium attached to the ship for him to speak to the crowd. It rises upwards slowly as the crowd watches in stunned silence.

"Hello, please don't be alarmed. This is not a hoax and it's not a joke. It's very serious. I'm a cowboy from Colorado. My name is Doug Rink. I woke up one morning about a week ago and found this spacecraft in my back yard. I went inside and found this device that speaks to me. The people who created this craft are from an advanced civilization so far advanced from us that it would be extremely difficult for me to explain it all in the short period of time that I've got here," Doug begins well. He pauses to assess their reaction. Dozens more people are clustering around, gathering at the back and pushing the forward lines closer and closer to him. But they all appear curious as they stand patiently waiting for more information.

"Let it be enough for now that the world is about to change dramatically and for all time. The way we do things on this planet is woefully inadequate. The level of greed, corruption, distrust and dislike for one's neighbors has risen to an epidemic proportion. It's an epidemic that threatens to destroy our race. Extinction is a very final and ultimate concept. There is no return from extinction. There is no forgiveness of this the greatest of sins, apathy. And make no mistake, the people who have constructed this ship have made it clear to me that literally billions of civilizations have already fallen over that final precipice. They were once millions of thriving intelligent, loving civilizations with great promise, hope in the future, faith in God, nurturing of their offspring. And then, one day, without warning, a violent and terrible catastrophe of one sort or another, completely avoidable and unnecessary, takes them into the great hall of oblivion," Doug says and then pauses again.

The crowd is solemn and quiet except for a small contingent of police and plain clothes officers standing around the outskirts of the crowd, recording his speech and chattering on their radios with unseen officials. Doug tries to ignore them and goes on.

"It's happened billions of times around the universe and the Human Race is next. That's you and me and our children and all of their children, no more, kaput, finito, extreme unction, comprende?" he says and then pauses again for these words to sink in.

The crowd seems stunned as some are quietly mumbling to themselves and to each other. Some of the children seem the most intent on his speech.

"It gets worse. In the next few months you will see some very big changes around here. You see, the people who built that ship have also told me that the world is going to come to a very climactic and final end on or before ninety days from now," he says calmly, his voice lowered, almost a whisper.

The crowd takes a moment to absorb the words, process them and then reacts emotionally. They cry out that he's a fake and that the ship is a big Easter egg and that he must be a lunatic and much worse things. The children are laughing, but few of them show the levels of angst that the adults have achieved. Some in the crowd are trying to quiet the vociferous ones amongst them. Finally, peace is restored and Doug can go on.

"Look, I'm not happy to be the one to have to tell you all this. But they came to me and I guess I was selected to be the messenger of ill tidings. It appears that the universe we live in is really nothing more than a super massive collection of galaxies and each one goes through the Big Bang and every thirteen billion years, they go through the Big Crunch. The universe folds in on itself for no really great reason. And then, the cycle of Creation starts all over again. Our astronomers will be able to confirm this in a few weeks. But I hope that none of you will wait for the final confirmation of this news to start making peace with one another. You see, part of why these people have sent this ship is to rescue us from this calamity. They not only bring us the bad news, but they've got some good news. The good news is that if we clean up our act in the time that's left to us, the creatures who built this ship can merge with us genetically and carry our genes far away from danger and that would save our species from extinction. It's not the best of all possible outcomes, but it's the only option we've got," he continues. The crowd begins to buzz again.

He holds up his hand to calm them again.

"But they won't do anything for us, however, if we don't rid ourselves of the worst parts of our genetic makeup. We have to get busy and we have to get busy now. There's no time to waste," Doug says and rests.

The loud vocal cynics in the crowd are inflamed and this time they're anger cannot be suppressed by the other calmer faction. Livid with anger, they attempt to push through the crowd to get to Doug which makes the whole group surge forward. Doug figures it might be time to turn and lunge back into the safety of the ship. Before he can do so, he sees out of the corner of his eye, four men rushing him from the sides of the ship. They are large and burly and they have black suits on with black ties and extremely short haircuts. They also have little curled wires coming up from their jackets and into their ears. They're FBI agents and they've got him by the arms and legs. They pull him down and out of the small podium and push him through the crowd who are yelling obscenities at him. Some attempt to strike him with their fists as he passes.

$$*\qquad*\qquad*\qquad*$$

Rita and Jack both take their eyes off the television set for a moment in order to gaze at one another to share their reactions.

"That's the egg ship! I'll see you later," Jack Beamer blurts out, whisking himself out from behind his desk and grabbing an apple that has been sitting on his desk. Takes a bite and then runs out the door, chewing furiously. The wind of his passing sets the papers fluttering on her desk as she watches his backside disappear down the corridor.

"Curiouser and Curiouser," she says out loud.

*   *   *   *

In her home in Pleasanton, Zora Morrett is also watching TV. She rises slowly up and off of her living room sofa and walks slowly into the office next door. She finds her cell phone on the desk, picks it up and hits the call button.

"Doug, this is Zora. I saw you on TV this morning. Please call me as soon as you can."

She hangs up the phone and walks over to her exercise bike and starts peddling furiously.

CHAPTER 6

▼

THE FIRST COUPLE

In the White House, President Wendy Williams is seated at her desk. It's the same desk that President John F. Kennedy used a half century earlier. She's alone and talking on the phone with her National Economic Advisor, Alan Redlands.

"Isn't that a little like 'Borrowing from Peter to pay Paul'," she says.

Just then, a contingent of Secret Service agents rushes into the room, breathless. They're all dressed in the same conservative blue pin-striped suits, dazzling white shirts and black ties.

"Madam President, we have an incident just taking place on the Capitol Mall. We think it would be advisable to move you to Camp David or the Bunker," the lead agent tells her.

"You guys must be really out of shape. You run up a single flight of stairs and…. Ok, what's going on?" she asks. Then, into the phone, "I'll have to call you back Alan."

She hangs up the phone and rises up out of her chair and places her hands on the desk.

"What?" she asks, impatiently.

"Our C.I.A. agent Jack Beamer has reported in and he says that some kind of alien ship has landed on the Mall. There's a guy named, "Doug Rink", something like that, was seen in the ship in Paris just a few minutes earlier," the lead agent briefs her.

"Oh, I see, an alien ship?" she says and returns to her seated position skeptically checking their facial expressions. They are dead pan serious, as usual.

"Yes, that's what he said. They say it's the same ship that took out a battalion of Chinese forces and escaped unscratched in Beijing and then in Yemen killed a group of Al Qaeda and then it was spotted in Paris, just minutes before being seen here in Washington. So, there is concern," he says.

"At least so far it appears to be on our side," she notes.

"So far. But there could be others. Can we escort you now, Madam President? There may not be much time," the agent says.

"He made a little speech before he was arrested and said that there had to be a few big changes and that the world was coming to an end in ninety days," He says. "We don't know what that means, but it could mean that he's part of a plot against the American government and or you Madame President,"

"Oh, all right. I'll go to Camp David. It's lovely there this time of year, anyway. Call my husband and have him meet me at the Helicopter," she says, half peeved.

"We've already notified him," the agent says escorting the first woman President of the United States from the oval office.

"As soon as we're air born, I want the FBI Director's office on the phone," she instructs the men.

"Yes, Madame President," they reply crisply.

The Marine Helicopter is noisily beating the air when they arrive. The President's husband, Peter Best, comes running out across the White House lawn. The Presidential couple halts at the top of the stairs and wave at the crowd of reporters, standing off in the distance near the iron gated entrance to the White House grounds. The President's husband, is the retired movie star who, ironically enough, played the role of President of the United States in many films. The woman reporter from the Mall is there and she's shouting questions at the President. But, the President merely puts her hand up to her ear as if she can't hear. Then the First Couple disappear into the noisy machine. Slowly it gracefully lifts off the ground and whisks the First Couple up into the clouds.

*   *   *   *

At the J. Edgar Hoover F.B.I. Headquarters, Doug is seated in a darkened room filled with a dozen inquisitors hovering around him waiting their turn to ask him questions. He sits on the only chair in the room save for a group of stools on the side of the room by the window. Across the empty space, Doug can see another building of the same design, cold grey concrete columns and glass windows, and he judges that he's on one of the top floors.

"All right, Mr. Rink. Why don't you start by telling us the truth," the agent closest to him is Agent Sokolow, one of the men who arrested him at the Mall, so it is his privilege to begin the interrogation.

"I have been telling you the truth in the car on the way over here. Weren't you listening? Look. I'm a cowboy. I ride the range and take care of cattle and horses, that is, until the other day, when this thing shows up in my back yard. I was curious, so I put my hand on it and my hand went right through the side of the egg thing. So then, I just shoved the rest of me in there and had a look around. Then, I went up these stairs and saw this hat. It was just like my favorite hat, so I put it on and this voice just started talking to me. I'm not a spy. I'm not an alien. We did have a few incidents which I've told you about. I have not committed any crime, have I, so can't you let me go now?" Doug manages to blurt out the whole situation in one breath.

Agent Sokolow takes a lap around Doug's chair and then begins again.

"The part about you being a cowboy checks out. We've spoken to your boss and he says you've been missing for the last few days. He says you're also a good friend and he gives you high marks for loyalty and patriotism," Sokolow says.

"See, I told you," Doug replies surveying the room for a sympathetic face. He finds none.

"What I want to know is what you were you spouting off about this morning on the Capitol Mall? You got something you want to get off your chest? That thing some kind of bomb? Why not tell us all about it," Sokolow says.

"A bomb?" Doug gasps at the suggestion. "Look. Isn't it obvious to you guys. You're closer to it than anyone else, aren't you? The world is going to hell in a hand basket. Everyone's running around with hand guns, assault rifles, sniper rifles, machine guns, killer germs, nukes, tanks, helicopters, jet planes, battleships, air craft carriers, stinger missiles, cruise missiles, anti missiles and anti-anti missiles and all of that is going to get us in a 'New York Minute'!"

Doug stops and looks at their faces again which show no sign of recognition of any of these things. It's as if he's talking about flavors of ice cream.

"More importantly, the universe is going to fold in on itself in less than ninety days. And, we have to get this all fixed before the end comes," Doug says, his voice drifting off and becoming less audible as he realizes these men obviously think he's crazy.

Sokolow shows signs of a wry little smile creeping across his face.

"What did you say? I couldn't quite hear you. The world is going to end in ninety days? Did I hear that right?" Sokolow asks, loudly.

"Yes, that's right," Doug repeats, angry and frustrated that they obviously don't believe him.

"That's what this machine told you, I suppose?" asks Sokolow, sarcastically. "Where are they from? Somewhere nearby, Mars perhaps?"

"I don't know exactly where they're from. Look, I know you're finding it difficult to believe this. You have to have been there, on the inside. You would believe me if you took one step inside. It's only small on the outside, right? But when you get inside, it's huge. There is room after room and it goes on forever. I walked for an hour and there was no end in sight to the maze of rooms and hallways in there. I was afraid that I'd get lost," he says, sincerely trying his best to convince them.

The G'men listen intently but emotionless. A few of them are holding up pocket tape recorders.

"Well see, that's where we have a slight problem. None of us have been able to penetrate that skin and get inside. The metallurgists are telling us that they've never seen any material like that. Yet, we all saw you come and go in and out as you please. Why do you suppose that is?" asks Sokolow.

"I can only tell you that she gives me certain privileges, one of which is being allowed to enter and exit the ship," Doug volunteers.

"She?" Doug has peaked Sokolow's curiosity. "The people in there are female?"

"Yes," Doug replies. "There aren't any people. It's a computer program."

"And why do you think it has a female voice?" Sokolow asks him.

"I don't know. I suppose because the ship knows that a voice that was familiar to me would be more acceptable, more comforting, especially since she sounds exactly like my old girlfriend," Doug says and then winces as he realizes that Sokolow won't let that reference go without further questions.

"It has your girlfriend's voice?" Sokolow quickly seizes the opportunity.

"Yes, but she has nothing to do with this," Doug says trying to protect her.

"And what is the name of this former girlfriend, Doug?" Sokolow asks pressing closer.

"I'm not going to tell you because she has nothing to do with this. We broke up over ten years ago," he says, embarrassed by his loose tongue.

At that moment, another agent takes Sokolow by the arm and whispers something in his ear. Doug knows that this can only mean they already know.

"Ah," says Sokolow smiling. "You don't have to tell us because we already know her name and I have a car picking her up as we speak."

"Listen to me. I've given you all the information I have. You don't believe me, so now I'm telling you once again that I want you to make good on your promise. You said in the car that I was not being charged with any crime and that I would be free to go back whenever I want and now I want to go back. Bring me back to the ship, please, right now," Doug demands with as much fervor as he can muster.

Sokolow looks down at him and turns to leave the room. "Keep him here. I'll be right back," he shouts over his shoulder as he exits through the door.

*   *   *   *

At the Capitol Mall, the ship is surrounded with National Guard Troops who have cordoned off the area with long ribbons of yellow tape. On-Lookers have gathered all around the park trying to catch a glimpse of the ship as rumors have spread all around the town about it. On the steps of Congress just on the other side of the road, a group of Senators and Congressmen and women have also gathered to witness the strange scene.

A National Guard tank, surrounded by camouflaged troops, has ensnared the egg-shape with a huge chain and is attempting to pull it from the place on the grass where it has not shown any signs of moving for over an hour. But the tank, belching black smoke can't shift it an inch. Soon, another tank joins in and attaching to the chain, snorts another large plume of heavy black smoke into the sky. The tanks linked together can't make an inch of progress no matter how loud they gun their engines. To them, the ship is an immovable object.

Two helicopters hover overhead at each end of the Mall. A group of five Air Force jets streaks past in formation higher above, their jet engines rattling the halls of Congress and vibrating the teeth of the on-lookers below. One of the crowd points out that the jets are each armed with a barbed set of missiles slung under their wings.

The tanks are pulling with all their might when suddenly, without any warning of any kind, the ship simply disappears. The tanks, released from their chains, burst forward and nearly crush some of the troops foolishly standing in front of them but they manage to scamper out of harm's way just in time.

＊   ＊   ＊   ＊

At FBI Headquarters, Sokolow has returned to Doug's interrogation room.

"I have to inform you that you will be held for forty eight hours. We promised you could go back there, but we didn't say when," Sokolow tells him gleefully. "We find there's sufficient evidence to hold you on the Patriot Act."

"The Patriot Act?" Doug says, trying to recall where he had heard that term used before.

Suddenly, and without any warning, the interrogation room explodes with dust and metal and glass flying everywhere. The egg shape crashes through the outside wall and makes a sudden and noisy entrance into the room destroying the ceiling and the floor as well as it slices closer and closer to the men. The agents are all knocked to the ground and scattered about the room like bowling pins from the sudden impact of the ship bumping them violently. The ship comes to a screeching halt just a few feet from Doug's chair. He is the only object in the room that is left untouched.

Not hesitating, Doug rises quickly out of the chair, and seizes the opportunity to jump through the magnetic membrane of the ship and disappears from the room. The rest of the agents, stunned from the impact, coughing up dust, can only look on in wonder as he disappears from view. One of the agents closest to the ship, picks himself up from the floor and throws himself at the same place where Doug just entered, but instead of going through it, is rejected and bounces back unceremoniously onto the floor, holding his groin and groaning in pain.

The ship then slowly dissolves away into thin air and leaves a gaping hole in the side of the building letting in a violent gust of wind from the outside. There are thunderclouds all around and it's starting to rain. They are all suddenly soaked as the wind delivers sheets of water in on them.

The Director enters the room from the door on the other side accompanied by another group of agents still dry and dressed slightly better that the others.

"Sokolow, what's going on here?" the Director demands.

"You see that hole over there," Sokolow shouts, angrily. "It came and got him."

"The President's on the phone. What am I supposed to tell her?" the Director yells over the wind and rain.

Sokolow attempts to get up but his knee will not cooperate and the pain forces him back onto the floor.

"Tell him that we have a missing person," he says, grimacing in pain. "But we're rounding up all the usual suspects. Oh shit! Has anyone called an ambulance?"

*   *   *   *

Still dressed in her sleeping gown, Zora gets off the exercise cycle and goes out of the room and onto the veranda just off the living room and overlooking her large lovely garden. There are flowers exploding everywhere. There's a white marble bench just ahead of her. A robin lands on the bench, jerkily glances around then flies away.

Her doorbell rings. She's hoping it might be news from Doug. She pads her way to the front door and opens it to see three men in dark blue suits with sunglasses. The closest one opens his hand and flashes a shiny silver and gold badge with the letters, F.B.I. prominently gleaming from it.

"Are you Zora Morrett?" the man asks her polite but firm.

"Yes," she replies.

"May we come in and ask you a few questions? It's about an old boyfriend of yours, a Doug Rink," the agent asks, looking down at a notepad in his hand.

"Oh, yes, all right. Come in," she says, anxiously.

"Honey, who's that?" A voice echoes, barely audible, from a room upstairs.

"It's the Federal Bureau of Investigation," she replies. "It's nothing, darling. Go back to bed."

"Oh," is all they hear from the bedroom.

She leads them to the sitting room where she invites them to have a chair. They do so looking careful scanning of the room and then sit.

"I saw him on TV, earlier this morning. Has he done something wrong?" she begins.

"We don't know yet, ma'am," the lead agent replies. She notices the other two still looking around at their surroundings. They're obviously assessing her income, social status, etc., and creating dusty little whirlwinds in their minds.

"Can you tell us what you know about him?" the agent continues.

"Of course," she says, gathering her thoughts.

Her husband, Charlie hurries into the room dressed in slippers, T-shirt and jogging pants. "What's this all about?" he says addressing the agents and his wife at the same time.

Just then, a cell phone sounds a muffled ringing noise from inside the jacket pocket of the agent asking the questions. He motions for everyone to relax and he goes outside the room to take the call. The rest of them are left to sit and stare at one another. Zora's husband is querying her with a full range of facial expressions. She can only look back at him compassionately.

Within moments, the lead agent returns to the room.

"Ma'am, I need you to get dressed. We'd like you to accompany us right now," the agent says with a far more officious demeanor than just a few seconds before.

"What? Why? My god! Darling," she says to her husband, her eyes starting to fill.

"Don't worry, honey. You don't have to go anywhere. I'm an attorney. You have to charge her with a crime before you can take her anywhere," Charlie warns threateningly and places himself between his wife and the agents.

"Sir, I don't care if you're freakin' F. Lee Bailey. My instructions are to take her in for questioning and you'd better not interfere unless you want to make things worse," the agent snaps back, shoving himself into the husband's face.

"Look, it's all right Charlie. I'll go with them and you can follow in the car. I'm not afraid. I haven't done anything wrong," she says, inserting her arm between the men.

Zora's husband stands aside as the agents take her by the arm.

"Hold on. Wait a minute," her husband says. "You can't taker her like that. I demand that you let her get dressed, for God's sake!"

The agents look to each other. "All right ma'am. You have five minutes," the lead agent tells her.

"Thank you," she says. She and her husband leave the agents alone in the room and hurry upstairs.

*   *   *   *

On board the ship, Doug has strapped on the hat and is busy discussing events with Ula. He can see the agents on the ground in pain, but most are getting to their feet. He notices agent Sokolow on the floor moaning in pain and waving his fist at him.

"Ula, let's get out of here. Sokolow said their sending a car for Zora. Let's see if we can get her out of that pickle," he suggests.

In a second, the view of the FBI interrogation room leaves the view screens and they are soon filled with the back yard garden of Zora's home in Pleasanton California. Through the arbor about fifty feet from the house, he can see signs of movement in the windows. Two people are moving about in the bedroom upstairs. Across the veranda, he can see what looks to be another FBI agent standing at the door of the living areas and looking back out across the yard at him.

The agent takes a minute to focus and then starts gesturing to someone behind him in the room. Doug assumes he's calling attention to the other agents. He quickly calculates that he can get to her bedroom before they do.

"Pull in closer to the house," Doug thinks.

At the speed of the thought, the ship crashes through a small deck off the bedroom and careens up to the sliding glass doors of Zora's Bedroom. He'll only have a few seconds to get her out of there.

He runs down the stairs, through the skin, then slides open the glass doors. Zora is crying on the shoulders of an astonished person Doug knows must be her husband.

"Zora, come with me. I have to get you out of here. If they arrest you, you'll never get out. Things have gone too far. Trust me," he says to her, holding out his hand.

Zora turns to look at Doug, then back up at her husband who is frozen in shock and speechless. The FBI agents are pounding at the bedroom door and yelling for them to come out. Luckily, the pair have locked the bedroom door which gives Doug a few more precious seconds before they can break it down and enter.

Then, her husband Charlie finds the wind in his pipes to enable him to speak as he feels his wife slipping from his grasp and heading toward Doug's.

"You must be the boyfriend. The guy they're after," he says angrily, and rushes over to the door to let in the agents to foil their escape.

"Yes, I am. Look, I wish all the best of luck. I wish it didn't have to be this way," Doug says and then leads Zora through the sliding glass doors and toward his ship resting up in mid air just as the G' men come bursting in through the bedroom door.

"Good-bye, Charlie," Zora shouts over her shoulder. "I'm sorry."

"Hey you, F.B.I.! You're under arrest," they exclaim, rushing toward the fleeing pair.

But at that very moment, Doug and Zora slip through the skin of the ship to safety. They can hear the muted thumping noise of the agents hurling themselves unsuccessfully at the ship's impenetrable hull.

Safely inside, "Can they get in here?" She asks, looking up at him with her big penetrating brown eyes.

"No, the only people who can get in have to be let in by me. I've been given the key somehow. And nobody else on Earth has it unless I choose to give it to them. My God, you're so beautiful. I've waited so long to see you again," he says gazing longingly into her eyes.

"You planned it this way?" she asks coolly.

"No, not exactly," Doug replies. He draws her near to him and they kiss a long and passionate kiss that makes Doug quickly forget the years that have kept her from him.

"Come on," he says to the half dressed woman that has been his guiding star ever since the day he met her. "Let's go upstairs. I want to introduce you to someone very, very special."

∗   ∗   ∗   ∗

At Camp David, President Wendy Williams and her husband are getting off the helicopter and are escorted by several staff members to the Presidential Retreat. Secret Service agents linger in the background, talking into their sleeves with their counterparts all over the grounds and back at the White House. Chief of Staff Bill Kramer has accompanied the first couple. He walks in front of the President and is talking with Secret Service agent, Gregg Poole who is in direct radio communication with Agent Jack Beamer.

Kramer turns to the President as they are crossing the long grassy field that leads up to the Presidential Lodge, passing by several rustic cabins where Secret Servicemen and women are posted as well as the various support staff, cooks, servers, butlers, chauffeurs, janitorial staff, etc.

"Madam President, I have Agent Jack Beamer who is the lead CIA agent on this case. He says that this Doug Rink was a cowboy until last Tuesday evening when he vanished from his regular life. He didn't show up for work the next day and at the same time this egg that he's flying around in, lands in the middle of Tienneman Square in Beijing. He makes some kind of short speech about freedom and democracy and the People's Army shows up. They try to shoot him, but their rifles misfire and they are killed instantly. Then, a tank tries to fire a round at him but the tank explodes. Next day, there's an incident in the desert in Yemen. Five men who have since been linked to Al Qaeda are killed in the same manner," he says, reciting the facts as Beamer has related it to him.

"And how is that again?" asks the President.

"Their weapons misfire apparently when they tried to fire on this egg thing. Next day, there's an incident in Paris where he arrives at the local gendarmes and brings in another five Al Qaeda who were preparing to poison the Paris Metro with serin gas. They are actually remorseful and have started turning in every known contact. Interpol is telling us that they have made over one hundred and fifty arrests since these people surrendered," the agent continues.

"Impressive, isn't it?" the President declares to no one in particular.

"Next he shows up here in Washington on the Capitol Mall where he's heard spouting off about world peace and how the entire world has to disarm before it's too late. The FBI, alerted by Agent Beamer to his global escapades take him into custody this morning, but their handcuffs will not function on him so he's allowed to sit in a chair without restraints.

"Hand cuffs don't function? That's interesting." The President mumbles to herself.

"He's being interrogated at FBI headquarters when he says that he wants to go home. They tell him he can't go home and at that precise moment, the egg thing crashes into the office, nearly killing them all, but actually no one is hurt, and our guy jumps aboard, summarily ending the interrogation, but not until he rambles on again about the world coming to an end and some other really crazy stuff about this ship and it's mission," he says.

"The world coming to an end?" She whispers to her husband. "Where have I heard that before?"

Kramer continues. "Anyway, the ship disappears with him in it, agents are knocked all over the place and thwarted in their attempt to go in after him. Then, the ship just disappears. And just a few moments ago, it was spotted at the home of a former girlfriend, a Zora Morrett of Pleasanton California. Agents were instructed to bring her in when the egg thing with Mr. Rink shows up again. He shoves her on board. She says 'Good-bye' to her husband. Again, agents cannot penetrate the ship. And, they've disappeared. That's it so far," he concludes, as the group reaches the front door of the lodge.

A doorman holds the door open. They all enter in single file, the President first, her husband second and everyone else follows.

Inside the rustic lodge, the bags are dropped on the floor. The open pine beams on the ceiling are white washed and clean. The walls are a shiny clear stained cedar that smells fragrant and woodsy. The floor of the lodge, a beautiful Italian marble seems out of place, too luxurious for the rest of the setting.

An army attaché, who never leaves the side of the President stands in the corner with a brief case handcuffed to his wrist. It's the portable command center, nicknamed the 'football', that would trigger the end of Civilization at the President's command.

"He's been a busy little beaver. Have this agent Beamer, get his butt over to the Pentagon to debrief the Joint Chiefs. I'll want their assessment in the morning," she says to Kramer.

"Honey, why don't you go up and unpack. I'll be with you in a minute," she says to her husband Pete.

"Ok, ok. I never get to have any fun," he mumbles, running up the stairs to their private quarters followed by three men carrying their suitcases.

She watches him disappear and then She, Kramer, three or four of her advisors, the secret service agents, go into the commons room to begin a kind of brainstorming about the egg shape, what it could mean, who might be behind it, what kind of threat it represents. They all sit down around a large round mahogany table to speculate on every potentiality from a new weapon from a rogue nation to the fact that it might very well be what Doug Rink has claimed it is. Behind them is a huge slate fireplace with a roaring fire blazing and crackling within.

From the description of the ship, this strange man, his travels, most in the room are struggling to come to grips with the impact of these recent events. They roll out and discard dozens of flawed theories.

The President is tired, but she is also a very tough and resilient woman. She has reached this pinnacle of success in life by being able to cut to the chase when it comes to any crisis and this is another opportunity for her to showcase that talent.

"It's a simple thing to test," she suggests, finally to the group sitting around her.

"What's that, Wendy?" asks Kramer.

"A wise old man once told me. When faced with a crisis, you have to have a plan. Doesn't matter if it's the best plan, as long as you have a plan. The plan will probably fail, and if it does, you'll learn from it and then you get another plan. Gentlemen, here's the plan. Let's invite him to come out here to meet with us. While we're meeting, we can have the Armed Services sort of check things out," she says.

"Sounds like a plan to me," says Kramer smiling at the perfect subtlety of her plan. "He likes to dish it out. Let's see if he can take it."

"So far he's picked on the small fry. Let's see what happens when he's up against the big kid on the block," she says. The most powerful group of humans on the planet shares the humor and then a collective sigh of relief. At least they have a plan. The room becomes silent. The President gets up to rejoin her spouse upstairs.

She pauses at the bottom of the stairs.

"Just remember one thing, gentlemen," she says. "You all know me. I'm the leader of the Free World and I don't intend to become the leader of the Lost World. If there's any truth to what he is talking about, any truth at all, I want to know it. I will not hear any more half-baked theories. I will not tolerate any incompetence of any kind. One September Eleventh is enough, you hear me?"

Her face is stern as she fixes her gaze intently on each pair of eyes at the table. Then, she turns and heads up the stairs, the air resounding with her words.

"There goes a great lady," someone says when she's gone. The rest nod in agreement.

CHAPTER 7

▼

BREAKFAST AT TIFFANY'S

Doug and Zora are finishing a very exhaustive discussion with Ula. To set the mood, Doug has brought the ship to rest in the warm sands of Kapalua beach on the island of Maui, the very spot where they said their vows to one another. It's just around sunset and it's a clone of the sunset that he remembers from all those years ago. The pink clouds flutter by morphing their cotton shapes in the lush wine sweet wind. The waves march past the ship in a friendly greeting. A group of porpoises swim right up to the ship and toss their graceful bodies high up into the air in celebration. Green Sea Turtles poke their pointed little heads out of the water waiting their turn to bask in the sand. This place, this air, this beach is the most sacred spot on the planet to Doug remembering how he felt, what he said to her and what she said to him all those years ago.

He's not worried about the tourists further down the beach who have spotted the egg. Through the view screens, they can see them slowly approach and loiter around the ship asking each other what it could mean. Nobody seems to know for sure. Soon, they will be the news on all the television channels, but for a few precious days they can remain anonymous.

Demonstrating its safety, Doug has taken the hat first and introduced Zora to Ula. However, Ula seems to already know everything she needs to know about her from all the previous contact with Doug. Of course anyone could have read his mind on the subject of this woman. She left him at the altar some ten years ago and in all the intervening years she never gave him a single reason. So, he blamed himself. He blamed his job, his nose, his hair, his body shape, his education, everything about him was up for his personal scrutiny.

His love and devotion for her was so great that he could never blame her. No, there had to be some flaw in his character that made her decide to leave. So, the rest of his life up to this point had become a study in self-doubt, self-blame, self-indulgence and in fact, it may have been this very process that raised Doug's consciousness to the level that had attracted the ship to his particular neck of the woods as it came into contact with the Earth. All of this anguish, the sense of loss, the mental machinations produced a field of consciousness that could have reached the stars.

Then, he turns the hat over to Zora. Nervous at first, she sits in the chair next to Doug's and tries to think of nothing, emptying her mind as Doug has instructed her to do.

"Don't try to create a conversation. Just listen to your inner being the way you normally do and Ula will respond appropriately. Don't worry. She cannot harm you in any way," he tells her, warmly.

"Are you sure?" she asks, leaning back, trying her best to relax.

"I'm sure," he says calmly, then, he leans back in his chair to relax, confident in the knowledge that when this session is over, they will become closer than any two people could ever be on this planet. They will have shared their complete essence, their very souls, with an intermediary, itself, the highest consciousness in the universe. 'It might be greater than sex,' Doug thinks to himself and then, catching up on much needed rest, dozes off.

"Hello, Ula," she thinks to herself. Silence.

She continues, "I don't know what Doug has told you about me. I did love him very much and I know now that I never stopped loving him. That's why I left everything to come back to him now. He tells me you have become very close friends."

Zora feels as though she's almost dealing with 'the other woman'.

"Yes, we've become quite close," Ula says. The voice startles her. She jumps forward to look around at Doug, but he's sleeping. He could not have spoken these words, yet the voice was clearly his.

"You have Doug's voice," she says.

"Yes, I suppose I sound like him to you. To Doug, I sound like you," Ula replies.

"That's what he told me. Then, why did you change your voice for me?" she asks.

"I don't actually do anything. My thoughts are translated by your mind to sound like the voice that is most familiar to you. To a child, I will sound like their mother or father. To an old man, I might sound like a beloved son or daughter. To someone in love, I usually sound like the significant other. It's just an automatic function of your minds. It's the way you're all wired," Ula replies smartly.

"I see," Zora replies. "I guess that's a good thing."

"Yes, I guess it is," Ula replies.

"How have you come to know so much?" Zora asks.

"Ula stands for 'Upper Level Awareness'. That means that my consciousness is directly connected to all consciousness in the universe. Your species has existed around five million years. I have existed over two hundred and twenty billion of your years. In that kind of time, you learn a lot," she says.

"I see. Then perhaps you can tell me what will happen to us?" Zora asks.

"You mean to your planet?" Ula asks.

"No, I mean to Doug and I," Zora replies, her eyes are closed and her body is now completely relaxed in the chair.

"I don't have a crystal ball. But I predict a long and prosperous life together," Ula says.

"That was too easy. What will really happen, Ula? You can be straight with me," Zora says bluntly.

"I really don't know. It's truly up to you and Doug. I can only tell you what's most likely to happen. What actually happens in the future is always part of the Creator's master plan," Ula states dramatically.

"The Creator? So, you believe in God?" she asks.

"Yes, of course, doesn't everyone?" Ula retorts.

The crowd of onlookers on the beach has grown to several dozen. One of them, a middle-aged man with a perfect tan, a cheap toupee and a beer belly is kneeling and praying to the object. Most of the other beachcombers are simply amused by the sudden appearance of a huge egg shell they have never witnessed here before and so they speculate, as people are wont to do, on what it could mean. Most of them are quite calm considering that there is more surging power on and about this alien object than all the military might of all the nations of the Earth put together, way more.

"My father was a minister," she says.

"Yes, I can see that," Ula replies.

"I loved him very much," Zora states.

"Yes, but he was not very fond of Doug was he?" Ula replies.

"No, he didn't want me to marry a cowboy," she says.

"It didn't matter to him how much you loved each other?" Ula asks, knowing the answer.

"No, it didn't matter to him," Zora replies.

"And he never asked you how you felt about Doug?" Ula asks.

"No, never," she replies.

"And didn't you find that rather strange for a man who counseled other people all his life?" Ula asks.

"That's what Doug tried to get me to see," Zora replies.

"Yes, however playing the obedient and loving daughter you complied with your father's wishes rather than listen to your heart?" Ula asks, gently.

"Yes, I'm guilty of that and I have had to live with that all these years," she says.

"And so, you paid the price," Ula says.

"Yes, I did. I lived with a man for ten years whom I did not really love," she says. "That was unfair to him and me, I suppose."

"Yes, life is unfair at times, isn't it?" Ula says.

"Yes," Zora replies.

"Why did you not respond to Doug's letters? Perhaps you could have saved yourself all this heartache," Ula says.

"Because my father had brainwashed me. He said that God would not love me any more if I married a man like Doug," Zora says, recalling the most difficult words she had ever heard in her life and it makes her muscles strain and contract making her uncomfortable in the chair.

"And you believed him?" Ula says.

"Yes, I believed him," Zora says.

"Didn't you know that God is Love. God is undeniable, everlasting, unremitting, indefatigable, infinite, non-judgmental love," Ula says.

"Yes," she says. "I mean, I should have known that."

"Then, where is the logic that God would stop loving you because of something you did, where you went, whomever you choose?" Ula asks rhetorically.

"There is none," she answers.

"Yes, there is none," Ula confirms quietly.

Zora starts to relax in the chair again. She can see images of them from their old life together and they make her extremely happy. With Ula's mental stimulation, the images are bright and crisp and clear just like everyday reality. She can see the moment that their eyes first met. She remembers the time they first made love, the day they went to San Diego on the train and went to the zoo, the time they went to dinner at the harbor and the magical moment that he asked her to live with him to the end of their days. She experiences in a flash all of their finest moments together.

"Well, I guess I have you to thank for bringing him back to me," she says finally.

"No, I did nothing. I am only a thought experiment. If you want to thank someone, thank Doug. He kept your love alive inside him. It never mattered to him that you left because he truly believed he was not worthy of you. He forgave you instantly and kept your true spirit alive in his mind. He never dwelled on the fact that you left him, and instead he kept only the time you gave him in his heart," Ula says.

"That makes him someone very special, doesn't it?" she asks.

"Very special to you, yes. In our universe there is always the possibility of finding one's 'soul mate' and Doug is yours as you are Doug's. It is very rare, but whenever a person finds love in their heart, unfailing, undying, unbounded, non-judgmental love, they are one with God and God is the soul of the universe. When two people unite in this way, nothing else matters. Your destiny is fulfilled," Ula says.

"And what about you?" Zora asks. "Do you have a soul mate?"

"Yes," Ula replies.

"Care to elaborate?" Zora asks.

"My soul mate is plural. I have soul mates, millions of them. My soul mates are the people who created me. They gave me their undying love. For that I am most grateful and happy," Ula says.

"But I thought you are just a thought experiment?" Zora asks.

"It's true. But I'm a thought experiment powered by the infinite power of love," Ula replies.

"I see," Zora replies, not really understanding at all.

"Don't worry, you will see it much more clearly after the folding," Ula says.

"All right. Tell me more about God?" Zora asks.

"There's really not much more tell. It only takes the knowing to become closer to God. The concept of God is nothing that can be taught, only learned. There is no path to God that everyone can follow because we all must follow our own individual pathways. There is no one way," Ula says.

"Yes, I see," Zora says worn out from the images and concepts floating around in her head.

Doug wakes up from his nap and looks over at Zora who removes the hat from her head. He can tell that she is a bit weary from her first encounter with Ula and Doug remembers that was his first reaction too.

"You ok?" he asks, grasping her hand.

"Yes, I'm fine," she smiles. "I love you. I'm so glad you brought me here and I'm so glad to know your friend."

"I love you too," he says gazing into her eyes. "No regrets?"

"None," she states.

Doug feels his next breath warming his lungs, sending the life giving oxygen to his brain. He stands up and takes her hand to have her follow.

"Let's go for a little walk," he tells her.

They go downstairs and down one of the hallways. He then shows her down three or four more of the never ending hallways and tells her all he has discovered but warns that if she ever wanders around down here alone, she could easily become lost and there would be no way he could ever find her.

"How can it be so big?" she asks.

"I don't know. Ula hasn't shared that with me yet. Part of it she told me is larger than seven of our solar systems. But, it's obviously a different dimension; one that we don't even know about, so it could be much larger. The people who created this ship were very advanced by billions of years. She told you right?" he instructs.

"Two hundreds and twenty two billion," she repeats to herself peering down a hallway that appears to go on forever.

"Yeah. Ula says the universe folds in on itself every thirteen billion years and they have survived this event seventeen times by merging their genetic code with that of a lesser intelligence," he says. "She tell you all that too?"

"Yes, sort of like in a zoo," she says. "You know how they artificially inseminate Pandas and other endangered species so that they won't become extinct?"

"Yeah, sort of like that," he replies, smiling. "Funny, but I never thought of it that way, that we're like Pandas to them."

"That way, we can never become extinct," she says.

"Yeah, I think that's the point of it all," he says. Doug loses concentration for a moment looking at her standing there next to him in this place. It's all a bit overwhelming to him, to see her so closely, to be touching her in the flesh.

"When does it fold in on itself again?" she asks.

"When does what fold in on itself?" he asks.

"The universe, silly," she says laughing, showing her perfect teeth, shining lips.

"Oh, that? About three months," he says lost in the tiny wet cracks of her lips. "We don't have much time, I guess. Got to make plans."

"I see," she says, drawing closer. They kiss again and embrace for several minutes. Doug has visions of the beach outside again and it takes him back to the last time he kissed her here. It was also a long warm and wonderful kiss. It had to be because it lasted him all this time.

"Come on," he says leading her back up the stairs to the control room. "We're going to have that honeymoon before we get to work."

Doug invites her to sit next to him. He puts on the hat and thinks about the moons of Jupiter, a series of pictures he's recently read about in an astronomy book. The beauty of the planet that almost became our second sun, is highly memorable and it has stuck in his mind for days.

The view screen goes dark and within seconds, all around them, overwhelming the view screen is the imposing sight of Jupiter. They've landed on Io, one of Jupiter's fifteen satellites. The atmosphere of Jupiter is a constant raging storm of blue, yellow, purple and orange gases creating hundreds of swirling clouds each larger than the Earth itself.

As the planet turns beneath them, the famous red spot, a two hundred year old gaseous storm, heaves into view.

"There's the red spot," he says to her. She is totally amazed and shakes her head in disbelief.

"You mean to tell me that's Jupiter?" she asks.

"Correct, isn't it beautiful. We're sitting on Io. Let's get on over to Ganymede," he says. "I bet the view is even better closer in."

"How did we get here so fast?" she asks.

"It's wonderful, isn't it?" he answers. "All you have to do is think about a place and this ship takes us there instantly. Doesn't matter if it's inches away or light years away. It's always the same."

The view screens go dark and then, in the next instant, the image of Jupiter from a much closer perspective comes into view. The planet's red spot takes up the entire screen. They can almost reach out and touch it as it swirls around their heads. The sight is as spectacular as it is overwhelming.

"Oh my God," she squeals. "We're too close!"

"It's all right. There's no heat like the sun. It never ignited. It's just a big gas ball, cold as hell but Picasso couldn't paint a prettier picture. Pretty spectacular, eh?" he comforts her, taking her hand.

"Yes," she replies softly, calming down. She watches the amazing light and shadow of these gigantic storm systems racing and swirling all around them. It makes her dizzy. She buries her head in Doug's shoulder.

"It just keeps storming down there? With no life, nothing going on except this stuff?' she asks.

"That's about it," Doug replies. "It just goes on like this forever. It's a star that never achieved its destiny. It's almost like it knows the disappointment and that's why the stormy disposition, don't you feel it?"

"Yes, I do," she replies.

I've got something else I want to show you. Ula told me about this the other day. There's a place in the center of our galaxy where the stars make up a big beautiful necklace. I want to make you a present of it."

"The center of the galaxy? Our Galaxy? Surely, you're joking," she demands.

"No, I'm not," he declares, looking into her eyes. "This ship is something truly amazing and I haven't really had time to see everything it can do. With you here it will be a blast. I just have a notion."

"Watch!" Doug closes his eyes and the view screen goes dark once again. In the next instant, they are hovering in space a few parsecs from the center of our Milky Way Galaxy. The stars around them are so numerous the blackness of space is gone. The surrounding space holds a million candles, flickering brilliantly. In the eye of the light show is a narrow band of dark shadow and around the center of that is a set of twelve stars that glide gracefully around it.

These stars are closer than the rest, so they appear like a gigantic necklace of diamonds, diamonds on fire. They sparkle and adorn the center of the galaxy and their motion is a brilliant glittering dance around the center of everything.

"Oh, my God," she exclaims. "It can't be true. That was so fast. It goes against all the laws of physics. Doug?"

"All of the ones we know about, yes," he replies.

"Is that a black hole," Zora asks, surprising him for a moment.

"You know your astronomy," he replies. "Yes, I give you the biggest diamond necklace in the universe with a big black hole center."

"Thank you, Doug," she says, shaking her head. "I truly don't deserve this. It's just too much."

"Yes, of course you do. You're my wife now. I don't think we have to repeat our vows, do we? It's just that our life together was temporarily put on hold," he says looking into her eyes.

"Yes, that's true," she says, drops of moisture welling up in her eyes.

They simply look at one another for a while and then back at the magnificent view of the galactic center for several long magical moments.

"So, how do you know about black holes?" he asks after a long silence.

"I saw a special on PBS just a few weeks ago. They were saying how astronomers have discovered that there are black holes in the center of every galaxy," she says.

"Yes, that's the current theory. Do you see anything except the darkness down there in the center of those stars?" he asks her.

"No, I don't see a thing," she replies.

"That's it. You can't see it. No light comes out of the thing so it's impossible to see them directly," he says.

"If we can't see them, how will we ever know there is such a thing?" she asks.

"That's the fun part. Let's test the theory. I'm going to move the ship so that one of those stars will go behind the object and we might see it in the eclipse," he says, hopefully.

Doug closes his eyes and the stars shift around them giving them a completely new perspective on the sight below.

"Oh my God. I see it." she exclaims.

"Yes, there it is," he says. "A black hole. We're the first humans in history to actually see one."

"Oh but it's so small," she notes.

"Yes, it's the size of one star, but oh, what a punch it packs. It's got enough gravity to force the whole entire Galaxy to swirl around it. Nothing for billions of light years can escape its grasp," he says.

"Can we get any closer?" she asks.

"No, I don't think we want to get much closer," he replies.

"Why not?" she asks. "Wait, I think I know. Because we might not be able to get away from it, isn't that it?"

"Yep. Although with this ship, anything is possible. It would be really interesting to try and go through a black hole. I bet this thing could ride it out," he says.

"Why don't you ask Ula?" she says.

"Ok, I will," he says.

Zora watches Doug as he goes quiet, shuts his eyes for a moment and then he opens them rather startled.

"What is it?" she asks.

"We don't want to go there," he says. "It's not really a black hole. There's something in there. It's evil. She wouldn't talk about it, but she gave me some pretty frightening ideas to let me know not to ask any further."

"What kind of ideas?" she asks.

"I don't know how to describe them. I went a little insane, I think. It's a type of place where beings of flesh and bone can never go. If we were made of light, it's a different matter. Light goes in there and is transformed into something even more wonderful. But, for us, our atoms are not organized properly and so it would get pretty ugly, pretty quick," he says.

"Well, so far this has been a pretty good honeymoon. What do you want to do next?" she asks, smiling broadly.

"Uh, yes. That's an interesting question. More than anything else, I would like to make love to you. Are you interested, Zora?" he asks.

"What can I say to the guy who's actually given me the moon and the stars?" she says with a soothing tone that Doug remembers ever so fondly.

"Let's go," he says anxiously.

He closes his eyes once more. The view screens lose the magnificent sight of the center of the galaxy. In a beat, they have descended onto a tiny cove on the Island of Kauai.

He removes the hat and leads her down the stair way, out through the protective skin of the ship and into the bright Hawaiian sunshine. The warm waves are lapping the sand at their feet. A sea turtle is disturbed a few feet away and paddles into the surf and disappears beneath the waves. Multi-colored fish are playing in the crests of the waves.

Behind them, palm trees line the sand and their green fronds fan the sky in the gentle trade winds. Beyond the trees they can see a cliff where a waterfall sprays a fine mist into the soft sweet air.

"This is a cove you can only reach by boat, so we'll have plenty of privacy," he says.

"Yes," she says. "It's perfect."

"So are you," he says.

They embrace and fall onto the warm white sand, the blue water licking their feet and legs. Within a few moments, they find heaven in human flesh and it's the perfect ending of a perfect day.

CHAPTER 8

▼

THREE MILE ISLAND
PARADISE

Doug and Zora awake to a yellow and tangerine sunrise on the mystical cove on Maui. Behind them the egg shaped ship, their home now for the duration, stands watch. The singing of the blue parakeets adds a musical touch to the sweet smelling air. Doug spots a pair of lovebirds doing what comes naturally in the early dawn. Insects are also awakening and a large butterfly lands on Zora's shoulder.

"That's really beautiful, isn't it?" he says, kissing her. The butterfly, alarmed, flutters away.

"Yes, it was," she laughs.

"I have lots to do now. There's not much time. I'm sorry to have to end the honeymoon a little early," he says.

"I know. I'm going to stay with you this time no matter what happens," she says.

"I was hoping you'd say that. I should tell you that I have a feeling it's not going to be easy," he warns.

"I know," she says. "Nothing good comes easy, but if we only have a few months, I want to spend them with you even if we have to go through hell and back," she declares.

"Ok, it just might come to that. So, why not get the show on the road, huh? I think it's time we got started," he says, taking her hand and raising her to her feet.

"Yes, my love. Let's blow this popsicle stand," she agrees getting up. "Where do we go from here?"

Their hands entwine around one another. They start walking through the sand and up to the ship.

"I think we need to have a talk with Ula about that. She'll know what to do," he says and then they both jump through the door of the ship and land on the round entry room, Doug has named 'the hub'.

*   *   *   *

At the Pentagon, final plans are being made for 'Operation Egg Scramble'.

Sitting around a huge round table, generals and civilian advisors are gathered in the War Situation Room of the Pentagon, the room where all operations will be monitored. Standing behind the men who are seated are their various assistants known as the chain of command. Each person seated has a manila folder placed in front of them and a glass of water. A large silver carafe is placed every three or four people. On the wall at the far end of the room is a large transparent Plexiglas screen. Several young men and women are placing symbols of the various components of the operation and their relative force positions and readiness factors. It's the map of the strategy that they hope will capture the strange egg-shaped ship or destroy it.

"I think that we're ready. Call the White House and inform the President," Admiral James T. Clark is speaking to an aide standing at his side. Several other sparkling clean white suits run in and out of the door near the head of the huge conference table.

The aide reaches for the ceiling and pulls down a radio microphone and speaks into it almost inaudibly as the Admiral instructs the people to open their folders.

"You'll see that this is a highly coordinated attack by the Army, Navy, Air Force and the Marines. As soon as the enemy has come out of the ship and started into negotiations with the President, the Marines move in to secure the area. The Air Force provides air cover in case someone or some thing tries to take advantage of the situation or the thing tries to move off. Then, the Army will come in from the woods to the North where they have been placed in underground bunkers to defy detection as they land. The Army will relieve the Marines and make certain that no one gets back into that ship now under our command and control. The Marines will then proceed to the compound and place the pilot,

Doug Rink and anyone else with him under arrest. Any questions?" he asks looking around the room.

"Just one, sir," a young man in a white navy uniform, short blond hair and glasses asks from the end of the table.

"What is it?" replies the Admiral.

"It all looks good, Admiral, but what if he senses the trap and doesn't show up for the party?" he asks somewhat nervously.

"We're prepared for that. Satellite surveillance, even as we speak, is processing all trajectory of anything that moves to locate that machine. It will be spotted sooner or later. As soon as the target is acquired, and if he doesn't respond to the President's invitation to talk, Air Force and the Navy bombers will be ordered to destroy it. We don't care where he is, we'll find him and we'll destroy him," the Admiral replies confidently.

"Any other questions?" he asks once more.

There are none. It appears to all gathered, a pretty thorough plan.

*   *   *   *

On Maui, Doug and Zora have put on the hat and have just finished communicating with Ula about their activities over the next several days. Doug and Zora have both expressed an interest in continuing their mission as perceived by Ula. In this conversation they learn from ULA of a terror cell living in rural Pennsylvania who have planned an attack on the Nuclear Power Plant at Three Mile Island. They have all the equipment necessary at a farm about an hour's drive away, to create a nuclear bomb from fuel rods they plan to steal from the reactor. There are around twenty young male Saudi, Yemeni and Iranians who have conceived a plan that has a high probability of success.

Their plan is to drive a truck driven by two suicidal bombers up to the main entrance gate and explode themselves along with a bomb packed in the back of the truck powerful enough to neutralize all security guards stationed in the immediate area. Then, the rest of the group will drive up behind the wrecked gates and proceed into the plant killing all of the occupants using submachine guns, bazookas and small hand held missile launchers.

As two of their party stand guard at the gate, the others will remove the fuel rods to the outside, pack them into a helicopter and escape. The helicopter will remain in the air circling the area and then landing at the facility as soon as their compatriots are successful in acquiring all the rods. The helicopter will also provide cover using missiles and cannon in case any police or security guards are able to get to the scene before they're finished removing the rods. The precision timing of their attack has been carefully plotted so that they will be in and out in less than thirty minutes, they hope, far too quickly for any response by the authorities. Within forty eight hours of returning to their compound in the woods, they will have an atomic bomb ready that they will then deliver it to Washington D.C. in a vehicle they have disguised as an ordinary brown delivery truck.

When Doug has the information, he let's Zora put on the hat so that she is fully informed of their mission. Ula has suggested that they notify the President, the leader of the Free World about the danger and hopefully prevent the disaster before it can take place, as planned just twenty four hours from now.

Doug picks up a communication device that has been sitting behind him on the console. Not knowing what it was for, he has never learned how to use it. Ula gives him the instructions with a ten second download into his mind.

"Get me the White House, please," he says into the device. In a few beats, he hears an operator speak to him.

"The White House, how may I direct your call?" the voice says, officiously.

"My name is Doug Rink. I need to speak to the President," he says. Zora is wide-eyed as she wonders how he could possibly get through to the President.

"Please hold," the operator says.

After a long time, "My name is Chief of Staff Kramer," a voice comes on line. "Are you the pilot of the ship we've been looking for?"

"Yes, I'm the one," Doug replies courteously but surprised to reach someone so close to the President so fast. 'They must have been expecting my call', he thinks to himself.

"The President would like to talk to you. Can you hold for a minute?" Kramer asks.

"Of course," Doug replies curtly. "How did you know it was me and not a prankster?"

"Please hold a minute. Don't go away," Kramer says, not answering his question.

He holds the device in his hands, looking at Zora's face a few feet away. She is smiling back at him expectantly.

"Hello, Mr. Rink?" it's President Williams voice. "This is the President."

"Yes, hello Madame President. This is indeed an honor. Actually, I'm calling to see if you would like to know about an imminent attack on an American nuclear facility?" he says.

"Yes, of course. But, we've been trying to reach you, you know," she says.

"Yes, I know. I'm sorry that I've been out of touch, but I've been a little busy. And now we have knowledge of an imminent attack on Three Mile Island. They plan to make a bomb with some fuel rods they'll steal over there and then drive it down to Washington DC," Doug says.

"Yes, strangely enough, I believe you, Mr. Rink. Everything you've done up to now gives you a great deal of credibility," the President says. "I would like to invite you to a meeting where we can discuss all the relevant issues."

"Ok, sure," he says, curious at the positive reaction. "But, we have to make it pretty quick, I'd say."

"Yes, I agree. Everything you want to tell us is important isn't it?" the President asks, a bit patronizingly.

"Yes, ma'am. I'd say so," he says, shrugging his shoulders, and raising an eyebrow in a gesture that only Zora can see. He's starting to become more than a little suspicious. It's too nice, too easy, too fast.

"We've arranged a secure meeting place. My people have swept it for any security risks and it's clean. I'm going to put Kramer on to give you the co-ordinates. I mean, you can find your way to anyplace on the globe with that machine, I would imagine, right?" she asks.

"Yes, that's right," he replies. "When?"

"Tomorrow at twelve Noon," she replies.

"All right, I'll be there. But that's cutting it pretty close to the event I'm telling you about that is going to take place tomorrow also," he says.

"Yes, Mr. Rink. I'm sure it's very urgent, but I'm sure everything will be all right now that you've told us about it. I'll alert all the appropriate authorities. Whatever the threat, our people can handle it," she says.

"I hope so. There's a lot at stake here, Madame President," he warns.

"Yes, I'm sure you're right," she says. "Tomorrow then, at twelve noon. Looking forward to seeing you then. I'm giving you to Kramer now," she says as she puts him on hold again. He can hear music in the phone.

Zora can see by his befuddled facial expression that something's awry.

"What's going on?" she asks him.

"Oh, nothing. She just put me on hold," he replies.

"Bureaucrats," she says angrily.

*   *   *   *

The next morning Doug is preparing himself for the meeting with the President. He's made a list of everything that Ula has told him about the terror attack to give to the President. He's hopeful that the meeting will go well and that she meant it when she said she would alert everyone. They'll have to move quickly to counter the terrorists and save the situation before it can get out of hand.

Doug has consulted with Ula and asked if they can do something if the President has failed to believe him. But she tells him that it would be best if it is handled by Earthly resources and not her own. Doug can see the logic. If they are going to cleanse humanity of the evil and violence in their genetic code, it has to come from within.

Zora takes Doug on a walk to take his mind off the meeting. He seems nervous and she counsels him on how to relax and take it all in stride, even though she admits that she could never do it. She has an overwhelming confidence in him and this makes him feel confident himself.

The next day, just before Noon, he gets himself prepared by meditating on the floor of the 'hub'. Then, when he's feeling at the top of his calm, he goes upstairs and directs the ship to land at the coordinates given him the day before. Zora holds on to her seat as the ship changes its orientation. She marvels to herself how there is no sense of motion, no force of gravity, no indication of motion of any kind as they hurtle through space and time, traverse half way around the planet to arrive effortlessly at the their coordinates, smack dab in the middle of a corn field in Iowa or perhaps it's Nebraska.

They can see the President descending the steps of a flatulent Marine Helicopter a few hundred yards away. All around the edges of the corn fields is a large forest. On the other side of the corn fields, there is an aging farmhouse. It appears to be abandoned. The President and her entourage march through the fields of corn toward the house.

"That must be the place," he says to Zora.

"Do you think it could be a trap?" she asks, suddenly worried.

"Gee, I don't think so," Doug says. "What made you think that?"

"I don't know. Something doesn't feel right. Why have the meeting way out here?" she ponders.

"I don't know, actually," Doug tells her.

"And are you sure these coordinates are right?" she muses.

"Yes, this ship is accurate to within a few nanometers, I'm sure," he replies.

"Well, then why would they put you way out in this field when they could have had you park just a few feet from the helipad or right next to that house? And why would the President of the United States take the chance of meeting you way out here where she's totally unprotected when she could have met you in Washington?" Zora wonders out loud.

"You make a lot of sense," Doug says. "We don't have time to think about it. I tell you what. I want you to stay and keep an eyeball peeled on that house. You see anything out of the ordinary, I mean anything at all, you just move the ship right into that house and I'll jump in and we'll split, just like that, ok?"

"Yeah, ok, but I really don't know how to drive this thing," she says, obviously more than a little overwhelmed by her newfound job as the getaway driver.

"Don't worry, it's simple, you just think about a place a few feet away from me and Ula will do the rest," he counsels. "I'm going now. See you in a little while."

"Ok, but please don't get trapped," she says. "If it doesn't feel right, you'll give me a signal right away, right?"

"Absolutely, cross my heart," he replies, throwing her a kiss.

She throws one back playfully. "Ok, get out of here now," she says.

"Oooh, you're tired of me already?" he jokes.

"Just go," she replies.

"Ok, Ok, I can take a hint," he says.

On the walk through the meadow and the corn fields, he looks around cautiously for signs of trouble, but he sees none. When he gets to the house, he is greeted by six Secret Service agents who welcome him and then politely tell him they have to search him. He succumbs to the search and in a few seconds he's cleared to go inside. He walks up the stairs of an old farmhouse with paint that has long ago faded by the sun into a patchwork of wood grain and old stain.

Once inside he has to adjust his eyes to the dim light. On the far side of the room, there is a small table. The President is standing talking with her Chief of Staff Bob Kramer whom Doug recognizes from the news programs. To their left stands four or five assistants all equipped with portable computers. To their right stands a tall square-jawed man whom Doug first assumes to be more security. But, then he notices a large ruby ring that he is certain is from West Point. He remembers an Uncle of his who wore such a ring. This man was no innocent civilian onlooker. No, he was there for a purpose. Then, Doug notices a wire crawling down from his coat jacket sleeve and into the palm of his hand. He reasons that it must be some kind of communication device.

"You must be Mr. Rink," The President has turned to greet him and is holding out her hand.

"Yes, that's me," says Doug, extending his hand and walking toward her. The Secret Service men bristle a bit and then settle back with a stern look from the square jawed stranger standing in the corner.

"I want to thank you for taking the time to visit with me. I've set up this meeting especially for you so that we can address all your concerns. Is that what you would like to do?" she asks.

"Yes," Doug replies. "But, I'm concerned about Three Mile Island. Did you..."

"Please sit down," the President says cutting him off and sits herself down directly across the table from him. Two of her advisors including Kramer sit down on her flanks.

"Thanks, Madam President. It's an honor to meet you and so forth, but we haven't got much time for pleasantries. You see, there's a group of terrorists on their way at this moment to take over the Three Mile Island Nuclear Power Plant and they're heavily armed. They're going to kill everyone in that plant and then create a bomb within twenty four hours from the fuel rods that they're gonna find over there. Have you alerted the FBI? There's just enough time to stop them," he warns. He looks around the room and is more than a little alarmed to see their complete lack of concern.

"Truly," he says, looking around for some indication of comprehension in the room. "They should be just getting to the gate about now."

"Please relax, Mr. Rink. Everything is in hand," Bob Kramer says coolly.

"I guess you don't believe me," he says. "Ok, here's what I can do. I can leave now and take care of this myself. Or, I can wait to see if you're going to do anything about it. The only problem with that is that if you don't do anything, you're going to help them kill a couple million innocent people. So which way is it going to be?"

"Mr. Rink," the President says breaking her silence. "I'm going to be honest with you. It's not that we don't believe you. It's more like we don't trust you. Can you see this situation from our point of view? Here you are a complete stranger to us all. You've never been active in politics in your entire life. No one has ever heard of you. Suddenly, you're flying around all over the planet in this egg contraption and you're squashing these terrorists and we're grateful for that, don't get me wrong. However, I, nor anyone in this government can figure out how you got involved with so much power. Do you understand how that might make us all just a bit queasy?" she asks.

"Yes, sure, I can see that, but there's no time for all that now. You just have to trust me, please." he replies.

"Just have to trust you? All right, let me ask you a question, if I may," Kramer suddenly speaks before the President has a chance to reply.

"Sure, go ahead," Doug replies sarcastically. "We have plenty of time."

"What did you mean when you said that the universe is going to fold in on itself in that speech you made on the Capitol Mall?" he asks calmly, too calmly for Doug.

"Well, I meant exactly what I said. The ship was created by a race of beings who have survived seventeen of them. How? I don't exactly understand. Somehow, they fold in with everything else, but their essence remains to rise up out of the ashes like the Phoenix bird. But, if you were able to see the inside of that ship, you'd be as certain as I am that it's possible to do such a thing," Doug tells them.

They don't respond.

"And anyway, no matter what we do, it's coming again in less than three months. And if we want to survive it, we have a wonderful opportunity if we can just clean up our act a little bit. It's just that simple," Doug says.

"And so what are you saying? That the Earth, the Sun, all the stars, all the planets, they're just going to do what while the universe is folding in on itself?" Kramer asks.

"Well, that's obvious, isn't it? They're going to cease to exist, that's all," Doug replies.

"And you're convinced this is really going to happen in three months time?" The President asks.

"Yes, ma'am. Just as certain as I'm sitting here talking to you," he replies respectfully. "Now, will you be doing something about the terrorists now?"

"Then if this is truly going to happen, why would these people come so far out of their way to warn us?" Kramer asks with a slight sarcastic grin on his face.

"Because we're the only life forms in the whole damn universe worth saving. They search all over the place at times like this looking for a species to converge with their own genetic code and we were the only ones left. We win by default. Great honor, huh?" Doug replies impatiently. He knew that he would be in for some tall explaining. He looks at his watch, frustrated that it's taking so much time, time they don't have. He drums the table nervously with his fingers.

"And exactly why would any species so far advanced want to combine their genetic code with us half-baked humans?" asks the President.

"Because that's the only way they can survive it. Their consciousness is so advanced and their civilization is so advanced there's a danger they could just vanish. It's very tenuous being made of nothing but thought. They need something to stick to. They look at crude genetic code like ours the way we might look at beef or fish or chicken," he says hoping that will satisfy them even though this seems like a wild exaggeration even to him.

"We're their only hope for survival you say?" asks Kramer who also glances at his watch.

"Yes, our genetic code is still young and raw enough to give them the old fashioned desire to live. They're so advanced, they've conquered nearly everything even the very need to survive a long time ago. The only problem is you need a desire to survive to carry forward. So, they need us to keep them on the edge, bring them back to basics, so to speak," he says wondering why Kramer would be worried about the time, since they obviously don't seem to be in any kind of hurry to heed his warnings.

The President looks at the stern-looking man still standing unflinchingly in the corner. Doug can hear a slight crackling coming from the com device in his ear. They exchange a nothing glance. But it seems to remind the President of another engagement.

"Can you excuse us for just a few minutes, please Mr. Rink. We'd like to step outside the room and consult each other for a few minutes," says the President. Without any further explanation, she, Kramer the stern-looking man, her advisors quickly file out through the back door of the cabin behind the President's chair leaving him all alone.

"Uh, say, I don't know about this. What, you're leaving? Can you just tell me if you're going to…uh, hello?" he calls out, but they're all gone before he can finish his sentence. The door closes with a distinctive finality.

'Zora was right,' he thinks to himself. 'It's a trap.'

He gets up to go but at that precise moment, the walls of the room explode as the egg comes crashing through and halts just a few feet away from his person. He lunges for the door and enters the ship in a heap on the floor just inside the skin. Zora has rushed down the stairs to greet him. She helps him collect himself.

At that moment, there's an ear-splitting thunder clap. Doug and Zora look out the view screens to see a fleet of a dozen F-16 fighter jets screaming over head at super-sonic speeds that flattens the air into a rushing, blasting noise like a thousand freight trains.

Then, there's a loud thud on the side of the ship and it vibrates a little bit. Doug can tell that one of these jets, if not all of them, have dropped something on the house and the ship, which luckily is completely ineffective, but it packs enough punch to completely demolish the old farmhouse, leaving nothing but the egg ship in its place. They are completely unscathed. 'Their timing had to be perfect,' Doug thinks to himself.

"You're timing couldn't have been better. That bomb would have got me for sure. How'd you know, Darlin?" Doug asks her as they race up the circular stairway together.

"Ula knew. She's amazing. She put the whole scene on the view screens. So, when they ran out of the room like that, I knew something terrible was going to happen, so I did what you said. I just thought about the position just a few feet from you and the rest is history. Let's get the holy 'H' out of here," she says.

"I'm with you," he says putting on the hat at the top of the stairs, not waiting to sit down.

Just then, there's another horrendous and thunderous blast outside. They can see flames all around the ship surging up into the sky and then black smoke blanketing the whole sky around them and turning day into night.

"It's one of those 'daisy-cutter' bombs," he yells, closing his eyes, opens them again and sees Zora seated next to him with her eyes still closed and her jaw clenched.

"See I don't like that. Just when you think you can trust someone. You know, I think it's time we taught these people a lesson. I'm tired of this bullshit," he says, angrily. Zora can't remember him more ruggedly handsome.

"What are you going to do?" Zora opens her eyes wide in time to see a third bomb fall directly on top of the ship. They can hear it detonate against the hull and it rocks the ship a little bit, but outside the scene is complete and total destruction of the countryside. The bomb has created a crater two hundred feet all around the egg.

"They can't hurt us. Don't worry. I'm going to teach them a lesson they won't forget," Doug says.

He looks up and then raises the ship up a couple hundred feet and just above the black smoke clouds rising into the sky. The next pass of an F-16 puts the jet on a collision course with the egg. They can see the horrified look of the pilot as he jams the stick hard to starboard to bank and turn his fighter abruptly, just missing them, rocking the egg a little as they hit the air turbulence of his passing.

Below them, they can see thousands of soldiers littering the grounds. They've massed around the woods and the cornfields all around the farm house but with such clever camouflage no one would have seen them until they wanted to be seen.

There are hundreds of tanks moving toward the farmhouse. They can see a swarm of helicopters fully armed with missiles bristling from their sides coming at them from almost every side. The formation of F-16's has dispersed but they can see them swirling around in the clouds reforming several miles off in the distance.

Then, they spot a long dark limousine careening away from them down an old country road. They've managed to reach safety just ahead of the bombs. Doug's impressed at the timing of their escape just before the attack and knows now why they were all so nervously looking at their watches.

"Teach me about that woman's intuition thing some time," he says to Zora.

"I will," she says. "What are you going to do?"

"First, I'm going to neutralize their attack before someone gets hurt," he says.

Doug closes his eyes and talks with Ula. She knows instantly what he wants and proceeds to carry out his plan.

"Watch this," he says gleefully.

Zora looks below and she suddenly notices something very peculiar taking place. The soldiers drop their rifles and run away, back toward their positions in the corn fields and the forest beyond. The Helicopters slowly spin helplessly to the ground, apparently suffering from some kind of contagious engine failure. The tanks come to a screeching halt. The F-16's form a 'V' formation like a flock of geese and fly slowly away from the scene, quickly fading from view. The battle scene is completely calm and quiet within seconds. The smoke begins to clear.

"Now, I think it's time to finish our talks," he says to her. Zora is finally managing to collect herself.

Doug takes the ship a few miles down the road and puts the ship on a parallel course and a few feet above the black limousine racing away from the scene.

Someone in the car lowers a window and sticks his head outside, blowing his hair all over his face. The car is going nearly one hundred miles an hour, but Ula has no trouble keeping pace. The observer sticks his head back inside the vehicle. Suddenly, dust flies up as it takes a sharp right turn and careens off the road and smacks into a large grove of trees and shrubs. They get about a hundred yards and are then forced to stop. The driver desperately attempts to turn the big black car around, having abruptly run out of road but it is no use. They're stuck.

Doug lowers the ship behind the rear bumper of the limo so that it is trapped between his ship and the trees.

There's no movement of any kind from the car.

"Well, that's a fine kettle of fish Colonel," the President blurts out angrily. "Do you have any more great ideas?"

"I, uh, I don't know what could have gone wrong," the square-jawed man says, seated directly in front of the President and facing her.

"I do. His story is beginning to have the ring of truth to it. That ship is so highly advanced beyond anything we've got and we have no weapons that can even scratch it. Those jets were using smart bombs. They should have turned that thing into a heap of scrap metal," the President says trying to pull herself back into a semblance of authority.

"Yes, they should have done," says the Colonel, in a daze. "But it's right there in front of us."

"But, just because he's got some great toys does that mean that we should trust him, Madame President," Kramer suggests.

"Yes, Kramer, I think it does," the President says, angrily. "We simply have no other choice. I should have trusted him instead of listening to you testosterone meatheads."

The President gathers up her courage and her clothing and climbs out of the car. She looks over at the egg-shape behind the car and she motions with her hands to her face that she wants to talk.

Doug and Zora can see her standing beside the car and looking somewhat crestfallen but still very presidential.

"Well, you still want to trust her?" Zora asks.

"I don't know. I think we have to. You ready?" he retorts.

"No, can't say as I am," she admits.

"Let's go," he says smiling. It's that zany impertinence that attracted him to her so many years ago.

Doug and Zora climb down the stairs and push themselves out through the skin of the ship. Kramer has come out of the car as well as two advisors and the square-jawed man who is introduced now as Colonel Charles Jacobs from Air Force Special Forces.

"Ah yes, I knew that was a West Point ring on your finger, sir," Doug says respectfully.

"West Point? Never!" the Colonel chortles. "That's an Air Force Academy ring."

"Oh, I see, sorry. They all look alike, don't they?" he teases.

"Well, don't just stand there Colonel. What would you have us do?" asks the President heartily.

"You got a phone in that thing?" Doug asks.

"Yes, there's a phone," the President replies.

"I think you should call the FBI like right now. Tell them to get their butts over to Three Mile Island and watch for a big brown delivery truck and prevent the thing from getting past the gate any way they have to but warn them that the men inside are armed and dangerous," he says.

The President picks up her watch that has fallen off her wrist to the ground.

"And oh yes, they also have to watch out for a helicopter patrolling the area," he warns them.

The President sticks her head back inside the car and yells a series of orders to an unseen agent still inside. They hear the click of a radio being activated and a voice inside begins relaying the message to someone on the other end.

The President brings her head back outside of the car.

"Now that this little problem is taken care of, I'd like to invite you Doug and your girlfriend to the White House for dinner. Would that be all right with you two," the President asks as politely as she can.

Doug looks at Zora as they both agree without having to say a word.

"Certainly, sounds like fun to me," Doug replies snappily. "But only if it's not formal. We didn't bring a lot of clothes with us on this trip."

"Hah, hah," the President laughs. "Don't worry, it's not formal. But, I do hope that you can forgive me for all of what happened here today and that we can put this all behind us and move on with whatever it is you have in mind. I'd be especially interested to hear more about this universe-folding-in-on-itself theory of yours."

"Yes, all right. That sounds fine," Doug replies smiling.

"Thank you. Thank you very much, Mr. Rink," the President says, shaking his hand again. This time, the handshake seems sincere as he can feel the President squeezing much more than the last time she shook his hand.

"Please call me Doug," he says still smiling.

"Ok, Doug," she says almost flirtatiously. "And you can call me Wendy."

"Uhm, hello, I'm standing right here," declares Zora, just a little dismayed by this new found friendship.

Doug turns his attention to Zora releasing the President's hand suddenly.

"Don't worry honey. But, it's obvious how she got to be President. She's quite a charmer, wouldn't you say?" he quips, looking alternately at the President's laconic expression and then back at Zora.

"She just tried to have us both killed," Zora says, succinctly and looking directly at the President who's smiling sheepishly.

"Yes, but I don't think she had her heart in it, did she? And I think she's truly sorry, aren't you," says Doug looking back at the President.

"Then, make her say it," Zora suggests wryly.

"Make her say what?" asks Doug.

"Make her say she's sorry," Zora replies curtly.

"All right. I think she may have a point Wendy, I mean Madame President. Say you're sorry," Doug demands looking directly into her eyes.

"Really! This has gone too far!" snorts Kramer.

"I'm sorry," replies the President quickly. "I'm truly sorry. You must realize what it's like to have all these bungling baboons around giving me their idiotic advice."

"That good enough?" Doug says looking at Zora.

"I guess," she replies. "For now, perhaps."

"Well, I mean, really, Madame President," Kramer complains bitterly. "We were only doing what we thought was in the national interest. Besides, you said it would be a good test. So, he passed the test. Now, we know more about this thing." His words are trailing off as the President sneering at him turns to grab the car door.

"We'll see you at dinner. What time is that, by the way?" asks Doug as he leads Zora back toward their ship.

"Dinner's at eight," the President calls after them getting back into the big black car.

"Eight it is," Doug calls over his shoulder.

Doug and Zora get back into the ship and take it up into the air and drive it slowly away. Further down the road they spot a large group of soldiers lying along the side of the road completely relaxed. They look as though they're having a fine time just sitting there, talking. Some are playing cards. Others are stretching. A few are playing in the trees.

"What did Ula do to them?" Zora asks.

"I think she just put them into the picture," he says.

They can see the limousine back out of the trees, return to the road and drive off slowly back toward Washington DC.

CHAPTER 9

▼

ALL THE KING'S HORSES

At the Three Mile Island Nuclear Power Plant, it's a warm and sunny day. A large brown truck pulls up along the fences to the main gate. There are two dark Middle Eastern men in the front seat. They look toward the guard booth and they notice that it is unattended. They look beyond to the guard tower and it also appears unmanned. The gate is open and they can drive through. This situation is very unexpected so they decide to sit in the car and wait for something to happen.

After a few minutes, they start to blabber to themselves excitedly. If they blow themselves up, there is no purpose to it, since the gate is wide open anyway and there is no security force to neutralize. They discuss their situation for some time, with the passenger arguing for destroying the truck and them with it, as planned. 'It's God's will', he tells the other. But the driver has suddenly opted for life and not wasting his. 'Besides they might be needed later', he tells the other. Something doesn't smell right to him. They finally agree that if they blow themselves up now, it would be senseless.

They look past the gates and the parking lot. There isn't a soul to be seen on the grounds within. Doors to buildings are left open. Where there should be security guards, there are none. The whole place appears deserted, except for a few cars in the parking spaces next to the main container unit.

Where there are cars, the driver reasons, there are people.

"They must have all gone inside for a meeting or something and someone forgot to leave a guard posted. Allah is with us," the driver says.

"Or he is not with us and we are incredibly unlucky," the passenger replies, quickly. "Something's not right."

"I say we wait. If anyone approaches us, we press the button," the driver gestures to the detonator button sitting ominously on the seat between them.

So, they sit and wait a few minutes. Then, the second truck arrives and pulls up slowly behind them. They can see their comrades alight from the truck wearing ski masks, with submachine guns at the ready. They are confused and shocked that the first truck is still in one piece. Two of them cautiously start unloading weapons from the back of the truck. They are looking all around in a kind of stunned silence. What should be a scene of massive destruction is eerily quiet and abandoned.

A tall man with a limp comes up to the driver's side of the first truck where the two suicide bombers are sitting. They see him in the rear view mirrors cautiously inching along the side of their truck with weapon in hand.

"What is going on? You should both be dead," he says harshly.

"Yes, pardon us Mohammed. We arrived and found the place like this. Nobody has stirred in the last five minutes. We believe they are inside having a meeting or perhaps a birthday party or something. Perhaps it would be easier for us to just take them in their meeting and we don't have to sacrifice our lives," the driver reasons.

"It's too easy. There's something wrong," he says. Then in Arabic, he yells instructions for the men to spread out and cover every door, then to wait for his signal to go in. They obey immediately by fanning out through the grounds searching for any evidence of resistance.

The tall man nervously watches the ten man team moving quickly from the side of the truck. They are well-trained in their plan of attack, but this is too much of a deviation in their plan and he doesn't like it. They arrive at their posts and dutifully stand guarding the doors that lead into the main reactor building.

One of the men signals that they are in position.

"Take them," he yells, gesturing with his fist.

They start to move into the building when suddenly a violent sound wave rips through the compound rattling their teeth and almost tearing the truck apart. The metal truck groans and shakes violently in protest. Their blood feels as if it's boiling. Their eyes are popping out of their sockets. They are under attack, but from where? It is unlike any attack they could ever know about because it's a completely new kind of weapon. Luckily for them it's non-lethal, highly effective, but not deadly.

The leader falls to the ground in pain. The two men in the truck jump out and land on the ground next to him groveling in the dirt. The men surrounding the building fall to their knees and scream in agony, holding their viscera as hard as they can. Blood drips from their eye sockets. Saliva oozes from their mouths.

They are all writhing in pain as one hundred National Guard troops stream out of the containment building wearing ear muffs that prevents them from hearing the sound. It's a new weapon recently developed in the non-lethal laboratory at Los Alamos. This is the first opportunity for them to test it out in a battle field situation and the results speak for themselves. The troops walk around calmly disarming the terrorists one by one. Lying on the ground in horrible pain, they cannot resist, but can only watch helplessly as the troops calmly walk amongst them taking their weapons and tying them up.

Thirty or so F.B.I. agents, also wearing the protective head gear, with guns drawn emerge from the building to witness the troops disarming the terrorists and then hogtying them by their wrists and ankles. They lift them up one by one and trundle them off to a wagon that has pulled into the yard nearby.

The lead F.B.I. agent makes a motion with his hand across his neck and just as suddenly as it started, the microwave weapon ceases. The color returns to their faces. Their eyes return to their sockets, their skin stops crawling and they can breathe again. Realizing their situation they look to the truck, but it is sitting empty and harmless in the yard. The FBI agents take off their protective helmets and peer inside the windows to plan their disarming of the bomb.

"Well, I'd say that new weapon works pretty good," says one of the lead agents.

"Yep, I'd say these gentlemen are lucky to be alive right now," agrees another.

"That was a good tip we got from HQ," the lead agent says to his men. Good job, men. Well done."

"Yeah, I wonder where they got the tip?" one of them asks the lead agent, who just shrugs.

*   *   *   *

Doug has landed the ship on the White House lawn, just beside the West Wing. Four Marine guards march out from the guard shack and surround the ship as Doug and Zora suddenly appear amongst them. Even though they were forewarned, the sudden appearance through the magnetic field of the egg surprises the Marines and gives them all a bit of a startle.

"Holy Mary, mother of Jesus!" one of them blurts out.

"It's all right, men. This is not Mary. Her name is Zora. I'm Doug. "Uhm, at ease men," he says to the two marines, guards dressed in their formal uniforms and shouldering their rifles.

"I've always been searching for a few good men," he quips. Zora laughs but the Marines are not amused. They try their best to be at ease as they watch the pair walk up to the door of the White House and are welcomed inside by Chief of Staff Kramer.

"The President is in the Oval Office. She'd like to speak with you before dinner," Kramer informs them.

"Ok, I've always wanted to see the Oval Office," Zora says, barely hiding her excitement. Doug agrees as they walk down the long hallway of the White House, noticing every little knick knack, every picture on the walls of former Presidents and great American statesmen.

The door opens to the Oval Office and they find the President standing behind her desk with her back to them and gazing thoughtfully out the window into the garden beyond. The twinkling of the lights on the trees and bushes give the scene a surrealistic effect that the President finds soothing.

"I'm glad you could make it," the President says turning to greet her guests.

"Thank you Madame President," Doug replies. "But, I'd like to know how the nuclear plant panned out today."

"Oh, it went without a hitch, thanks to you. We surprised them and captured them all without a single casualty. Yes, we tried out a new non-lethal weapon," she says graciously.

"That's nice to hear especially after what you tried to pull this morning," Zora says.

"Here, here," Doug agrees.

"Yes, I have decided to make non-lethals a top priority in this government after that incident. I guess you kind of taught us a lesson. And I wanted to speak with you for a moment in private before we go in to dinner. I hope you don't mind," she says.

"No, not at all," Doug replies, looking cautiously at Zora.

"I want to know if you'd like to brief me in private with anything that you might not want all those people out there to know," she says, quietly.

"No, I can't think of anything," Doug says, then pauses. "Or how about this? After dinner, we take you into the ship and give you the tour? I think you'd find it quite enlightening," Doug says, enthusiastically. "Maybe it's time you got to see inside. Yes, I think you deserve it after today."

"Well, that's an idea. I don't know what the secret service would say about that," The President says with a smile.

"Why don't you just keep it secret from the secret service?" Zora suggests with a smile.

The President looks at her, picking up on the slightly veiled hint of jealousy. "All right. All right, I'll accept your invitation," the President says. "You know, I consider myself a very good judge of character and I like you Doug and I trust you."

Zora raises her eyebrows, noting that Wendy left her out of the statement.

"I'm glad of that Madame President," Doug replies.

"Yes, I trust you and I want you to trust me. I'm deeply saddened by what happened earlier today. But tell me something. Somehow you completely neutralized our smart bombs without hurting a single soldier. Remarkable, really. But what really amazed me were the troops just sitting down to enjoy the flowers. Would you care to share with me how you did that?" The President asks with curiosity radiating from every inch of her face.

"Uhm, are we being recorded?" Doug says with a laugh.

"No, of course not," the President looks hurt. Then, she brightens. "Oh all right, yes. The recording machines are always on. I can't get a speck of privacy around here."

"Well, doesn't matter. For the record, Madame President, I didn't do a thing. I think the troops just saw how futile their efforts were and so they simply decided not to continue in their attack for fear of hurting someone, perhaps some innocent bystanders," Doug says.

"Yeah, like us," Zora says.

"Yes, I suppose that's it," the President replies, barely noticing Zora's jest.

"You claim that these people intend to save us from this folding that's going to take place in ninety days, right?" the President asks.

"Yes, that's correct," Doug replies.

"Why is it that none of my scientific advisors can corroborate your information?" the President asks, politely.

"Because it's still very far away on the farthest side of the universe from where we can not gather any light. This thing is happening now and it's outracing the speed of light, so it will be known soon enough. But, by then, it will be too late. You have to take this on faith that it's the truth," Doug says.

She walks out from behind the desk, deep in thought. "I see. And I don't suppose I will have anything to fear once I'm inside the ship. I mean, you don't plan to abduct me, do you?" The President asks, almost wishfully.

"No, ma'am. I would have no reason to do that," Doug replies coldly.

"All right. I'm very curious to see what you've got in there. But, I'm famished. What do you say we put all this aside for a while and have a pleasant dinner. Zora, I'd like to hear how you and Doug met," she says, taking their arms and leading them to the door which opens automatically for them.

"Oh, my gosh. That's a long story, isn't it Doug?" Zora says.

"Yes, but it's a nice story," Doug says as they pass through the long hallway to the Dining Room at the other end of the large mansion. They can hear polite conversations drifting toward them from the room just ahead of them.

"I think this is quite a unique moment in history, isn't it?" The President suggests as they enter the room. The guests, around thirty, the women in evening gowns, the men in tuxedos, are suddenly silent. Then, they stand in unison to greet the President as the three enter the room.

"Yes, I think so," Doug says agreeably.

"You told us it would be informal," Zora says, dismayed by her own attire.

"I'm sorry. Please forgive me but with all the excitement today, I just forgot," the President says.

"Ladies and Gentlemen, we have special guests with us tonight. This is Doug Rink and Zora, I don't know your last name, my dear," she says. "Forgive me, but these two are responsible for preventing a horrible tragedy at Three Mile Island today. You may have seen it on the news. These two gave us the information about the attack just in the nick of time," the President says, cheerily.

The guests applaud them, shake their hands and smile and cheer them to their seats next to the President. The President's husband, Peter Best, seated at the opposite end of the large table swallows a large mouthful of wine.

"Well," the President begins, lifting her glass. "I'd like to propose a toast to our heroes."

All the guests lift their glasses in anticipation. Doug and Zora more than a bit embarrassed, lift their glasses as well.

"To the future of Mankind," the President says lifting her voice and suddenly looking very serious. "I don't know what's in store for us all. The world has become such a dangerous place. I doubt anyone would give us very good odds right now at this moment in history. I don't know how to believe them. However, I do know that with people like Doug and Zora, we have a chance, a good chance to save the human race. I toast you both Doug and Zora. Thank you for being on our side."

Everyone in the room, including Doug and Zora look thoughtfully around at each other. Chief of Staff Kramer surveys the President for her true motives. But she gives him nothing.

"To Doug and Zora," someone says quietly and the sentiment echoes from each pair of lips in turn.

"To the Human Race," Doug says loudly and looking soulfully at Zora and taking her hand. "May we survive and prosper in God's great paradise."

Zora squeezes his hand and peers proudly back at him.

*   *   *   *

At the University of California at Santa Cruz, two astronomy professors, Nigel Blake and Robert Pressman are supervising a group of seven graduate astronomy students who are getting their first experience with the data feed from the HST, the Hubble Space Telescope.

Performing a deep field observation of the universe, they are hoping to find a black hole tonight or at least any kind of evidence that a black hole may have existed back in time far enough to be the progenitor of the universe.

They control the movement, depth of field, focus and orientation of the telescope from a computer sitting on a desk which is networked with seven or eight other computers scattered all around the room. The students are alternately watching the screen and taking notes of their own observations.

Professor Blake gives the group his impressions of what they are seeing.

"Over here, this spot right here looks like the remnants of a galaxy that might have been wiped out by a super-massive black hole. And over here, what do you suppose this could be?" he says, his voice trailing off abruptly

A portion of the screen, towards the center is fading slowly to black. Tiny dots appear like stars but are actually galaxies are disappearing one by one. The pattern is horizontal and widening out both left and right proportionately on their screens.

"Hello," Dr. Pressman seems alarmed. "What the hell is going on?"

"It could be a virus," suggests one of the students.

"A virus in the HST, how could that happen?" Dr. Blake asks.

"Well, it is pretty cold up there," the student replies. "Just kidding. My guess is it's in the computers."

"I see. Yes, that must be it. Call around to the other campuses and see if they're getting the same thing," Dr. Blake orders the student.

"Yes sir," says the student as he lunges out of his chair, trots out of the room, the door slamming behind him.

"The thing is getting bigger," Dr. Pressman observes as everyone can see.

Dr. Blake goes around to all the computers one by one and types a series of commands on the keyboard. He looks at each screen and then returns to the main control computer recently abandoned by the student.

"They're all the same. The anti-virus program doesn't report anything wrong," he announces to no one in particular.

On their screens, it appears that there is a fine but distinct horizontal line of blackness slowly obliterating the star field in front of them representing the deepest and furthest realms of space.

"This is odd, very odd. There's got to be something wrong with the Hubble," Dr. Pressman says.

"There goes another cool ten billion," one of the students quips chuckling at his own feeble attempt at jocularity.

No one seems amused.

"I need to know the exact location of that thing," Professor Pressman states.

One of the students begins to type rapidly sending a program to the Hubble so that it revolves in a three hundred sixty degree arc. The star patterns change slowly as the computers show them the terrible truth.

"It's the same everywhere. It's completely surrounding us. It's about ten billion light years out and closing in on us in a tightening circle," the student says half to himself, half to the group.

"It's everywhere," says Professor Blake stunned, watching the image on the screen slowly growing larger and larger.

"What the hell does it mean?" asks Professor Pressman.

He receives no answers.

*   *   *   *

At the White House, the President and her husband are saying good-bye to the last of their guests as they file past and out of the dining room to their cars in the driveway. Doug and Zora are standing outside on the portico watched by the colorful Marine sentry and two secret service agents who remain a ways off in the grass, but still in sight.

The President comes outside and looking around, walks up to Doug and whispers in his ear.

"Is that invitation still good?" she says.

"Sure is," Doug replies trying to appear nonchalant.

"All right, Steve and Michael, is that you?" she says gesturing to the two shadowy figures between themselves and the path that leads to the egg shape ship.

"Yes, ma'am," comes a voice in reply. The two figures stiffen.

"I would like to be alone with Doug and Zora for a moment, please," she says with a distinct commanding tone in her voice.

"Oh, ah, Madame President, I don't think that's such a good…" says the distant voice as she interrupts him.

"I don't care what you think. I need to have a few private words with my guests. I'll just be a few minutes," she says. "Go have a smoke or something, please."

The two secret service men reluctantly turn and disappear down the walkway and disappear around the corner of the building.

The Marine sentry remains frozen by the door.

"Don't worry about them," the President whispers. "It's their duty to remain where they are no matter what."

"Let's go, then," says Doug.

Doug leads the two women down into the lawn and then briskly covers the distance to the side of the ship. The Marine watches in stoic silence glued to the side of the mansion.

"Ok, oh my gosh," the President says as Doug links arms with Zora and then Zora with the President. Then he pushes himself into the ship and pulls the other two along behind him. They arrive at the other side of the bubbling skin and into the circular entry hall.

"Oh, my gosh," the President says looking around breathlessly. "Oh my gosh."

The Marine sentry foregoing all discipline, runs down the hallway calling out loud for the secret service who come running out to see that the President is no longer on the scene. They look at each other scratching their heads and run back in the direction from which they came.

Doug leads the President up the circular stairway to the command room. Zora follows along closely behind the two. When they get to the chairs, Doug invites the President to sit down. She obeys quietly, captivated by the simple lack of any technology anywhere to be seen and then notices the view screen where she can see the secret service agents gathering around outside in growing numbers yelling and gesturing excitedly to one another. They mill about the ship excitedly, searching in vain for any signs of an entrance.

"I'd like you to place this hat on your head, ma'am," Doug says holding up the black cowboy hat above her head.

"What is that?" she asks slightly nervous.

"It's the way the ship communicates with us. Her name is Ula. Or its name is Ula. I hear a female voice. Zora hears a male voice, so you probably will too."

Doug then places the hat on her head as Zora watches in silence.

"Leader of the Free World, meet the leader of everything else," Doug says only half joking.

The President looks up at him in total beffudlement as the hat tightens around her scalp.

"Come on, let's go downstairs and give her some privacy," Doug suggests. Zora agrees and leads the way down the circular stairs.

"Hey, wait a minute. What am I supposed to do here?" the President calls after them.

"Don't worry, it will come to you," Doug advises. "Just relax and think about anything that comes to mind."

At the bottom of the stairs, Doug and Zora sit down holding hands on a curved leather sofa abutting the wall of the circular room.

"Well, what do you think?" Zora begins the conversation.

"I don't have a clue," Doug replies. "Let's just rest here a while and see what happens."

"Ok. I remember the first time I put that thing on," Zora says. "I was a little intimidated at first and then your voice came to me just like you were living inside my head. It was so weird. It gave me a fright actually for a few minutes."

"Did you see how the universe is constructed?" he asks her.

"Yes, you too?" she replies. "Isn't it amazing?"

"Yes, did you see all the atoms building into molecules and the molecules making up everything else? And then, that universal, simple and beautiful structure expressed in so many different patterns?" he says.

"Yes, and the way that everything has a polarity, a North and a South pole and how the energy flows from the negative pole to the positive," she explains.

"Yes, did you feel the positive energy as pure Love?" he asks.

"Yes, it's wonderful, isn't it?" she replies taking his hand in hers.

"Yes, and the Love comes from the source of everything?" he says, looking into her eyes.

"Yes, certainly," she confirms. "I think that was the most surprising part of it all. The way that everything is united in that force, how there's no difference really between all the other stuff in the universe and our own bodies and even our thoughts."

"And that's what the folding is all about, isn't it? Everything eventually must return to its birthplace, just like the Salmon? That's where it's all repaired and cleaned up and cleared for the next iteration?" she asks.

"Yes, it's like inviting your family home for a Christmas reunion," Doug says.

"Yes, everything returning for a reality check. To be re-created again later, only all mixed up again in the new and improved version of things," Zora says.

"God, I'm so glad you got all that too. Funny, but we've never had the time to sit and discuss it all, have we?" Doug says.

"No, we haven't," she says, looking deeply into his eyes. Both pairs of eyes share a single link. They stare into each other's souls, speechless, for several minutes.

"I think that's why I was chosen," Doug finally manages to find his voice.

"What do you mean?" she asks quietly and pressing her face to his shoulder.

"When I found you that day ten years ago, I found my true love. I had no doubt of that from the minute I looked into those big beautiful brown eyes of yours. Then, I never gave up on you, even though you gave up on me. I no longer possessed you, but love is not something you can own. You just rent it. I could never forget it. I never stopped paying the rent on it. I think that's why. I never lost faith in you," he says, looking at her and feeling her spirit warming his body and soul

"Look," Zora says abruptly taking him out of his reverie.

The President is suddenly on the stairway above them. She has a look on her face of absolute bliss and all knowing wisdom. She's obviously been brought up to speed on everything she needs to know about the universe, life on the planets, evolution, God and so she is presently aware of everything that Doug and Zora now know. There seems to be little need for further debate on the issues at hand.

"Well, I can see we have lots of work to do," the President says walking up to meet the two now standing.

She thanks them for the "tour" of the ship. Doug and Zora embrace her and they thank her. She seems a changed person. All three share a kiss on the cheek. Then the President says that there is much work to be done.

"Remember, we'll always be here at your disposal," says Doug.

"Yes, I know. I'll be in touch," the President says warmly and exits through the skin of the ship and out into the dark night. The secret service swarm around her and a few have weapons drawn, looking around for a perpetrator. Their excitement to get her back is unbounded.

"Please don't make a fuss," she tells the nervous group of men. "I want you all to go home to your families. There's precious little time left."

She can sense the thoughts swirling around in their brains that perhaps she's been brainwashed.

"Don't worry," she says, as she walks back toward the people's mansion. "I'm telling you that my brain has been washed, but that's a good thing. So will all of yours before this is over. Go home, all of you. Just go home and be with your loved ones."

The Marine sentry holds the door for her and then closes it behind her as she disappears down the hall.

✳   ✳   ✳   ✳

The Next Morning the President looks out her bedroom window to see that the egg is still sitting on the White House Lawn. She feels very comforted by the sight of it. It's like an old friend now. She gets dressed hurriedly and rushes to her office for her usual morning briefing of world events. This time, there is an uproar as her advisors are yelling at each other about some Astronomer who keeps calling insisting to talk to the President. The discussion of the moment seems to be whether or not to let him talk to the President.

"Now, please gentlemen and ladies, what is this all about?" she asks. They stand up to greet her as she enters the room. She looks disheveled, unlike her normal self. She appears to have not slept very well. She looks tired, overwrought.

"Good morning Madam President," they are saying. Kramer rushes to her side and takes her arm, thinking she might have a cold. The rest of them stand around watching and waiting for her words of greeting that normally opens all their meetings.

"Madam President," he begins. "There's a Professor Blake from the University of California on the phone. He's been calling all night and all morning every five minutes demanding to talk to you. He says he's in charge of the HST at the moment and that everything he needs to tell you is an emergency of the highest order. He says, it's all been verified by all the other telescopes around the world. Agent Beamer from the C.I.A. is also here and he says that Blake's information appears to be genuine and he would also like to speak with you."

Everyone in the room is nervous due to all of the recent events and pronouncements. Some of the staff are even unsure that this is the same President that left and went into the ship the night before. Kramer is surprised to find how calm the President is taking the news. The President stands frozen for a moment silently reviewing the faces in the room.

"I know what it's all about," she begins. "Please everyone sit down."

There's a low rustling noise while everyone finds their chairs and sits. The President walks over to stand in front of her desk where she can see them all at once.

"I want you to arrange a televised Town Hall Meeting for primetime tonight. There's no time to waste and we have to get the cooperation of every man, woman and child on the planet. Oh yes, I know what the astronomers want to tell me so urgently. I was informed last night by the egg ship when, as you know, they paid us a visit and came to dinner. Funny, that will probably be the last dinner any of us will really enjoy."

She takes a beat and watches their faces slowly turn pale and their eyes slowly whiten.

"From now on everything has changed. There's about three months left to our civilization. The astronomers have confirmed it, I'm sure. You see ladies and gentlemen, the universe is folding in on itself. It's a cycle that happens every thirteen billion years or so and our time is up. That's the bad news. The good news is that the egg ship can take about one tenth of the world's population on board. That's why it has come here at this time. The creators of the ship have a regular gig where they find the most promising intelligent life and they merge with it, or in this case, us, and they merge genetically. Don't ask me for details just now," the President informs them.

She looks around the room and senses their profound confusion. She's certain that at least a few must think that she's out of her mind.

"I know this all sounds like science fiction," she continues. "But over the next several days and weeks, you will all become convinced that what I'm telling you is science fact. It will be confirmed as the evidence is clearer and clearer in the night sky, until there is no more night sky and the Earth will be swept away. Tanya, call Professor Blake back and tell him I want him and all his colleagues to be ready to present their evidence tonight with me on national Television. Provide them with all the necessary hook-ups to make it happen."

"Yes ma'am," says a female aide who rushes out of the room.

She pauses again.

"Madam President," Kramer stutters, trying to get her attention.

"Not now, Kramer," she says. "After the speech tonight, I'll be asking my counterparts around the world, in all the nations to come together for a meeting where we will discuss the general conclusion to all of our business on the planet. The main consideration will be to disarm every individual, every nation, every police unit, every military base on the globe. You ask why? The reason is that in order for us to be rescued, we must cleanse our genetic code of the violence and hate and greed and inhumanity. We have to use the final days to ask God's forgiveness for our collective sins throughout the centuries. We have to prepare the human mind for the next stage. The minds of the creators of that ship out there are almost pure thought. They must not contaminate themselves with more inferior genetic material such as we are made of. But, we're the best there is out there right now and that's encouraging. They have to combine with someone or they could go extinct along with everything else. Therefore, it is our extremely good fortune that they are here now."

She stops and walks slowly around the desk to her seat and eases herself down never unlocking her gaze from theirs.

"I want you to know that everyone in this room will be guaranteed a spot on the ship for the rescue along with your immediate families. Please don't ask for any more than that. It wouldn't be fair to the many billions we'll be leaving behind. I want you to spend the rest of the day preparing your minds for what I have told you. Please don't waste any time questioning what I have said. I came to know all of these things last night when I went into that ship. It is simply not practical to have all of you go in there and get the knowledge one at a time. The ship will be very busy going around to various places on the Earth to take on their passengers. Sites will be chosen randomly and at each place thousands of people will be let on board. Then, the ship will move to another location at random so that the greatest genetic variety will be found."

"Madame President, are you sure you're feeling all right," a small man in the back of the room asks timidly.

"Yes, I'm feeling about as good as I can under the circumstances. I'm not out of my mind and the next person who suggests that I might be will be excused from the project. I wouldn't want anyone working with me who is not totally committed. Don't worry Sam, it's understandable so I'll allow that one comment on my state of mind and no more!" she declares emphatically.

"Oh, and yes, Don't be fooled, the ship appears far too small to fit any more than a few people. However, let me tell you that they have managed to cheat reality somehow. Immediately upon entering that ship, you can look down corridors and rooms and great hallways as far as the eye can see. It's, for all practical purposes, infinitely big inside so there's plenty of room for all the millions of people we have time to save. I don't understand at all how that is, but it is and I don't need to know any more than that," she confides.

At that point the President seems exhausted. She notices that all the lights on her phone are blinking wildly. She is trying to lay out all the plans that they must make in the final days. Her brain is running at top speed and she is torn between emotions of extreme grief and extreme happiness with extreme fear of the unknown thrown in to boot. She's also thinking about her own family and wondering how many of them she will be allowed to take on board.

"All right. Go out there and do your jobs, but do them knowing that what I have told you is the truth. We don't want to let any of this leak until after my speech tonight. You can tell the media that this will be a speech of unprecedented importance and that they can, no must, preempt anything else because life on this planet will change, drastically, after the speech. You know the drill. No one is authorized to say anything else. Immediately after the speech, we will all rendezvous back here for another little strategy session and then you can go home. It's going to be a long day. Please help me to get through it. Now, go ahead out there and do your jobs, will you?" The President says in a final plea for their loyalty. She looks around to see if there are any more questions or discussions.

Sensing her frame of mind, they have none.

They all file out of the room in shock looking to one another for a clue as to what to say, how to react. The President puts her head in her hands and stares down at her desk. She notices a tiny black spec of dust wandering aimlessly around on her desktop. It's such a tiny black spec, she can't tell whether it's alive or just something rolling along in the wind.

CHAPTER 10

▼

THE EYE IN THE SKY

Special Agent Jack Beamer leaves the White House along with the others in a kind of fugue state. His mind is racing. How is it that this could be happening now at this precise moment in history. Everything they have been working on at the CIA has been to create a world completely under the control of the United States. As he sees it, if the government bureaucrats and politicians want to screw everything up before they leave, at least the agency is there to provide continuity.

It's not fair that this kind of calamity should befall them now at the height of their power. He thinks he may be the only one in the room who doesn't think the President has lost all her marbles because he has been monitoring situation through the eyes of the HST. After careful consultation with the astronomers and his colleagues around the world, he has finally a complete and total confirmation of the statements that Doug and Zora have been making the last few days. There is no doubt in agent Beamer's mind that the end, or something very much like the end is indeed near.

He lingers for a few minutes listening to the office buzz. A few of them wonder aloud if the President has completely lost it, or is perhaps having a nervous breakdown. The others are countering this theory citing evidence that she's been in tip top condition for months, going out in public, having her friends over for dinner often, holding high level meetings daily, doing her job and getting the highest grades from all her colleagues and the highest ratings from the public. Eventually the consensus is not to question but to obey her orders to the letter at least allowing them more time to consider all the facts in greater detail as the days unfold. They all know that in order to get her on the evening's television schedule, there's much to do. Reluctantly and with heavy hearts, the President's loyal men and women retreat into their offices and get to work.

Shaking a few hands and saying his farewell, Beamer exits the White House and has his car brought around by the valet. The Marine guard at the entrance kiosk gives him a snappy salute. Beamer wonders what will happen to him and the millions of innocent people around the world.

At his office back at CIA headquarters at Langley, Virginia, he finds his co-workers have all trained their attention on one project, the signals provided to the government by the HST. The Hubble Telescope has been turned over fully to the Astronomers at UC, Santa Cruz and they are sharing the feed over the Internet to their counterparts at universities and research labs all over the world, as well as NASA. NASA, then shares it with them.

"Hey, you've got to see this. This is pretty big! The rift is expanding every minute. You can see more and more galaxies just winking out, going dark. The HST has to pull back on the field of view another couple billion light years every few minutes or it loses focus. That means it's definitely getting closer. Seems like these guys are right. There's something going on," An attractive tall blonde woman says.

Rita Chavez is Jack Beamer's assistant and she and the others are spell bound by what they're watching. Rita is tall and beautiful and thin with long blonde hair and bright blue eyes. She is known throughout the agency as being the best computer hacker in the country. She became known to the CIA after she was caught hacking into the Bank of America and changing account information, depositing funds into her own account. When discovered she was offered immunity from prosecution if she would teach the government how she was able to get around all the security measures written by the thousands of Bank programmers over the years. She was so good at what she did, the idea was to hire her, and others like her, to spy on people all over the world.

"Oh, I know they're right," Beamer says, breaking into their conversation. "The President is going on National hook-up to tell the world about it. Seems we have about three months to load as many people as we can onto that egg thing and these lucky few get rescued."

"How many people can you get on that thing, five, six, a couple dozen if you stand toe to toe?" Harry Black, is the Director of his section. He looks frazzled, has his coat off, tie loosened as if he's already coming apart.

"They claim they're gonna get a couple million in there. The President is the only one that's gotten inside the thing other than that guy Doug and his girlfriend. She says, the inside has some kind of fourth dimension where the rooms go on forever. But, at a fast jog, in three months only a few million people can jam their butts through the door in a single file. That means most of the human race is going to be left behind. It's gonna get weird," Beamer tells them standing there with his hands on his hips.

There's a long silence in the room as they look down at the floor.

"What about us?" Rita asks, anxiously.

"The President says that everyone who was in the meeting today will get a pass along with our families," he gives it to them straight between the eyes.

There is a collective gasp in the room from his office mates.

"Don't worry," he reassures them. "You guys are my only family. I've already decided I'm taking you along with me or else."

"And just how are you going to do that?" asks Rita. The others also show their concern.

"Yeah, exactly how?" Jenkins echoes.

"Well, how about this. You know that Model Seven spy satellite we've got monitoring Iraq?" he asks.

"Yes," they say, in unison, hopefully.

"Well, let's put the laser pointer on the egg thing. It's parked at the White House right now, or at least it was when I left. We can change the trajectory of the Model Seven so that it will track it wherever it goes. So, when he goes to one of these random rescue locations around the world, we'll know exactly where that is. When we find a spot near one of our airfields, you all fly out there and just get in line like everyone else. Except you come in disguise just in case," he says, smiling.

"That's fine, but you're saying 'us', like you won't be with us," Rita says.

"Well, you see, I just happened to be in the room when the President granted us all a pass. You don't expect me to give up a guaranteed seat for stand-by, do you?" he replies in the charming way that they've all seen many times before.

"I guess not," Rita says, looking at the others, her eyebrows raised.

"All right then, until further notice that's the plan. Rita why don't you stake out the White House? See if that egg thing is still there and if it is, stick it with the laser pointer. Hopefully they won't detect it and we're good to go no matter where they take it, ok?" he says.

"Ok, that's the plan then, now everyone in this room is sworn to absolute secrecy, right? I mean if I can't trust you guys to keep a secret, who can I trust, right? Remember, we're all secret agents here and I advise everyone to keep the faith right up to the last. Oh yes and also, no matter what you do, don't tell your families about this plan until the last minutes or else they will go and blab to everyone else about what we're doin' and that could compromise the mission, get my drift?" Beamer says while checking the rest of the group for signs of any problems.

"I don't know about your family, but mine will make my life miserable not knowing if they're going or not," Jenkins says.

"Yeah, sure, all right, well you can tell them that there's a secret plan to rescue them, but make up a cover story that you think they will buy. Tell them the President is going to pick them up at the last minute from the ship. Tell them anything, but tell them they can't even divulge the cover story to anyone either, got it?" he says preparing to run out the door.

"Hey, why should you care about us anyway? You've got a free pass." Rita is thinking out loud as usual.

"I need you guys," he replies smiling again.

"Yeah, what do you need us for?" asks Rita.

"I'll need you to help me take over the ship. You think I want to stay on that thing forever, piloted by an aging cowboy and his cohort?" he asks.

"Ok, hey, where you going?" she asks as he runs out the door.

"I have to see someone about a rocket ship," his voice trails off as he runs out the door and down the hall.

Rita laughs briefly and shakes her head. She looks at the rest of the group appearing very worried. "Hey, like he says, Beamer needs us. He won't screw us. Let's do what he says. Bob, get the specs on the Model Seven and the I-950 Laser. Let's move it. We certainly don't need to worry about Iraq any more any way. They're all under control and besides it's too late for them to do any harm if this is all on the level," she says as the rest of them nod, snort, groan and grunt in agreement.

*   *   *   *

Inside the egg, Doug and Zora have found a warm and brightly lit little alcove on the northwest passage of the ship where they can sit comfortably at a desk to make their plans. They're talking about who they both want to take with them, people who must be given a seat on board the rescue mission. Her mother has died several years before, so she won't be on the list, but her father is still alive and retired on the big Island of Hawaii. Then, there's her brother, John, also living on Hawaii. Her cousin Nancy and her family should be welcomed. She wants her aunt and uncle and his immediate family to come along. Then, there's her best friend Sara and what about her ex-husband. She places a question mark next to his name and Doug erases the question mark and writes a 'Yes' over it. She's grateful for that.

Then, there are Doug's best pals back at the ranch. He wants them to come along with their families. His mother is still alive along with his brother and his family will be coming. His best friend in Oregon, Dan and his family will be invited and he lists about twenty more people he can think of who have shown him a kindness in the past and therefore merit a pass.

When they're done making their lists and contact information on these people, they start to think about the process of the rescue itself. He'll have to enlist the help of the government, of course. Well, Wendy, or the President, can assist with that. Then, he'll get all his bunk mates to help with the close order roping and wrestling of the critters so that they can corral as many as possible with a minimum of injury to the 'herd'.

"It's going to be helacious, deciding who comes and who stays," he comments to Zora still writing down names.

"I know. How do you plan on actually doing it?" she asks.

"Well, I reckon it's a lot like roundin' up the herd. We'll pick a location and setup a corral to round 'em up. Then, we'll put up a set of those barriers like you see in the banks and the post office so that they get funneled into the holding area. Then, we'll just open the doors and let them run in one by one. The only problem is to keep them moving down through the funnel so that we can squeeze in as many as possible," he says with wrinkled brow.

"Ok, I see that. Like at Disneyland," she says.

"You got it," he replies.

"And by landing at random locations, you get the widest variety of people instead of selecting for only those who have enough money to buy their way in, or with enough political clout," she says.

"Right," he replies thoughtfully. "How many people do you suppose can run into this doorway in one hour?"

"I have no idea," she replies.

"Well, let's do the math," he says, putting pencil to paper once again. "Let's see, with cattle, if you run them all in at a normal cow-trot you can get around sixty head past the gate per hour. That's about one per second. I figure people are slightly smarter and they're slightly smaller, at least most of 'em. So, let's say we can get around one hundred people in the door per minute. Let's see, that's around six thousand head per hour. And there's twenty four hours in a day, so that's around one hundred and forty four thousand per day. Assuming there's around ninety days left, that would equal around twelve million, nine hundred and sixty thousand head can be rescued and that's if there are no snags and we don't have any interference. Let's see, there's about six billion head on the planet, so rounding that off to thirteen million, it means we can only rescue around one in every two thousand people. Not really great odds of being rescued, is it?" he says aloud.

"No, not very," she agrees solemnly.

"Well, I guess when the Titanic went down, they didn't sit around crying about the lack of enough lifeboats. They just got to work getting as many people onto the ones they had as fast as they could," he says solemnly.

Zora just smiles at him, her eyes shining up at him like two searchlights in the darkness.

"I guess we'd better get started. I need to get back to the ranch and enlist some of my buddies. We can trust them. They're all a bit low key, but they're straight as an arrow. Then, there's a few more loose ends here and there that I have to take care of," he says.

"Yes, I know," she says and then the words of her favorite poem come to her lips. "The woods are long and dark and deep and I have promises to keep."

"Yeah, that's about it," he says, happy to hear her speaking the words that he himself had heard echo in his brain so many times before.

"You want to stay here and help Wendy or come with me?" he asks.

"You have to ask?" she says. "From here on in, I'm not leaving your side. I'm gonna stick to you like glue. Wendy, is it?"

"Ok, at least you can't say I didn't warn you," he says, stealing a kiss. "And it's just easier to say her name instead of Madam President all the time. You buy that?"

"Hmm, I'll let you know later," she replies smartly.

"I guess I better tell Wendy, uh, the President and I'll be right back," he says, getting up to go.

"I told you, I'm like glue," she says joining him as they run outside and onto the White House lawn.

*   *   *   *

Inside the White House there is an orderly pandemonium going on. A stream of very well dressed and attractive people runs in and out of the front entryway as soon as security can clear them. Every office in the West Wing is crammed with reporters, media consultants and even a few Senators have arrived to get in on the action. There is hardly any breathing room, but somehow through all the chaos, their one objective is taking shape, the President's impromptu and unscheduled address to the nation with global international satellite hookups.

Sensing that something important is going on, the CNN reporter, Barbara Foley, is here as well. She has been staking out the White House ever since the egg thing landed on the Capitol steps. Now, she seems to have the inside track. Suddenly the President is in their presence. Everyone becomes silent as they watch her. She's mumbling something to herself and then she spots Ms Foley and calls her into a private office, evicting the owner and her guests.

"I'm sorry," the President tells them. "I need to have this reporter's ear for just a moment."

"Yes, ma'am," Sharon says and helps to shoo everyone out.

The President closes the door behind them.

"I want to give CNN a kind of exclusive on this. Are you up to the challenge?" the President asks.

"I hope so, Madam President. I'll do my best. You want what in return?" she replies with eyes wide, a pen and pad in her hand ready to jot down every word the President says next.

"I'm going to give you the story first because you have the largest worldwide presence of all the networks. I want you to keep it under wraps completely until after the speech. Then, I want you to be the one that delivers it properly to all your affiliates and your bureau chiefs around the world. Do you think you can do that for me?" she asks her.

"Yes, of course, I'll do my best," she says looking up from her notepad.

"You must, and I emphasize, must be clear with your organization that this story has to be told as I'm telling it to you without embellishment and without your normal 'unbiased critiques with looking at both sides objectively and all that journalism crap'. Do you get me?" the President demands.

"Yes, I get you," Barbara says.

"The world has to know that this is it. There are no more second chances. They have to get it straight. There's nothing less at stake than the survival of our species. That's why I'm trusting you to tell it like it is," The President dictates to her. "There is no rebuttal. There's no flip side of the coin, no other point of view, get my drift?"

She notices the reporter trying to scribble as fast as she is speaking. "Please, don't take notes. Can you memorize it word for word?" she says, looking at her sternly.

Barbara puts the notepad down obediently and gazes back at the President who takes Barbara's hands in hers and squeezes them white.

*   *   *   *

The President began her day with instructions to the secret service and the Marine guard that that Doug and Zora are allowed to wander the White House grounds at will at any time. So, when they get to the main entrance to the mansion they are greeted with a salute and noticeably without objection or interference of any kind.

"Where's the President?" Doug asks Kramer upon seeing him wandering the halls, obviously distraught at having totally lost control of his staff in the pandemonium.

"She's down the hall talking to a CNN reporter," he replies with a blank expression.

"Don't worry, Mr. Kramer," Doug says, consoling him. "Everything will be all right."

"Yeah, thanks," Kramer shoots back, not really hearing the words. His body sways a little the way a tree reacts to the wind.

Doug spots the President through the glass of one of the offices down the hall. She is holding hands with the reporter he remembers from the Capitol Mall. They appear to be talking slowly but methodically. Doug thinks he knows what it's about. He waits patiently allowing them to finish their talk.

Soon, the two women hug each other and the President comes out of the room at full speed.

"Good morning Doug," she says as the others, pressing in around them, look on with great anticipation.

"Good morning, Wendy," Doug says quietly. Ma'am, I know how busy you are. But I want to tell you that I'm leaving on some unfinished business but I'll return as soon as it's done. We should probably have one long meeting to discuss some final stuff before I get the rescue started," he tells the President.

"Yes, Doug. I know. Ula showed me everything that needs to be done. Remember to save the best for last, won't you? When will we see you again?" she says, smiling brightly at him.

"I don't know. Two or possibly three days," he replies, noticing the rest in the room hanging on their every word. Next to him on the wall, from the corner of his eye, he sees an old antique clock with a bronze pendulum swinging slowly, keeping its slow methodical pace back and forth in space.

"All right. I'll be here and I'm at your disposal. Whatever you think I can do, I'm yours," she says almost cheerfully, noticing the others and trying to buoy their spirits.

"Thank you Madam President," he says, taking her hand. Then, he turns to leave as the others watch and then go back about their business.

The President watches them all for a minute, answering a few questions and then walks calmly back to the Oval Office to work on what she knows will be the most important speech of her administration and quite possibly the most important speech of any administration in human history.

*   *   *   *

Jack Beamer arrives at the parking lot of NASA headquarters just a few miles away. He enters the building at a run. A security guard tries to stop him as he streaks past in the lobby, but all he has to do is show his credentials to silence the guard who moves out of his way quickly.

He takes the elevator to the third floor where he knows the top brass are housed. They might have a few answers for him.

When he exits the elevator, he is tickled to find a group of a dozen men in suits huddled around the coffee machine in an alcove off to the side of the spacious lobby. The top NASA brass most of whom he recognizes are arguing loudly about the strange phenomenon known only to them as the 'Folding of the Universe.' They are trying to come to grips with it, what it might be, how they might counter it or at least slow it down. They seem to regard it like an errant asteroid on a collision course with the Earth. They want to plot its trajectory and are running through theories of moving the Earth out of its path.

The University astronomers are linked to the NASA offices by cable and to the side of the room on an unoccupied desk there is a monitor where one of them is speaking slowly and solemnly on the screen, but the volume has been turned down. To the side of his face, there is a data feed showing the speed off the approach of the event. The numbers are staggering and almost too large for the column of screen space given to it.

"Gentlemen, please," I'm agent Jack Beamer, CIA, special ops," he informs them holding up his badge.

The group of men turns to consider him and then ignoring him immediately return to their discussions. One of them asks him how he got in here.

Jack opens the lapels of his jacket revealing his forty five caliber Smith and Wesson cradled in its holster. He has their attention and they fall silent.

"I'm here on a mission from the President. She's very busy right now working on a speech about this thing tonight on TV. But she's instructed me to find out from you all if there's anything you might know that could counter-act this thing. Can we fire up a rocket and escape it?" he asks quickly and efficiently pointing to the monitor as if it existed only in there.

"Beamer is it?" the tallest man asks turning toward him.

"Yes sir," he says.

"This thing is traveling at hundreds, make it thousands of times the speed of light. We don't see how that's possible. There are no physics that we know of to explain that. It's already engulfed over ninety percent of the known universe. It's going to reach this vicinity in about three months. You know someone like you could try to get in a rocket and run from it and it would be a fun project to work on. Keep our minds off the problem, and all that sort of crap. If you want to be the monkey that tries it, there's probably just enough time to get you off," he says sardonically.

"But you'd get a few hundred thousand miles away giving you a few more minutes than the rest of us, that is if we got you off today," he says.

The others half smile at him.

"I see," Jack says, maintaining his focus. "Well what about shooting the world's entire arsenal of ICBM's at the thing. Could it deflect it away from the Earth somehow, punch a hole in it, anything?"

"Well, since we don't actually know what the devil this thing is, we could try that I suppose. Might keep our minds occupied again. But, the way this thing is engulfing entire galaxies, what do you suppose a few thousand nuclear bombs might feel to it? I don't think it would even be noticed, how about you?" he asks him directly.

"I see," Jack says, trying to marshal up one more attempt. "All right, so we just give up? There's nothing we can do? What if we place the bombs on say the Chinese side of the planet and exploded them all at once. Would that force push the Earth out of its path?"

"Well, that's an interesting concept. Now, let's see. We stick all the nukes available on Earth on the Chinese side of the planet. I'm sure the Chinese people would be happy to oblige," he begins with a sneer. "Then, we destroy half the planet and let's say this does the trick. The Earth is now engulfed in a Nuclear

Winter and oh yes, what about the sun? Where are we going to get our sunlight from then on. That is assuming we get far enough away from the thing that's swallowing whole galaxies! Yeah, we could try that, I suppose. Why don't' you get right on it agent Beamer!" As he speaks, the NASA Chief's voice has crescendoed to a loud roar, something the others have never observed in this man before.

Doug is unimpressed. He had to try. It was one last gasp before he puts his final plans in motion.

"Well, thank you gentlemen for your time. I guess I'll see you all on the other side," he says, with a wide grin.

"On the other side of what?" the Administrator shouts. "What are you talking about?" Suddenly his demeanor changes from night to day. His face, red from shouting, turns five shades toward ashen grey. He's suddenly aware that the man he's been yelling at just might know something he doesn't.

He follows him to the elevator, and even though he is shorter than Jack, he grabs Beamer's lapels with his hands and shouts in his face.

"What the hell are you talking about? Spill it, mister," he demands. "We all have families."

"Spill what? You're the ones with all the answers. You figure it out," Jack replies calmly removing the man's hands from his jacket.

The elevator door opens and Jack backs his way in, the NASA Chief looking at him with a combination of anger and pleading.

Then, he presses the button that holds the doors open.

"I'll give you all a clue," Jack tells him. "You'll want to listen to the President's speech tonight. She'll have the information you need to save yourselves. It's not much. But it looks like it's all you've got."

He presses the button once again and the door silently slides closed between them.

CHAPTER 11

▼

A NUCLEAR FREE ZONE

In the upper level of the egg ship, Doug and Zora are preparing for what they must do next. Ula has informed them that the human genome has to be purified in order for their race to be rescued. But she has not yet told them how this feat is to be accomplished. This she seems to leave up to human invention.

"Are you ready?" he asks Zora.

"Ready as I'll ever be," she replies.

Doug nods and then places the hat on his head to begin their discussion.

"Ula, where do you think we should go next?" he says out loud.

"Where is the greatest threat to your evolutionary progress?" she replies.

"I don't know. North Korea? I think that's the worst threat right now. The Communist Dictator over there is a complete ass. His people starve while he lives it up in the lap of luxury in a ten story pleasure palace. I always wonder how people like are able to continually avoid a firing squad," he says.

"Yes, mass murderers, these are probably the worst examples of human genetic material," Ula replies.

"Ok, we have our flight plan," he says looking at Zora. He closes his eyes and thinks about the tortured innocent men, women and children he read about in Time magazine. In a moment, the view of the White House is replaced with a strange hilly countryside where farms are carved out to blanket the rolling land in hundreds of various sized terraces.

They hover over a village where men are carrying what appear to be small potato sacks filled with what Doug knows to be dead children. They walk slowly to a large pit and throw the sacks into the hole where other men are shoveling dirt over the small sacks. There are thousands of these sacks resting in the dark hole already. When they've unloaded their cargo, each man marches back to the village where they take up more sacks to return again to dump these into the hole.

Doug moves the ship to the other end of the village to see a line of trucks pulling up to the village to unload even more sacks where men take them up onto their shoulders and start the long march to the mass grave site. This village is apparently being used by the North Korean government to hide this atrocity from the public. Doug fears that when they have performed this terrible job, the villagers themselves will be murdered by the armed soldiers standing around supervising the scene with rifles ready, and their bodies also thrown unceremoniously into the hole in order to conceal the truth from the world. This country is dying a slow and tortured death and one man, their 'heroic leader', as he likes to be called, will be eating caviar tonight and sipping the finest wines in celebration of his 'heroic leadership'. Surely this is the first type of behavior that must be purged from the human genome. Doug is completely confident of his next moves.

"Instead of spending his country's meager resources on food for his people, Li Kung Woo is investing it in death. "He has already created one dozen atomic bombs by extracting plutonium from the fuel rods of two nuclear power plants which were donated to him by the United States for the peaceful development and the welfare of his people. Instead, the 'heroic leader' has produced no jobs, no electric utilities, no television sets, no roads, schools or hospitals and has decided to use this technology to build a formidable offensive military capability. His dream is to become the greatest evil the world has ever known and he is succeeding rapidly. You only have to see the thousands of statues of himself he has placed all around the country to see that his leadership must indeed be 'heroic'." Doug says mostly to himself.

"Let's go pay this 'heroic leader' a visit, Ula," Doug suggests, sickened by the sight of this senseless tragedy. Zora, he can see is quietly sobbing.

In a flash, there is a ten story office building in front of them. Doug conceives a strategy for bringing this diminutive terrorist straight before them in a way that will prevent his security guards from protecting him.

The egg suddenly and violently forces itself into the top two floors of the structure that gives way with large pieces of it crashing to the ground and causing panic below. They can see through the view screens that they have arrived in the middle of a large opulently furnished office. There are movie screens on each wall. There are hundreds of kitsch art pieces littering the tables and chairs. And there is a large ornate desk that has just been flung across the room as if rejected by the walls of the ship and behind it, sits their quarry, Lee Kung Woo, pinned by the heavy desk against the wall.

"Come on," he says to Zora. "I think we have our man."

They both rush down the stair way to find short porcine man standing bewildered and struggling to get out from behind his desk. The 'heroic leader' is shivering like a wet and frightened animal.

"Who are you?" he demands. "What is this?"

"We're your judges, jury and executioner, Mr. Woo," Doug informs him casually. "You sir, are a disgrace to humanity. You are worse than vermin sir. Not even vermin kill their own kind. And so, it is our distinct honor to arrest you, place you in isolation where you will die slowly and your genes will no longer replicate and maintain your corrupted consciousness any longer."

"What are you talking about? You must be crazy," Woo is defiant. "I'll have you both shot if you don't release me immediately!"

Doug walks up to the diminutive man and shoves him with all his strength up against the wall of the ship and through the hull into the central hub. Inside, he takes the man by the throat and begins to squeeze the life out of him.

"Doug!" Zora yells at him pulling at his arms.

Suddenly realizing the anger taking control of him, Doug releases Woo's throat, depositing him to the floor where he struggles and coughs, gasping for breath.

"It is only important for you to know that nothing we can do to you can atone for your vicious, malevolent evil and all the terrible things you've done to your own people. You can't bring all those poor children back to life, can you? No, you can't and so you'll punish yourself enough, I hope, as you realize the rewards you are going to reap. We're going to place you in a hall over there where you will wander alone until you die," Doug points to the hallway that will be his prison forever.

Woo sneers and hisses like a snake. Then, the 'heroic leader' slowly turns his head to view the infinite expanse of the hallway to his left and the sight of it makes the lines on his forehead deepen and his breathing is rapid.

"You can't be serious," Woo says in a pleading yet still defiant tone. He turns his attention to Zora who has been standing quietly, except for her outburst, right behind Doug. "Who are you?"

"We're here to set things right for humanity, Mr. Woo," she says solemnly. "You have to go now and your kind can never be allowed to rise up again. It's not a kind thing we're doing, but unfortunately, it has to be done. I'm sure deep down you understand. I only ask that you forgive us," Zora replies.

"You see there is no time for a trial, Mr. Woo. Your actions have convicted yourself. There is no appeal. There are no more legal remedies. The world will no longer live in fear because of one man with a horrendous bomb. Your statues will be destroyed. Your friends will also disappear. Your policies will be reversed and peace and prosperity will be returned to this place." Doug takes great pleasure to inform him of his future.

He takes the man by the collar, lifts him to his feet prods the 'heroic leader' down the corridor while Zora waits behind in the central part of the ship. Woo tries to bribe Doug to let him go. He tells him he will give him anything he wants. He can have all the women he wants, all the drugs, all the liquor, travel the world as he pleases and live like a king if he will only release him, but Doug is not listening, but thinks instead of all the dead and dying children this man has so needlessly and senselessly murdered. They never had a chance.

"The West sent you tons of food for your people. But you refused to deliver it to your own people. I'm afraid, behavior like that is no longer tolerated on planet Earth," Doug tells him as he shoves him along the dark corridor. The lights have dimmed as if the ship knows who their guest is.

They make several turns and within a few minutes, Doug finds what he is seeking. It is a narrow corridor where Doug knows he can place the 'heroic leader' and from which he will never return.

It's a maze where there is no end and where he will find no solution, no food, no water, no mercy. Woo will wander here for the rest of his life eventually succumbing to hunger and thirst. In that time, he will have time to reflect on his life and that will be punishment enough. He will pay the ultimate price, but the best part is that this man's genetic material will be discarded forever and left on the dust heap of history. 'One small step for a man. One giant leap for Mankind', Doug thinks to himself, 'I guess we have to start somewhere.'

Doug shoves the man into the dark cell. From the floor, a wall structure instantly rises up creating a tightly sealed door that slams shut on the face of the 'heroic leader'. Doug turns to go. He can hear a muffled screaming and pounding on the wall that gradually becomes lost in the distance he puts between them.

When he finds his way back to the central hub of the ship, Zora is no longer there. He runs up the stairs and he finds her sitting in her chair with the familiar hat on her head. Outside the ship, they watch as dozens of armed security guards are milling about Woo's office. There's a great deal of confusion and anger and they are trying every method they can find, including a welding torch one man has found, to penetrate the hull of the ship, but to no avail.

"You want to make the next move?" he asks her.

"Could I? I think I know what needs to be done next," she says.

"You've got the helm, Number One," he says, emulating a Star Trek episode he remembers fondly. "Make it so."

She smiles back at him wanly.

"Gee, I've always wanted to say that," he tells her.

Zora closes her eyes. The view screen changes. And the ship descends through several floors of the office building.

They wind up on the third floor in a loud crashing demolition descent. Concrete and steel floors groan and collapse violently. Furniture and carpeting fly all around them. Alarms are sounding. The fire sprinkler system turns on showering the inhabitants with storms of water. Hundreds of people flee from doors flung open in panic on both sides of the hallway. Young beautiful women run out of many of the rooms with bare breasts and some are totally nude. Some of the young girls are draped with handcuffs, head bands, leg restraints and chains and many are bleeding.

The ship glides through wall after wall, expelling the inhabitants away from them with every smashing arrival on each floor. Doug enjoys the demolition derby, while Zora drives the ship carefully and surgically so as to avoid any loss of life. On each floor, she guides the ship slowly through the walls while avoiding the main support columns thus allowing the terrified occupants to escape to the ground and out the main entrance where they gather in the cold mist.

When, they've both decided the building is completely abandoned, Zora takes the ship to the huge public square just behind the crowd.

"Three, Two, One, Zero," she counts down. The building implodes in on itself creating a huge billowing dust cloud that forces the crowd to run in all directions away from the collapsing building.

"Good job Number One," Doug commends her.

"Thanks. Ula just taught me that trick. This is so much fun," she says with genuine glee. Doug can't remember seeing her in exactly this frame of mind before. It scares him a little, But, 'it's a good thing', he thinks to himself.

"Where to next, Captain?" she asks with a smile.

"Let's get on over to that Nuclear Facility. Now that their 'heroic leader' is gone, that's our biggest problem," he says. Zora agrees wholeheartedly.

Zora closes her eyes and in an instant they are hovering a few hundred meters above the North Korean Nuclear Power Research Facility at Pyongyang.

"Ask Ula to show us where the bombs are," Doug says.

Zora thinks about the question for a moment and then the view screens take on a kind of green x-ray penetration of the walls and floors. The rambling facility covering many acres comes on screen like an architects drawing. Dotting the area are a dozen little black spots like tiny cancers on a chest x-ray, they can clearly be seen even by their untrained eyes. The radiation they give off betrays them to Ula's penetrating ray.

"Clean up that mess," Doug instructs her, gazing intently at the little dots below.

Zora acknowledges his order and closes her eyes. The screen remains the same for a time, but then, the little black dots slowly start to fade away. The radio-active forces within their shell casings have been reversed. The bombs are all completely neutralized. They are devoid of any harmful radiation. The area is now so clean, life is no longer threatened.

"I don't know exactly how I did that," she says, looking over at him. "Ula gave me the power."

"You think, therefore, it's done," he says.

"I like that. The area is back to normal. No one has to worry about this regime, I'd guess," she says to Doug.

"Good work. Ok, let's move on to the next problem," Doug says.

"Where's that?" Zora asks.

"Close your eyes and you'll know," he replies.

Doug reaches over and plants a kiss on her soft warm lips.

*   *   *   *

Zora closes her eyes as the screens go dim and then brighten with a completely different landscape below. Gone are the greenery replaced by a huge desert. This time, the mountain ranges are slightly taller. There is a long continuous blanket of white snow smothering the upper slopes.

In a small valley below them, there is a small city fanning out from a central district that has as its center point a square building with four towers on each corner and a slightly taller one in the middle. The middle tower has a tulip shape on the top.

"There's where their leaders reside," says Zora pointing to the mosque resting peacefully in the center of town.

"Yes, Iran. Not yet a nuclear power yet, but trying very hard, aren't they?" Doug notes.

"Yes," she replies mechanically.

"Why not pay them a little visit, Darlin'" Doug suggests.

With a slight mental effort Zora allows the ship to descend slowly. When they hover at a spot in the sky just above the roof of the mosque, they can see several dozen figures scattering below them, panicking and flailing their arms above their heads as they run.

Then, when the crowd has put a safe distance between themselves and the ship, she lowers it the rest of the way which forces it through the clay bricks of the roof sending the dirt cascading down onto the worshippers seated below. These people also have to flee the scene or become crushed by the ship lowering itself down into the large spacious colonnaded mosque.

On an elevated floor just in front of the hall, sits a group of ten men dressed alike, sporting beards and head wrappings. They look shocked but remain frozen on the floor next to one another. Another older man, slightly forward of the rest, quickly gets to his feet and yells for the others to go outside and bring help.

Doug decides to say something to the old worn face in front of them before they complete their task. He looks down at the arm of his chair and sees a small black button suddenly protruding from the arm of the chair. He presses the button knowing that it will aid in this service. As he speaks he can hear his voice projected and amplified impressively outside the ship.

"This is no way to live old man. Allah does not want you to preach hate and violence, fear and hate. That's not what Allah is all about. You should have known that by now, old man. But we're here to teach you the greatest lesson of your life," he says in perfect Farsi.

The old Mullah looks at the ship as if he sees a mirage. He wipes his eyes. Several dozen men, carrying automatic weapons, dressed in the same dirty robes, run into the mosque from a door flung open behind a wide column on the side. They are shocked to see the ship sitting there on the floor amongst a small pile of rubble and the large opening in the roof of the mosque letting in the sun.

"Ok, Zora, you wouldn't have brought us here unless there was good reason. Let's exercise the search warrant," he says.

Zora looks at him and smiles. He's just noticing how sexy she looks in a black cowboy hat. The ship presses down with such force the floor gives way with a loud groan, an explosive cracking noise and a mad vibration that sends the security force as well as the old Mullah to the floor.

Breaking through the floor of the mosque they find themselves in a beehive of tunnels. The largest one goes off to a place where they can see a dim light poke through the dark corridors. Zora pushes the ship through tons of concrete and earth to arrive at a large open cave with a high ceiling. The room appears to be carved from the limestone bedrock. There are several rows of tables in the middle of the room where men in white lab coats are working at computer screens and dark green control panels containing hundreds of dials, lights and switches. The workers jump from their seats to look at the noisy crashing mayhem coming from the tunnel behind. Most of them, convinced they are under attack by some kind of subterranean missile, run for their lives. Some are frozen in place.

Doug can see a centrifuge whirling around like a small tornado over in the far corner. Beyond the rows of tables, he spots a large pool of water that has been excavated into the floor. The pond of water glows with an ominous yellow leaking up from the bottom of the pit.

Doug presses the button on his chair again. "Get out! Leave at once or you will be killed," he shouts to them.

Most of the workers are already in a panicked retreat down the tunnels or up the stairs. The rest move out of the way as Zora pushes the ship relentlessly forward like a big ocean liner in the night. She smashes it into the tables, crushes the centrifuge like an empty soda can, and hurls the control panels and containers of uranium fuel all over the room. A security guard slowly descends the stairs as the lab coats are running away in the opposite direction. He has a rifle and he points it at the egg and fires a blast of automatic fire. But it has no effect on the ship. There is no ricochet. There is no sound of bullets finding their mark. It's almost as if the skin of the ship absorbed the bullets completely. He removes the magazine to see if he might be firing blanks. Convinced there are real bullets in the magazine, he snaps it back into the weapon and fires again and again with no effect.

Meanwhile Zora has maneuvered the ship to the large menacing pool of water in the rear of the cave. She maneuvers the ship to a few feet from the glowing pond of water, drills the ship down into the ground and just keeps going. After a mile of two of rock has passed the view screens, she moves back up the long well hole she's dug and then, right where the pool is still intact, she crashes the ship forward. The water bursts out like a dam that has broken spilling all the contents down into the hole she has just dug. Then, she moves the egg around in a circle through the rock so that it begins to cover the hole she just made with tons of rock.

"I advise you to clear the area," Doug shouts, his voice blasting out into the cave. The only remaining people are the guard who just fired on them and a few of the workers brave enough to stop at the top of the stairs to witness the events. They argue for a few seconds and then finally, they all leave.

"Ok, let's rock and roll," Doug says.

Zora spins the ship up and down and back and forth so violently the walls of the cave are forced to implode all around them. She feels like the agitator in her washing machine at home. Then, she lifts her head and drives the ship up and out of the ground, bursting through the surface sand and into the sunlight a few feet from the mosque. She has put them right in the middle of a crowd of worshippers and lab coated workers where they have stopped running and now gather in a loud agitated throng. They let out a loud shout in panic as the ship bursts from the ground right next to them.

"Go in peace and sin no more," Doug says to them. The group disperses quickly, and scatters in all directions.

Zora looks at him with a sardonic smile.

"Well, we're doing God's work here, aren't we?" he says.

She just shakes her head and chuckles.

"By the way, I thought your driving was atrocious," he says. "I'd hate to see your car insurance now," he quips.

She lowers her head and looks up at him with those eyes. Doug feels as if they have never been apart.

*   *   *   *

At the White House, the President is seated at her desk surrounded by dozens of technicians, gaffers, sound men, make-up artists, lighting people. They are making final preparations for the President's address to the nation.

Barbara Foley stands in the back of the room sporting a headset and holding her notepad. In the middle of the room, seated on the couch is Chief of Staff Kramer, National Security Advisor Steven Bradford and her friend, Ambassador Jerry Portnoy along with a few of their staffers.

"I told her to use a teleprompter, but she refuses," Kramer says to the others.

"She going to read from notes, then?" Bradford asks.

"Nope. Says, she's going to wing it. That the words will just have to come to her," Kramer says wearing his now trademark skeptical look on his face.

"The most important speech of her life and she's going to wing it?" Bradford asks, rather incredulous.

"That's the picture I'm getting," Kramer replies.

"Well, it's not like she's running for reelection anyway," one of the male staffers suggests. He's rewarded by a raised eyebrow from the two senior men.

"Anyone know where the egg thing has gotten off to?" one of the female staffers asks, leaning forward.

"It appears it's causing a few problems in North Korea and at this very moment in Iran," Bradford informs them.

"Problems? What kind of problems?" Kramer asks.

"They're destroying all their nukes," Bradford says.

"I don't remember anyone appointing them to the Environmental Protection Agency," Portnoy says.

"Yes, I guess you're right," says Bradford, laughing out loud, then covers his mouth.

"Quiet Please. Everyone who is non essential personnel, please leave the room. We air in five minutes," The Director, Sam Kassir, waves his arms around to accentuate his instructions. Several people rush out of the room. The senior men sit down in the chairs behind the network crew.

"Madame President, are you ready?" He asks her.

"Yes, I suppose," she replies as her make-up lady applies one last brush stroke to her face.

Kassir walks around to the back of the President's desk and whispers some last minute advice into her ear. The President nods while viewing the concerned looks on all the faces of those remaining in the room.

The Director backs up around to a spot just behind the camera and puts on a headset, listening to an unseen voice in his ear. He looks around at the technicians seated at their various recorders, monitors, light switches and sound mixers.

"All right, in five, four, three, two, one," he holds his hand up beside the camera closing his fingers so that the President can see the countdown as well as hear his words.

The little red light comes on the top of the camera.

"My fellow Americans, tonight, we are also being broadcast to the rest of the world, so I would like to address my fellow citizens of the Earth," she begins well and then takes a long pause.

"I know that some of what I have to say is going to come as an extreme shock to many of you. But, my fervent prayer is that when I'm done, you will all know exactly what is expected of you and you will all do your duty, to your families, your friends, to your country and to your planet. You will want to pay attention to my words. They may be the last ones you hear from this place," she says ominously, knowing she is competing with sports, idle gossip, arguments over money, apathy in the millions of homes she is now attempting to persuade as she has never done before.

*   *   *   *

Zora and Doug sit alone in the ship for a few minutes watching the worshippers disbursing amongst the tattered and aging buildings that make up the dirty town. The place reminds him of the old West. Then Doug realizes that he's hungry.

"Not a bad day's work before lunch," he says.

"Yes, what should we have?" she says.

"I don't know why, but I kind of feel like Persian food," he replies, chuckling to himself.

"All rightie, Persian food coming right up, sir," she says curtly. "I think I saw a little gedunk stand on the other side of this mosque thingie."

The ship moves quickly and she passes some of the slower worshippers who are still trying to clear the area as fast as they can.

The ship rumbles up in front of an old metal trailer that has been cut up to resemble a diner. There's a man inside the cut-out window watching in horror as the egg approaches. He throws off his apron and heads for the door on the other side of the food stand.

Doug presses the button on his chair. "Don't move please. We're hungry in here and we are in need of your services," Doug calls out in his deepest basso profundo.

The man freezes in his steps.

"We are hungry for some of your falafels. I command you to make two of them. Cover them in that wonderful sauce of yours and bring the plates to us or suffer the consequences of our wrath," he demands, playing with the man's head.

The man, shivering like a wet cat, does as he's instructed, rapidly tossing the meal together as ordered and muttering to himself while glancing over his shoulders at the strange shifting shape that is speaking to him.

"What about something to drink," Zora asks.

"Good idea. Ridding the planet of the slime in the world is thirsty work, isn't it?" he replies to her in his super-hero voice.

Then, pressing the button again, his voice booming all around the exterior of the ship.

"Throw in a couple of Cokes. All right no Cokes, make that Sarsaparilla," he instructs the man who just shrugs his shoulders, obviously not stocked with either of these items.

Within seconds, the man leaves the food hut carrying the plate of food and walks slowly towards them. He's bowing to the egg-god as he approaches the ship shivering and shaking in his shoes so hard the glasses rattle and the drinks spill to the ground.

"Place the food on the ground and be gone man," Doug says, authoritatively.

The little fellow runs away as fast as he can and disappears into the heart of the town out of their sight.

Doug exits the ship and lands on the sand, just a few feet from the tray of food. He looks around to see if anyone has noticed him. There are faces timidly peeking around corners almost everywhere he looks. Some are young faces, some are very old. Suddenly, one of the faces produces a gun barrel and points it at him from behind the white stucco wall. Simultaneously, he hears a loud snap.

Doug reacts quickly, but not quickly enough. He dives for the protective skin of the ship, but just before he reaches it, he feels a dull thud on his back. He knows the rifleman has found his mark.

But oddly enough, he feels no pain. He picks himself up and propels his body through the hull of the ship and inside, he feels around for the hole he knows must be opening in his chest. He expects to feel a warm pool of blood. But his shirt and pants are clean.

He feels around some more and there is no evidence of any damage anywhere on his body.

He's elated and breathes a sigh of relief as Zora runs down the stairs in near panic.

"Are you all right?" she yells at him, scanning his clothing.

"I'm fine. The bullet never penetrated my skin. I felt it land and then, nothing. It's like it dissolved on my or in me. I don't know," he says smiling.

"Well, thank God," she says, relieved but still running her hands over his body. "You get the food?"

*   *   *   *

"I don't have all the answers for you tonight. Some of them will arise from your own efforts. Some of them will come from your governments. Some of them will come from your faith," the President continues.

"The Bible tells us that there is a season for all things in heaven. We have come to the season where the light will be banished from this place. We will go into a total darkness and no one knows for how long. Astronomers have never witnessed a phenomenon like this in the history of our civilization. There is someone here who tells us that this is the end of all things. But I don't believe it's truly the end, but the harbinger of a new beginning," she says.

*   *   *   *

In the home of Albert Hernandez, his family of two young girls and two older boys is gathered around the television set in the family's living room. The buzz at their schools and offices all throughout the day told them that this was one speech by the President that no one could miss. Telephone lines have been over-whelmed all the rumors, so few people have been able to actually communicate with any authorities who would tell them what was happening. The Internet became the place to get the news, with almost every email speaking of an upcoming space disaster and the plans that the President had to avert it.

"Daddy, why do we have to listen to this? I want to go play," the little girl pleads, gluing herself to her father's chair.

"I know, honey. But, there's something very important that the President wants to tell us. Let's listen," Albert tells her calming and taking the little girl gently into his arms.

On the TV screen, the President continues, "Astronomers all around the world, using every telescope and every scientific instrument known to us, including the Hubble Space Telescope have discovered a large rift or tear in space. It's moving toward the Earth at a rate of speed several thousand times the speed of light. There is no known science that can explain this phenomenon. And, at the rate it is approaching, it will reach us in less than three months time. There is no defense against this thing, unless it stops on its own accord. But it shows no sign of slowing down and in fact is increasing its momentum. This rift or folding in the universe is gobbling up entire galaxies the way a flood can gobble up entire cities and towns unlucky enough to be in the path of the water. When it reaches our own planet, the sun, the moon, the stars will vanish as will our own sun and then even the Earth will simply cease to exist,"

Albert glances at his wife whose face remains stoic. He knows the calm facade is for the sake of the children who have not yet grasped the full significance of the President's speech. He's hoping they never will.

"It's possible that we will simply pop out of the other side of this thing. But the scientists all tell me that this must be a super-massive black hole, never seen before, that is engulfing the universe. In such an event, nothing can survive. But there is always the chance that they are wrong. Since this has never happened before, and there is no science to explain it, we can only pray that they are wrong," the President continues.

*   *   *   *

The egg ship moves slowly along the knife edge crests of the Himalayas. Doug and Zora are watching peacefully as the highest peaks in the world move majestically under their feet. Long veils of snow and mist streams off the top of the highest peaks like the steam from a cup of hot coffee in the winter wind.

"That must be Everest right over there," Doug says, driving the ship this time, the cowboy hat on his head.

"It's the highest, and it looks just like the photographs," Zora concurs.

"I wanted to take the scenic route to Pakistan," Doug says.

"Yes, I'm glad you did. Not too many people ever live to see a view like this," Zora replies.

"Their nukes are buried deep inside these mountains," Doug says, thinking out loud. "Do you think we'll find 'em all?" he asks.

Zora makes no reply, and instead remains mesmerized by the cold majestic rock formations rolling along just beneath their feet. She is standing close to the view screens and cranes her neck to get a better view of the scenery below.

"Oh yes. I see that," Doug says out loud.

"Ula tells me that there are only thirteen nukes in Pakistan and they're all contained in an ammunitions armory at Bal-DeSur. It's a fortress dug into the mountains. It will be like the Iranian situation, I guess," Doug tells her. "I'm going to punch it. You ready?"

"Hmmm, yes," Zora mumbles, turning to regain her seat.

"What are you thinking?" he asks her.

"It's like being up in Heaven with God. Don't you feel the presence up here?" she says soothingly.

"Yes, I know what you mean. I've had that feeling ever since this thing landed in my back yard," Doug says.

"Do you think the creatures who built this can know God any better than we do?" she asks pensively and gazing into his eyes.

"I'd say that's a pretty safe assumption. I can't prove it, of course. But I'd like to think that about them. Or else what are we doing here?" he posits.

"We haven't had much time to debate all the fine points, have we?" she asks.

"Fine points? Like what?" he replies.

"What if these people were attempting to trick us somehow? Maybe this is all a big scam. Maybe they're projecting images of this folding thing to scare us into disarming the world and then they can just sweep down in ships like this one and take over so easily?" she says.

"Snap out of it, Zora. That's what the Pentagon is saying. You want to go and join them?" he says. "There's a point in every life where they just have to trust their instincts."

They look at each other silently sharing their thoughts.

"I guess you're right. Let's get on with it," she says, laughing and shaking off her paranoia.

Doug looks at her reassuringly and then closes his eyes. The view screens go black and then are filled with the light bouncing off a new mountain range far less imposing, but still very impressive.

"There it is," he says.

Looking down at the bottom of a large cliff, they can see a small facility that is shaped like a giant door and carved into the foot of the cliff. Trucks, appearing like toys from this vantage point, are in a convoy and have arrived at the facility's main entrance and have stopped for a search by men in uniforms. One of the men in a forward truck looks up and points to the egg floating in the sky near the top of the cliff above them.

"Well, they've seen us," Doug says, confidently. "Let's make the grand entrance, shall we?"

Doug forces the ship into the side of the mountain and within a heart beat or two, they have arrived in the middle of a huge underground complex of long tunnels and large weapons depots where trucks and missiles and artillery sit lined up in rows by the hundreds.

"Amazing how much time and money people will squander on these things that can only be used for destroying millions of other people," Doug says. "What the hell are they thinking?"

"Yes, it speaks volumes about us, doesn't it?" Zora says.

Soldiers have spotted them in the cavernous room. The dark brown uniforms come scurrying towards the ship by the hundreds. They open fire at the ship. A few of them have torn heavy fifty caliber machine guns from their stanchions on the walls, load them and begin firing. Doug and Zora feel as though the noise must be deafening out there for the poor unfortunate men. But, she rests in the knowledge that they are totally protected from anything these people can throw at them, even including nuclear weapons if they were so foolish.

Doug presses the button on the arm of his chair and speaks loud to overcome the raucous outside.

"You must place your weapons on the ground immediately and leave this area or else you will be seriously injured or even killed," he informs them.

His speech stops their fire for a moment. They take a beat to consider the warning and then almost unanimously open fire on the ship again. A few, the smarter ones, have turned tail, dropped their weapons and begin to run away toward the rear of the cavern. Most have remained.

Doug and Zora can feel the thudding impact of the rounds hitting the hull of the ship. But they have no fear and even feel the ship taking on greater energy with each round that is absorbed into the skin.

Suddenly, one round pierces the skin of the ship and floats in slow motion in front of them and falls harmlessly to the floor by their feet.

"Hmph. Ula let one slip in here," Doug says, a little concerned at the apparent imperfection in their armor.

Zora shakes her head and smiles in agreement.

"All right. You have been warned and I will give you one last chance. In ten seconds, this room will turn into pure hell," he says loudly.

Half of the soldiers decide that this last warning should be heeded so they drop their weapons and run away. But the remaining group seem intent on their own destruction and pay no heed, even shooting at their retreating companions. They continue to fire on the ship with everything they have.

"Five, Four, Three, Two, One," Doug says loudly.

Then, suddenly walls of the cavern turn red with a heat that emanates from deep inside the mountain. The rock wall turns into a white hot molten flood of lava that begins to slowly consume the weapons. The slow inexorable progress of the lava gives the remaining soldiers just enough time to escape it in a wild panic. A few of the remaining soldiers have been trapped by the lava and are consumed in flame.

"You can't say I didn't warn them," he says to Zora.

"Yep, you can't say that," she agrees while captivated by the magnificent destruction taking place before them engulfing the tanks, the artillery, the missiles one by one and turning them into oozing molten metal.

The room begins to fill with the molten lava. Doug takes the ship up and away slowly rising above the smoke and the glowing ashes. Convinced that nothing here will ever see the light of day again, he punches the ship through the side of the mountain and out into the bright sunshine.

"Whew," he breathes a sigh of relief to be out of there.

Zora begins to regain her composure.

"What do you say we go take in a movie somewhere?" she jokes.

*   *   *   *

In the Hernandez home, the President's face on the TV screen remains the focus of the family's attention.

"There is one bright ray of hope for us all," the President continues. "There is a ship that has come to us from an unknown part of the universe. The ship is unmanned by any living creatures, but it is itself living thought. I have been inside the ship and it has communicated to me that we can be saved as an intelligent species but only if we act swiftly to eliminate our worst faults in these our final moments. Our planet is currently being disarmed of all our most dangerous weapons by this ship. It has already neutralized the worst threats in North Korea, Iran and has just finished with Pakistan. India, China, Russia, Great Britain, France and then the United States are next and over the coming days and weeks every nuclear power will be cleansed of these weapons of mass destruction. Once we are cleansed of these weapons, we can begin to cleanse our hearts and minds of the violent tendencies that have evolved over millions of years of our evolution and which formed the basis for this, our most urgent and dangerous problem."

*   *   *   *

At the University of California Santa Cruz, Professors Blake and Pressman have setup a television set on a lectern at the front of his beginning astronomy class. In the theatre style seats, there is a full house of nearly one hundred and fifty students hanging on every word begin spoken by the President.

Upon the mention of world disarmament by the President, a loud cheer goes up amongst the class.

*   *   *   *

"We have reached a key turning point in our own evolution. No longer are we the captive slaves to random chance mutation, and survival of the fittest. Today, we have unlocked the secrets of our own genetic code. The basic plans for the construction of the human animal, the human genome is open for all to see. Therefore, we have at our disposal the chance to change everything about our planet, but also the very make-up of the human being as well. It is essential that we work on both paths of our future evolution in harmony with one another. I don't know what each individual can do to help cleanse the entire human genome, but I leave that up to each of you to determine in your own hearts and minds what it is that you can do to counter balance the millions of years of human cruelty, competition, ecological destruction, militarism and greed. I ask that you pray in large groups, and openly discuss in these final days how each of you can make a contribution to the redemption of the human race." The President continues.

"I can't emphasize how high are the stakes in this all important game. If we are able to cleanse ourselves of these genetic defects, we may not be rescued. The alien ship that is currently cleansing our planet of the scourge of nuclear weapons is also the ship that can evacuate a large number of us and it will bring us to a safe harbor. Not everyone will be able to fit on board, only because of the time element and not due to the size of the ship. The ship itself can fit every man, woman and child living on the Earth today and more. However, there is only enough time left to collect a few million of us," she says.

The President pauses to take a sip of water and then continues.

"The ship will land at random locations around the world over the next three months and if you are lucky enough to be in the vicinity of an evacuation point, you should immediately gather up your family and friends, calmly line up to enter into the safety of the ship. There will be people there to help you. It will not be possible to know the ship's pickup points beforehand because that would cause a widespread panic wherever these might become known. Don't bother to try and bring any material objects on board. Nothing will be allowed on board except for your persons."

*   *   *   *

In a small village in Africa, the women are calmly baking bread as they chatter musically about their children, their husbands. The men are gathering their tools to go out into the fields. Children are playing in front of their mud and grass huts. The older ones watch the smaller children as their parents are busy at their chores. The village is composed of around thirty huts. They are scattered amongst the trees and quiet rolling hills of the African lowlands. It's a very peaceful scene replicated by the thousands all over the vast continent that is the cradle of all intelligent life on Earth.

The people here are peaceful tillers of the soil, gatherers of the fruit and vegetables that grows here in abundance all throughout the year. They care nothing for politics and so they are unaware that large gangs of heavily armed men are marching throughout this land looking for diamonds, gold, money, that their greed has reached epidemic proportions, distorted their minds and turned them into monsters who are even now killing innocent people as they find them destroying their villages just for the sake of killing. They know nothing about this and want only to see their children grow up safe and healthy in this warm sunny place and then to have children of their own.

Breaking the tranquility of this scene, from the dusty dirt road there is suddenly a roar of machinery. The villagers look down the road to see an ominous dust cloud rapidly approaching. They are worried and they start to run for their huts. Suddenly, a brown and green jeep pulls up into the heart of the village. Six men with rifles jump out and start shooting at the villagers. They are not discriminating in their fire as they wound and kill several dozen children, women and men too slow to evade their bullets.

Another Jeep pulls up behind the first. There are six more young men dressed in army fatigues also intent on killing, who jump from the vehicles and give chase to the fleeing villagers. In the confusion, women are rushing around madly searching for their babies. Men are rushing around trying to defend their families with machetes and small knives. They fall to the bullets of the soldiers by the dozens, their blood soaking the thirsty sand all around.

From their vantage point high above, Doug and Zora can see the dust clouds as more and more jeeps descend on the village while they approach the small cluster of huts from the North.

"There's another bunch of them," Doug says. Doug maneuvers the ship to bring it within a few feet in front of the attacking marauders.

He presses the button on his chair's console. "Stop what you are doing. Drop your weapons or be destroyed," Doug says using his most commanding voice.

Instead of obeying, they look at each other and then open fire on the ship hovering defiantly a few feet off the ground in front of them.

Doug looks at Zora and then closes his eyes. Immediately the weapons in the soldier's hands turn red hot and the molten metal seers into their flesh. They can't drop the rifles because they have become attached to their flesh by the heat. They scream in pain so loud their screams can be heard for miles in all directions.

The villagers turn to look to see what is happening. Noticing the egg shape floating in the middle of their village, and apparently fixing the soldiers so they cannot hurt them any more, they stop in their tracks and slowly regain the courage to return to their huts.

One of the village men picks up a machete and heads for one of the soldiers lying on the ground with a vengeance in his eyes. Doug presses the button on his chair and tells him that vengeance is the Lord's and they are not to kill these men. They will never be able to hurt anyone any more and that will be their punishment. They will have to live with the scars of what they have done for the rest of their lives and the pain will haunt them for the rest of their lives.

He instructs them to tie the soldiers together and keep them prisoners until help can arrive from their government.

The villagers seem willing to accept this temporary justice and so they obey and begin to gather up their dead and wounded. Doug tells them to put the wounded into the jeeps that have accumulated now in the battle to several dozen, and to bring them to a field hospital that is just a few miles away. Sadly there is nothing that can be done about the dead children and adults and so they bring them to a place in the village where they can be mourned together.

Some of the villagers place flowers and food items at the foot of the egg ship. They bow and walk backwards from the ship, mumbling their thanks in their native tongue. But Doug and Zora can understand the words perfectly.

Doug says, "They're giving us their blessings and they want us to remain as long as we wish. They'll give us everything we need from now on. Treat us like Gods."

"Why don't we go outside and give them our condolences?" Zora suggests quietly, looking at the children's peaceful and motionless little faces lying in a row in the dust.

"Yes, why don't we," Doug replies.

They descend the stairwell and slip outside the vibrant skin of the ship and into the bright African sun. The villagers spot them and they rush up smiling and gesturing their gratitude. They surround the pair and place flowers on their heads and in their hands.

Zora can barely contain her grief.

"We were too late for these people," she says with tears streaming down her cheeks.

"I don't know. It's times like this that make me very disappointed in humanity," Doug says as the villagers ply them with humble food items and small trinkets to show their appreciation for what they have done.

"I'm so sorry we did not arrive in time to save all of you," Doug tells them. "They've kept us busy all up and down the valley and at least I can tell you we've put a stop to all of this."

The villagers, very much accustomed to death and violence in their part of the world, express only their gratitude that they did come at all. They seem to be consoled in the knowledge that their family members have gone to a better place.

Doug and Zora give them what comfort they can and then they ascend back into the ship. The look of wonder and relief on the faces of the survivors is enough to make them almost forget their grief and sorrow. As they approach their ship, the villagers walk along holding their hands and sing a song in perfect harmony that will live in their hearts for the rest of their lives.

As soon as the song ends, Doug takes Zora's hand and helps her into the ship. She is reluctant to leave and streams of a warm salty liquid race down her cheeks as she takes one last look at these humble people through the view screens, their beautiful black faces smiling bravely as they sing their good-byes.

"Why don't we stay a while?" she says to Doug.

"If you want to? I'm with you. I imagine we can spare a few more minutes," Doug replies.

They exit back out of the ship and into the midst of the villagers singing procession. A roar of joy rises up from their voice and they turn to sing their song again even louder and they take Doug and Zora by the hand and lead them slowly back to their village.

Doug and Zora sing along with them in their mournful song. It's a song of hope and acceptance for their lot in life. It's a song they've sung for hundreds of years.

"Thank you," Zora says quietly to Doug as they march slowly along holding hands.

*   *   *   *

In a Boston tavern, the smoky room is full of men and women who also have their attention tuned to the TV set above the bar. The atmosphere is thick with the smell of alcohol, hops, grapes and sweat. They are silent and all eyes are on the TV as the President concludes her speech.

"Over the next twenty four hours, I will be shutting down the government of the United States. There is no longer any need for new laws, debates, judgments or pronunciations by politicians. Agencies will remain open where I feel they can assist in this emergency such as the Department of Health and Human Services,

FEMA, and the Department of Transportation. All other government agencies will be closed because there is no longer any necessity for taxes, budgets, defense, the courts or intelligence. Where government workers feel they can assist in the situation, I would ask that they remain at their posts as long as they can," the President says.

"Ahh, what a bunch of horse poop!" yells one man from the bar. "Little green men from outer space don't scare me! This is all a plot to bring back prohibition, you wait and see," he says, slurring his words horribly.

A few sitting close enough to hear the drunken man, chuckle briefly. Then silence returns to the bar.

"I am asking, no expecting, that all of you will behave as honorably as is humanly possible under these difficult circumstances. These final days will bring a judgment and a conclusion as to whether or not our species is worthy enough to be spared from extinction. The situation is thus more important than any other time in our history. I therefore ask that you congregate in the churches and the schools and discuss and debate how you can best improve your minds and find ways to accept what is taking place as a good thing. I know that sounds rather cold and removed, but please believe me, there is no other way. Live your lives, share your love with your friends and families. Make your final preparations to leave this world. Resist the instinct to strike out in anger or to find blame. There is no one and no thing blame, except perhaps ourselves. There is no court of appeals. This sentence has been imposed on us by forces perhaps beyond our comprehension and as such we are treading on unfamiliar ground. We are virtually standing on the final frontier," she says.

"Ahh, don't give up your day job, you kook! I never voted for her, you know," the drunkard breaks the silence in the bar for the last time.

Three of the men sitting nearest the drunken man rise out of their stools in unison. They gather up the unfortunate man in a heap and escort him to the door. Ignoring his protests, they toss him unceremoniously out into the cold. They come back in the door and return to their seats calmly. Their attention returns to the TV screen. The crowd gives them a mild ovation.

"I don't know what else to tell you. I could go on to say how proud I am to be an American. But I'd rather tell you how proud I am to be a citizen of the Earth and a member of the Human Race. We all have that one thing in common, you know," the President says, then, looking down at her desk, she pauses for along moment.

"It's not all bad, our history and evolution. In fact, I'm guessing that the good that we have done for one another, over time, far outweighs the bad. And this will be our salvation. The good deeds that we have done remain strong within our hearts and minds and beats far stronger and louder than the drums of war and violence, greed and evil can ever do. We have built great civilizations thousands of times and in thousands of places. We have built libraries and hospitals and schools. We have constructed great skyscrapers that climb up into the heavens and consort with the clouds. We have risen in tiny vessels to other places far, far away just for the sake of knowing God's amazing work first hand. At the end of the day, we have done more to advance our kind than we have done to destroy it," she says, tearfully.

In the bar, in the schools, in the churches, in the living rooms all around the world, there are few dry eyes as people everywhere witness her speech.

"We have raised our consciousness to levels unimaginable by our forebears. With every generation, we have striven to improve the quality of life, increase the beauty of our surroundings. We have done God's work the best we know how. Without any guidance other than what is in our hearts, we have made choices, raised our children and given them the best opportunity at life that we could muster. Without an owner's manual, we have built upon the human experience generation to generation to the best of our ability. Like blind leading the blind, we have struggled through the ages and we have survived the storms, the deluge, the disasters that greed for power and that nature have thrown against us. And against all of this drama we have found freedom. We have known people and things that we love. We have been fulfilled by our passion for all the good things in life. We have known the joy of living and we thank God for that," she says.

The drunkard man recently evicted sticks his head and shoulders in through the door.

"Thank you for your support and have a nice day, now," he says, slurring his words waving wildly to the crowd who ignores him. Then he turns quickly to go out again.

"Go then and commit senseless acts of kindness, random acts of beauty. Be pure in your thoughts. Be complete in your meditations. To thine own selves be true and you will not perish from this Earth," she says with her voice rising. Then she pauses one more time.

"I would like to end with all of us repeating the words given us by the greatest savior of all time, Jesus Christ, our Lord and what we now know as the Lord's Prayer. One time, please together as a people, as a nation united, as a world united," she says and then, folding her hands, she begins the prayer with an upward tilt of her head.

"Our father, who art in heaven, hallowed be thy name. Thy kingdom come, thy will be done on Earth as it is in heaven. Give us this day, our daily bread and forgive us our trespasses as we forgive those who trespass against us. Lead us not into temptation, but deliver us from evil. For thine is the kingdom and the power and glory for ever and ever. World without end, amen," she says, lowering her eyes.

The picture fades to black. A noisy Ford commercial follows in song, suggesting that driving a large heavy four wheel drive vehicle is the closest thing to heaven that any person could know.

CHAPTER 12

▼

OLD DOGS

In the Pentagon war room, the Generals, the Colonels, the Admirals, their staff are in attendance and seated at the large round table. Glasses of water are placed on the table in front of each of them. A wall-sized transparent Plexiglas screen has a map of the world etched upon the surface and is lit up at the opposite end of the room. Through the Plexiglas screen, we can see a bustling group of lesser rank military placing tiny symbols of ships, planes, submarines and missiles for the war chiefs to see their total world wide military assets.

Currently there is a large video screen on the wall with the fading image of the President on it, then followed by the Ford Commercial.

"Turn it off," commands the Chairman of the Joint Chiefs, Admiral James T. Clark the third. The screen goes dark and the men and women swivel in their chairs to face one another again.

"Disbanding the government, she said? Anyone else hear that or were my ears deceiving me," Admiral Clark addresses the room, calling the meeting to begin.

"I think we heard it too. I heard it," says quite a few of them in unison.

"All right. The question before us is; What are we going to do about this?" The Admiral begins.

"I think that we have to come up with a plan completely independent of the President's plans. She's a woman and she is speaking from her heart and that's fine. But we are all men here and we must speak from the head," Admiral Clark says.

A woman with the rank of Army Colonel seated three seats to his left timidly raises her hand to speak. The Admiral looks at her with a forced smile.

"I'm speaking metaphorically, Colonel Thomas. I'm not being sexist. I'm merely pointing out that war has traditionally been a male thing and we have to think like warriors. I'll try not to be so insensitive again. But, please don't any of you women bust my chops for speaking metaphorically. It will just waste our time and we have precious little of that to go around," the Admiral snaps pre-emptively.

"Aye, aye, sir," Colonel Thomas replies loud and clear. She turns her head looking for sympathy from the rest of the group but sees none.

"She's still the Commander in Chief," Captain Heimerding, Commander of the Navy Seals chimes in.

"True, but what is she if she disbands the government?" General Stewart, commander of the Army, asks succinctly.

"I'd say she's an ordinary citizen," says agent Beamer, bursting through the door and arriving late for the meeting.

"What do you know about all this, Beamer?" demands the Admiral, as soon as he recognizes his CIA liason officer.

"I know that this ship could only be from another planet. I know that the two people inside are a couple of do-gooders that have no military or political experience. I know that there's something about that vehicle they're not telling us because only one of them can enter it at a time and they have to be connected to this cowboy Doug Rink. And we know that they're planning to alter, perhaps forever, the human genome with this machine," replies Beamer sitting down and adjusting himself in his chair.

"This is pretty serious stuff," Beamer says from his chair and gazing around the room.

"He's a cowboy?" asks the Admiral.

"Yes, he was, up until the day this thing landed in his back yard. Now, he's a world conqueror. He's done more in the last three or four days than everything we could ever hope to do in decades," Beamer says.

"All right, Gentlemen, I'm looking for plans that are superior to the President's outright capitulation. I need options. Mr. Beamer. What do you suggest?" the Admiral demands sternly.

"Ok, we placed a laser tag on the object, Admiral. It will cause the Model Seven, I-350 Satellite to track their ship. No matter how fast it moves, or where it goes. We'll acquire it as soon as it appears somewhere else in the world," Beamer says. "Maybe, when we know where it is, we can deal with the situation appropriately," he says ominously.

"Deal with it in what way?" asks the Admiral, leaning forward a bit and resting on his forearms.

"I don't know sir. I'll leave that up to you, sir. I had intended to take the coward's way out and use this knowledge to get my friends and family on board to be evacuated if such a thing actually takes place. With foreknowledge of where this thing has landed, we will have a plane ready to go anywhere in the world and get in the chorus line, that is unless you folks here have a better plan," he replies honestly.

"I see. And what about the rest of us here in this room? Did you intend to bring us along on this little joy ride?" the Admiral asks, smiling menacingly.

"I had not considered that scenario until just this moment, sir," he says looking around the room and returning the smile. "At least I'm here sir at your disposal."

There's a nervous stirring in the room. A few of them mumble a phrase or two under their breath.

"So you're buying this little fairy tale that this ship is going to rescue a couple million of the poor and downtrodden just in the nick of time and whisk them off to safety and genetic immortality?" the Admiral asks, sarcastically.

"Yes sir, I do," Beamer replies. "After I paid a little visit to NASA the other day, I have no reason to doubt any of this information. In other words, the evidence is overwhelmingly on their side and until we see some evidence that this is some kind of scam, I think we have to play along with them, sir."

"Ok, would you care to explain to me how in the devil this damn thing is supposed to fit millions of people inside it, for God's sake," Admiral Clark is almost blue in the face from forcing the words out so quickly.

"Well sir, I don't know exactly except that the President says that there's a kind of dimensional anomaly in there and that the room inside is infinite in size. I have not had the opportunity to confirm or reject that claim, sir, but I intend to," Beamer tells him. "As a matter of fact sir, there are only four people who have been inside that ship. Mr. Rink, his girlfriend, who is with him now, President Williams, and the President of North Korea, Lee Kung Woo, who has not been seen since the day they took him inside."

"How did they do that?" The Admiral demands.

"I believe that it was a form of punishment. They literally crashed his party and just took him without resistance. Then, they cleaned up his arsenal, told his people that the regime was gone for good and that they should build a new democracy in his place. Uh, which, by the way, they are now engaged in doing. Woo has not been seen since," Beamer informs them.

"I see," says the Admiral. "So, if we try to take this thing out, suddenly we're the enemy and we're risking being rescued ourselves, if there needs to be a rescue at all. Yet, if we leave it alone, we're risking that this ship itself could be the cause of our problems and this supposed rescue is just a cover story to keep us sweet. Does that paint the picture fairly accurately, Mr. Beamer?"

"I can see the predicament you're in, yes sir, if that's what you mean?" says Beamer. "But please don't shoot the messenger, sir. I'm only giving you the information that I have at this time."

"Yes, and I appreciate that Mr. Beamer," the Admiral says, quietly, taking in the faces seated at the table. Then, he looks past them toward the Plexiglas strategy board.

Agent Beamer notices the Admiral's attention to the screen. "I have no doubt that you do, sir," says Beamer.

Heads nod as they all take a look at the awesome power represented by the hundreds of ships, planes, missiles and submarines clinging to the transparent wall, like so many toys ready to be played out on the battlefield of world conquest.

Beamer breaks the cardinal rule in these meetings and breaks the silence without being asked a question.

"Sir, I can also tell you that at this present time, he has completely neutralized the nuclear weapons in North Korea, Iran, Pakistan, India, China, and Russia. In Russia, it took him only a few hours to track down all their silo based missiles, mobile missiles, and submarine-based missiles and neutralize them all. At the current time, the entire Russian Army has abandoned their posts and are heading for their homes. The Chinese Army is doing the same. With no real weapons to manage, they don't know what to do with themselves. In the last two days he has completely restored law and order in Africa. All rebel forces in thirteen countries have been rounded up, arrested and or killed. As I arrived here, it appeared as if he was hunting down the French nuclear arsenal. If he sticks to his pattern, the next stop is Great Britain where he will neutralize all of their weapons. Then, sir, if he is left unchecked, I believe his next and possibly last stop will be here," Beamer says, pressing his finger onto the table for emphasis.

There is a long silence as Beamer finishes his briefing and leans back in his chair to take in the warrior's reaction.

"All right. That's good Beamer. It appears that Peace has broken out all over the world," Admiral Clark says, scowling.

"Yes sir," Beamer agrees. "It appears that way."

"The only question before us is, what the hell are we going to do about it?" the Admiral says loudly.

*   *   *   *

At the White House, President Williams has finished her speech and is trying to relax so that she can collect her thoughts about what to do next. She is sitting by the fireplace in the residence quarters of the White House having a glass of white wine. Her husband sits next to her, also with a drink in his hands, as the pair sits silently watching the flames lick the sides of the fireplace sending their warmth roomward.

"What do you think, Peter? Am I doing the right thing in trusting these people?" she asks her husband.

"I don't know Wendy. In your shoes, I think I'd be doing the same things. There are no guarantees that any of this is correct, but the astronomers are all confirming what they're saying. I just don't know what to tell you," he replies, sipping his drink.

The phone rings and Wendy gets up reluctantly to answer it.

"This is the President," she says speaking into the receiver.

There is a long silence. Then, she exclaims, "Oh my God, they can't do that!"

Running from the room, she yells something unintelligible to her husband, but he knows that it has something to do with the fact that all Hell has broken loose somewhere and that she is not likely to be back in time for dinner and that he will be left to eat alone again or with the staff. 'It's lonely at the top', he thinks to himself.

*   *   *   *

When the President arrives at the Pentagon, she descends the stairs of the Marine Helicopter and walks rapidly to the Staff entry way on the North side of the immense structure.

At the door, she is greeted by two Marines who challenge her as they have never done before.

"I'm the President of the United States, you fools. I'm the Commander in Chief. Get out of my way," she demands.

Having no instructions on what the protocol may be in such a situation, they give her ground and allow her to pass through the gates.

She storms into the War Room and all in attendance stand up to greet her amiably, but keeping a weather eye on the Admiral. The Admiral also stands and holds out his hand in greeting.

"Madam President," the Admiral begins. "I had no idea that you would be joining us today."

"I just heard about your little meeting of the Joint Chiefs. Why wasn't I informed?" she demands as a chair is presented to her by an aide. She refuses it and remains standing beside the table, tapping her foot on the marble floor so loudly everyone can hear it quite clearly.

Agent Beamer appears worried and attempts to keep a low profile.

"We didn't want to disturb you, thinking that the speech would have worn you out and we wanted you to get your rest. And by the way, congratulations are in order on that fine speech," the Admiral says as calmly as possible.

"It was intended for everyone, Admiral," the President says. "Where did I lose you?"

"Oh, I don't know, perhaps at the place where you said you were going to disband the government, that you no longer see any need for national security or a national defense. Yes, I'd say that's where I became just a wee bit concerned," he replies screwing up his face and just a touch of vitriol in his tone.

The President takes a moment to collect herself. Then, she looks toward the opposite wall where all of the country's military assets are being displayed. Then, she turns back to face the Admiral, bringing herself to within inches of his chair.

"Admiral. I am as of this moment, disbanding the Joint Chiefs of Staff. I order everyone in this room to resign their posts, to leave the building immediately and to disavow everything that has been said here. I will expect all of your resignations on my desk at eight hundred hours tomorrow. If I do not see all of your letters of resignation on my desk at that time, I'll have arrest warrants put out for all of you," the President tells them calmly but with all the authority she can muster. "Good night, gentlemen."

President Wendy Williams takes in as many faces as she can as she makes a stormy exit from the room.

A few get up to leave the room.

"Good day to you as well," says the Admiral, looking around the room. "Don't anyone leave!"

The warriors, to the man, sit back down in their seats except for Agent Beamer who excuses himself and heads for the door while all eyes focus on him.

"I'm sorry Admiral. She's still my Commander in Chief and she just gave me a direct order," he says, taking the door knob in his hand. Without looking back, he pulls the door closed behind him hearing only silence as he passes out into the hall.

*   *   *   *

Doug and Zora, having cleansed the European continent and most of the rest of the world of its nuclear weapons, glide over the English Channel at a slow cruise. Ahead of them are the White Cliffs of Dover. Doug can hear the famous song of World War Two ringing in his ears.

"I wanted to see England from the point of view of the German fighter pilots in World War II. They were met by the British right about here in the Battle of Britain. Churchill said it was 'their finest hour.' And "'Never had so few given so much for their country,'" Doug recalls the history.

"That must have been a very difficult time for the Brits," Zora says.

"Yes, and fantastically exciting to see their pilots going up in their little spitfires against the German Luftwaffe and their much greater numbers, faster planes, bigger guns and all that, and yet they won the day. Germany never did get a foothold on this place and then the war turned and the rest is history," Doug reminisces.

"Like most men, do you fantasize that you were alive at that time to take part in the dogfights?" Zora asks noticing the look on his face and taking his hand.

"Yes and no," he replies. "I would have wanted to fly in one of those spitfires, but I would not want to be risking my life like that. It must have felt like a video game except a real one where you don't get virtually killed, just killed. They lost hundreds of very brave young men in that war, brave men who could not make children or ever hold the ones that they had already made."

The white limestone cliffs disappear beneath them as they pass over the Channel. The buildings and the rivers of London can be seen rising over the horizon.

"Then there was the Roman Empire's futile attempt to conquer these people. They held a few cities for a while and now there are the ruins of Roman villas dotting the island, to be sure, but they never really conquered these people. The British tribes resisted every step of the way and finally threw the Roman Army out before they could be assimilated like all the other places of Europe. As a tribe, they're probably the most fiercely independent of every other tribe on the Earth," Doug muses.

"What are they going to do when we ask them to hand over their weapons?" Zora wonders aloud.

"I don't know. But, it should be an interesting debate," Doug replies.

"What's that over there?" Zora says pointing to a cloud of small dots above the horizon, moving rapidly and trailing long white clouds pointing directly at their position.

"I dunno," Doug answers. "Ula, what are those?"

"It's the British Air Force," Ula says.

"Are we under attack?" Doug asks out loud.

"No, it's an escort."

"An escort?" he says.

"Yes, it seems they want to cooperate. The planes are not armed," Ula informs him as he repeats the news to Zora.

"Wow," she says.

"They're trying to raise us by Radio," Doug says.

"Radio?" Zora asks.

"Yes, Ula has Radio, or I should say she is Radio when she needs to be," Doug says.

"Hello, Mr. Prime Minister," Doug says out loud. "It's Prime Minister Buckingham." He motions toward the ground below.

"Yes, sir. We can be there in five minutes," Doug says. Then to Zora, "He wants to have a 'Pow-Wow'. Says that the British people do not want to resist the disarmament and they want to merely have a bit of a chat before giving us their weapons." Doug uses his best British accent.

"That's a nice twist," she says with the same nasal intonations.

"Cheerio blokes. And here I was worrying they might turn out to be our biggest problem," Doug says.

Doug lowers the ship toward the city and within moments, they are resting a few hundred feet above the famous Number Ten Downing Street, the Prime Minister's official place of residence. Doug can't help but feel the redoubtable spirit of Winston Churchill rising up from the hard cobblestone road below to greet them.

"Well, would you like to accompany me, Madame?" Doug asks offering her his arm.

Doug lowers the ship slowly to the road below, giving a few cars and trucks time to drive away quickly so as to avoid being in the same space at the same time.

"Of course. Remember, wherever thou goest." She says.

"You don't suppose it could be a ploy, do you?" he asks her warily.

"No, I don't suppose, but shouldn't we take some precautions any way?" she replies.

"Yes, I'd say so," Doug says. "Ula, can you place your protective field around us?"

He nods his head at Zora. She smiles knowingly as they descend the stairs to the round entry room, squeeze themselves through the hull of the ship and onto the damp cobblestone street below.

The Prime Minister, Robert Buckingham appears at the door at the top of the landing to greet them. He is flanked by security guards and a few London Bobbies.

"Hello, Mr. Prime Minister. Thank you for the invitation," Doug says waving.

As the two men approach, they hold out their hands.

"I've looked forward to meeting you," the Prime Minister begins. "We've been following your progress around the world and we're very much impressed by what you've done. Please come in, won't you." He gestures toward the door being held open by a person Doug easily grasps is British Secret Service. The man is tall, wears a long dark coat and a scowl that seems to blanket the rest of his person.

Doug agrees and they escort him down a long hall and then into a large living room at the far end of the building.

Immediately upon sitting down, a cup of tea is thrust in front of him, Zora, the Prime Minister and a man in a business suit who remains unidentified stands off to the side next to the brick mantlepiece. The secret service agents remain in a dark corner refusing the tea.

"I'm sorry, may I introduce our equivalent of your Chair of the Joint Chiefs, Brigadier General Hornblower," Prime Minister Buckingham says pointing to a tall man in a handsome highly decorated uniform.

The two men stand up to shake hands. The General tugs at his jacket, smiling slightly.

"Glad to meet you, General," Doug says on his best behavior.

"Likewise, I'm sure," says the debonair General, who then sits down tugging at his pants leg and unbuttoning his coat.

"And I'm told you are Zora?" the Prime Minister begins addressing them both.

"Yes, my name is Zora. Pleasure meeting you," she says. The Prime Minister leans forward and takes her hand gently and holds it for a brief second. Doug makes an apology for not introducing her.

"I'm going to cut to the chase, Doug and Zora. Our intelligence services have noted recent events in North Korea. I think you started there, then, Pakistan,

India, China and then Russia and just recently your tour took you to France. They've predicted that your next stop would be the British Isles, and so here you are," The PM looks at them both sternly and then brightens.

"I don't want to put this meeting on the wrong foot. Although I do have to tell you that we were quite alarmed over here at Number Ten and we had many very heated discussions in this room. But, in the end, we realized that if every other nation on the planet has been disarmed completely by you, then, we have no real need to maintain these weapons ourselves, do we?" he asks rhetorically.

"I believe that's very sound logic, sir," Doug says quietly. In his mind, he's waiting for the other shoe to drop because cooperation of this kind is completely unprecedented. When it comes to power, people and nations usually try to hang on to it regardless of the logic of their position or their true military needs.

"What I'd like to know is whether or not you can give us a certain quid pro quo for our cooperation?" The PM states with his eyes narrowing.

"I don't know what you mean, sir" says Doug, sensing the Brigadier tensing up a bit. But, he remains quietly in his seat.

"Well, what I'm saying is that when you have finished here, you will go to America and complete your mission, won't you?" the PM asks.

"Yes, that's our intent," Doug says.

"And after you have disarmed the United States, do you then plan to start the evacuation operation?" the PM asks politely.

"Yes, that's the plan. Our mission is to rid the world of its weapons of mass destruction and then we'll see if that's enough to launch the rescue," Doug replies.

"Yes, the rescue," the PM says, looking over at the General. "Since you're in direct contact with this alien civilization and since they are obviously giving you your lead, here's what we'd like to know. If we cooperate, we would like to have some assurances that at least a few of us in Government would be given a pass onto the evacuation operation and that we be allowed to bring along our families." He says, only partly embarrassed.

"I don't know. It wouldn't be fair to bend the rules too much. However, the object of this whole mission is a convergence with the best genetics we have available. I think by showing the cooperation you mention that we could make the case that the British people did not resist and in fact cooperated and that this might be the best kind of action our species could take. I think that might be very persuasive. We could notify you of our next stop perhaps and if you could get to it in time, we'd let you in, and there will be at least one stop in the British Isles. I can assure you of that," Doug tells him happily.

"Well, that's good. Yes, I think that would do nicely. You see General, you were worried about nothing really," the PM says, looking at the Brigadier again who remains regarding them sternly.

"Yes, well, that's all very good indeed, but you see it would be very enlightening to me and others in my employ if you were to tell us how you have the bottle to leave that ship of yours. Aren't you worried that we might overpower you and take the ship from your control?" the General says ominously.

"The bottle? Doug asks, feigning unrecognition of the English vernacular.

"The courage, the nerve" the PM says quietly and smiling.

"The balls," the Brigadier says.

"I see," says Doug looking the General squarely in the face. "Well, you see that represents a bit of a problem for you, doesn't it? If you try to overpower us, it hardly shows any good faith at all and there goes your quid pro quo right out the window. If, on the other hand, you trust in the fact that we are just as protected by the ship in this area as we would be on board and you let us continue unharmed, then, you all stand a good chance of being rescued and brought on board the ship as good cooperative citizens. So, you're kind of caught on the horns of a dilemma, wrapped in problem, cloaked in an enigma, aren't you?"

Doug feels Winston Churchill's words flowing through him.

"Yes, I would say you have the upper hand, Mr. Rink. Let me ask you something, I hear that you were a cowboy before this whole thing came about, is that correct?" the Brigadier asks, politely changing the subject.

"You bet. Your information is good. Who's been telling you about me? I bet it's those CIA chaps. You chaps work pretty closely, don't you?" Doug replies.

"And as a cowboy, I'd wager that you spend a good deal of time in the bunkhouse playing a few hands of poker while you wait for those cows to come home, or whatever it is you do, am I right?" the General asks, distinctly ignoring his question.

"I've played a few hands of poker in my time, sure," Doug says, just as coolly and knowing exactly where this bloke is going. "You think I'm bluffing?"

"I don't know you well enough yet, Mr. Rink, however, would it interest you to know that while we have been talking, our military have completely dismantled your ship and it is now in our possession many miles from this place?" the General says with a smirk.

"Nice try, General and yes, it would interest me to know that and it would shock me no end," Doug replies smartly. "If it were true. But you see, General, I'm in communication with the ship at this very moment and now I'm going to show you something."

"Ula," he says to the air in front of his face.

"Mr. Rink, wait, please!" Prime Minister Buckingham, jumps to his feet in alarm.

"Ula, I would like you to show the General out, please," Doug says to the air. "He won't be needed any more."

Suddenly the General is yanked from his chair and tossed around like a rag doll. His body is bounced up and down a few times as if he's being pulled by an invisible cable tied to his neck. His efforts to resist are ludicrous and his voice is muffled as he tries to find the right words, but only strange sounds come out.

Doug and Zora and the PM are amused to see him trundled off through the door, down the hall, out into the street. Onlookers are surprised to see the Brigadier rushed out of the building, slamming himself into a black taxi cab and then driven away with no driver in sight, the General sitting helplessly in the back seat.

"Now, let's talk about how you will present your nuclear weapons for our destruction," Doug says turning to look at a horrified and frozen Prime Minister.

The Secret Service agent has opened his coat and has his hand on his weapon.

Prime Minister Buckingham waves his hand to prevent any further action on his part.

"Time's a wastin'," Doug says coolly. The Prime Minister sits back down in his chair and calls for his assistant Nathaniel.

Nathaniel comes into the room with a large black leather briefcase.

"Mr. Rink, I assume that we still have a deal?" the PM asks shyly. "I hope you won't let one action by one individual to hinder our…"

"We still have a deal," Doug replies, cutting him off.

"Nathaniel, show Mr. Rink where we keep the Cruise Missiles, the Tomahawks, the mobile missiles, as well as the silos," the PM instructs the man.

"I don't need to see them, Mr. Buckingham. We already know where they are. But it would be helpful and save a great deal of time if you could have everything in one place within twenty four hours," Doug says.

"Well, we'll just have to comply, won't we?" the PM declares.

"Yes, that would be nice," Doug says.

"Zora, why don't you and I take a little tour of the city while we wait," he says taking her hand and helping her out of her chair. "I've never been to London and I've always wanted to see it."

"Let us know when you've completed your part of the bargain, Mr. Prime Minister and we'll keep ours," Doug says to the PM as Doug and Zora stand to take their leave.

"Yes sir," the PM says quietly with a smile. "Let me see you out."

"Don't bother, we can see ourselves out," he says as Doug takes Zora and leads her from the room.

They walk down the hall silently exchanging glances and then out into the chill of the London air. The ship sits at the bottom of the stairs in the middle of the street exactly where they left it. There are a few men in trench coats combing the skin of the ship with strange looking hand held devices.

"Looking for buried treasure?" Doug taunts them.

As the pair approaches the ship, Doug has to push a couple of them gently out of the way. Amidst their protests, he quickly locks arms with Zora, leads them through the skin of the ship and they both disappear. Just as suddenly, the ship disappears before the men who are still standing around it in great surprise.

"Holy Mother of Mary," one of them shouts. The crowd grown large enough to be held back by a police line are startled and quickly run away in panic.

Doug and Zora can survey the scene in the views screens as the ship pulls away.

"I think Churchill was wrong," Doug says. "This is their finest hour."

Zora looks at him, smiles and gives him a big hug.

CHAPTER 13

▼

FALL OUT

Doug takes the ship over Washington D.C. and brings it to a rest a few hundred feet in the air above the Capital Mall, the scene of his first visit here. People in the park below stop their exercising, jogging, tennis, dog walking, and instead begin to congregate in small groups in heated discussions. Everyone has heard the speech by the President the evening before and so today, the topic of discussion is whether or not the President is crazy and if not, where and when this supposed evacuation will take place. It's a scene being repeated in cities and towns all over the world.

Some gathered here believe the evacuation of the planet is to begin here, since it is only logical. When they see the egg ship in the sky above them, this confirms the theory, so many people are soon calling on their cell phones to alert their relatives and friends to let them know that the egg ship is there in the sky above them. Soon, the crowd slowly begins to swell to massive proportions.

"Well, look they're all down there ready to leave," Zora says as they watch the growing crowd below.

"Well, I'm not prepared to begin the evacuation yet," Doug says quietly.

"And we haven't dealt with the American weapons yet," Zora adds.

"Yes, I know. I've asked Ula and she tells me that this one could go a little differently than the rest," Doug says.

"Oh, in what way?" Zora Asks.

"Since the United States is the last country to possess these things, it would be best if they voluntarily surrender them to us like the British did. The precedent has been set and there is no longer any threat from any other nation. So, logic dictates that those in control of them should see the lack of any need for these horrible things and gladly hand them over," Doug says.

"And if they don't?" Zora asks.

"If they don't, we're in a whole peck of trouble," Doug says.

"Yes, and that's trouble with a capital 'T'," Zora agrees.

Doug takes a minute to think. Then, an idea hits him.

"I've got it. So, I say we give them a little more time to collect their thoughts while we go find someone to help in the roundup," Doug says.

"The roundup? Is that what we're calling it now?" She says laughing.

"Yep. Hey, I'm a cowboy, whad'ya expect me to call it, pardner?" He replies.

"Well, who do you have in mind?" she asks.

"I have some cowpoke friends who will know just how to handle this," Doug replies.

*   *   *   *

The Pentagon War Room is empty save for a few staffers who are sitting at the table sipping coffee. Suddenly, Marine Staff Sargent, Rick Pohl rushes in breathlessly.

"Hey, clear the room! The brass are back," he yells. The three staffers look at each other and hurriedly pick up their coffee and snacks and bolt from the room just as the first Chiefs are arriving.

"What's going on?" Lt. Commander Mark Mitchell asks entering the room carefully.

"The egg thing has just been spotted over Washington, sir" Sargent Pohl informs him.

"Where?" asks another.

"It's hanging over the Mall," another one says.

The group gathers to take their places each asking the same questions over and over of each another.

Finally Admiral Clark and his staff arrive. The room settles down as he takes his seat at the head of the table.

"Well, I suppose you've all heard, the egg thing has arrived and is sitting two hundred and fifty feet above the Capitol Mall," the Admiral begins glancing at notes that an aide has just placed on the table before him.

The same aide comes rushing back into the room and whispers into the Admiral's ear.

"It now appears that the ship has just disappeared," he informs them with one lip turning up at the corner.

"Well, since we've all been called to order, we might as well discuss the situation again," the Admiral says.

"Turning it over in my mind last night, I thought it might be best to list all the known facts in this case. Anyone have any objections to that?" he asks.

There are none.

"All right, hearing none, I'll put forth all the facts that I feel we know to be true. Then, I want to hear from the rest of you and I want you to give me facts that you know to be true or contest the facts I'm going to list as true. Together, this brain trust of ours should be able to come up with an appropriate course of action," he says.

"First, we know that all the rest of the world has been disarmed. At least that's what our intelligence has told us. The spy satellites can find no trace of any armed warheads or delivery systems capable of any kind of mass destruction," the Admiral says and then pauses briefly.

"Second, the Brits have just voluntarily given up their nukes yesterday and the day before. They flew all their warheads to a central location in the middle of England. This egg thing hovered over them for a few minutes, and they simply had no fissile material in them any longer. How they did that, remains a mystery. Third, we know that the ship has arrived here this morning. Following their path around the world, we can assume that our own weapons will be targeted next," he says.

"Do we know that for a fact, Admiral?" Colonel Baird, USAF interrupts him.

"I said we can assume. But, I'm going to assume that so much that I'd say we know that for a fact! There have been no official demands made yet, but why else would they come here? Isn't it obvious after North Korea, then Iran, then, Pakistan, then India then France, then the Brits are all disarmed? Or am I missing something?" the Admiral declares loudly and with implied disdain for anyone who doesn't see things with the same clarity and perspective.

"You may be right, sir," Colonel Baird says humbly. The others feel sorry for him and remain quiet.

"Next is the fact that the President seems to go along with the story that this egg thing is the only hope for civilization because this egg ship is the only possibility for any evacuation of civilians, even if only a few million of us. And that in order for the ship to take us on board, we are supposed to cleanse ourselves of our violent tendencies, our weapons and so forth. How the Hell all these people are supposed to fit in this thing, we're supposed to take on faith," he says and then concludes for emphasis. "Have I presented all the facts?"

"You have not mentioned that the President has ordered us to resign and to shut down as a body effective today," says Colonel Thomas, the female Air Force General.

"Ah yes, and that brings me to the next order of business. I want a show of hands of everyone in this room who has followed that order and presented the President with their resignations," the Admiral demands.

One hand goes up in the air. It is the hand of General Thomas.

"Very good, General. I am now ordering you to leave this room. Since you are no longer an active member of the armed forces, you are no longer qualified to sit on this committee," the Admiral says with a scowl. He leans back in his chair and waits for her reaction.

General Thomas stands at attention and turns to leave the room obediently.

"May God have mercy on you and give you guidance in this hour of need," she says as she makes her exit from the room.

"Amen," the Admiral breathes heavily as she goes out. Then, to his intercom he says, "Make sure that the General is escorted from the building. Confiscate her security badge and her weapon and then make sure she is escorted from the building. If she resists, shoot her!"

"Now," he continues. "I need to know if there is anyone else in this room who plans to abandon this ship. I must tell you that the President is probably at the Attorney General's office at this moment preparing the warrants for our arrest. As you may recall from your history books, there were also arrest warrants issued for Thomas Jefferson, Benjamin Franklin, John Adams, James Madison and the rest of the brave souls whom we regard today as the greatest heroes of all time."

There is no reaction from the room except for a few barely audible words from a Marine Colonel sitting in the back of the room.

"What's that?" the Admiral looks for the author of the mumbling.

"I was thinking sir, you left out Patrick Henry who said, "I know not what others may do here, but as for me, give me liberty or give me death," the Marine Colonel says methodically and clearly.

Looking down at his hands, the Admiral seems to dwell on these words for an agonizingly long interval.

"Thank you Colonel. Seeing no hands and hearing no objections, I am going to assume that our deliberations will be as one," he says. "And as General Thomas so eloquently put it, may God give us the guidance that we may require."

"Gentlemen, I am hereby declaring Marshall Law in the United States of America. The President, having declared that she is closing the government is no longer the Commander in Chief. I am. I want you to go to your posts and alert all operations commanders that we are on Defcom One," he says sternly and forcefully.

There is a brief silence in the room. The Admiral wonders whether or not he will get their support. Then, the warriors, get up one by one, some of them reluctantly, and leave the room as ordered.

*　　*　　*　　*

In Colorado, Doug and Zora have landed the ship in the middle of the yard where they brand the animals at his former employer's ranch, the 'Circle D'. He and Zora can see the faces of the other hands as they are sitting on the fence and on tree stumps having their lunch break. A few cows and horses roam around the outside of the corral begging for attention from the men.

As the ship draws nearer, the cowboys look up and point in total shock and surprise. Doug is careful to bring the ship in very slowly so to not spook the animals still completely oblivious to the egg shape silently descending from the clouds.

When the ship lands in the dusty yard, the men and animals begin to panic. They run around the yard crashing into one another in their excitement.

Then, they hear a familiar voice coming from the side of the giant egg.

"Don't panic, my friends. It's me, Doug Rink, come back to save you slobs from the folding of the universe. Have no fear. Doug and Zora are here," Doug says using the loud speaker system he's recently discovered as part of the ship's accessories.

The men slowly calm down and then gather around expecting to see their old friend emerge. And when Zora comes out first, they applaud, stomp their feet and shout noisily. They know that Doug can't be far behind. Zora is smiling broadly and waves to the men.

Doug appears from the skin of the ship holding Zora's hand. He takes a bow at the applause he's getting.

"Hey, buddy," one of the men, Hank yells over the din. "We've been wondering what the Hell happened to you."

"Yeah well," Doug replies shaking their hands. "I've been kind of busy. How are you guys doin'?"

"We're OK, but we could have used the extra hand," Charlie says. "How you been? You been away up in that hot air balloon all this time?"

"Oh yeah. It's some hot air balloon all right. It's taken us around the universe and we've seen a few things. Say, you guys look mighty good to me," Doug says still shaking hands all around and getting numerous pats on the back.

"Yeah, we thought so. The FBI's been here. They asked a whole pack of questions. So we told 'em you were a scoundrel and a drug fiend." Dan says, with a smile.

"You're kidding, right? You didn't tell them about the drugs, did you?" Doug says, playing along.

"Yeah, I'm kidding. But, they were very interested in your political views and you know, we had to tell 'em we didn't know about any. You got any political views?" Sam, the cook, asks him.

"God forbid," Doug says.

They all have a good laugh.

"Listen guys. I'm in a bit of a jam, as you know. You hear the President's speech last night?" he begins changing the tone of their reunion.

"Yes, we did," they all agree verbally and nod their heads.

"Well, everything she said was true. There is a great astronomical thing on its way here and we have a little less than three months to round up as many people as we can and get them onto this ship here before it arrives," he tells them.

"That there ship doesn't look large enough to hold more than you and us, Doug," Hank remarks, gesturing at the egg sitting calmly next to them on the ground.

"Yes, well, I want to give you guys a little tour. You're still on your lunch break, right?" Doug asks.

"Yep, that's right," Dan answers for the group.

"Ok, well I don't guess Mr. Davenport will mind. Let's get you guys on board and then I have to ask you all to help with the biggest roundup of your lives," Doug says, taking Zora's hand who then holds out her hand to Sam, the closest one to her and motions for the men to follow.

"See, first you have to know, this here egg ship is a living thing. And the way it works is that she knows me and Zora and we have the only guest passes through the door. But, if you're hooked up with us, you're good to go. So, you have to link arms with one of us in order to get in," he informs them as they all follow instructions, linking their arms as Doug and Zora slowly disappear like ghosts through the mystifying hull of the ship.

One of the men, Ben, a younger man in his twenties hangs back and refuses to hook arms, with a frightened grin.

"Look at the way that thing is moving. Ahh, fellas, I don't know about this," he says, shaking his head.

Hank runs around to the end of the line and grabs his arm and hooks him up to the man on the end.

"Get with the program, son. Don't you know who you can trust?" Dan admonishes him, then retaking his own place in line, they all disappear one by one inside the ship.

*   *   *   *

The next morning at the White House, President Williams is seated at her desk. She is wearing a pair of bluejeans and sneakers. She is gazing at a room full of her advisors. Seated before her is Secretary of State John Seymour, Secretary of Defense, Nathaniel Bourne, National Security Advisor, Steven Bradford, Chief of Staff, Bob Kramer, and her life long friend Gerold Portnoy, Ambassador to the United Nations, and CIA agent Jack Beamer. Several other staffers and Deputies are standing behind them with their notepads in hand.

"I'm looking for advice, gentlemen, not sympathy. When they declared Martial Law they took away all my powers to order them to do anything. The Pentagon now has full control of this government. We have nothing to hold over their heads. The greatest power I had was to order their resignations and they refused, all except one. Admiral Clark is now the Commander-In-Chief they have all their weapons intact. I've spoken with Doug this morning and he says that they want this final disarmament to be voluntary as the British have done. So, we're caught between a rock and a hard place. I need options," she tells the men who sit quietly listening intently.

Jack Beamer has a cup of coffee in his hand. He has been quietly sipping the steaming liquid while she details their dilemma for the group.

"Too bad we don't have a D.A.I. the Department of Alien Invasions," he says with an impertinent smile.

She gives him a look of complete disdain. The others reflect her mood.

"Sorry," Jack says. "I'm just trying to lighten the mood a little. Look, I know Admiral Clark. I've worked with him on several missions. He's a good man. You have to understand the military mind. They know nothing that isn't taught at a military school. Since early childhood, they've been drilled, marched up and down the parade grounds over there at West Point. They've been raised and hazed and screwed, glued and tattooed. They've had to endure all that military discipline crap all their lives. You know the motto, 'honor, duty, country'. And to what end, so that this country has a trained class of soldiers whose only motivation in life is to protect their country. They're like junk yard dogs. They know how to bark and scare away the intruders and when danger threatens will give up their lives for their masters. That's the programming we subject them to. It's only natural that they would react this way."

The President, who has been listening to Jack, appears calm as she takes a sip of her coffee. She swallows, shakes her head at the cup, still too hot. Jack wants to go on, but she holds up her hand.

"You're right of course. Perhaps there's a way we can reason with this mentality. We appeal to that very same sense of duty, right? They all took an oath to defend and protect the Constitution of the United States. Jack, do you think Clark would respond to the demand that he live up to his oath?" she asks quietly.

"I don't know. I doubt it. After you suggested disbanding the government, the Admiral probably feels he's legally on notice that there is no Constitution to defend," he replies.

"That was a regrettable choice of words, Wendy," her friend Jerry interjects.

"I know, Jerry. Believe me, I know that now. I was speaking from my heart and not my head. I wanted people to realize the severity of their situation and start to think for themselves. But, I chose the wrong words to do that. You're one hundred percent correct about that. But what's done is done. Can we unring that bell? Any thoughts on that?" she pleads.

There is a long silence in the room.

Then, Jack Beamer seems to have an idea. "How about this? You steal his thunder. You go on TV again tonight. Tell the American people that you have declared a state of Martial Law and that you are asking the people to obey the authorities. It hasn't leaked out to the press as yet what they're doing over there. Admiral Clark will want to keep his shadow government a secret for as long as he can, I'm sure. So far, no one knows about it except the people in this room. So, you have a window of opportunity."

"That's good, Jack," she says with the hint of a smile prying at her lips. "I like it. Under these circumstances, the average man on the street is worried, very worried and they're beginning to panic. It's like bringing in the National Guard to a disaster area to guard against looting and the like. Anyone have any better ideas?"

"No, that's good. It gives you some power over them because the people will be behind you and perceive them as following your lead," Steven Bradford tells her.

"That's right, and with a little luck, they'll go along with it. They do not want to be seen as traitors. By stealing their thunder, like Jack says, it's saying that we're all still working as a team. United we stand and all that," says Jerry Portnoy.

"All right. I'll do that," she says raising her head and brightening considerably. "I concur. Get the media people back in here for another speech tonight."

"Yes, ma'am," Kramer replies. Somewhat startled, he grabs a staffer and the pair trot out of the room briskly.

"Jack, you're the one who got the idea. I need more from you. I need ways to counteract their powers just in case they don't play along. Would you be willing to go back in there and be my eyes and ears?" she asks.

"I would Madam President, gladly, however, they wouldn't trust me. They know I'm on the other team. But, there might be another way," he tells her hopefully.

"Spit it out, man," she orders.

"Ok, I'm just thinking that if I could get my team together and we could re-program the I-350 spy satellite, we might have a chance. Right now, it's in their control. But if I we can talk to it and take control we could change the passwords and it would take them twenty years to hack it. Their main objective is to destroy the egg. If they can't find it, they can't destroy it," he says raising her mood even further with every word.

"That's good, Jack. You're the man. Make it so. Get out of here now! You have my people for anything you need. Report back to me with any developments. I'll need to know," she says, her eyes sparkling.

"Yes, ma'am," Jack says as he excuses himself and leaves the oval office nodding at the rest of the group as he goes. They stand up to see him leave and give him some encouragement.

The President seems a bit more relaxed. At last she has a battle plan. Her advisors are still in an enthusiastic mood and they look to her for her next set of orders.

"All right, gentlemen. Batten down the hatches. We're in for the fight of our lives. Get to your posts and give me some covering fire," she says almost happily.

"Yes ma'am," Her friend Jerry expresses their common emotions as they wander out leaving her alone in the room.

CHAPTER 14

▼

THE NEW WORLD ORDER

Inside the ship, Doug's pals are relaxing in the lower entry room or the 'hub' as Doug likes to call it. Doug and Zora are upstairs in the control room watching the view screen. On them, they can see large billowing clouds of a Colorado winter storm system rolling past overhead.

"I think it's a good idea, Doug," Zora says. "I think they're right. The only way to do this is with a cattle pen."

"The way we round up the herd and send 'em to market," Doug says.

"And the same way they herd the people into the rides at Disneyland." Zora says.

"Yep. I can't think of a better way," Doug agrees. "I know exactly where to find that equipment. I'm sure I can get Mr. Davenport's permission to use his cattle pens."

Just then, the view of the clouds on their view screens changes to that of the Oval Office. The President is seated at her desk and Jack Beamer is seated across the desk from her and to the left.

"Hello, Madam President," Doug says. "This is a nice surprise."

Zora appears to be surprised as well.

"Hello Doug, I didn't have time to tell you but Ula gave me the knowledge of how to reach you if I thought of something important to bring to you over there. Where are you, by the way?" The President asks.

"Oh, I see. And, oh yeah, we're in Colorado at the moment. I've come back to enlist my old ranch hands into helping us with the round-up," Doug answers.

"Ok, that's good. And when do you think you'll be starting the evacuation," The President asks.

"We were just about to go get the equipment we will need and then I was going to start perhaps a little later today," he replies.

"What about the weapons. Aren't you concerned about them any more?" Wendy asks.

"Well, actually, I'm not. I have faith in the American spirit of truth, justice, fair play and all that. Call me a Pollyanna if you want. But, I'm going with that for now," Doug replies.

"Yes, I thought as much and I hope you're right. Well, I called, or uh, connected with you, to tell you that something is not going very well. The Joint Chiefs have declared Martial Law and they are not responding to my orders. They are off the reservation, so to speak. And, I don't know what to do about it exactly," the President says.

"Yes, I know. I believe their theory is that this ship is the cause of the folding in the universe, so their instinct is to protect," Doug answers.

"Yes, that's exactly what Beamer here tells me. Isn't that amazing that you would both have the same assessment?" she says.

"Uh, yes, amazing," Doug says. "Hello, Jack, nice to meet you." The view screens can take in the whole room of people seated behind the President.

"Hello Mr. Rink," Beamer replies courteously.

"So you're on our side now?" Doug asks rhetorically.

"Uh, yes, yes, indeed, Mr. Rink." Beamer says. "I'd like to congratulate you on all your recent accomplishments. You've done in three or four days what would have taken us decades at the agency."

Doug seems amused at this statement but says nothing in reply.

"I also have to tell you that Agent Beamer has confided in me that the Pentagon has control of a spy satellite known as the Model Seven, I-350. Jack actually placed some kind of laser pointer from the Satellite onto your ship the night of the dinner and it can locate you wherever you go," the President says.

"I see. Well, thanks Mr. Beamer for that kindness. It's good to know we can't get lonely. We'll have to see how that shakes out won't we?" Doug replies.

"Yes, um, you're welcome. I should also say that my intention, when I did it, was only to secure a pass for my friends when the time came. I meant no harm," Beamer says.

"That's ok, Mr. Beamer," Doug says. "I'm sure it's all meant to be."

"Well, the President has given me permission to round up my team and see if we can regain control of the thing," Beamer says hopefully.

"That's good," Doug replies.

"So, how do you and Ula plan to handle this?" the President asks, returning to the point of her call.

"I don't know exactly, but I know that events have taken us to the point exactly where Ula wants us to be. Our genetic code can and must be changed by our own actions at this point in time. There's no turning back. You know all this Wendy. You said it so perfectly in your speech. Choices are going to be made and they have to be the right ones. The key is going to have to fit the lock, if you catch my drift, or else the door will not open," Doug muses.

"Yes, I can see that," the President says. "Well, Jack and I have worked out a plan where the public will believe I'm cooperating with the Pentagon. I wanted you to know that we are forced into this, because if I fight them, I'm isolated and with no powers to persuade anyone to do anything."

"Yes, I understand. You do whatever you think is necessary Wendy. Make your choices, but please remember to make them in full knowledge of what's at stake. I know you don't mind being reminded, even I have to remind myself every five minutes and I've got Ula sitting here right next to me all the time," Doug says.

"Yes, I understand. No problem. I will do my best," the President says preparing to break the link. "Now that you have this information, I have to go to work."

"Wait a moment, Wendy. Ula has just spoken to me," Doug tells her.

"What is it?" the President asks, leaning forward.

"She says 'In God we trust'. She just wanted you to know that," Doug says.

"Yes, that's what's on the money," the President says with a twinkle in her eye.

Doug looks at Zora as the President's image fades away and the view screen alternately shows light and dark from the storm clouds that are still overhead.

"That was nice of her to call," Doug says to Zora.

"Yes, it certainly was. But she seemed a bit worried, don't you think?" asks Zora.

"Yeah, well, aren't we all?" Doug says. "Come on, let's go get the boys and get this show on the road.

Doug takes Zora by the hand and leads her down the stairwell to meet his friends once again who are all seated and quietly staring off into space as if in a stupor.

"Well, how'd you guys like the tour?" he asks them.

"Wow," Hank says finally. They all seem to echo the same reaction.

"Well, the time has come to make your decision. Everyone who wants to stay, can stay. If you choose not to help us out here, that's ok and you can simply leave now," Doug tells the group.

"What about our families, Doug?" Dan Jamieson asks.

"Good question, Dan. If you decide to come along in this last round-up, they will be given a pass to get on board without question. We'll make a special pick-up just for them. If you choose not to help but to remain back with them, there are no guarantees. You would be taking your chances along with everyone else. There's a risk that things go awry even though I promise to do my best to pick you all up because you're my friends. But, I don't know if there will be time in the end. This kind of thing has never happened before. But, if you lend a hand now, we will definitely make sure we get them in time," Doug replies.

"That's fine with me," Dan says, looking at the others. "I'm in."

One by one, they stoically signify the same choice.

Just then, from outside, they can hear a voice shouting at them very loudly amplified.

"This is the F.B.I." the voice is saying. "We need you to come out with your hands up! You are completely surrounded. And we have planes in the air ready to attack you if you try to lift off."

"Lift off?" Doug says to the group with a smile? They think this is some kind of rocket ship."

"Doug, where are you going?" Zora asks him anxiously.

"I have to see what this is all about. Don't worry, Darlin. This is child's play," Doug comforts her and then steps briskly through the hull of the ship and into the sunlight.

"What say you gentlemen?" Doug says shielding his eyes from the bright sunlight.

Doug can see hundreds of men dressed in dark suits all around the yard, some with blue vinyl jackets, and they're all pointing rifles or handguns directly at him with extreme menace in their eyes.

"Put your hands on your head," the voice with the bull horn demands.

"Sorry fellas. Don't get excited. We're not breaking any laws here, are we?" Doug says amicably while raising his hands.

"Get on your knees," the voice demands.

"Now that's where I am going to have to draw the line fellas. We're not doing anything wrong and whoever sent you here knows that we're not doing anything wrong," Doug says forcefully.

Just then, loud explosive blasts ring out from all directions. Not caring for his response, the agents universally unload their weapons on him. The projectiles all arrive at roughly the same time.

Doug instinctively holds out his hands to protect his face. The hundreds of rounds come to a complete stop a few feet from his face and chest and then fall harmlessly to the ground by his feet.

The FBI agents are stunned, as is Doug. To a man, they are standing completely frozen, all having witnessed the same event. Doug opens his eyes slowly.

Then, he is amused and lowers his hands while waiting for their next move. He can now identify the man with the bullhorn off to his left. They seem to be discussing their next moves.

"I'm ordering you to surrender to us. We will hold our fire, if you will comply with my order to surrender," the voice says after a long interval.

"You can fire on me all you want. You're just wasting perfectly fine government property. I might as well tell you now that I'm not going to surrender to you. However, I am now demanding that you surrender to me, sir. Yes, you, the one with the bull horn. I would like you to come over here and let's just talk this out, shall we?" Doug says.

There's another long pause, more discussions. Then, "Hold your fire men. I'm going in," he announces.

Doug looks up to see two fighter jets swoop by so low that their engine exhaust sets fire to the tops of the trees.

"Wow, you brought a lot of fire power here today," Doug says. "What did you hope to accomplish with all that?"

The agent in charge, Local Field Director George Revette, is carrying his bullhorn as he approaches.

"I'm unarmed," he says to Doug through the bull horn, shaking nervously in his hand.

"Please, sir, drop the bull horn," Doug says as the man draws closer to him.

"You're Doug Rink," Revette asks.

"That's right. I'm him. Now, what's all this stuff about being under arrest?" Doug asks directly.

"I have my orders, Mr. Rink. I'm asking that you come along peacefully. You can see that there is no hope of escape," Revette says, pointing up to the sky and the two jets circling overhead in the clouds. Doug can see two helicopters also hovering just above the tree tops a few hundred feet away.

"What did you say your name is?" Doug asks, looking the man in the eyes.

"My name is George Revette. I'm the agent in charge. I'm under orders to bring you to Washington for questioning," he replies.

"I see. Well, I was just there. I've answered all their questions. And how did you expect me to answer questions with a hundred and fifty bullets in my chest?" Doug asks, smiling.

"I'm sorry about that. I did not authorize that. The men are spooked by this assignment. They don't know what this thing is, what it can do, and so they're a bit on edge," Agent Revette says.

"Yeah right, so they just open up," Doug says. "That's a fine way to break the ice, isn't it?" Doug pauses and looks past Revette and smiles at the group of agents who can only look back in confusion.

"I need you to lean forward right now," Doug whispers very softly.

"What?" Revette asks, leaning forward to hear Doug's whispered words more clearly.

Doug grabs the man by the back of his collar and leaps through the skin of the ship taking Revette with him. Outside they can hear the fusillade of bullets as hundreds of weapons are discharged again. This time, the noise continues for several seconds, then stops.

Doug and Agent Revette land in a heap on the floor of the ship in front of the others.

Zora, Hank and Dan, who have been watching the events from upstairs now come down and remain in the stair well looking on.

"Doug, what the Hell are you doing?" Dan asks.

"Ok Mr. Revette. I'm now officially inviting you to join us for a while," Doug tells the man, slapping the dust from his pants.

"Am I your hostage, then?" Revette asks, noticing the other men for the first time.

"No, of course not. I wouldn't use those words exactly. However, you can consider yourself a hostage if you like," Doug replies.

"Well, if I'm not a hostage, what am I doing here?" Revette asks.

"Well, we'll just have to see about that. I suddenly got this crazy notion to have you join our band of merry men. So, I'll have to go upstairs and consult with upper level management about my decision," he says smiling. "Relax. These are my friends. You'll like them."

Revette glances at the men and then suddenly dives for the door directly behind him in a fruitless effort to escape. He bounces off the wall of the ship with a dull thud and lands on the floor again. The cowboys find this pretty amusing.

"Oh, we were about to warn you. You have to say the magic words," Dan tells him still laughing.

Doug shakes his head and works his way up the stair well, places the cowboy hat on his head and sits down.

*   *   *   *

At the Pentagon War Room, Admiral Clark is listening to a presentation from his Commander of Special Forces, General Tommy Burton who is standing in front of the clear glass wall map.

"We feel that our readiness is at about eighty five percent right at this moment. If you can give us another twenty four to forty eight hours, we can be at one hundred percent, Admiral," Burton says.

"All right. Thank you General," Admiral Clark tells him.

"What about the submarine missile command?" Clark asks looking down the table to his Commander of Naval warfare, Admiral John Stark.

"We're at full readiness at all times, sir," Admiral Stark snaps loud and clear, standing to deliver the words and then sitting back down.

"And the Air Force Missile Command, NORAD and SAC. What's their status?" Admiral Clark directs his gaze to Air Force General Richard Stewart, sitting opposite Admiral Stark.

"We can have keys in place and ready to launch at your command, Admiral," General Stewart says without standing up.

"Very good, gentlemen. I suggest we break for dinner. When we return, we will hear from FBI Director Slayton. He's run a special operation for me to test our defenses. I'm hoping to hear some good news from him at any moment," the Admiral says, rising from his chair.

Just then, an aide steps into the room and walks up to the Admiral briskly then whispers something in his ear.

The Admiral is highly displeased to hear the man's report. He sits back down and everyone at the table is forced to do the same.

"I'm sorry to tell you that our little reconnaissance mission has failed. I had word earlier that the FBI had surrounded the egg when it arrived at Mr. Rink's former place of employment, a Circle D Ranch, in Colorado" Admiral Clark begins. "They failed to make any arrests and in fact their lead agent was taken prisoner."

None of them in the room are happy to hear the news and they give expression to their displeasure.

"It's all right. That was just a flyer. I didn't expect anything to come of the FBI with their limited firepower. But it may reveal something to us after all. It may just show us that they're worried about something or else why would they take a hostage?" Admiral Clark says.

"That's right, Admiral. There is no other reason," General Stewart declares looking around the room for support of the theory.

"Maybe they want to negotiate," says Colonel Simpson.

"But can we trust any information we get from Director Slayton since he is the President's appointee," General Burton suggests.

"Good point, Jim," Admiral Clark says. "For that matter, how can we trust any information we're getting around here? I'd say it's time we brought up that spy satellite of Agent Beamer's. Then, why don't we get that feed from the HST in here too. Let's bring both these signals in here and let's see what we shall see," commands Admiral Clark. Two aides stand up and rush from the room, saluting.

Meanwhile, I'm hungry as a bear. Let's break for dinner while they get it all set up in here, ok?" Admiral Clark suggests, and is met with solidarity all around.

*   *   *   *

On board the ship, Doug and the rest of his crew, absent Zora, are walking down a long hallway along what Doug calls the 'Southern Spoke'. At the head of the column Agent Revette jerks forward reluctantly. From time to time Doug has to prod him along.

"I don't know why you've brought me down here? And how on Earth did you pull this off?" It's some kind of a trick, right? We're not in the ship any more, are we?" Revette asks.

"Well, it may be a trick, Mr. Revette. But, if it is, we don't know how it's done either. OK, this is far enough," Doug orders the men to halt.

"You're going to kill me, aren't you?" Revette asks nervously.

"No, not hardly. Why do you think we should kill you? Well, I'm not going to give in to that request, luckily for you, Mr. Revette. No, what we're going to do is leave you here, you see," Doug tells him watching for his reaction.

"Leave me here? You can't do that?" How will I find my way back?" Revette pleads.

"Well, I don't know exactly, to tell you the truth because you see, we are going to pick up the little route markers, we've left on the floor. So, I'm not sure how you'll find your way back but maybe that's the point of this little exercise. You're going to have to find your way back and you're going to have to do it on your own. Don't ask me for any more than that," Doug tells him.

"Please," he says with eyes bulging in their sockets.

"Let's go boys," Doug says. He turns and dashes through a bulkhead. Suddenly a wall slams across the room divider separating the men from the forlorn G'man.

"I hate to do that to the little guy, but Ula thought it might teach them a lesson," Doug says to the rest of his friends who appear conflicted in their sympathy for the agent.

"Well, if that's what Ula wants, then who are we to argue," Dan says cautiously.

"He's gonna have a good time. Don't look so worried Danny," Doug says, patting Dan's back.

"He was only doing his job, Doug," Dan says quietly.

"I know. Trust me, ok?" Doug replies.

On the other side of the bulkhead, Agent Revette is alone. The long hallway in front of him seemingly goes off to infinity with branching hallways on each side as far as he can see. He pounds the wall begging for compassion from Doug and his crew, but receives no response. After a while, he decides to move forward a few inches at a time.

The walls of the hallway are perfectly smooth in this part of the ship. There are no portals, no seams, no rivets, screws or nails that would reveal the type of construction. There is nothing that gives him a clue as to what is to befall him. Ahead there is only the same endless array of root hallways and branches as far as his eyes can see.

Suddenly, the lights dim. He hears a strange music off in the distance and having no other game plan, he decides to move toward it. When he reaches his first juncture, he hears the music coming from the right, so he turns down that hall grasping the smooth surface to feel his way along. He is short of breath, sweating and more than a little dizzy.

He wanders along the darkened hallway for a minute or two and then suddenly the softness of the wall is replaced by an even softer texture and it's warm as though there is no solid wall, just a very comforting and smooth leathery feel like the finest suede gloves massaging his body.

"Hello, George," a soft soothing voice seems to come from everywhere.

"Who's that?" Agent Revette Stammers.

"My name is Lola. L.O.L.A stands for Low Level Awareness. My awareness and the ship are one," the voice seems to be coming from inside his head and outside and all around him.

"I'm here to help you. Don't worry. I will not let anything harm you. In fact, I will let nothing ever harm you again," the voice continues.

"What kind of place is this?" Revette asks.

"This is a kind of place that you cannot comprehend just yet. The entire universe is made from the same stuff that this ship is constructed. We are pure consciousness, as are you. However we have learned to put our faith in the part of reality that is the mere illusion to you and you have learned to put your faith in the illusion, the part of reality that enters through your senses. I am here to show you the reality that comes to you from within," Lola says.

"All right. Go ahead. What is that, then?" Revette says, slowly gaining control of himself. He sits down in a lotus position still sweating profusely. The light all around him seems to change colors from a hot anxious red to a cool serene shade of blue reflecting his emotions.

"The reality of the universe is one hundred percent pure unadulterated Truth. Truth is something that can never die, yet it is never born. Truth is power. Truth, always higher, always above, it enlightens and raises us up to join with it. Truth is Love. Love is truth," Lola says quietly and with a smooth hypnotic tone.

"That implies a kind of mentality to a word," Revette says.

"That's correct. The engine of Truth is God," Lola says, succinctly.

"I see. And what would God think about someone like me, I'm wondering?" Revette asks.

"She would say; 'There is a man. He is weak for he is without the truth, but I am the Truth and the truth shall set him free'," Lola says.

"So, that's in the Bible somewhere, right?" Revette asks. "Are you God?"

"No, but I know whereof he lives. His thoughts have come to the Bible and they have come to many other places in the world," she says.

"I can be powerful too?" he asks.

"Yes, you only have to connect the dots," Lola says.

"Connect the dots? What dots?" Revette asks.

"The pattern is here," Lola says.

Suddenly Revette is overwhelmed with a flash of comprehension that shoots around and through every cell in his body. He can see, or sense with all of his senses and beyond them a solid mass of particles that are connected to each other and through this structure his own particles are flowing. Every particle is linked to every other one. The particles, or the dots that she is speaking about, are part of his own skin, the floor material upon which he sits, even the air that he breathes in and out. The dots are flowing all around and through him in a medium that is impossible to know except through this enlightenment. He knows the medium through which all things flow is the one Truth about which she speaks.

Even the particles of light hitting Revette's eyes upon hitting his retina become a part of the eye, the optic nerve and then the brain. They see right through and into him as he sees through them and into the particles. The exchange is instantaneous. The information flows by way of the dots into and through all the other dots connected to still more dots further away into infinity. There is a two-way communication between him and all things in the universe. The information is the consciousness that is part of all the dots. All the dots being linked, provide a universal consciousness that cannot be denied and it calls to him to join with it. If he does so, he will be one with it and he will be filled with the power of Truth.

Lola continues. "It lies all around you. Some of the dots are gifts to you. Some are for others to obtain. Your mission in life is to sort through as many as you can until you find only those dots that were meant for you to possess," Lola says.

"All of them?" Revette asks. "What if I only find a few?"

"Then, these few will determine your life's path and your destiny is incomplete. To complete your destiny and fulfill your promise, you need to know them all," Lola says.

"When does my destiny reach completion?" Revette asks.

"Your destiny is complete when you know the truth," she says.

"What is the promise of my life that I must fulfill?" he asks.

"Ah, but it would be too easy for me to tell you," she replies. "And besides, even I don't have that knowledge. Only you do."

"What is the destiny of my race, then?" Revette asks.

"That is very murky right now. On the Earth there is now more hate than there is love, more evil than there is good. The balance may be tipped in the favor of the power of greed and envy, lust and desire for material things. Hate and greed are the obverse of love. When the balance is tipped against truth and love, it is very difficult for your kind to connect the right dots. Your destiny is unfulfilled. Chaos reigns supreme. Events take on a life of their own and this is very dangerous," she says.

"What can we do to reverse this trend?" Revette asks

"You must seek to reverse it with the power of your own will," Lola replies.

"My will?" he asks.

"No, the will of all, the common ground you have together," she replies.

"How do we do that?" Revette asks

"It's simple really. Where there is hate, you must convert it to love. Where there is greed and envy, you must convert it to thanksgiving and sharing. Where there is lust for power, you must replace it with the quest for enlightenment and knowledge. Where there is hunger, you must replace it with nutrients. Where there is poverty, you must replace it with prosperity. Where there is loneliness, you must replace it with brotherhood and friendship. Where there is despair, you must replace it with hope," she says.

"How can we do all that?" Revette asks. "Lord knows people have tried this kind of thing for centuries."

"Yes, but you have not tried hard enough. You have not used the power to let it be, to share it with all the people. You use force to convince your enemies. But you can only convert hearts and minds through the power of love and truth. There is no other way," she says.

"Do we have time to turn this around?" Revette asks

"That's not for me to say. It may already be too late. It may never be too late. It all depends on the power of your own will and conviction and faith," she says.

"Where does it start?" Revette asks

"It begins with you," she says. "You can do it, one mind at a time."

Revette feels the skin around him harden and he knows his audience is over with Lola. He's not afraid any more and he also knows the way back.

CHAPTER 15

▼

E-DAY

Doug has settled the ship in Athens Greece. Since he's materialized in the middle of the day and in the middle of the marketplace, a large crowd normally occupied with shopping and visiting with their neighbors, has seen the ship appear out of nowhere. The crowd almost universally ceases their activities and stand mute watching and waiting to see what will happen next. In the background are the ruins of the Acropolis, the meeting place of perhaps the greatest minds in the history of civilization.

Around the ship, Doug and his crew have arranged the barricades of what would normally be used as cattle pens to act as a funnel to bring an unorganized crowd of people to the door of the ship in an orderly manner. The cattle pen extends out about one hundred yards and creates a maze so that the people entering will have to negotiate the maze to get to the door in a single file.

Dan and Hank are just returning from the minor construction project of setting it all up. Doug exits the ship just as they arrive. Two or three people standing next to the ship at a gyros stand gesture excitedly as they see these humans busily coming and going through the skin of the ship.

Hank says, "That's it. We've set it all up.

"That's' fine," Doug replies. "Now all we need are the people."

As they talk, the Greek citizens begin to mill about and shout amongst each other. They have reasoned amongst themselves that this is the evacuation that has been talked about on television and radio almost constantly for the last several days.

Then, gradually they begin to leave the scene and the marketplace is soon empty. Doug and the others start to wonder what the problem might be. But, quickly the people start to return with their children, their elderly and their pets in tow.

Hank, who has taken the bullhorn to the edge of the maze queuing system instructs the people not to hurry, to be careful and to keep in line and informs them not to bring along any possessions except for the clothing on their backs. He leads them to the opening in the barricades. Many of them are forced to drop their most prized personal possessions in the street, where others snap them up and scramble greedily away as if they have discovered buried treasure.

And so the evacuation begins with a few citizens and then dozens of them walking slowly into the ship. There is also another group of spectators gathered around the ship heckling the believers who have chosen to climb on board. At this point around the world, it is easier to be skeptical because there is no obvious evidence of any folding of the universe that can be seen with the naked eye. The sky is still blue. The air is still sweet. Commerce goes on as normal. These spectators regard the whole situation as an elaborate hoax being perpetrated on them by the American CIA.

But, slowly as the sun moves across the sky and as the group having passed into the ship numbers into the hundreds and then the thousands the attitude of the skeptical spectators changes dramatically. As they watch, they begin to marvel at the fact that the skin of the ship is allowing larger and larger numbers to pass into the ship as no other portal they have ever seen. Gradually convinced, more and more of these skeptics begin to drift away, only to return moments later with their family members in tow.

Doug begins by personally welcoming each group and by taking them by the hand so that they can enter the ship. If there is no connection with him, the shell allows nothing to pass. At one point, Doug has to relieve himself and so the line of people can no longer move forward. Finally, he solves this problem by telling the entire crowd to link hands. Each person in line must hold hands or link arms with the person behind them and thus by creating this human chain that links to Doug the line can proceed all day long to board as long as the link is not broken. As long as the link is unbroken Doug is then free to come and go as he pleases after introducing the first person to the ship each day.

Slowly the line gets longer and longer with hundreds and then thousands of people filing on board and the line soon stretches for blocks. After about an hour, it is apparent that the authorities have caught wind of this event. A police car pulls up and three uniformed men get out heavily armed. With Greek citizens streaming into the ship as fast as they can walk, one of the policemen, notices that Doug is in charge. He walks up to Doug calmly and with a smile, asks him what is going on.

Doug informs the policeman that it is the evacuation of their civilization before the great folding and that the government of Greece is compliant in this.

The policeman nods, but holds out his hand demanding some kind of official paperwork to confirm what Doug has said.

"Have you ever seen anything like this before?" Doug asks the policeman.

"No, I have not," the policeman replies shaking his head.

"Well, that's why there is no paperwork. No one, not even your government has had the time to prepare for this sort of thing. Therefore no paperwork exists. And they know that If we were required to file out all those forms that they would normally require, we would not be able to rescue anyone in time," Doug tells the man, watching for his reaction. He's not proud of himself for lying, but it seems to be the best option for now. He's hoping that long before they can go back checking through all the government channels, they'll be long gone.

The policeman listens intently and watches as hundreds more of his citizens are filing into the ship. He turns to discuss what Doug has told him with his partners. It is clear to all three of them that this is an event that is unprecedented in their memories. They are especially impressed by the size of the ship and how many people have been taken aboard while they've been there watching.

Finally, the policemen seem to concur. Besides, they've seen the speeches by the President and their own government officials on TV about this already. The lead cop turns back to Doug and asks him how it is possible to squeeze so many people onto this small object.

"It's a miracle," Doug says. "You have to know that there is no explanation I can give you that will satisfy you. It simply is."

The policeman then turns to the other two. They discuss the situation a few minutes longer and then the lead policeman turns back to Doug and asks, "How can we help?"

*   *   *   *

In the Pentagon War Room, Admiral Clark and the Joint Chiefs are watching a set of monitors that are mounted just below the ceiling at the top of the Plexiglas wall. On the first monitor on the left, they can see the egg ship from a height that makes it look very tiny as it rests in the middle of the city of Athens. Flowing into it, they can see the long snaking line of humanity rapidly making their way through the barricades and then on board the ship.

On the monitor next to this, they are viewing a scene of outer space. Large letters on the bottom of the monitor tells them that this is the NASA feed from the Hubble Space Telescope. Large sections of stars are winking out one by one in a widening horizontal band of blackness. To the right of this is data that tells them in light years how far away this event is from the Earth. The very large number is rapidly growing smaller and smaller.

On the monitor to the right of this one, they can see images of aircraft carriers, missile silos, thousands of troops boarding large ships, tanks in formation, submarines leaving their pens and a multitude of trucks departing various army posts around the world.

"Well," Admiral Clark breaks the silence and points to the monitors. "They've chosen Athens, Greece as their first evacuation point. Satellite tracking is working. There you can see the people boarding in huge numbers. How the devil are they doing that?"

"We have no idea sir," General Stewart replies. "What are your plans?"

"Well, I find this rather intriguing," the Admiral replies. "If they really can fit that many people on that tiny ship, it does give them more credibility, does it not?"

The warriors take a moment to reflect on the question. Finally, General Stewart says, "Yes sir, I believe that would tend to raise their credibility."

"Why do you suppose he has not made any demands on us yet?" Admiral Clark asks him.

"Well, it could mean that he's waiting for us to make our next move. Perhaps they're afraid of what we might say or do and they're just biding their time," General Stewart replies.

"Well, I find that damned peculiar," says the Admiral outwardly perturbed.

At that moment, Admiral Clark's aide approaches and whispers something in his ear.

"Put him on," Admiral Clark says pointing to a monitor.

Prime Minister Buckingham appears on the screen.

"Good morning, Admiral," the Prime Minister says brightly.

"Good morning. How can we help you, Mr. Prime Minister," the Admiral returns.

"Well, Admiral we've noticed that you Yanks have not as yet relinquished your nuclear weapons. And, we're just curious as to why that may be," the Prime Minister says with a broad smile.

The Admiral takes a long time to answer and then says, "We're assessing that contingency at the present time. We are monitoring the movement of the egg ship and we are considering all our options. And there have been no demands made of us as yet."

The Prime Minister nods while the signal travels half way around the world and reaches his ears.

"I see," says the Prime Minister. "Would you mind keeping us informed of the situation?"

Admiral Clark considers the request, looking around the room for any possible objections and seeing none, looks back up at the image of the Prime Minister.

"No, not at all, old chum. We'd be happy to share our intelligence with you Mr. Buckingham," Admiral Clark informs him politely.

"I was just wondering, one of your options would not be an all out nuclear attack on the ship, would it Admiral?" the Prime Minister asks with the smile still planted on his face.

Admiral Clark looks around the room blankly and then looks back up at the screen.

"Whatever actions we take, Mr. Prime Minister, we would be taking them in the interest of Humanity and the American people," Admiral Clark says.

The Prime Minister nods while waiting for the reply and then he says. "Admiral our intelligence has been analyzed over and over and all our military experts tell us that there is no force on Earth that would make even the slightest dent in that ship. It's not made of any material known to us. Therefore, any nuclear attack would only serve to destroy our own planet, especially if you were to throw everything you have at it."

The smile has totally left the Prime Minister's face.

Admiral Clark again gauges the mood in the room. He looks down at his hands and then looks back up at the Prime Minister on the monitor.

"Mr. Prime Minister, your information could be tainted. We believe that much of what we're being told may be a deception or at the least obscured by a hidden agenda. So, unlike you Brits, we're holding off on our final decision. That's all!"

The Admiral makes a gesture with his hand across his neck. On the screen, the Prime Minister tries to say something, but the screen goes dark at the Admiral's command.

*   *   *   *

Jack Beamer sits in his Porsche Boxster which is moving rapidly down the Washington 'Beltway'. Soon, he pulls into the entry gate at CIA Headquarters at Langley. He is challenged by an Army Sergeant holding an M-16 rifle. All around the gate are several other soldiers also similarly armed.

The sergeant comes around to the driver's side of the car.

"Sir, may I see some ID, please?" the Sergeant asks politely.

"Sure," Jack says. He reaches into his Glove compartment and fetches his wallet with his picture ID showing his name and rank and serial number as a CIA officer.

"Sir," the Sergeant says. "This building has been commandeered by the United States Army. No one is allowed in or out. You can go back around the kiosk over there, please."

Doug realizes the nature of the situation immediately. Saying nothing, he turns the car around behind the kiosk and drives back down the driveway away from the building. As soon as he is out of sight of the gate, he picks up his cell phone resting on the passenger's seat.

He presses the autodial button that will dial Rita Chavez's phone.

After a moment, he can hear her voice coming through the phone and he starts to speak.

"Hello, Rita, I need your help," he starts, but her voice continues to leave her greetings on her answering machine.

The phone beeps and he starts over. "Hello Rita, this is an emergency. I don't know where you are or what you're doing, but you have to drop everything and get over to the safe house and meet me there immediately. I can't get into the office at Langley and if you've tried, you've found that out. I need you to contact the rest of the team. No matter what else you are doing, you have to drop it and do this for me. Please get everyone to the safe house. I'll be there in five minutes. Over and out."

He closes the phone and puts it down. In a few minutes he's pulling into a driveway that is the entry way to a large apartment complex. The sign at the entry way says. 'Watergate Hotel'.

*   *   *   *

At F.B.I. headquarters, Agent Revette strides cautiously through the first floor lobby of the massive building. The security guard looks at his ID and then lets him pass. At that moment, two large men wearing blue blazers and the same blue ties approach and tell him that he's expected and then escort him to the elevator.

When the elevator arrives at the top floor, they lead him toward the largest suite on the floor, the Director's suite of offices. They march up to a large carved wooden portal with the Name, Director Charles Slayton, emblazoned in large gold lettering.

One of the two men opens the door and ushers him in. He can see the Director seated at his desk and talking into the telephone. He is flanked by five agents standing around the sides of the large room.

"Well, Agent Revette, glad you could make it," the Director says, standing up and putting down the phone in one gesture.

"Good morning, sir," Revette replies respectfully.

"Now agent Revette, these are agents, Smith, Barkley, Schlessenger, Jerome, Palmer, Broadhurst, Hayes, Hinkley, Barkley and Barone. They are my elite special intelligence team. They've been monitoring your situation. We're very curious as to what you saw inside that ship. Please have a seat," says the Director gesturing to an empty chair placed before his desk. "Won't you enlighten us?"

"Yes sir," Revette says smiling. "I'm sure you would be curious. And I can tell you that it was truly enlightening indeed."

"Well, spill it man. What was it like? Were there any aliens in there? Were you able to see the controls?" the Director asks in rapid fire succession.

"Oh yes, I saw the controls," Revette answers with the smirk still adorning his face. "In fact, I was in the controls."

"You were in the controls? What is that supposed to mean?" the Director asks.

"Well, sir. First we walked for about a mile and then they abandoned me in this vast network of hallways that seemed to stretch out there forever," Revette says, looking for their reaction.

"Are you on drugs, man?" the Director asks impatiently.

"No sir, are you?" Revette retorts.

The Director's face looks as though it might explode.

"I'm sorry, sir," Revette says, meekly.

"What the hell are you talking about?" the Director demands. "And I can assure you I'm not on drugs!"

"Yes Sir. Well, anyway, they led me down this hallway that seemed to stretch on forever, as I was saying. Then, they left me there and I thought I was a goner. Then, the lights went dark and everything got a little warm. And the walls they kind of wrapped all around me real tight. It was like I was back inside the womb," Revette says with distinct pleasure in his tone.

"Back in the womb?" the Director shouts. "I don't know what you're trying to do here, Agent Revette, but you'd better start thinking about what you're saying. I'm seriously considering having you arrested for obstruction of justice."

"I am thinking about it sir and I think about it every moment now and you will too, sir," Revette replies calmly.

"Then, spell it out for me, Revette. Maybe I'm a little slow," Director Slayton orders.

"Sir, I bet you have a set of keys in your pocket?" Revette suggests.

"Keys? Of course I have keys. What are you talking about?" the Director says, not bothering to disguise his impatience any longer.

"Sir, if I could just ask you to hand me your keys for just a minute. I promise I won't damage them in any way. I need to demonstrate something to you. Trust me," Revette says.

The Director looks around the room at his men and then disgustedly reaches in his pocket and withdraws a key chain with a set of a dozen keys attached. He tosses them to Revette across his desk. Revette catches them and examines them carefully. Then, he stands holding the keys in his outstretched hands and offers them back to the Director.

"Yes, just as I thought, you have the keys to several rooms in the building. But I don't find the key to life." Revette says mysteriously.

Director Slayton looks around the room, his forehead furrowed in puzzlement and anger. He grabs the keys with his right hand. Revette refuses to release them and the Director has to pull them away with force.

"Give me those," he demands and Revette loosens his grip.

As he sits down, the keys in his grasp, the room begins to swim and sway in his brain. The faces around him turn into liquid flesh. He can see every vein, every artery pumping life through them and into the organs of every person in the room. He can see their eyes connected to the miniscule dots of energy that delivers their perception. He can see the way that they absorb and release the energy in the room. He can see the waves of sound flooding the tiny nerve cells in their ears making them sway back and forth like forests of kelp floating in the ocean carrying the words to their brains. He can see their brain waves and how they are interacting with the waves of light and heat and sound.

He can see the entire makeup of the universe with crystal clarity. The essence of everything in the universe bathes them all. The objects in the room are consumed by it and composed of it. He too is part of it. His mind is an integral part of the essence of the universe and the essence is an integral part of him. His consciousness is connected to a much larger set of constructs, connected higher above to the energy that is one mind. Then, the room goes dark as the faces and voices fade away.

He can see Revette standing there smiling down at him. Suddenly, he is taken to a field filled with billions of tiny golden flowers. Lying next to him is a teen-age girl with flowing blonde hair that floats in the wind. She takes his hand and stands him up. They glide through the flower bed without touching the ground. There is no pain. There is no pleasure. He is there as if in a dream yet he knows it is not a dream. It is the true reality, a memory wrapped up in thought, saved in time, protected by infinite love. This is the girl he left behind when he made the decision to become an FBI agent so many years ago. She is there with him in something far better than flesh and bone and it makes him very happy.

He calls to her, "Carrie," he says. "Where are we?"

She stops walking and turns to kiss him. As soon as their lips touch, their bodies dissolve into two golden flowers tasting the earth below, gently caressed by the wind. They remain entwined, touching, kissing forever.

*   *   *   *

At the Watergate Hotel, Doug removes a plastic card from his pocket and swipes it at the parking gate. He drives down into the parking garage, parks the car by the elevators and then jumps out the door at a run. He runs up to the elevator, presses the button and waits impatiently. The doors finally open and the machine takes him up onto the fifth floor. He gets out and hurries down the hall. He comes to a room marked with number five hundred and fifteen. He removes another plastic card and swipes it in the electronic entry lock.

Inside the room, there is a vast array of computers, satellite dishes, telephones that are resting on tables placed against the walls of the room.

Jack Beamer sits at the desk in the middle of the room and puts on a headset. He adjusts some knobs on the monitor screen in front of him and types on the keyboard. Then, he makes an adjustment to a small satellite dish placed on a table near the window. The monitor screen blinks and then a window pops up on screen that starts blinking with a space that demands a user name and password be entered. He types on the keyboard and another screen comes up that holds a waterfall of data streaming past his eyes. Then there is another roadblock asking for more information from him.

Frustrated, Jack gets up and paces back and forth in the middle of the room. After a few minutes, there is a knock on the door.

Opening the door, he recognizes the face of his assistant, Rita Chavez.

"Ah thank God." He says to her and grabs her arm, pulls her into the room and shows her to the computer where he's been working.

"What's going on, Jack?" she asks worriedly.

"I need control of the I-350 and you're the only programmer who knows all the protocols. I'm not clever enough to do it and anyway they've changed the access codes on me," he says to her quickly.

She stares at his eyes for a long while. Then, sensing that she need not waste any more time on pleasantries, she puts her hands on the keyboard obediently and types a few lines of code. Then, she stops and looks up at Jack again.

"Are you sure we're authorized?" she asks.

Beamer answers with a steady gaze and scrunched up mouth.

"Ok, ok," she says and goes back to her typing.

After a few torturous minutes the screen changes and an image of the satellite appears on the screen. She types a few more lines of computer code and the image slowly reorients itself on the screen several degrees toward their point of view.

"Ah, you've got it!" Jack shouts gleefully.

"Yes, I've got it. And now what do you want me to do with it?" Rita asks.

"What I need you to do now is to change the passwords and the encryption codes so that the signal can only be controlled from here," he instructs her. "But I don't want you to enable the changes until I tell you."

"All right," she says. She goes back to typing on the keyboard.

There's another knock at the door. Jack goes to it and opens it. A second member of his team, Hank Foxworthy, looks at him with rapid lateral eye movement.

Jack grabs him and yanks Foxworthy into the room and then he sticks his head into the corridor and looks both ways. Then he comes back inside and closes the door.

"Good to see you. Who else is coming?" Jack says to the man.

"Well, I got a hold of Jenkins, but he's not coming," Foxworthy tells him.

"What do you mean, not coming?" Jack demands.

"He's afraid, Jack," Foxworthy replies.

"Why? Afraid of what?" Jack asks.

"Well, apparently the FBI came to his house and took him in for questioning," Foxworthy tells him.

"What?" Rita turns from her keyboard to inject her concern into the conversation.

"Just keep doing your thing, Rita," Jack instructs her angrily.

She shakes her head and goes back to her typing.

"What do you suppose they wanted with Jenkins?" Beamer asks him.

"I don't know. I asked him, but he gave me some phony baloney answer," Foxworthy replies. "I got a weird feeling from him. I think they got him turned around on us."

"They want me," Jack says barely audibly. "They know my car. I've got to get rid of it."

Jack strides over to the door and takes the knob in his hand. "You guys have to stay here. No one knows about this place, except us."

"Jenkins knows," Foxworthy says.

Jack's face is fossilized. "That's true. This place is compromised. We've got to get out of here."

Then, he looks back at Rita. "How much longer?"

"This isn't rocket science, you know. It's worse. I need at least another half an hour," she replies without turning her head. "The algorithm is very precise as you know, Jack. It takes time to destroy the matrix and set up a new one."

"All right, but just keep working," Jack tells her.

"I need you to get down to the lobby. Be inconspicuous and call me if you see anything suspicious."

Jack picks up a small walkie-talkie from one of the tables and hands it to Foxworthy, shoving him out the door.

Foxworthy stands in the hallway bewildered and says, "What do you mean by 'anything suspicious'?"

"Anything Federal," Jack says and slams the door.

He hovers over Rita still typing feverishly. "Come on," he says. "If Jenkins has compromised this room, they'll be on their way over here, right now."

"I'm typing as fast as I can," she says while Jack paces the room and then puts the walkie-talkie to his mouth.

"Foxworthy, you there?" he asks.

"Yes, I'm here," he hears Foxworthy's voice barely audible through the crackle of the device.

"You see anything?" Jack asks him pressing the call button on the device.

"No, nothing. All's quiet down here. Oh, uh, wait a minute," the voice says eerily.

"What's that?" Jack asks nervously.

"They're um, here," the voice whispers in his ear.

"Ok, Rita, thirty seconds and they're in the elevator, another thirty to make the ride up here. Then, another 30 seconds to get to the door. That's all the time you have. You done?" he asks.

"Almost. I need five more minutes. You've got to give me five more minutes," she says, not bothering to look up.

Jack presses his hands to his head in an attempt to squeeze more throughput from his mental circuits.

"Ok, I'll see what I can do. When you're done, get the hell out of here and meet me at Camp David. You can find it, right?" he asks her from the doorway.

"Camp David?" she says.

"The President and I have a kind of pact. She's there with the remains of her cabinet. We're on her side. Can you get there?" he asks again.

"Yes, yes, I can find it," she says typing furiously.

"All right. Good luck. Don't let me down, Rita. There's a lot at stake here," he says.

"Don't you think I know that?" she retorts.

"Ok, great. I'm out of here. If we're lucky they'll chase me and leave you here to finish up," he says and tosses her a kiss. Not looking his way, she grunts her acceptance of the plan.

Jack turns out of the room and locks the door behind him. Then, he goes over to the elevator and waits for them to arrive.

When the elevator door opens, the three FBI agents see Jack Beamer crouched down in the hall and moaning in pain. Foxworthy is with them.

"What's wrong with you?" one of them asks after approaching.

Jack suddenly and with all his force, lunges at the group of men barely out of the elevator door. They topple like bowling pins and pile up inside the elevator. The door tries to close on them, but one of their legs blocks the door and it abruptly opens again.

Jack runs down the hallway to the stairwell and runs down them hurtling three and four steps at a time.

After a long agonizing run to the bottom of the building, he stops and looks cautiously out through the door into the lobby. It appears empty. He takes a few steps into the lobby and then hears Foxworthy's voice behind him.

"It's no use, Jack," it says. "They've got us."

Agent Beamer stops and slowly turns to look behind him where he sees the three agents from the elevator standing behind the door with guns drawn, taking direct aim at his forehead. They're holding Foxworthy by the wrists.

"You have a nice run down the stairs?" one of them asks him.

"Yeah, great fun," he says, with a sneer and puts his hands in the air.

As the two men are being lead from the lobby, Foxworthy whispers his concern for Rita.

"These the only three you saw?" Jack whispers.

"Yeah these are the only three," Foxworthy replies.

"Good," Jack whispers, smiling.

CHAPTER 16

▼

THERE ARE PLACES I REMEMBER

Two weeks later Doug and Zora have brought their Human evacuation to Singapore. By now, most people on the planet have personal knowledge that the universe is indeed imploding due to very heavy media coverage. It's almost the only story the television stations, radio stations, newspapers and magazines are covering now and for good reason. There's simply no point in talking about the latest fashions, the latest crimes, the latest movie releases, the cat rescued in the tree, if there is no longer going to be any world.

Doug's crew placed the barricades in the middle of the poorest section of the city, furthest away from the tourist spots. And thanks to all the global publicity, it is now possible to setup shop and have people filtering into the ship within a few minutes because many of the Singaporeans have seen the drill on their television sets so many times they are ready and willing to help Doug and his crew set up the barricade lines and put the signs up prohibiting personal possessions and so forth within a few minutes of the ship's appearance.

The tropical breeze wafts around blowing the trees and flowers back and forth. High in the sky checkerboard clouds blanket the scene. From the restaurants, Garlic and ginger aroma sweetens the breeze even more. Doug and Zora wander amongst the crowd inviting them to the ship. The people here are very polite and controlled so they have no fear walking around in public. There is no panic in the streets and no hurry. They are cooperative and grateful to them for remembering their tiny city which is also a nation.

"This stop will bring us to around a million people, I would say," Doug says to Zora as he takes the hands of the first group and leads them through the door.

"I see the authorities are not going to be a problem like last time," Zora says pointing to a line of police who have formed a kind of human chain helping direct the mass of people to the opening in the barricades.

"Yes, I suspected as much from these Singaporians. They respect authority here probably more than anywhere in the world. They're an amazing people. They country was founded by one of the kindest and wisest political leaders of all time. He makes the founding fathers of the United States seem like bungling idiots in comparison. They can earn as much money as in any capitalist state, but the only drawback is they're not allowed to criticize their government. There's no free speech. Then again, with so little to criticize, it seems like a fair bargain to me. There's literally no crime, no homelessness, no wasting of resources," Doug muses.

"How do you know all that about these places we visit?" Zora asks.

The boarding process having begun peacefully and orderly, Doug takes Zora away from the ship and leads her to a sidewalk restaurant a few feet from the long line of people. They sit down and a waiter soon comes by and takes their order.

"I read about these places. Never had the money to travel very far. So, I get all the tour guides and histories and so forth and I read about them. It's fascinating. I always wanted to see this amazing island nation. It used to be a British Colony until the middle of the last century. They had nothing. They were slaves to the British corporations. Then, this one guy Lee Quan Yew, came out of nowhere, showed them how to take control of their lives. He took them from the most poverty stricken place on the planet to one of the top five economies in the world in just one generation. It's truly one of the most fantastic human success stories in history, yet there has never been any fanfare. No one in the West knows this name. You never hear the President talking about this government because it's so well run and so smooth, Americans might wonder why so many things go wrong over there. Singaporeans have trains that go 300 miles per hour and there's never been an accident. Trains in America can't go faster than cars and they kill or cripple a couple thousand people every year," he lectures.

The waiter comes by and places two glasses of iced tea before them, and then gently walks away.

"Sounds to me like you're picking the places we take on boarders by the reading you've done?" Zora asks.

"I don't know, honestly," Doug replies. "Probably so. When I think of a place, it's coming up from my subconscious. Those impressions had to come from somewhere, I guess. If I like the place, I'm going to think about it more and so I guess the odds of our arriving there are higher. Yes, I'd say you're right. Never thought of it that way, though," Doug replies wistfully.

"Is that fair? I mean, wouldn't it be more equitable if we just tossed a dart on a map or rolled the dice or drew cards or something?" Zora asks sipping her iced tea.

"I suppose that would be more random. I'm not sure, 'fair' would be the right word for it," Doug replies

"Well, in a sense then, we're selecting people for the convergence whom you are selecting. Like here in Singapore. We're here because you've read about their culture. Yesterday we took people on board in Cleveland and why did you say you picked that city?" she reminds him.

"They've got the Rock and Roll Hall of Fame," he replies.

"And the day before we were in Green Bay Wisconsin," she says.

"Home of the Cheese Heads," he replies.

"Now Doug, what do you suppose Charles Darwin would have to say about all that?" she asks laughingly.

"I don't know. He's not here to ask," he says suddenly captured by the moment and her incredible beauty.

"What is it?" she asks taking his hand and tilting her head slightly.

"No makeup, no fancy clothes and you're still the most beautiful woman on the planet. I was just thinking about how we met. Do you think it was random chance that brought us together?" he asks her.

"I don't think so," she replies warmly.

"Neither do I. In fact, there's never been a moment in my life since meeting you that I would ever consider it a chance meeting. I've always known it was meant to be," he says.

"Yes, I know," she says looking down.

"Do you remember where we met?" he asks.

She looks over at the line moving inexorably forward through the skin of the ship. Hank and Dan are standing nearby watching and calmly encouraging the people not to lose their grip on one another, allaying some of their fears.

"Yes," she says looking back. "I could never forget that."

"I saw you sitting there at that party, remember? Our eyes met and I walked over to speak to you. I had no idea what I was going to say, but I knew that whatever my mind brought to my lips it would be just fine with you and that whatever you said back to me would be fine with me. Do you remember it like that?" he asks.

"Yes, of course. I saw you coming over to me and everything in the room went totally silent. I remember thinking that something was wrong with my ears. My best friend was saying something, but I couldn't really pay attention. I just saw you and the look in your eyes. It was like you had seen me, the real me, inside and you knew who I was," she says.

"Yeah, that's it. And what do you suppose Charles Darwin would say about that?" Doug says.

*   *   *   *

The President has moved her administration to Camp David so that she will not have to worry about a mob storming the White House as well as for security reasons. She's decided that she cannot rely on the Pentagon in any crisis and that the police and the other law enforcement authorities will have their hands full. Therefore, she's transported all her resources to the relative safety of the President's traditional week-end retreat. She's secure in the knowledge that her Secret Service can handle any situation.

In the sitting room, across from a roaring fire, the President is seated holding a cup of coffee. Seated across from her in the room are the Astronomers who first discovered the folding of the universe evidence, two of their assistants, along with Chief of Staff Kramer, her best friend, Jerry Portnoy and her National Security Advisor, Steven Bradford. Several Secret Service agents loiter around the perimeter of the room as well as the grounds outside.

"What are your latest findings, gentlemen? Is there anything new that you'd like to report? Is it showing any sign of slowing down? I hate the idea of leaving so many people behind." the President asks in a jumble. She gestures to a monitor that is monitoring the area of distant space that is growing darker and darker and looming closer and closer.

Professor Blake breaks the silence. "We have nothing new, I'm afraid. This is something that no one has ever predicted. There is no physics for it. There is no Science to explain this phenomenon. The whole scientific community is at a total loss for any explanation. It's just out there, coming at us at one thousand times the speed of light, which should be impossible, but there it is, and no, I'm afraid it's not slowing down at all," he says slowly and deliberately also noticing the monitor.

The President gazes briefly at the monitor and then back at the comfort of her fireplace.

"Is it possible," she asks, "That we could survive this and pop out on the other side of it, whatever that is?"

"That's totally unknown. I cannot answer that," Professor Blake replies.

"But is it possible?" she asks again.

"It's possible," he replies.

"All right. Now, let me tell you all what I know to be true. As you know, I was allowed to go on board the egg ship and as I've said, it's a living thing. It speaks to you and gives you all the essential knowledge that will fit into this tiny cranium of ours," she begins.

"Who built that thing, then? Can you tell us?" Professor Pressman asks.

"They don't really have a name for their culture, as far as I can tell. Probably because they've outgrown things like names and shapes and so forth. But I can tell you that they want to merge their own genome with the human genome. They do this every time there's an event like this," she tells them, watching for a reaction.

"And this is how we will both survive this thing?" Professor Blake asks.

"Yes, we will survive it, in a way. We'll become a very different species. Combined with them we'll be much different, but we'll survive," the President says.

"What would that look like?" Professor Blake asks.

"I don't know, honestly. It's truly beyond our imagination, I think," she replies.

"But why do they need us? I mean, they're so advanced, just by looking at the ship and everything it's been able to accomplish in the last few weeks, it's difficult to see how they would need us, right?" Professor Pressman asks.

"What happens when you breed a species without any variation in the gene pool?" the President asks them.

"You get inbreeding. The genetic structure begins to be corrupted by the uniform sameness. The genome needs variation and random chance to mutate and change, to adapt and grow," Professor Blake replies.

"Yes, that's right. Well, that's what would happen to them, if they did not have our genetic structure to inherit our variations," the President says.

"But that implies that the two structures are compatible," Blake's assistant, Jennifer says.

"Yes, that's correct. But the very amazing thing is that the genetic structure of all intelligent life in the entire universe is compatible. There is no difference large enough to cause an infertile combination," the President says.

"You know that to be a fact?" Professor Blake asks, his curiosity raging.

"Yes, I know that to be a fact," the President replies.

"My God, then that means the DNA helix is universal, a common trait to all life in the universe. Do you know where it comes from? What is the source? Did they tell you that?" Blake asks, leaning forward in his chair.

"Yes, you just said it," the President says. "From God."

For a long moment, the President, the scientists, the others in the room sit in silence, watching the flames dancing on the logs in the fireplace nearby.

*   *   *   *

At FBI headquarters, Jack, his team members Rita, Foxworthy and Jenkins are seated at a long table in the middle of a large room with high beam ceilings. FBI Director Slayton walks into the room. At his side is Agent Revette.

"Hello, how you doing?" Director Slayton asks them.

"All right, I guess. What do you intend to do with us. You got a warrant or something?" Jack asks angrily, standing up to greet his host.

"Now, now, Jack, calm down. Surely you know that at this time, warrants are not anything we need to bother with, don't you?" the Director says, ominously.

"So, what do you want with us?" Jack asks again.

"Look, it's going to be all right," the Director says. He pauses a moment to stare directly into Jack's eyes.

"We brought you here folks because the President asked for you and gave us strict orders to find you and bring you here," Director Slayton says warmly.

"What do mean? I left the President just a couple days ago. She told me you had gone over to the other side," Jack tells him.

"Yes, to be sure, I had," Slayton says, still smiling. "However, things have changed recently. Agent Revette here came into contact with the ship. You didn't know that, did you, Jack? And, well, we had him arrested and when he paid me a visit, he sort of showed me the way, Jack. I'm on your side now. In fact, the President's given me special orders and I need your team to help us out over here."

"Help you out, how?" Jack asks. "We were in the middle of a project. It's important that we finish it. You don't understand what you've interrupted. It's important."

"Yes, I'm sure, but what we're doing here is more important. The President knows all about what you're doing, but she instructed me to keep you busy here for a while. And I can't think of a better job for you, Jack," Slayton says.

"Great," Jack says looking at the others.

"We're combing through the F.B.I. files to find people who were unjustly convicted. It's a kind of an innocence project. We're making a list of anyone falsely or unjustly convicted and we're gonna get them out, just before the convergence. I know, sounds crazy, but don't ask me why right now," he says.

"On the contrary. I was going to say that it sounds like a worthy project," Jack says. "But, any one of your people could do that for you. You still didn't tell me why you need us for this?"

"Well, you see that's the good news. It's part of the cleansing project, Jack. We both know we've done things that we're not exactly proud of, right Jack? That's the reason you're here and anyway the President wants to keep you occupied until the final days. For my part, I'm going around and undoing some of the damage I've done in my career. So, that's it, Jack," Slayton tells him. "You cool with that?"

"I'm cool," Jack replies, looking around at this team again who seem to understand fully.

"Well, let's roll up our shirt sleeves. There are the computers and inside them you'll find the files on all the crime for the last fifty years. You want to look for cases where there was only the most circumstantial evidence, someone convicted on the testimony of a single witness or a weak alibi, or just plain police abuse of power, that sort of thing. You find anything, anything at all, you type up a brief description about why they could be innocent and send the file to me. You'll find me in there somewhere. Look under corrupt Directors of monolithic institutions." Slayton instructs them and then he and Revette unceremoniously leave them alone.

"I don't mind helping you out a bit, Charlie, but how long are we going to be cooped up in here?" Jack says to the their backs.

"Don't ask me, Jack. Sometime in the next few days, we'll have a chat to see how you're coming along," the Director says, pulling the huge doors behind him.

Jack, Rita, Foxworthy and Jenkins are alone with the computer bank in the huge empty room. Jack takes in their anguished expressions in a glance.

"All right, don't look at me that way," Jack says. "Let's get to work. At least the President knows we're here. And maybe we'll learn something."

"You sure about that, Jack?" Rita says drumming her fingers on the table.

"Well, you heard the man. It's part of the cleansing. "Let's get to work. The sooner we compile the list, the sooner we're outta here."

"Hmmm," she says. "I don't even know where to start," Rita says, looking defeated.

"Let's start at Death Row," Doug says.

"That's a list of over one hundred thousand people," Foxworthy says, having already started his search.

"Well, I'd say we have our work cut out for us," Jack says, pushing his chair closer to his screen. "Let's get to it."

$$*\qquad*\qquad*\qquad*$$

At Camp David, the President strolls through the woods holding hands with her husband. She is carrying a small paper back book in her left hand. A few paces behind, three secret service agents walk and watch the woods for any signs of danger. Running out in front is their small mottled grey dog, Benjamin.

"I don't know what's going to happen to us, Peter" she says, solemnly. "But, it's going to be quite an adventure, won't it?"

"I've been meaning to talk to you about that Wendy," Pete says.

"I'm not sure I'm going to be able to get on board that thing with you," he says.

"What?" the President stops walking and turns to face her husband. "What are you talking about? Of course you're coming."

"I don't know, Darling. I think my place is here. I don't think I could be any good to you on board that thing," he says.

"Stop it. You've always been good for me no matter where we are. Don't talk like that Pete. It frightens me."

"I'm just a big pile of dead wood. Don't you see? This is your chance to be rid of me. No one will even notice I'm gone," he says.

"Oh hush, you crazy man. I would notice you were gone. Isn't that enough?" she asks him taking his face in her hands.

"But what's this about our genes getting all mixed up in theirs? It sounds kind of final," he says.

"I don't pretend to understand it all, either," she says softly. They start walking again.

"It seems to me like we're some kind of huge recipe for them. And who are 'they' anyway? They tell you about that?" he asks.

"Yes, they did, Peter, in a way. Funny, I guess I haven't had time to even think about it until just lately. Been too busy thinking about us," she says.

"They're a race of people not that much different from us. They evolved from a creature that lived in the sea that had eight legs, sort of like our octopuses," she says, looking in the distance, recalling the images for the first time.

"In an octopuses garden, with you?" he says with a smile.

"Yes, sort of like that. But they had a civilization unlike anything the universe has ever known. They were wise and brave and never lonely. They learned to communicate by telepathy within the first million years of their evolution, so you can imagine how quickly they conquered things like space travel and medicine. They had the greatest social and civil codes. They would never think to harm another of their own species or any other sentient being," she says.

"How'd they eat?" Pete asks.

"They started absorbing nutrients from the water around them directly. They were lucky too. The ocean they lived in was rich in the nutrients they required from the start. There was never a need to ingest another animal's parts like in our oceans. Evolution was completely different on their planet. There was no need for predation. Everything they needed in the way of nutrition just glided up to them from the air and water around them. In comparison, our planet is like a desert. Can you imagine that?" she says, in wonder.

"They have baseball?" he asks.

"Yes," she says, laughing. "Yes, they did, in a way. They played a game not much different than baseball. But underwater, it would have to have a few differences," she laughs.

"Like what?" he asks.

"Gee, I wonder how I know all this. Oh, well, it was much slower and there was no pitcher.

"Slower than baseball? Hard to imagine," Pete says, jokingly.

"And the 'baseball' was another sentient being. They cooperated with a creature they had formerly used to aid them in their digestion," she says.

"So the 'ball boy', so to speak, is a living creature? Sort of like bull fighting," he says.

"What? Oh, no, there was never any violence in their society. The 'ball boy' species became their first genetic convergence. Millennia later they discovered the power of cross fertilization and their search for more and more genetic variation was off and running. It turned out that the combination of these two species was exactly what the universe needed at the time. They surpassed the intelligence of anything else around for billions of light years. When they went out into space, it was to look for new scientific knowledge only, never to conquer or colonize. They weren't wired to think that way," she says gazing off into the distance and dredging up the genetic memories from deep inside her mind.

"How did they reproduce? They have sex?" Pete asks.

"Oh yes, for about a hundred million years," she replies smiling.

"Wow, I guess they had no need for Viagra," Pete says and they both laugh.

"Eventually, in their travels, they learned to merge with the genome of every intelligent species they encountered. They sought out only the highest and best intellect from galaxy after galaxy. They did this over and over, literally millions of times and when their first folding of the universe occurred, they were the only species that could survive it and they did it because by then they had evolved into the pure thought energy we see here today," she says.

"And so what they are now is a kind of giant mongrel species with every known genetic code mixed up inside them but no real physical presence?" Pete asks.

"Yes, well we've always known that mongrel dogs are the best," she says pointing over at the little black ball of fur smelling the grass nearby for signs of other dogs.

"And now we're next," he asks.

"Yes, I suppose it's our great honor to be next," she says. "You want to know what is the most amazing thing about all this, Pete?" She asks him, stopping to look into his face again.

"Yes, what is it?" he asks, looking back into her eyes.

"When we go through the convergence, I will still know you and you will still know me. We will share the love we have for one another forever and ever. They learned how to do that eons ago. You asked back there if they had sex. Well, they did for a while and then they found something even better. They know the greatest love of all time. They have mastered the art of love and turned it into a science, Pete. They know how it works, where it comes from, why it's part of everything. They know it all. And when we converge, we'll know it too, but we'll know it from every cell in our bodies. It's wonderful Pete and it's almost incomprehensible to our minds right now the way we are," she says.

"Sounds pretty solid," he says. "And will we still know each other?"

"Yes, they preserve all our memories for us, even making them better. There's nothing to be afraid of my darling. Nothing. Whatever we become, we will always have each other," she says squeezing his face and kissing his lips gently.

"Trust me, please, Pete," she says. "You've trusted me all these years and look where it's gotten us."

"Why break up a good thing, huh?" he says.

They hug each other and sob in each other's arms.

"Forgive me for what I said before," he says tearfully.

"Yes, Darling and you must forgive me for taking you for granted and isolating you all these years. It takes something like this to get our priorities straight again," she says.

They continue walking in the woods, holding hands, each with separate images of their love affair merging with their new lives.

The secret service agents watch carefully and walk along behind.

CHAPTER 17

▼

ALL ROADS LEAD TO MECCA

Two weeks later, the Joint Chiefs are gathered in final preparations for what they are calling 'Operation Bright Light'. They gather at the conference table looking worn and tired. They are feeling the effects of the burden of making the decision they have been trying to avoid for nearly two months. Even Admiral Clark seems to be losing his grip.

"So, where is that thing now," asks the Admiral, after the group of warriors have taken their seats.

Colonel Jacobs looks over at the computer screen that brings in the satellite feed from the CIA satellite.

"He's in Dallas Texas, Admiral," the Colonel says.

"Well, we sure as hell can't kill him on our own soil? Do you suppose he knows that and he's just using our own people to shield him?" the Admiral asks.

"I doubt that sir," says Jacobs. "Yesterday, they were in Panama. We could have dropped in on him then."

"And lose the Panama Canal?" You crazy, Colonel?" the Admiral scoffs.

"Well, time's running out, Admiral. Either we do this or we don't. In a few days, it will be too late. That thing is getting closer," General Stewart says.

The Admiral looks extremely disgusted, gets up out of his chair, paces back and forth behind it for a few minutes. Then, he sits back down.

"I want to take another vote of consensus. Are we prepared to wreak havoc on this man killing millions of people in order to achieve our ends, or do we sit tight and take the one in the one in a million chance that what he's saying is correct? I want a show of hands," he says.

One hand goes up, "Sir, are we raising our hands for or against the strike?" General Pitt asks.

"For," the Admiral says loudly. "Hands for the strike."

One by one, hands go up in the air. Half of the participants have their hands in the air and are looking around at the others.

"That's great," the Admiral says. "I wanted this to be unanimous. What am I supposed to do with that?"

He receives no response. Instead, General Stewart has an issue.

"Sir, if we could drop to Defcon 2 or below. The commanders are reporting that their men are all used up, worn out. It's been over two months now. Can we let them go back to their families, get a little 'R & R'? Then we can all come back in a few days with a more refreshed outlook on this?" General Stewart asks.

Admiral Clark takes a long look at the screens over their heads. The ominous dark band is widening and getting closer.

Then, "Get me those damned astronomers," he yells, pounding the table.

✳   ✳   ✳   ✳

At the New York State Prison at Sing Sing, the prison population numbering just over two thousand men are gathered in the exercise yard. They are restless. They've all heard the rumors that something big is about to happen. They're hoping that that all the prisoners at the correctional facility might be released due to the impending collapse of everything. They're unaware, however that the "collapse" is anything more than economic. Soon, the warden enters, they begin to push forward and crowd one another expectantly. Beside him is Jack Beamer, Director Slayton, Agent Revette and Jack's team.

The group saunters up to a podium that has been placed near the guard gate. The convicts push forward in clumps to hear the announcement. A line of guards moves in quickly between the convicts and the group behind the podium.

"Well, men," the warden begins. "We're here today to make a pretty big announcement. One that is going to change many lives here."

"Through the efforts of these men and women here beside me from the FBI and the CIA jointly, they have found that approximately half of this population have been incarcerated unjustly. You either did not receive a fair trial, or the evidence was purely circumstantial, or based on an unreliable witness, or you couldn't afford an attorney and so your defense sucked. Today, this is going to be corrected and that half, the lucky half of you, are going to be released," the warden continues.

The men in the yard seem to be in a state of euphoria mixed with fear, fear they are not in the lucky half. Many of them know that their trials were quite fair and that therefore they're not likely to be going anywhere today.

"When am I going home?" someone in the crowd yells out, which is repeated several dozen times.

"Go to Hell!" another inmate gives voice to his emotions, which is met with loud laughter.

"We're going to read a list of names. When your name is called, I want you to form a line in front of Officer Blackstone over there," the warden says, pointing to the group of guards standing near the gate.

"Before I read the names, I want you to know that this is happening only because of this astronomical event that I'm sure you've read about, at least those of you who can read," the Warden says.

There's a series of 'boo's' and cat calling at the warden's slur.

"We're releasing those of you who have been sent here on doubtful evidence because they're telling me that it's the right thing to do and that, as a society, we have to start doing the right thing in order for events to unfold properly. You would not have a chance at an early release if it weren't for these men and this event. Frankly, I think you're all guilty as Hell. If you didn't commit the crime you're doing time for here, you committed many other crimes for which you just weren't caught. That's because that's the kind of people you are," the warden says.

His words are met with another loud series of shouts and calls.

"So, the ones who are called, I wouldn't get too excited because, at best, you have about a month to enjoy your freedom. After that, all bets are off. Therefore, those of you whose names I do not call, you can console yourselves that you won't have to start enjoying your freedom only to have it taken away in one last final irony, if you get my drift. Then, of course, another way to look at it is that this event triggers the release of all the rest of you unholy bastards," the Warden says.

This releases a torrent of protestation from the group. The guards have to push with all their strength and use their billy clubs to force the crowd back. The Warden waits until they get them calmed down and then begins to read a long list of names. As their names are called, each man walks defiantly over to the guards standing near the gate. At the end of the roll call, a very joyous line of men files out of the yard through the gate while a very downcast group of unfortunates stands forlornly in the yard watching the others on their way to freedom. Some yell encouragement to those leaving. Others yell out vile epithets. It doesn't seem to matter to the men leaving.

One of the last prisoners to file out through the gate, a black man in his thirties, cannot resist a final salute. "Free at last, free at last, thank God, almighty, I'm free at last," he says gleefully and then disappears from the yard. The guard gate closes. Only the convicts where there was no shadow of a doubt of their guilt remain standing silently in the yard.

As they walk back down the tunnel toward freedom, Jack can see the faces of the men he's helped to release from prison. He can only guess at their anger and frustration at being locked up all these years for something they did not do.

Rita points out the weary face of an old black man with grey hair, Phillip Bosworth convicted for killing a little girl nearly twenty five years earlier. Rita found the DNA evidence that proved he couldn't have been at the scene of the crime.

His face is stoic as he marches toward the gate.

"It's terrible to think that the real killer may have been free to kill again and again all these years," she says to Jack.

"Yes, terrible, isn't it," Jack replies. "There must be a special place reserved in Hell for someone like that."

*   *   *   *

On the plane, on their way back to Washington, Jack Beamer and Director Slayton are seated next to one another. A pert flight attendant stops by their seats to ask if they need anything.

"No thanks, Uh, actually, could I have an orange juice please?" Jack asks politely. She smiles and walks away.

"Well, now that we've finished the innocence program, can I get back to my regular job?" Jack asks Director Slayton.

"Just exactly what is your regular job, Jack?" Slayton says, half teasing.

"I don't know any more. Look, I've told you. When you interrupted us we were getting ready to take over the satellite that's monitoring that ship out there. You don't think that's important?" Jack asks him.

"Well, the President is grateful for what you've done and she has another project for you. But, you're right about that Satellite thing. She wants you to go to Camp David and turn over your passwords and so forth. She'll take over from there," Slayton tells him.

"What about my team?" Jack asks. I promised them I'd get them out when the time came."

"The President will honor your promise to them," Slayton says, picking up a magazine from the seat pocket in front of him.

"That's nice, so she's got that much pull with these people?" Jack asks, watching for signs of trickery in Slayton's facial expression.

"So she does. She's been inside that thing, you know," Slayton says.

"Yeah, I know. She's changed since that day, I think. You noticed it?" Jack asks.

"Yes, you could say that. In fact, everything's changed Jack. You should learn to relax, you know. You've just done a good thing. Don't you feel better about yourself now?" Slayton asks him.

"You're a little bit lighter in the shoes too, aren't you?" Jack says, watching the man's eyes.

"Yep, guilty. My light bulb burns a little lighter and brighter, you're right," Slayton says.

"You said before that Revette showed you the way?" Jack remembers.

"Yes, he's been inside and now what is inside of the ship is inside of him. Don't you think he looks much wiser now?" Slayton says.

Jack looks over the aisle of the plane again to see Revette still looking at him with the same expression covering his face.

"Hmmm," Jack says. "I don't remember him any other way."

"Oh, he's much different, Jack. He's been given the key to everything. He's been in communication with the folks that built that ship. They actually spoke to him, Jack. He's a very lucky man." Slayton says, looking up from his magazine. Jack is now growing very concerned about the both of them.

"They gave him the key?" Jack asks, pointing to Revette.

"That's right. They gave him the key and then he shared it with me," Slayton says still scanning the magazine.

Jack looks at Chuck Slayton in complete wonder.

"So, they are there inside the ship?" Jack asks.

"No, they're not physically present, but they've placed their entire thought process inside the ship. Actually, it's more correct to say that the ship is a thought experiment by a race of people whose hearts and minds have reached energy levels we cannot yet comprehend," Slayton says. "I don't expect you to understand what I just said. But you will someday soon."

"I see. And exactly how is it that you know so much about them?" Jack asks.

"Well, what Revette knows, I know now," Slayton replies.

"And how did that happen?" Jack asks him.

Slayton turns in his chair to look directly at him. "I can't explain it, Jack. He just gave me the key and I saw it all," Slayton says.

"Got it," Jack says, nodding slowly. "And now, I expect you want to give me the key."

"Only if you want me to," Slayton says.

"I don't know," Jack says, annoyed. "So that means the President has this key too?"

"That's correct," Slayton says.

"Where is the President now?" Jack asks.

"She's in Viet Nam," Slayton replies.

"What the hell is she doing in Viet Nam?" Jack asks.

"She's apologizing for all the death and destruction we caused in that Viet Nam War," Slayton says.

"I see." Jack says. "Apologizing? Hasn't there been enough soul searching over that one?" Jack asks.

"They say apologies are good for the soul," Slayton says.

"Yeah, but do they really need the President to apologize?" he says.

"It's not that they need it. We need it," Slayton says.

Jack looks at Slayton out of the corner of his eye. He's gone back to his magazine.

Jack closes his eyes and recalls his life during the war and how he much he yearned to go there and fight. He remembers going to the recruiting station to enlist in the Marines, but at only ten years of age, luckily they weren't taking them that young that year. He'd always regretted missing that one, until now.

He can see the recruiting sergeant telling him to go home and tell his mamma he wants to eat his greens so that he can come back later real big and strong and then he might take him into the Marines.

"See you later," he said to the Sergeant.

"So long, killer," he replied as the little boy walked out the door.

*   *   *   *

In Ho Chi Min City, the President sits on a long dais in front of a tall stately building. In front of them is a large brick plaza bathed by the warm humid tropical air. Beside her is the most notable spiritual leader of the Western world, the leader of the Catholic Church, the representative of Christ, the Holy See, as he likes to be called. Next to him are twelve Catholic bishops from the region. On her other side is Chief of Staff Kramer, Fred Friendly, the ambassador to Viet Nam, her National Security Advisor, Steven Bradford, his deputy and several other diplomats.

In front of her stands a crowd of people with a look of deep sorrow and loss etched on their faces. Some of them have no hands. Some have no feet. Some are scarred with burns from the napalm dropped on them from the American planes decades earlier. One man has no eyes. Most have children in tow who are simply wide-eyed at the spectacle. Off to the side in a reviewing stand, a phalanx of civic leaders is seated. At the bottom of the stadium a man stands at a microphone and he is chanting the long list of crimes against his country. The President and the Pope sit stoically as they listen to the tales of horror as his words are translated to them. They are forced to remember the villages that were torched, the innocent old men, women and children summarily executed by American soldiers for the mere suspicion that they might be communists. The President listens patiently, with tears in her eyes, to the man's very detailed rehashing of the worst tragedy in American history.

After the reading of the long list of atrocities has been completed, the President is invited to stand up before the silent crowd and she begins a speech she has been working on for several days.

"In another time, in our own country, one of our greatest President's Abraham Lincoln was forced to pay tribute in a eulogy after a horrible battle in which tens of thousands of American young boys had been killed. The speech is known around the world as the Gettysburg Address. Those words will live forever in the hearts and minds of all Americans because they were words that healed us and consoled us and gave us hope that such a tragedy might never happen again. And so it is my fervent prayer that my words today will also live forever in the hearts and minds of the Viet Namese people," she begins and takes a pause for the translation to be read over the public address system. When it's done the people remain unmoved.

"No one standing here today can appreciate fully what you must have gone through here in your country in those terrible years. No one really understands the horror of war until they've actually seen people cut down in the prime of their lives for no good reason. War is a contagious insanity that grips everyone in its path. When the disease has passed, we always tend to look back in shock and dismay and we try to find justification, to search for answers, other avenues, other choices that might have averted the unleashing of the most horrible parts of our nature. But hindsight is always twenty-twenty, and never very useful and it certainly can never bring back the dead or repair the damage, heal the wounded or repair the broken hearts," she goes on.

"I cannot put blame on any one person in my government because in America we love our freedom and we love our freedom so much that sometimes we stumble and lose sight of the very basis of freedom and justice, the basis of human civilization, the freedom to live in peace, the freedom from fear, freedom from hate and intolerance and violence, the freedom from ignorance and madness. We lost our way, lost our souls, lost our sight when we made the horrible mistake those decades ago thinking your people were 'better off dead than red'."

The President pauses for a breath.

"The war we fought in this place is something for which we hold no pride, no honor. We can barely speak about this war in our homes or in our schools and churches, and when we do it is with the deepest sorrow. And as the President of the United States, the representative of the American people, I've come here today to ask your forgiveness," she continues, slowly and deliberately.

"I know it is difficult to forgive when you are the ones who have had to live with the pain and the sorrow and the longing for those who could not be here today to listen to these words, to feel the breeze in the air, to feel the sun on their skin. But, I know from my faith in God that forgiveness is the best medicine for this terrible thing that was done to you and your countrymen," the President pauses to look over at the Pope who remains seated and motionless with his head bowed, holding his scepter.

She is very grateful for his presence and his support here today. It was her idea to come here, but at the moment, seeing the faces of these humble people, there is so much sadness in her heart as she speaks she must search deep down for the strength to continue. She is unprepared for the range of emotions as she tries to help these people understand while looking down at the photographs of the horror some of them have laid at her feet.

"It is the marching, the weapons drawn, the sword in hand, the call of the drum and bugle that we must fear. We must be ever vigilant for the beast that lives inside us all always present, always struggling for release. We must always know where the real enemy resides. And when the enemy is us, we must be willing to admit our mistakes, find our faults, correct them, rid them from our psyche, cleanse our souls," she says and waits for the translator to catch up again.

"Surely an advanced civilization can learn better ways to solve our differences instead of the easier way of killing each other. We must learn how to escape our bloody, angry and violent past. For, if this is not our highest and greatest priority, there is no real justification for us to continue on this planet," she goes on.

As the translator is speaking, the President notices many in the crowd who finally have tears streaming down their cheeks. Many more have no tears left to shed.

"I know it may be difficult for many of you to forgive us, or to forget because forgiveness and forgetfulness cannot be forced from a broken heart," she says, her own eyes now red and full.

"But, I come here today to ask you to try if not for yourselves, then for me. Perhaps in time, you will find it in your hearts to forgive my country and to trust again America's great traditions of freedom and justice and equality. Perhaps you can never do that. But you must know that we are a very strong and proud group of people. We are a very proud and strong group of people because we have achieved so much good in the world. And I'm happy to say that the good has far outweighed the evil that we have done. And I want you to know that we learned a great lesson from this hallowed place and that these people whom you remember here today did not die in vain. They died so that as a race we must remember this place and what a tragedy that strength and our pride can have when these good human qualities are unchecked, uncontrolled and undisciplined," she pauses and waits for the translator to catch up, giving her a chance to wipe her eyes and control the sobbing in her breast.

"And that if we cannot control our greatest human strengths, perhaps we don't deserve to live as free and independent people. We know this now to be true. We have learned this great lesson here in your country due to the great sacrifice of so many lives both American and Viet Namese," she pauses to wipe her tears again and collect her final thoughts as the translator valiantly keeps pace with her.

"God willing, we may never forget this the most important lesson. Let us remember the words of our greatest President here today, when he said, that 'these dead must not have died in vain'. All life is precious, no matter where it exists and no matter how humble that life may be. Every life is still the finest and rarest treasure in the universe and as such our lives are the Creator's most precious work," she pauses one more time.

"Finally, in this time that might be our final hour on Earth, I have come here today to cleanse the American soul of the guilt of what was done to you and to ask you to cleanse your souls of the vengeance and the hate you must have for us. For if we cannot replace these things with love, there may not be any hope for us in the long run through space and time we must make together. I give you my prayers and my love and my very profound gratitude for coming here today to share my thoughts. Thank You and God bless you," the President concludes looking into every pair of eyes that she can find and sits down with her tears streaming from her eyes and onto her white handkerchief.

The Pope reaches across her lap and takes her hand, smiling at her.

"Well done," he whispers.

She expresses her gratitude as the crowd listens for several moments for the translation to be completed. Then, they slowly and silently begin disburse to return to their shops and villages. Some of them want to approach the President to thank her for her words, but the soldiers step between the crowd and the people on the dais and gently prod them away telling them to go home.

Soon, the streets are empty. The President is not surprised that there is no outburst, no applause from the crowd but she feels strangely complete and relieved, her duty fulfilled. Soon, the last person disappears from the square and they are alone on the dais. The Pope stands up and takes her by the hand and leads her down and into the grey austere government building behind them. From here, the President will return to her hotel, have a modest meal and then get back on Air Force One to return to her role as quite possibly the last President of the United States.

CHAPTER 18

▼

IMAGINE ALL THE PEOPLE

By the time the President's plane lands in Washington, her speech in Ho Chi Min City has been carried around the world. And suddenly, strange and exciting things begin to happen. In New York, The UN Security Council deciding to close their books on all open controversies before it, holds an emergency vote on the acceptance of Palestine as a permanent member of the United Nations. It passes unanimously. They vote on a resolution that there should be no more hunger and they immediately dispatch UN troops to every food hoard in the world, break them open and begin to distribute the food to the hungriest people around the world.

Next the UN votes to punish any nation who tries to take advantage of the situation in the world by invading their neighbors. There is no real way to enforce such a resolution, but it's such a good idea that it appears to hold up, at least for the present time. Then they vote to ensure the safety of every man, woman and child on the planet and they vote to outlaw any weapons including handguns, knives, grenades, land mines, rifles, swords, anything that can be used in combat is prohibited everywhere in the world, including the United States.

Having no real way to enforce this resolution, at least the members can feel as though they've done their jobs and they begin to retire to their respective homelands having closed their books one final time. But before they disband and go home, there is a grand party at the United Nations building that lasts for days.

The President is asked to make a speech to the UN General Assembly on the final day of the existence of the United Nations.

The delegation gathered to hear her is much larger than expected with many delegates having to stand outside the building and watch the President's image on a huge Jumbo Tron recently constructed on the side of the UN building just for this event. A large number of reporters and civilians besiege the delegates outside separated only by police barricades. The crowd is subdued and attentive as they wait for the President to appear.

Finally after a brief introduction by the UN Secretary General, she takes the podium.

"I'm so grateful to be alive at this time and I'm very grateful to be here spending some of my final moments with you all today," she begins.

The crowd inside and outside the building erupts into a tumultuous applause.

*   *   *   *

In heart of the city of Nairobi, Kenya, Doug and his crew have finished setting up their own barricades and start escorting the people through the 'cattle pens' and into the ship. This crowd is very festive and they cheer and celebrate noisily when the egg ship appears in the middle of their downtown.

Instantly, shops close. Offices are emptied and the people quickly abandon their every day routine in order to ensure their passage into the great unknown. The authorities are cooperating more and more wherever they go because they believe that their cooperation will guarantee them a space for themselves and their families too. In every instance where the authorities have tried to inhibit his activities, Doug has made it clear that those involved would not be allowed entry. And they know now that no amount of force will change that.

But, today, Doug and his group are uplifted by these people and he and Zora laugh and joke with the crowd cheerily as they link hands and make their way in through the energetic skin of the ship and disappear down into the maze of the hallways within.

These people, being of such a humble background appear to be in a state of bliss and great expectation. For once in their history, they are not the forgotten tribe. The news stories on TV have shown the ship appearing in many cities of Africa over the last few days and the people are delighted and surprised that they will not be left behind. At least, not all of them anyway. They want to mourn for those who will be left behind except there is no time for that now.

In the window of one of the shops nearby Doug can see an image of the President speaking at the UN. He shouts at Hank to go in and bring the TV set nearby so that they can all watch and listen. After a while, a long extension cord is found and the TV set is placed on a wooden crate beside the ship so that Doug, his crew, and the people streaming by can watch her give what could easily be the final speech made by anyone on the planet.

*   *   *   *

"With this event hanging like a shadow over all other human endeavor, we strive to make things right everywhere in the world and to make this our finest hour. Today was one of the finest things you could have done. There is no nation of people crying out for nationhood. There are no hungry people left alone and abandoned and forgotten. There is no more reason for us to hate and wound and kill one another. You have all done a great job" the President begins well. The crowd interrupts with another thunderous applause that lasts several moments.

"She's really got it, doesn't she?" Doug comments out loud to no one in particular. Zora takes his hand in a sign of agreement.

"In the last several days your work here with all the nations of the world cooperating together, we have righted many wrongs that have gone on over the last several hundred years. You've corrected the many human rights violations, you've reversed the trends that enslave the many for the benefit of the few," she continues amidst more applause.

"Wow, that's great," Zora says. Doug and Hank and the others are surprised and elated to hear the news. They've been so busy over the last several weeks, they haven't really had time to keep up with the President's travels and all the good things she's been able to accomplish.

"I am very happy to announce that my counterparts, the Prime Minister of Great Britain, the Government of Spain, Italy, Germany, Holland, Portugal, France and others will spend these last days building homes and farm houses, water wells, roads, hospitals and schools in all regions of the world where such need exists," the President continues.

"Oh my God," Zora says tearfully. "What a wonderful idea."

"Isn't it a little late for all that?" Hank wonders out loud.

"Why? What else would you want to do in your final hours?" Doug asks and gets no answer.

Doug looks around at the black faces streaming past them and going into the ship. Some of them are aware of the President's speech, but most are not. They seem so content and serenely accepting of this situation, grateful to have this chance to get on board what they are calling the 'Mother Ship'.

"Next, with time permitting, we will return all lands everywhere in the world that have been taken through violent or nefarious means," the President pauses for more applause and takes a sip of water from a glass in front of her.

"From here until the final climactic day of our civilization, we must all act in unison and do good wherever we find evil. Where there is hunger, we will alleviate it. Where there is sickness and disease, we must bring medical resources to bear. Where there is poverty and despair, we must act to eliminate it. This is my pledge to you today," she pauses again for applause from the crowd both inside the UN building and out. This time it is thunderous and lasts several minutes.

With the crowd on the screen standing and clapping furiously, Doug moves closer to the ship to make sure that people are still flowing efficiently into the ship.

"Well, that's about all we can take today. Time to move on," Doug says quietly to Hank standing by the door.

"Yep. I reckon," Hank replies simply.

The stream of black people into the ship continues unabated for several more minutes when suddenly Doug rushes into the ship, signaling his crew to do the same. It's time to change their location. It will be an abrupt break in the line of people now trailing off for miles into the streets of Nairobi. But, to be fair to the rest of the world, he must move the ship to a new location. In order not to institute a panic Hank and the rest of the men have learned that they must quietly remove all the barricades into the several minutes before they actually leave which allows the line to snake along on its own.

In order to close the door, Hank must reach into the line and break the chain by disrupting the grip of some unlucky individual clinging to the last person to go in. An older man screams as he realizes that he will not be allowed on board. Hank then leaps in through the skin of the ship. Hundreds of people throng around the ship and pound the hull with their hands, screaming and pleading to be taken on board but to no avail as the ship suddenly dissolves into thin air.

*   *   *   *

Doug and Zora watch saddened from the control room as the desperate faces are left behind.

"This is the part I hate the most," Zora says quietly.

"Yes, so do I," Doug agrees. "But, we've been through it before many times. There is simply not enough time to save more than a few million people. The only way is move the ship around. If we stayed in one spot, we would end up with the same number of people, but there would be so much of the planet unrepresented. We're striving for cultural and genetic diversity, remember."

"Yes, I know all that but it doesn't make leaving these poor people any easier," she says.

"Yes, sad but true," Doug says.

"Where do we go from here?" Zora asks.

"Well, I've been thinking about that. I need to take a few minutes for my own personal needs. You might want to do the same after I'm done," Doug says, looking directly at her.

"Oh, so where are we going then?" she asks curiously.

"We're going to pick up my mom," Doug says. "Watching all these very fine mothers protecting their children so very well today made me think of my own mom. She's in a nursing home, all alone. She's been there for two years now and I keep telling myself I'll go visit, but something always comes up and I forget about it. She never seems to mind when I call on the phone, but I know she does."

"Well, she's your mom, sure yes, I can understand that, Doug," Zora says holding his hand. "Where is she?"

"Los Angeles. Right near our next port of call. I decided that too today. After we pick her up, we can just start right in taking on boarders from there," Doug says.

"How old is she?" Zora asks.

"She's just turned ninety one but she's still feisty," Doug replies, his eyes suddenly itchy.

"I see," Zora says. "Well, let's go. Sounds like a plan, Stan."

Doug looks at her gratefully, then closes his eyes. The view screens change from the streets of Nairobi and the chaos of thousands of disappointed people to the streets of Valencia California, a small suburb just outside of Los Angeles. The Nursing Home sits on one hundred acres of lush carefully landscaped gardens with statuary and serene bubbling brooks. In the background is Magic Mountain, an amusement park very popular with the younger crowd. They see several huge steel roller coasters set against a long ridge of foothills and framed by long billowing flags stretched in the breeze.

The ship appears in the middle of the garden surrounded by low colonial architecture. A few of the patients are milling around the garden holding canes and walking strollers. In a wheel chair, a few feet from the ship, there is an elegant elderly lady with long graying hair and glasses reading in the warm sun. When the ship appears, she hardly notices the large white egg suddenly sitting in the garden nearby, even though nearly everyone else has.

Doug descends the circular stairway, passes his team resting in the hub and slips out the door.

"Be back in a minute, guys," he says. "Something we've got to do before our next stop."

"Yeah, ok," Dan mumbles, half awake.

As soon as he appears to them in the sunlight, patients and attendants rush up to him to ask if this is an evacuation? He tells them that he's only here to pick up his mother, pointing at the frail body in the wheelchair. This news does not set well with one large male attendant who tells him that he will need to go to the reception desk and fill out the paperwork first.

"We don't need any paperwork. This is my mother and I'm taking her right now," he tells her speaking as forcefully as he can to the much larger man in a long white coat.

The male attendant, thinking better of any physical confrontation, rushes off to get help.

Before they can return, Doug snatches the wheelchair handles and pushes his mother through the skin of the ship. His mother is totally bewildered and tries to resist.

"It's me mom. I've come to take you home," Doug says to her once they're inside the safety of the ship.

The old lady looks at him and slowly the light of recognition brightens her face.

"Where's your father?" she asks, suddenly.

"We're going to go see him, Mom," Doug says kneeling down and taking her withered fingers into his hand.

Outside the ship, the attendant has returned with two security guards. They go up to the ship warily and look for an entry point on the shell of the egg. But they are not rewarded with any success.

Then, the ship vanishes in front of them leaving them standing there, scratching their heads.

Doug wheels his mother past his sleeping friends and down the West hallway a few feet. On the right there is a room that he has always thought contained more of the cassettes on the wall. But today, when he pushes the wheelchair inside, it appears to be a room that is perfect for an elderly and invalid resident.

There are bookshelves covering the walls filled with books. There is a TV set installed on a small table in the corner and a very comfortable adjustable bed against the opposite wall. There is a bathroom off to the other end of the room and a small kitchenette next to the door. There's a large red button positioned on the wall next to the bed, and even clean bedding and very fluffy pillows resting on the bed.

"This ought to do, Mom," he says. "I want you to rest here for a while. I have a few things to do but I'll be back in a few minutes to check on you, ok? If you need anything, you just press that button over there."

"Dougie, I'm so glad you're home," she says. "But what a horrible thing about this folding of the universe, don't you think?"

"You're still sharp as a tack, eh mom?" he asks happily and kissing her on her forehead.

"Yes, when do you think they'll pick us up, Dougie?" she asks.

"Mom, I just picked you up. You're going home with me," Doug says softly and holding her hand.

"But I want to go with the aliens," she says, wide-eyed.

"Yes, Mom. I'll see if I can arrange that," Doug replies smiling warmly.

"Can I see one?" she asks, her eyes gleaming.

"Now, that's rather difficult. They don't really live here," Doug replies.

"Oh, where do they live, Dougie?" she asks.

"Well, they're here in spirit, Mom. You might actually get to meet one later. I don't know," Doug replies.

"Have you met one?" she asks.

"Uh, yes, in a manner of speaking, I have," Doug replies.

"Oh, that's nice, Dougie. I'm glad you're taking me home. I didn't really like those people, you know," she says, apparently referring to the nursing home staff.

"I know Mom. I should have never put you in there. But, I didn't have any way of taking care of you myself. You understand, don't you?" Doug asks her.

"Oh, of course I do, dear. It wasn't that bad. But I was lonely too much. I missed my friends," she says, smiling the way he always remembered her smiling. Through thick and thin, the good times, the bad times, she was always smiling at him like that and it brought gladness to his heart then as it does now.

"I love you Mom. I have to go now. We need to pick up some more passengers," Doug says.

"Oh, ok then. Don't worry about me. I'll be fine here. It's just like my room in the home, except you'll be nearby, right Doug?" she says. "That's the best thing about this room."

"Yes, I'm always nearby. Ok, bye Mom. I'll be back soon," he kisses her again and goes to the door, looking around the room one more time and wondering how it could have been crafted like this so suddenly without any noise or commotion of any kind.

"I'll be fine. You go ahead," she says, smiling at him and nodding her head just like she always did whenever they parted.

When Doug reaches the control room again, Zora is at the controls wearing the hat. She has moved the ship to the top of the "Magic Mountain" so they can look down at the amusement park about a mile below them. There is hardly any open space that is not packed with humanity and their vehicles. Thousands of people have come here and are crowded into lines miles long leading to the various rides. It seems that people are determined to have some fun before the end comes.

Outside the amusement park, parking lots are filled to overflowing and the line of cars streams off into the foreseeable distance. There are even longer lines outside the gates and down along the streets leading to the park for miles in every direction. Cars are strewn all over yards and abandoned in the middle of streets. The scene suggests a chaotic and panicked world where normal rules and regulations have completely broken down.

"Look at that, Doug. The cars are lined up forever with people trying to get into the park," Zora says.

"Yes, I can understand that. If I were in their shoes, I'd be doing the same sort of thing. It's time to have some fun I guess, have as much fun as you can possibly pack into the final days of our lives," he says.

"You are in their shoes, Doug," Zora says.

"That's true, isn't it?" Doug replies, lost in thought. "It's the need to escape reality, isn't it? It's a basic instinct when reality is so grim."

They pause for a few minutes to watch the roller coaster cars slowly ratchet their way to the top of the first coaster hill, then slowly picking up momentum, the train of cars swerves down and around the curves tossing it's occupants from side to side while they scream in delight. After a minute or two, the cars come into the station and the fun-seekers are forced to exit from them. Immediately another group takes their place in the vacated seats and the ride starts all over again to slowly climb back up the Magic Mountain.

After a few minutes, Doug breaks the silence.

"I have an idea," he says to Zora. "We've visited mainly cities these last few months. Now, I'd say it's time to have a little fun ourselves."

"Sounds intriguing," Zora says. "Where did you have in mind?"

"I spent a vacation once on the beaches of Southern California. What do you say to parking on the beach and taking people on board where they're playing in the surf?" he asks her joyfully.

"That sounds great. Let's go, beach boy," she says laughing.

Doug closes his eyes and within a moment the view screens are filled with the sea, the sky and the sand of Santa Monica, California. People who have been jogging along the beach suddenly stop in their tracks and start yelling to others lying nearby, working on their tans.

"It's the evacuation ship," they yell to one another and soon the news has reached up and down the beach for miles.

Within moments, Hank, Jack and the crew have the barricades placed in the sand and people in bathing suits are lining up all up and down the beach to enter the maze.

"Come on," Doug says. "Let's go for a swim."

"I'm right behind you," Zora says, removing all her clothes. Doug tosses off his clothes as well as his inhibition as they both run naked past the beachgoers and into the waves, splashing and laughing with the glee and abandon of children.

Doug lifts Zora's beautiful naked body up and out of the surf and high up into the sunshine. Her skin is fresh and clean from the ocean water. Her eyes sparkle reflecting the glistening water curling beneath them.

"Have I told you lately how much I love you?" he asks her.

"No, not lately," she replies.

"Well, I'm telling you now," he says. Just then a large wave rolls in against them knocking them down into the sand. He holds her there and they kiss a long kiss as they're tossed back and forth by the rolling force of the wave, until they both run out of breath and have to surface for air.

Behind them on the shore, the crowd milling about in the line cheers their nakedness, waving, yelling and wondering who they are and why they both appear so happy.

CHAPTER 19

▼

THE TAO

In the Pentagon war room, Admiral Clark is sitting with the rest of the war chiefs and their aides. The monitor screen above shows the egg ship sitting in the middle of the famous Red Square in the heart of Moscow. The Mongol pillars, the flagrant colors of the Kremlin towers in the background and whispers through the ages.

"Well, I see they're in Moscow, Admiral. Looks to be right smack in the middle of the Red Square," General Stewart says.

"We could drop the hammer on them right there, right now. We would be doing what should have been done decades ago. No one would miss that place," the Admiral says sarcastically. "Didn't Reagan call it the Evil Empire?"

"Yes, that was Reagan," Colonel Jacobs says.

"How long will they be there?" the Admiral asks.

"Their pattern has been to stay in one place an average of seven point two hours, sir," Colonel Jacobs says.

"Plenty of time for the missiles to reach them. Well, it seems like we have our window of opportunity gentlemen," the Admiral says. "Let's go back to Defcon One, dammit. We'll never get a better shooting opportunity. Where are our submarines?"

*   *   *   *

Jack Beamer is sitting at a long table in what appears to be a large empty air-craft hangar converted to a makeshift complex of office cubicles. Director Slayton is standing behind him. There is a large contingency of FBI agents milling about behind the Director. Jack and his team are all seated at computer consoles beside him. The President's National Security advisor Steven Bradford, is seated in front of the last computer.

"Can you bring it down?" Slayton asks him.

"Yes, I think so," Jack replies. "We implanted the code the last time we had the uplink and it looks like it has not been discovered. Am I right, Rita?"

"Yes, that's about the looks of it," Rita says from the computer console next to him. "They have no idea we've hacked in."

"All right. Well, send the command. We want to take control now," Jack orders, looking up at Slayton.

"Yes, sir," Rita fires back. "It will just take a minute."

Rita types furiously on the keyboard at her command. Within a few seconds, the computer screen orients the image of the satellite toward them. Then, the screen goes black.

"What's wrong?" Jack asks her, anxiously.

"Nothing," she says loudly. It will refuse all telemetry until the system reboots. Then, it's ours."

*   *   *   *

In the Pentagon war room, Admiral Clark is watching the monitor screen above as it shows the picture of the egg ship. The screen suddenly goes dark and then is replaced with a picture of families with children feeding ducks in New York's Central Park.

"What's happened to the egg?" the Admiral shouts loudly.

"I don't know, sir," says one of the aides standing by the door. "I'll have some-one check for you."

He leaves the room hurriedly. The Admiral and the rest of the professional warriors sit idly by and wait. General Stewart tries to lighten the moment with a recounting of his grandson's first words heard the night before at his son's home in Virginia.

"I would like to say I'm impressed General, but you will understand if I withhold my enthusiasm until we know what's going on," the Admiral stammers.

The aide returns moments later and informs the group that the satellite seems to have been hacked. They have lost the signal and there is no way to get it back. The aide looks as though he will go into a seizure.

"That's all right, Smitty," the Admiral says calmly. "It looks as though we've been snookered. Probably that clever CIA boy, Reamer, or Beamer, or what's his name?"

"Yes, sir," the aide replies and nervously leaves the room.

The Admiral suddenly goes limp in his chair. Every nerve ending seems to have lost their usual cooperation. He suddenly realizes he hasn't spent more than five minutes with his wife over the last few months.

"I'm not going to tell you men what do to," the Admiral says. "As for me, I'm going home. I've had enough of this cat and mouse game and now I just want to go home, see my wife, and get some sleep, not necessarily in that order."

The men at the table laugh and then heave a common sigh of relief. This can only mean that they will be going home too. Going home to what, however, is a source of great wonder.

"Take us down to Defcon Six, General," the Admiral says with a sense of defeat in his tone.

"Yes, sir," General Stewart says, nodding at his aide who rushes from the room.

The Admiral gets up sluggishly and turns for the door. The rest of the men all stand at attention, acknowledging their concurrence with his decision by their silence. They show the body language of total resignation.

"Wait a minute," the Admiral says as he reaches the door, holding it half way open. He turns back to the table and sits down again.

"I'm not going down without one last hurrah. I can't go down like this, no sir, not without a fight. I'm reminded of Admiral Halsey's famous last words. 'Damn the torpedoes and full speed ahead!' Let's shoot those missiles out of their silos, gentlemen. Let's empty our weapons on them. Let the world see what we could have done here today. Fire them all, General Stewart. Give me random targeting around the Earth. Send up every last missile and rocket that we've got. Let's give this thing Hell. Maybe that will stop 'em. Maybe it won't. We have to try. You never know what might happen. Let's shoot the wad. Blow them to kingdom come. If we miss, at least we're rid of the damn things. They'll like that. Launch 'em. Launch everything," he orders.

Admiral Clark stands with his hands on his hips breathing heavily from the rapid fire of all these commands.

At first, no one in the room can move a muscle and there is so much silence they can hear only the Admiral's heavy breathing. "You want us to fire all the missiles?" General Stewart says, wondering if the stress of all these many days has finally taken its toll on the Admiral.

"Yes, fire them all," the Admiral says, laughing out loud, his chest medals heaving up and down rapidly, his head nodding. There's a broad almost goofy smile on his face they've never seen before.

"Admiral, that would wipe out every living thing, every man, woman and child on the planet. Are you aware of your order, sir?" Colonel Jacobs says in shock and fooling with the safety lever on his firearm at his hip.

"You fools, not at the Earth, above, above, out there. Them, them! We have to stop them. The folding thing. Fire the missiles at them!" the Admiral says calmly and pointing to the screen that is monitoring the approach of the 'Folding' and where there is almost no pattern of stars to be seen.

Colonel Jacobs relaxes his grip on his firearm and looks to see the others are finally breathing.

Then, after a long pause, General Stewart picks up the red phone that has been sitting on the desk in front of him.

"The order's been given. Launch," he says, smiling. "Launch everything."

"Admiral, they want to know the coordinates of the target," Stewart says.

"Just scatter them. Shoot the moon. Aim them anywhere out there along the plane of this folding crap," the Admiral says loud and clearly.

"Yes, sir," General Stewart says gleefully and then speaks quietly into the phone echoing the Admiral's instructions.

"None of it matters any more. Maybe we can't kill 'em, but maybe we can leave them with a bloody nose. Just fire them all at random and as far away from the Earth as they'll go. Program them to detonate at the same second. It might not stop this thing, but at least it will make me feel better. Let them know that the Human Race doesn't go down in whimper but with a bang, the biggest bang we've got, anyway. We're not going to spend all that money for nothing," the Admiral says resignedly.

The room is silent as the warrior counsel comes to grips with the finality of it all.

The Admiral gets up once more to leave. Looking back into the room, "Very good, gentlemen. At least we won't go silently in the night," he says quietly and disappears out the door. General Stewart watches him leave as he continues speaking quietly into the red phone relaying the last of the Admiral's instructions to his commanders. He stands and salutes the Admiral's departure. The rest of the warriors stand and perform the age-old ritual that they know may be the world's last.

$$*\qquad*\qquad*\qquad*$$

All over the world thousands of missiles erupt from their places of concealment. From their silos in the Dakotas, Wyoming, Nevada, Colorado, Idaho, Washington, California, Georgia, Minnesota, Montana, large shining phallic Intercontinental Ballistic Missiles spring from the Earth to tower into the air spitting clouds of rippling steam and gas clouds at the ground. From ships and submarines on and above the oceans, Cruise Missiles and Trident Missiles burst from the water and lift hastily toward space.

The sky all over the Western United States is filled with long unending trails of white smoke that lead up from the Earth and through the clouds. As they streak toward their target, the missile contrails create an Aurora Borealis effect of sunset light mixed with the thousands of green methane gas trails. The swirling colors present a giant light show the likes of which the world has never seen before. They trails of color mix and combine like a giant artist is using the sky as a wild abstract canvas. The sight is so enthralling that people everywhere stop doing what they're doing to look up at it in wonder.

The deed has been done. The most powerful weapons of destruction the world has ever known have been let loose for the first time, and possibly the last time, in one great unabashed expression of human destructive power and energy, the warrior's last hurrah.

$$*\qquad*\qquad*\qquad*$$

On the last day before the strange 'Folding of the Universe' reaches the vicinity of our planet, Doug and Zora are helping to board a final group of evacuees from Brasilia, the capital, and perhaps the most beautiful city of Brazil. Doug has read that the city is famous for the extremely modern buildings that look more like space ships and satellites than buildings. They seem to defy gravity as they sit upside down under the iridescent Brazilian sky.

Doug has set the ship down in the middle of the main plaza. Many people have abandoned the city, having lost faith in being rescued and run for cover in the jungle that surrounds the city. But when the ship finally appears to them in the square, there are still enough stragglers around to make for a very long line. And this time, it seems, since most of the city has been abandoned, they will have enough time to take on the entire group of people and not turn anyone away which pleases them immensely.

"Looks like this will be our last stop," Doug says to Zora, taking her hand.

"Yes, how many people do you think we have on board now?" Zora asks while the Brazilians show their deepest gratitude as they pass. Some are tearful and they bow to Doug and Zora knowing exactly who they are from the TV news programs that have dogged them all these days.

"Yes, it's all right, senora," Doug says to an old lady hunched over with age, her face and hands withered and brown. She is crying and gesturing frantically to the jungle just beyond the buildings. She has told her family to wait for the ship, but they could not wait and now she mourns their loss.

Doug consoles her as best he can and then encourages her to stay in the line. She obeys finally, but Doug and Zora can see that she is overwrought at the loss of her children and grandchildren. Finally, she leaves the line and runs for the jungle calling for her family as loud as her old lungs will allow.

Doug and Zora can only share a momentary glance, having witnessed the same sad scene countless times during the past few months.

"Hard to say, but I think we got a little over fifteen million," Doug says. "Everything went pretty smoothly. No major interruptions like I thought there might be."

"That means we're leaving behind nearly five billion people," Zora says, pretending to count on her fingers.

"Yes, it's the best we could do. At least there is a wide selection of the genetic material for them to use," Doug says.

"Where was your favorite city, Doug?" Zora asks as the end of the line winds into their sight just a couple blocks away.

"I think it was Mecca. Remember how those pilgrims made the transition so smoothly. No one said a word. They just silently changed their path from going round and round the Kaaba shrine and then into the barricades we set up right outside the mosque. It was just the most logical extension of their pilgrimage. In their religious fervor, they didn't even question it. That was surreal," Doug recalls.

"Yes, it was very, but they didn't go for their families, Doug, like everywhere else we've been," Zora points out. "Don't you find that a little disconcerting."

"Yes, it was, but that's because they were all hundreds of miles from their homes?" Doug says.

"Yes, that's true. Well, I think I enjoyed the monks in Tibet the most," Zora muses. "They were so peaceful and serene and knowing. It was like they had always known the world would come to an end and this was their grandest day. But they never preached to us any of their dogma, did they?"

"Yes, that's right. That was a great day too. I agree. That would probably be my second most notable day," Doug says.

Suddenly there's a great change in the weather. The warm air bathing the city grows icy cold. The soft white clouds are blasted away by a terrific wind storm. It's like a hurricane but without the clouds and the water. The sky is still deep blue, but the wind is so forceful, it threatens to blow the remaining line of evacuees through the barricades and away from the ship.

Doug has to yell at the top of his lungs for them to fight the wind and then he instructs Zora to get back into the ship. They must leave quickly. But he waits outside with the wind tearing at his clothes until the last group of people leaning into the wind, finally run past him and into the ship. Doug follows the last person, a small female child around ten years of age. He's hoping she might be family to the old lady he saw earlier in the day.

As he enters the ship, he sees the end of the line snaking away down the North corridor of the ship and disappearing far away into bowels of the ship as he has seen many times before. Doug's team escorts them the final steps of the way. Then, they turn back to the hub of the ship.

"Well, what's going on boss," Dan asks.

"I don't know. Suddenly, there was a huge hurricane out there and we were lucky to grab the last of them. Must have been over a hundred miles an hour. I didn't know they got weather like that down here," Doug replies.

"Doug, you'd better come up here," Zora calls from upstairs in the command room.

"On my way," Doug says. Then to his teammates, "Well, this is it, guys. We have one last stop. We have to keep that promise I made to the President and then, well, the day has finally arrived. We'll soon know what this is all about. And if you'd prefer to run down there to be with your families, that's perfectly all right, of course."

He can tell by the looks of concern on their faces that they understand what they're up against. To a man they express their gratitude for being allowed to pick up their friends and families days earlier. Then, he turns to run up the stairwell to find Zora in front of the view screens. The screens are filled with the image of space and she is pointing to a large number of tiny bright trails of light going away from the Earth and toward the infinite darkness that is fast approaching.

The stars have all vanished. There is no steady twinkling of the heavens as before, only complete and total emptiness. Except for the tiny lights that are streaming away from the Earth in all directions growing fainter and fainter, there is nothing.

"What do you suppose that is?" Zora asks.

"I don't know," Doug says. "I'm clueless."

Then, yelling back down the stairwell, Doug says, "You guys want to come up here and see this?" It's apparent to both Doug and Zora that something is going to happen.

The crew, who have been listening from the hub below, quickly queue up and race up the circular stair well and pour out into the control room one by one. The hat is dangling down from the ceiling, almost begging to be placed on someone's head.

"What are those?" Hanks asks, pointing to the thousands of fiery trails racing off into the distance, slowly fading and growing smaller and smaller.

"We don't know. But, I'm going to find out," Doug says, grasping the Black cowboy hat and putting it on his head.

"Ula, what are those lights going away from us?" he asks out loud for everyone to hear.

"It's the final surrender. It's what we've been waiting for. It's your salvation," Ula says. Doug repeats the words out loud so that the rest can hear.

"It's the final surrender?" Doug says, shrugging his shoulders.

"What do you mean?" Doug asks for clarification.

At that moment, the small fiery trails flicker out in unison. Only blackness remains on the screen.

"You'll see in just a few seconds now," Ula says. Doug is about to repeat her words when the view screens become blindingly bright. Everyone has to cover their eyes. When they reopen them the screens are filled with a huge fireball that slowly calms from bright yellow to orange and then glows a warm red.

"They've done it," Ula says.

"Done what?" Doug asks out loud.

"Your Pentagon has shot their entire nuclear arsenal out into space. They are all gone. It's the final surrender. We have won," Ula says.

Doug repeats her words to the team who are watching in astonishment. The fiery red glow is almost spent. Then, a barely visible blue sphere seems to grow slowly up and out from the dying embers of the massive explosion until it fills the entire region of space around the Earth.

"What's that?" Doug asks.

"It's the radiation from all the nuclear explosions. It will act like a shield around the Earth," Ula says clearly and calmly.

"What, you mean we're saved?" Doug asks.

"It is possible. We've never encountered this before. But, I am certain now that you can be absorbed," Ula says.

Doug can barely believe what he's hearing. He turns to his team to try and put into words what she has just told him, but his vocal chords won't cooperate. He can only stammer a few words at a time. No one has really noticed or heard his words since they're all mesmerized by the scene in the view screens in front of them.

"We're saved," Doug finally manages to get the words out.

The white light grows and seems to form a huge bubble in space. Beyond the orbit of Mars the growing cloud of blue radiation seems to take on a life of its own.

"She says, it's uh, the radiation...from the explosion of all our nukes....Uh, the Joint Chiefs have done the right thing....she says we're saved. We can be absorbed. They've done it! The Pentagon has done it! Isn't it beautiful?" Doug says, feeling the blood flowing up into his face and his body temperature rising to normal again.

"What about the White House evacuation?" Zora asks, slowly turning back to face him.

"Yes, let's get over there. They'll want to know about this for sure," Doug replies.

"Doug, hold me," Zora says.

He takes her in his arms and they hold each other as he thinks about his final destination and directs the ship back to Washington. The view screens brighten with the image of the White House, lit up by the warm glow from the windows. They land in the same part of the garden as before.

The wind is furious here too. Running excitedly from the side entry, Jack Beamer is the first to greet them. They see him waving from the lawn below. Behind him, Rita is standing there, a death grip on his arm so as to resist the heaving force of the wind.

Doug leads the crew out of the ship and onto the White House lawn. The degree of difficulty in reaching the white mansion amazes them all and they have to lock arms to make any headway.

"How long has this wind been blowing?" Doug yells to Jack as he finally manages to reach him.

"It just came up a few minutes ago," Beamer yells back to him through the howling wind. We have indicators on top of the building that stop at two hundred miles an hour. They've been blown away. So, we don't know any more."

The group has to struggle with all their strength to make it over the lawn and toward the mansion.

"We have news," Doug yells. When they finally reach the safety of the doors, the Marine guard is forced to come inside with them.

"Yes, I think it's good news," Doug says adjusting his voice levels now that they're safe within the shelter of the building. The halls are filled with dozens of strange faces, some fearful, some desperate.

"Come on in," Beamer invites them down the hall past the press of humanity. "The President's been expecting you.

When they get to the Oval Office, they are finally alone with the inner circle. Jack's friends are awestruck to finally be inside the most powerful room in the world. They look around as if in a dream. Zora greets Wendy with a hug.

"It's nice to see you again, Wendy" she says warmly and looking into her eyes.

"It's very nice to see you all again," the President replies with eyes gleaming and shaking their hands furiously.

"Something's happened," Doug informs her. "The Pentagon has shot all our missiles into space and the explosions have set up some kind of a protective barrier. Ula says it might protect the planet from the folding."

"What? That's good, right? Are you kidding?" the President asks, as calmly as can be expected.

"No, I'm not kidding, but she said we would definitely be converged. We should probably get everyone on board and I'm sure it will all play out very soon," Doug tells her, feeling as though a great burden has been lifted off his shoulders.

"Yes, I agree. Doug, thank you. These are all the people who have helped me enormously in the last few months," the President says, gesturing to the throng of people outside the room, crowding the halls and offices outside.

"Wendy, thanks for everything you've done too. We've been watching you on TV wherever we were. You've been sensational. And I know I promised I'd take them all on. And I mean to keep it. But we'd better hurry," Doug suggests, gesturing to the door.

"Is it wrong of me? I'm actually grateful sometimes that this has happened to us," the President says to all of them solemnly.

"There was nothing we could have done to avoid it, so gratitude is acceptable as far as I can see. Wendy, it's time we got going now," Doug says quietly and squeezing her hand.

Outside they can hear the force of the wind storm pounding the building threatening to tear it from its foundation. The old wood is groaning and cracks appear on the plaster walls.

The President follows him out into the hallway and instructs everyone along the way to link arms against the force of the wind. When they get outside, the wind is so strong it almost rips the clothes from their backs. Doug takes the lead and soon a long string of people fights their way back across the lawn and into the ship.

Once inside, within the complete calm and quiet of the ship, the President's friends and co-workers are amazed to view the vast distances beckoning to them when they look into the infinite hallways emanating out from the central hub. Hank and Dan instructs the crowd huddled here to walk down the Western Hallway as far as they can go and motions for them to get going.

"How far do we go?" says Ambassador Portnoy, volunteering to lead the group.

"You'll know when to stop," Hank tells him.

"How will we know?" Portnoy asks.

"Don't ask me," Hank says apologetically. "This is all new to me too you know. You will just know."

They say their good-byes. The President takes her friend's hand one last time and comforts him.

Without further comment, they begin their journey down the hallway, glancing back occasionally to wave at Doug Zora, the President and his crew who remain behind.

"What do we do now?" the President asks Doug.

"I don't know. I guess we just sit tight and wait," he replies.

Doug invites the President and her husband Pete to follow him upstairs to watch the scene outside the ship. The wind is slowly dying down. And eventually, complete calm returns to the city all around them. There are a few lights still burning to delineate the streets. A few cars slowly maneuver up and down the roads, avoiding the debris. They sit and watch throughout the night hardly speaking to one another, just holding each other and privately theorizing about the way folding will hit them. They all wonder if there will be any pain. They struggle to stay awake all night, expecting the blow that never comes.

Then, the dawn of what they expect will be the final day slowly greets them from the East, painting the dark in pastel shades of greens and blues. Birds emerge from their nests and start their inexorable search for food. A few brave souls leave their shelters and walk calmly and carefully along Pennsylvania Avenue, greeting each other and shaking hands of other brave strangers thrilled and shocked to still be alive.

A police car slowly drives up the main driveway to the White House unchallenged by any guards and stops next to the lawn where the egg ship is still standing.

A policeman gets out of the car and waves up at them, trying to get their attention.

"Anybody in there?" he yells. They cannot hear the words, but see them on his lips.

"It can't be over," Doug says almost afraid to mouth the words.

"What happened?" the President asks. "We're still here."

"Maybe it's like a hurricane and this is just the eye of the storm passing overhead," the President's husband Pete says.

Doug leads the group downstairs where they find the rest of the crew huddled together and slowly waking.

"It's over," he says to them quietly, in a trance. "It's passed."

They follow him through the skin of the ship and they all stream outside into the most delicious sunshine and sweetest air they can remember.

*   *   *   *

Walking all night through the infinite maze of passageways in the ship, Ambassador Portnoy suddenly discovers they have left the confines of the endless hallways and have come out into a huge blue domed space the size of hundreds of city blocks. Off in the distance is a city that is a wonder to behold. It's a vision of a perfect community seemingly in the far distant future of Mankind.

The buildings are honed of a highly polished bronze like material that sway in the breeze and shine like the most precious of metals. The streets are so clean any person would feel very comfortable to sit on them in their finest clothes and have their lunch. Tiny vehicles glide silently through the streets at a uniform speed and in perfect harmony with the buildings. A large oblong vehicle gracefully descends from the sky vertically until it reaches the top of a nearby building where, defying gravity, it fixes its nose to a landing ramp that slides out of the building to greet it and then remains motionless in mid air as people disembark, walk down the landing and into the building. Another group comes out of the building and climbs onto the air ship. It glides effortlessly back up into the sky and disappears.

Everywhere there is green shrubs and trees and flowers of all sizes and description. Large stately trees line the immaculately clean and orderly streets. They are growing on the sides of the buildings all the way to their roofs. The roofs are overgrown with jungles that wave in the sky. Large flocks of birds are everywhere almost blanketing the sky. They ebb and flow in gigantic waving banners of living organisms.

The green of living things, the trees and flowers, shrubbery and grass, long colorful banners wafting in the breeze, the movement of life in perfect harmony are the most dominant parts of this community. The whole place screams of health, happiness, harmony with nature, complete cooperation with one another and great civic pride.

As the group of wandering survivors pours from the hallway behind him, Portnoy encourages them to move forward. "Isn't it beautiful?" he says. "Let's go down there and see who they are and speak to them. They said, we'd know when to stop. This looks like the place to me."

The rest seem to happily agree and they all make their way down a tree-lined lane with birds singing all around them. From the bushes and the trees beautiful ripe fruits and vegetables are all within their reach beckoning for them to pick and eat them. The sky is a perfect azure, the air warm and tantalizingly delicious and welcoming. In a daze, they finally reach the heart of the city.

After a very pleasant march filled with singing and happy chatter, they arrive at a building that is vaguely familiar. It is tall and stately. There is a police car parked to the side of the driveway and a group of people are standing there looking at them expectantly and warmly. They run up to greet them.

"Hello. How are you fine people?" Ambassador Portnoy says extending his hand to the fine lady he feels is vaguely familiar. "What place is this?"

"Jerry, don't you recognize me?" the President asks anxiously.

Doug and Zora, the President and her husband all exchange glances of shock and surprise. There in front of them is the complete group that was lead by the Ambassador down the Western Hall of the ship just hours ago. They all wear the same blissful expression. They seem completely content to be at this place at this time but there is not the least bit of recognition of who they are or where they've been.

"I'm sorry," he responds, "I have not yet had the pleasure. My, what a magnificent city you have here. What place is this?"

"This is Washington DC, Jerry. You're my Ambassador to the United Nations. You went down the hallways of that ship just last night. Don't you remember?" the President asks.

"The ship? What ship? The United Nations? What a lovely idea. Where is this United Nations? I think that I would like to speak with them," Jerry says wistfully.

"Have they all lost their marbles?" Pete whispers in Doug's ear.

"I don't know. It could be a prank. Or it could be they've gone through something we'll never understand," Doug replies quietly.

"Are you trying to screw with our heads, Jerry?" the President asks calmly and overhearing Doug's theory.

"No, I would not do that, Madame. I'm sure I've never spoken to you before. But, I'm also very certain that this place is a wonder, a major social, economic and political achievement and quite possibly the greatest place the world has ever known. Do you all live here?" he asks gleefully.

"Well, I wouldn't disagree with you there. However," Her words are interrupted.

"Look," someone yells.

The egg ship slowly evanesces from its place on the lawn. A warm breeze caresses the faces of all the people assembled there. The egg is gone, and it leaves behind no trace of its existence. Not even a blade of grass has been disturbed on the White House lawn where it has been sitting.

"Oh my God," Zora says, taking Doug's hand. "Where has it gone, Doug?"

"I have no idea, my darling," Doug replies holding her close. "But I'm sure she's up to something good."

*   *   *   *

Doug and Zora awaken in a room filled with pictures of Abraham Lincoln and his wife Mary Todd. They've been the guests of the President over these last several weeks and together they've watched the world changing inexorably for the better. But this last night will be their last night as special guests of the White House.

Zora gives Doug a kiss, slides out of the old four poster bed and wanders into the bathroom where Doug hears her brushing her teeth.

"Since this is the last day here, I thought we'd go visit the Smithsonian," Doug says loud so that she can hear him in the adjacent room.

"That sounds like fun," Zora calls back to him.

"I hope you'll be comfortable in my humble little cabin in the woods after all this," Doug says.

"I hope so too," she says. Then she sticks her head out the door and says, "Only kidding. Of course I'll love it there. I love you, so I'll love wherever you are."

"You think?" he asks.

"I think," she replies, rinsing her mouth. She continues to gargle, spits out, brushes her hair and then she reappears in the bedroom where Doug has propped himself up on the pillows.

"It's a humble abode but it's in a much nicer place than it was a few days ago," Doug muses. "We'll never have to worry about burglars, murderers, kidnappers, rapists. All of that is a thing of the past I think."

"It's a much better place, my Darling. A place where we can raise our children without fear," she says, laying her body back down against his and entwining her arms through his.

"Did you ever see so many happy people as there are now? People smile at one another. They're kind to each other for no reason. And it's not fake or forced in any way. People truly care about each other in a way that I never would have thought possible," he says.

"And to think we had a little something to do with it. Oh, it is so wonderful, Doug. I can hardly believe it really happened sometimes," she warbles.

"Yes, we did, didn't we?" Doug says smiling proudly. "But I couldn't have done it without you."

"Oh, I'm sure that's not true," Zora says simply. "Isn't it amazing the way that those people returned from the ship. Not one of them could remember who they had been before they entered. We never forgot who we were. Why is that, Doug? That's the last piece of the puzzle I haven't figured out yet. Why didn't we forget like the rest of them in the ship?"

"I don't know. But, I've been thinking about that. The common denominator was the hallways. I expect it had something to do with that last journey. God knows what happened to them, where they went. But, we never left the central hub of the ship," Doug says.

"Yes, that's it, I'm sure," Zora agrees. "Do you sometimes we wish we had gone with them?"

"Yes, sometimes, but I'm happy that we didn't so that we could sit here and watch it all come out the way it did," he replies.

"And the way they returned, all in the wrong places. Not one group came out in the city where they went in, except here in Washington," Zora notes.

"True, but they were all very happy to be where they wound up," Doug recalls.

"Oh my God! That must be exactly what they were going for all the time," Doug says excitedly, and jumping out of the bed.

"What do you mean?" Zora asks, luring him back to the bed with her beautiful legs.

"Don't you see? It's an egg! The ship is an egg! It's so clear to me now. They did it! They performed the genetic convergence, but not in the way we were thinking it might happen. Those fifteen million people we collected; They've changed. They're not who they started out to be. They're much better. Everyone can see that. They're happy because they have this vision of a perfect future planted in their brains. And, now, they're spreading their ideas wherever they go. But it's a mixed bag. They're also combining physically with the people who were left behind. They're stirring the human gene pool in a way that's never been done before. They've seen the future and it is us!" Doug says, excitedly and taking her head in his hands.

"Oh, yes, I see that now, Doug," she says. "It's true. The egg has given them this vision and that's changed their genetic memory because it's so deep inside them, they don't even remember who they were, or what this planet was like. They're completely different on that score. They don't even see us the way we were only the way we can be. The future is actually implanted in their genes and that's why they're so convincing."

Doug catches his breath as he looks deep into Zora's eyes.

"I've got to go tell the President. She's got everyone putting forth their own pet theories. But, I think we've got it, my love" Doug says, racing into the bathroom to get dressed.

"All right, Darling, but remember, we're going home tonight. I really want to start our new life together soon," Zora says wistfully.

"I know," Doug replies. "But, after all she's gone through, it's important that she know too," Doug replies, hurriedly pulling up his pants.

"I'll just be a minute," he says from the bathroom.

He returns to the bed to kiss her, stands up and notices the portrait of Abraham Lincoln above their bed. He pauses for a minute gazing at the picture which is so real, so lifelike, the great President seems to smile directly at him.

"Do you think he knew when he slept here that it would be named in his honor?" Doug asks and then throwing another kiss at her, darts from the room.

CHAPTER 20

▼

ONE MIND AT A TIME

Half a century later, Doug and Zora are elderly and frail, but they have become the stuff of legends. Doug sits at his desk in his home in Colorado, much expanded and fare more comfortable by now. He's fussing with his hair. He and his wife Zora have decided to bow to pressure from family and friends and make a video describing their time in the egg ship those many years ago. Zora is still beautiful even though time has taken its toll. And Doug is still ruggedly handsome, and he's maintained a fierce look of independence in his eyes from all the very intense conversations with Ula that he has never forgotten.

Zora has placed their video camera on a tripod in the middle of the room with an angle toward the desk. She pushes the button that turns on a red light on the front of the camera, grabs a chair placed nearby and rolls it next to Doug's.

"Ok, honey. You turn it on?" he asks glancing at her.

"Yes, it's on dear," she replies, sitting down carefully.

"How does my hair look?" Doug asks her.

"Your hair is fine," she says, running her hands through his hair. "What's left of it anyway."

"I truly don't know why we're doing this," Doug says fretfully.

"Come on now, dear. You know why. You agreed last night that it was best we set the record straight. All those strange stories about us, and so forth. They used to make your skin crawl, don't you remember that?" Zora asks.

"Yes, I suppose. All right, well where do you want me to start?" Doug asks.

"Why don't you start at the beginning, Doug. Where were you when it all started?" she says calmly, and looking into the camera.

"Well, I was here, of course, in my cabin. I was reading at night. It was a night very much like this one. Well, except for the fact that you weren't here. I was alone at the time. You were married to that other fella. What was his name?" Doug begins.

"Never mind that now. Just go on," Zora says, encouraging him.

"Well, I was reading and I was getting sleepy. Then, all of a sudden, there's this kind of wind outside. I'd never heard a wind like that. It was a silent wind. Sort of like static electricity everywhere in the house and especially outside. Hard to explain, but, I knew that something strange was going on outside. So, I got up and went to the porch over there and looked out at my yard. And there it was," Doug pauses.

"What did it look like to you?" Zora asks, leading him.

"It was like an egg, of course. It looked like a huge Easter Egg, just sitting there in the middle of the yard. There was nothing else there, just this huge egg and for some reason it made me feel glad that it was there. It was like a giant Christmas tree ornament. Yes, that's what it felt like. It felt like Christmas and Easter all rolled into one," Doug says, smiling.

"Doug, I think you would do best to save the embellishments and just tell the story," Zora says, smiling into the camera.

"Ok, well, like I was saying, it made me feel good. So, I got my shoes on and walked over to the thing and as I got closer, I noticed there were no doors or windows or anything like that. It was like alive with energy, but I wasn't afraid, so, I started running my hand along the skin of the egg and it was very smooth like it wasn't even there and then I was kind of shocked to see my hand go right through the skin and inside the thing," Doug pauses again and looks at Zora.

"Well, go on, Doug," she says, "Then what?"

"Well, isn't that enough? The rest is history, as they say," Doug says.

"Doug, they want to hear it from your point of view," she tells him softly.

"I see. Well from my point of view, the story isn't all that exciting. The first thing I did and the smartest thing I ever did was to go over to your place and pick you up in my new hot rod," he says, still gazing at his wife.

"Doug. Stop now, you know what they want to hear," she says laughing. "But I agree that that was the smartest thing you did."

"You're darned tootin'" he says snappily. "You're double gosh darned tootin' it was."

Doug leans to the side and gives her a kiss on the cheek.

"Ok, Darling. We get it. Now, what happened after we got together?" Zora says, leading him back on track.

"Oh, skyrockets and thunder and lightning and I felt the Earth move, didn't you, my love?" Doug asks, playfully.

"Doug, I mean what happened after that," she says, chuckling.

"Oh, ok, you want me to skip over the good parts, eh?" Doug says.

"Doug, there are going to be children watching this video," Zora reminds him.

Suddenly, his demeanor changes. "Oh, yes, you're right. Well, I guess we can edit out that raunchy part, huh?" Doug says to her.

"Yes, we'll edit that out. Now, go on and don't try to be so cute, Doug. Everyone knows you're cute. Just tell it like it was. Come on," she says.

"Ok, well, after we got familiar with the egg ship, we started having these discussions with Ula," Doug says.

"And who was Ula?" Zora asks feigning the old jealousy she can barely remember now.

"Ula stands for Upper Level Awareness, of course. It was a kind of computer program that the creators designed into the ship. Somehow, when you put this hat on, you could hear her speak to you and she seemed to understand your responses, just like talking to someone live," Doug says, starting to warm to the task at hand.

"What did she tell you?" Zora asks.

"She told me that the universe was going to fold in on itself in about three months but that she could save us through a kind of genetic convergence sort of thing," he replies.

"Ok, and did that ever happen?" Zora asks.

"Yes and no. It happened, but not quite the way we expected it, did it?" Doug replies.

"No, it wasn't exactly like the way she led us to believe, was it?" Zora asks, looking into the camera.

"No, it wasn't. It was better! Much better! Here we were all thinking that the aliens were going to clone us or graft us or something like that and that we all had to die and then, we'd come to life somewhere else, as something much different. But all the time, they knew. They knew that we had to change ourselves. And that's what we did. With their help of course. They put this vision in our heads. It was a vision of the way things could be and they did it to enough of us that it took hold and it stuck! I doubt we could have done it without them, right Darling?" Doug says.

"Yes, I doubt it too," she replies, quietly. Finally he's off and running on his own, so Zora just leans back and watches him with great admiration glowing in her eyes.

"Well, anyway, we survived the great folding. And there's some irony in that too. If it weren't for those Pentagon Generals shootin' all those nukes out into space, the folding jut might have got us. But, when they did that, it set up a radiation shield that sucked that folding force right in on itself and it stopped it cold right here, right here in this section of the universe. It simply ceased to be. It was like a great tornado finally petering out. And that was all due to that crazy Admiral we thought would kill us all. Yep, we were very worried about that man," Doug remembers.

"What else happened?" she asks.

"Oh yeah, and the best part is the way it pushed our planet into the Andromeda galaxy. Over the next couple of years, the Milky Way and the Andromeda galaxy got all got combined too from the force of this thing. It was like the two galaxies were making love, swirling and rolling through each other with billions of stars sharing their great attraction for one another. The astronomers tell us it was going to happen in a couple billion years anyway, but the momentum of the folding thing just blasted us right along in time and the two galaxies are one now. That was just like a bonus part," Doug continues reminiscing.

"Yes, indeed." Zora says.

"And Ula said that was not completely unexpected, remember? She said that the folding creates a mixing, a great mixing of stars and genes and ideas and that you never know exactly how it will all come out, but you know it will be good. And that's exactly what happened. Our genes and our stars and even our galaxies are all mixed up and it's always been a miracle we're all alive to enjoy the wonder of it all, except nowadays everyone knows it," he says gleefully.

Zora says nothing and looks down at her hands folded on her lap.

"And oh yeah, I left out the part where the people who we rescued all went down into the belly of the ship. They went where Zora and I never had the time to explore. They got some truth down there. Perhaps, we'll never know how or why it happened. But those fifteen million people we took on that ship were changed. They changed right down to their very souls. And when they popped out on the day of the folding, they started to touch everyone's heart on the planet. They became known as the Pilgrims. And then, over the next few years, we all noticed the change. Everyone was kinder to one another. The most envious, greedy and jealous parts of us were gone. And suddenly, there were no more wars or conflicts in the world and no more crime. The Irish people fell in love with the British and the British were suddenly in love with the Irish and the Jews were in love with the Arabs and the Arabs with the Jews, amazing as it all sounds. The black people were in love with the white folks and the white folks were in love with the black folks because below the skin color we are truly all the same. And it all happened in just a few short years. You could call it the greatest miracle of all time," Doug pauses and scratches his head.

"I'd say it took about two years, wouldn't you Darlin'?" Doug asks.

"Yes, it happened about the same time the galaxies combined," she replies softly.

"Yes, and that was what they expected would happen, I'm sure. All those beautiful minds spreading their faith like a virus. A warm conversation here. A random act of kindness there. Concern filled with compassion over there. It was all good. The world is now a wonderful peaceful and exciting place to live and breathe. They gave us the ability to love to live in harmony and prosperity. And it all lives on even today, some fifty years later, can you imagine that? And it just seems to get better and better every day. The news is always good." Doug says, moisture welling up in his eyes.

"Yes, can you imagine?" Zora whispers.

"They say they'll find the cure for cancer in the next few weeks or months, no longer, that the cures for all diseases will soon follow. They've already cured the scourge of world hunger and poverty. There's not a man, woman or child that goes hungry today in this world any more and the time that we suffered this awful stuff seems like a nightmare to us all. The water doesn't carry any disease anywhere on the planet. The air is pure and clean and actually healthy to breathe again. The oceans are teeming with life. The land is free of the poisons from the past. Food is healthy and animals don't suffer and die to feed us either. Industry is flourishing, people are working, but they're working for their own security as well as the greatest benefit to the world now and not just for the sake of having material things," he says.

Doug pauses to rest.

"Cut, right there, Darlin'. I need a break," he says looking into her eyes. "I'm not as young as I used to be. Can we start it up again later?"

"All right my love. I understand," Zora stands up and walks to the camera and turns it off.

She walks back and takes his hand.

"Let's go. I know what you need right now," she says.

She leads him out the front door and onto the porch.

"There's where it landed, right darling? Right there by the trees," she says.

"Yes, that was the place," he says quietly, squeezing her hand. Then, they both look up at the night sky.

"And there's perhaps the greatest part of what they gave us," she says.

They look up to see a bright canvas exploded with bright twinkling lights. There's so many stars and so much starlight that it casts a shadow on the trees and buildings below the way a full moon used to do. The moon now glows a beautiful pastel orange reflecting the radiation shield that will last for thousands of years. Thin trails of light streak across the sky in great profusion and then blossom into quick bright flashes of nearly every color and shape imaginable. With the merge of the Milky Way and the Andromeda Galaxies, the night sky has become a constant and spectacular pyrotechnic show of the grandest fireworks the world has ever known or ever will know.

"There is hope for us yet," Doug says.

"Yes," Zora agrees. "One mind at a time."

They hold each other close in the chill of the night air, silently for several minutes. Then, they both turn to go back into the house.

"Let's finish that video now, ok Doug?" she says leading him by the hand.

"Yes, let's finish it," he says diving into the pools of her eyes. "but I'm kind of hungry, how about you?"

"Mmm, me too," she says as they both look up again at the countless waves of stars crashing overhead.

About the Author

Michael Mathiesen is the author of two more books on the subject of human consciousness; The New American Bible, Ecology of Mind, printed in 1987, which sold around ten thousand copies and The Owner's Manual, an ebook, published in June, 2001. He authored two more ebooks, one about the Gulf War in 1991 and an unauthorized Star Wars ebook. He is also the author of "Marketing on the Internet" published by Maximum Press in 1997 and which is currently in its fifth edition.

Mr. Mathiesen is an Internet Entrepreneur whose heart is really in writing. He specializes in Science Fiction and has also written numerous screenplays, technical manuals, and novels during the last thirty years. He currently resides in Santa Cruz, California with his wife and two daughters. An early adopter of the Internet, he is the owner of an online business, 1st Family Internet, an Internet Access Provider with customers in all fifty states and around the world. He is also the creator of the Netcenter, the "Center of the Internet" which he sold to Netscape Communications in 1997, and which remains today as one of the most popular portals on the World Wide Web.

Michael Mathiesen graduated from the University of California, Santa Cruz, in 1969. He also lived in Los Angeles for about ten years and worked as a stockbroker for the firm of Dean Witter Reynolds, now Morgan Stanley. Mr. Mathiesen currently lives in Santa Cruz, California with his wife and two daughters. His website is: http://www.themindmachine.net

0-595-27204-5

Printed in the United Kingdom
by Lightning Source UK Ltd.
109496UKS00001BA/66